"What is it?" Hatch asked from the doorway.

It was a picture of Lia Grant, stared up at her, a red X slashed across her face. Grace checked the envelope. No return address. Her hands shaking, she squinted at the handwritten notation along the bottom of the photo:

Me: 1
You: 0

"Grace? What the hell?"

"I..." ds on her shoul tire body shook eone used her t X, horror sendi s. "It's a game r a phone programmed to call only me. I was supposed to find her, but I struck out."

The lack of oxygen was making her head dizzy. Names, hundreds of names, spun through her head. She'd spent the past decade putting bad people behind bars. All day Grace had struggled with anger and shock and profound sadness.

But now a warm wave of powerful relief surged through her. If someone was indeed playing a game with her, bring it on...

Acclaim for *The Broken*

"Coriell's Apostles series launch is a true roller-coaster ride of romantic suspense...The gradual attraction between Hayden and Kate is believable and intense, as their flaws make them all too human. And the suspense is top-notch, with so many twists and turns that even the most astute reader will be riveted to the stunning conclusion."

—*Publishers Weekly* (starred review)

"4½ stars! Top pick! Coriell's latest grips the reader from the first page. An engaging, intriguing plot...a definite must-read."

—*RT Book Reviews*

THE BURIED

Also by Shelley Coriell

The Broken

THE BURIED

SHELLEY CORIELL

FOREVER

NEW YORK   BOSTON

Copyright © 2014 by Shelley Coriell
Excerpt from *The Blind* copyright © 2014 by Shelley Coriell
All rights reserved. In accordance with the U.S. Copyright Act of 1976, the scanning, uploading, and electronic sharing of any part of this book without the permission of the publisher constitute unlawful piracy and theft of the author's intellectual property. If you would like to use material from the book (other than for review purposes), prior written permission must be obtained by contacting the publisher at permissions@hbgusa.com. Thank you for your support of the author's rights.

Forever
Hachette Book Group
1290 Avenue of the Americas
New York, NY 10104

www.HachetteBookGroup.com

Printed in the United States of America

First Edition: October 2014
10 9 8 7 6 5 4 3 2 1

OPM

Forever is an imprint of Grand Central Publishing.
The Forever name and logo are trademarks of Hachette Book Group, Inc.

The Hachette Speakers Bureau provides a wide range of authors for speaking events. To find out more, go to www.hachettespeakersbureau.com or call (866) 376-6591.

The publisher is not responsible for websites (or their content) that are not owned by the publisher.

To Bea Coriell

CHAPTER ONE

Momma was wrong.

Good things didn't happen to good girls.

Tears seeped from Lia Grant's eyes, and she inched a bloodied hand to her cheek and brushed away the dampness. She couldn't see the tears. Or the blood.

Too dark.

But she felt the slickness running down her palms and wrists, the slivers of wood biting into the fleshy nubs of what was left of her fingers, and the heaviness pressing down on her chest, flattening her lungs.

Yes, Momma was wrong. Bad things happened to good girls.

A thick, heavy fog crept across her body, pushing her deeper into the earth.

She always tried to be a good girl, just like Momma wanted. Church every Sunday. Straight As in her first year of nursing studies. A job as a volunteer greeter at the Cypress

Bend Medical Center. But that was far away from the dark, cold place where she now lay.

In a box.

Underground.

Somewhere on the bayou.

Chunks of earth thudded onto the wooden box that encased her body. She pressed her face to an ill-fitting corner and breathed in the sweet decay of the swamp above, a place where kites and warblers cried, gators splashed, and people walked and talked.

And breathed.

She pushed back the fog. Fought for another ragged breath. "Let me out. Please let me out."

The thudding stopped, and a voice from above said, "I'm afraid that would be against the rules."

Rules? There were *rules* that governed bad people doing bad things?

A scream coiled in the pit of her stomach and rushed up her throat. She beat her fists against the rough-hewn lid of her tomb.

Thud.

She kicked her sneakered feet.

Thud.

She bucked her hips and shoulders, her body a battering ram. Soupy earth oozed through one of the uneven seams, blotting out a ribbon of blue. She clawed at the sky. "No! Come back!"

Thud. Thud!

The whispers of air seeping through the gaps thinned. The fog pressed harder. She inched her arms above her head, easing the ache in her lungs. Something clattered, like bones rattling in a coffin. Was it a hand? A foot? An elbow? Dear God, she was falling apart.

She spread her fingers and found something cold and hard, small and square. Not a bone. More like a deck of playing cards. Did the devil who'd buried her alive want her to amuse herself as she suffocated?

Her sticky fingers slid over the small box, and a half breath caught in her throat. A phone. Had her captor dropped a phone? Would a phone work underground? She fumbled with the power button.

Light, glorious light, glowed on the face.

"Momma, oh, Momma! I'm here. Your good girl's here." Lia Grant reached up from her cold, dark grave and with bloodied fingertips punched in Momma's phone number.

* * *

Grace: 345. Bad guys: 0.

Grace Courtemanche always kept score, a relatively easy task at this point in her career.

"Hey, counselor, one more picture." A photographer from the Associated Press motioned to her as she stepped away from the microphone centered on the steps of the county courthouse.

Grace turned to the photographer and smiled. Lips together. Chin forward. Left eyebrow arched. Her colleagues called it her news-at-eleven smile, and tonight it would be splashed across television screens and newspapers throughout the Florida panhandle, right next to the stunned mug of Larry Morehouse. Morehouse, the former commander-in-chief of the state's largest ring of prostitution houses masquerading as strip clubs, had just been slammed with a few not-so-minor convictions: conspiracy to engage in prostitution, coercion, money laundering, racketeering, and tax evasion. As lead prosecutor, Grace had dealt the blows, swift and hard, and she'd loved every minute of the fight.

Her step light, she wound through the buzzing crowd to the offices that housed the team of prosecutors from Florida's Second Judicial Circuit. She pushed the button on the elevator that would take her to her third-floor, garden-view office and to defendant Helena Ring. Ring was the twenty-four-year-old meth user who'd given birth to a son in a rest stop toilet off Highway 319 and left the newborn to die amidst human waste. *Florida v. Morehouse* was over, and she couldn't wait to dig into *Florida v. Ring*.

The phone at her waist buzzed. Call display showed RESTRICTED NUMBER. She banished the call to voicemail where it would be saved so she could forward it—and the six others she received today—to the sheriff's department. Again she jabbed the elevator button. The calls from restricted numbers had started months ago when the Morehouse camp had approached her with a bribe, suggesting she offer the whorehouse king a deal down. She laughed then and now. The day she took a bribe was the day she dined with alligators. Both were dumb and dangerous, sure to bite you in the ass. With the elevator stuck on the second floor, she spun on her gray sling backs and took the stairs.

Inside her office, a man sitting in silhouette on the windowsill bent in a sweeping bow. "I shall buy you furs and chocolate bonbons and place diamonds at your feet," her boss, Travis Theobold, said.

She switched on the light. "I'm sure your *wife* will take issue with that."

"Nah. She knows you too well." A man with a mop of silvery hair and a politician's easy grin, her boss served as the state attorney for Florida's Second Circuit. "Damn, Grace, you buried that son of a bitch and made us look brilliant."

Some called her a justice-seeking missile. Those with less tact called her the Blond Bulldozer. In her youth her father had simply called her a winner. For the briefest of moments, she raised her gaze heavenward and allowed the corners of her mouth to tilt in a grin that wasn't practiced, a little girl smile that came from a heart some defense attorneys claimed she didn't have.

See that, Daddy, I won.

"Why don't you knock off for the day? Come to Jeb's with the rest of the team and celebrate?" Travis asked.

"Can't. Helena Ring needs my immediate attention." She settled behind her desk and switched on her computer.

Travis cupped his hand over hers. "You're off the Ring case."

She jammed her hair behind her ears. She must not have heard correctly. "Excuse me?"

"It's about the bribe."

"You mean the one Morehouse's people offered and I didn't take?" She made no attempt to keep the sharp edge out of her voice. She was fed up with Morehouse and his minions.

"This morning I received information about a bank account in Nevis in your name. Deposit records show a six-figure transfer from one of Morehouse's companies."

In her dreams. Until payday she had a whopping fifty-six dollars to her name. "This is clearly a twisted case of identity theft."

"I agree, and when we're done investigating, I hope to rack up a few more counts against Morehouse, but for now, I need you on *vacation.*" He held out his hand and waggled his fingers. "Keys, please."

She recoiled as if those fingers were five baby cottonmouths. "You can't be serious."

His hand slithered closer.

Ten years ago, when her personal life had been slammed with a class five hurricane, this job had been her refuge, a safe place to land, a solid foundation on which to rebuild.

"Work with me on this," Travis said. "Anyway, after the Morehouse case, you deserve a vacation."

Her computer stared at her with its giant, unblinking blue eye. In the decade she'd worked at the SA's office, she hadn't taken a single vacation day. "Exactly what do people *do* on vacation?"

Travis gave her a devilish grin. "How about something with your new housemate?"

"Hah!" Last week her new *housemate* ruined her favorite silk suit, and this morning he broke the back door. "He's about to be evicted."

"How about your new place? Doesn't construction begin soon?"

A hint of a smile chased away her scowl. Four months ago she'd been a player in a bidding war for the old Giroux place, twenty prize acres of land on the Cypress Bend River near Apalachicola Bay. There she planned to build her dream home, a two-story Greek revival with tennis courts and a tire swing.

Another win, Daddy. See it?

Travis had a point. It might be good to be home for a few days to oversee the start of construction. "Earth movers begin clearing tomorrow morning," she said.

"So go home, drink champagne, and celebrate that you, dear Grace, are living the dream, that you are one of the privileged souls who gets everything you ever go after."

A face with eyes the color of a July sky flashed into her head. No, not everything.

She jerked open her briefcase, dug through the mountain

of papers, and finally unearthed her keys. As Travis plucked them from her hand, her phone vibrated again. With a jab and a glare, she sent the call to voicemail.

"Another Morehouse crank?" Travis asked.

"Eight calls today from a restricted number. Fits his M.O."

"You'll report this to the sheriff's office?"

"Of course." She was independent, not stupid.

"Seriously, Grace, be careful out there. Your new place is remote, and with Morehouse in jail, his people are riled."

With Travis's footsteps fading in the hall, she turned to her computer and flexed her fingers. If she was going on vacation, Helena Ring was going with her. She typed in her pass code and hit, *Enter*.

Denied.

She rekeyed the information.

Denied.

After ten years, her boss knew her well. "Okay," she said with a laugh, "I'm going on *vacation*."

She turned off her computer, and her unknown caller buzzed again. Cranks thrived on reaction, but she might as well see what she could get for the sheriff's office. "Grace Courtemanche."

A pause stretched along the line followed by a sharp intake of breath, almost a gasp. "G…g…grace, is it really you?" The voice was soft and female, low and scratchy. "I've been trying to reach you, but no one answered. Got your voice mail. Over and over. Why, Grace, why didn't you answer your phone?"

The words pricked at the base of her neck. "Who is this?"

Raspy breath. "L…Lia Grant."

"Listen, Lia Grant, or whoever you are, I—"

"It's cold. And dark. I can't breathe." Hollow rattling

poured across the line, like stones rolling about a wooden box.

"I don't know who you are or what you want—"

"Help! I want help. I'm in a box. Underground." A cracked sob, as if the caller's body had been torn in two, followed. "I need your help."

Grace ran her fingers along the scattered pearls at her neck. Not just help. *Your* help. Which made no sense. Grace didn't know Lia Grant, had never heard of Lia Grant, and there was no reason for Lia Grant to call her if she was in trouble.

"Please, Grace, help me." The whisper burrowed deeper, the hushed words bone-chilling cold. If this was the Morehouse camp orchestrating another crank call meant to unnerve her, they'd hired a damn good actress. "Tell Momma I tried to be a good girl. I tried..." Another strangled sob poured out of the phone followed by a long, broken wheeze.

Cold shot across Grace's body, freezing any further arguments. "Lia?"

No words, just a faint push of breath.

"Lia. Where are you?"

More breathy whispers.

"Lia, talk to me. Tell me where you are."

Click.

The lights on Grace's phone flickered out. Lia Grant was gone. The air in her office thinned. No, Lia Grant was not entirely gone. She called up her voicemail, her heartbeat quickening at the eight messages. She pushed, *Play.*

Beeeeep. Dial tone.

Beeeeep. "Um...my name is Lia Grant and I need your help. Please call me as soon as possible. This is"—*cracking voice*—"an emergency. Um...thank you."

Beeeeep. "It's Lia again. Call me. Please."

Beeeeep. "Listen, Grace, I need your help. This is going to sound crazy but someone put me in a box and...and buried me. The box isn't airtight, but it's getting harder to breathe. I'm not sure where I'm at, somewhere in the swamp, maybe near Apalachicola. Please call me. Please."

Beeeeep. "Dammit, Grace, pick up your stupid phone!"

Beeeeep. Sob. "I'm sorry for yelling. I'm in a bad place, Grace, really bad."

Beeeeep. Dial tone.

Beeeeep. Cough. "Hey, Grace. It's me again. Lia. The phone, it's dying." *Choky sob.* "This may be my last call. Please call my momma and tell her I love her. God bless."

Click.

The tendons at Grace's wrist strained under the heavy silence. In her ten years with the State Attorney's office, she'd encountered real fear and real terror in the voices of victims who'd been violated and in the whispered truths of witnesses who'd come face-to-face with evil. And there was something about Lia's voice, something grave and desperate and *real*.

An uncharacteristic tremor rocked her hand as she retrieved her contacts on speed dial.

"Franklin County Sheriff's Department, Criminal Division," a cheery voice answered. "How can I direct your call?"

CHAPTER TWO

Gulf of Mexico, Off Florida Coast

Hatch Hatcher adjusted the jib, propped his bare feet on a five-gallon bait bucket, and tilted his face to the sun-soaked sky. He had steady winds, low chop. Should be straight-line sailing. At this rate, he'd arrive in New Orleans with time on his hands.

He ran a hand through his hair. Too long. He should probably get a trim before his presentation in the Big Easy. He was giving a talk to regional law enforcers on crisis negotiations and would be representing the Blue Suits. He tugged off his T-shirt and balled it under his head. Or not. He grabbed an icy longneck from the cooler at his side. Natalia lived in New Orleans. Clara, too. He uncapped the beer. His was a good life. A job he loved, beautiful women in every port, and time to travel the world on a boat called *No Regrets*.

He raised his beer, toasting the sun and sea.

His satellite phone rang. Caller ID showed a number from Cypress Bend. The bottle froze midway to his mouth. He knew one person in Cypress Bend, but she wanted nothing to do with him. She'd made that clear ten years ago when she'd sent him sailing from Apalachicola Bay. His fingers tightened around the bottle, the veins in his forearm thickening and rising.

Nope. Not going there. Because he wanted nothing to do with her, either.

He pushed away the past. Gathered in the peace.

Always peace.

As he reached for his fishing pole, the call went to voicemail and he noticed the blinking light on the phone. One other message, this one from the Box, headquarters for the FBI's Special Criminal Investigative Unit. His team. He couldn't ignore that call.

"Hey, Sugar and Spice, miss me?" Hatch said when his teammate Evie Jimenez answered the phone. Evie was the SCIU's bomb and weapons specialist, and he loved getting her fired up.

"I refuse to feed your gargantuan ego," Evie said. "You may have every woman east of the Mississippi charmed by that syrupy drawl, but not me, *amigo*. Speaking of your ego, we got a call from Atlanta PD. The kid you talked into giving up his boom box at the high school got a seriously mentally ill designation. He's in a treatment center and getting his life together. One of the Atlanta news stations wants to do a feature on you."

"Tell 'em I'm on assignment." Hatch's role as a crisis negotiator was simple. Get in. Defuse. Get out. "Park around?"

"Yep, but he's in the communications room with some techie. Computer crashed again."

Hatch grinned around another swig. The Box was a huge glass, chrome, and concrete structure on the rocky cliffs of northern Maine, and while the SCIU's official headquarters looked like an ultra-modern marvel, it had a notoriously cranky computer system.

"I'm returning his call," he said. "You know what he wanted?"

Evie paused, which sent warning sirens blaring through his head. His fiery teammate never paused for anything.

"Okay, Evie, what's up?"

Another beat of silence. "Have you checked your e-mail?"

"Not today." Technically, not for a few days. His work featured long, intense moments of negotiation with men and women in the throes of crisis, insanity, rage, or a soul-sucking combination of all three. So when time allowed, Hatch set sail, which was why he'd ended up with Parker's team. His boss understood his need to disconnect. Hatch had spent the past week anchored near the sugary sand dunes of Islamorada in the Florida Keys hunting for buried treasure.

"Then you haven't heard about Alex?" Evie continued.

"Alex?"

"Alex Milanos." The quiet stretched on. "Your son."

A burst of laughter shot over his lips. "Good one." He was careful about these things. He didn't do long-term commitments, and his disastrous relationship with his old man had cured him of any parental longings.

"This isn't a joke, Hatch. A woman from Cypress Bend contacted the Box and insisted on talking to you. Parker finally took her call. Name's Trina Milanos, and she claims her daughter, Vanessa, knew you, as in the biblical sense, and that Vanessa's thirteen-year-old son is yours."

Hatch studied an icy bead on his longneck as if it were

a tiny crystal ball. Vanessa Milanos? He couldn't picture a face. The name didn't ring a bell either, and he certainly didn't associate it with Cypress Bend. Cypress Bend was Princess Grace's kingdom. Grace Courtemanche was royalty, and he'd told her that every night as they lay intertwined on the deck of *No Regrets*, drenched in sweat and moonlight.

But this call from Cypress Bend had nothing to do with Grace Courtemanche. Some other woman claimed he had a thirteen-year-old son. He did the math. The timing could work. In his college days, he'd spent a number of summers on St. George Island, one of the barrier islands below the Florida panhandle. He'd taught sailing to kids at a posh summer camp, and before the summer of Princess Grace, he'd had a string of women on his boat and in his bed. But he was careful about these things.

"At the risk of being blunt, I don't leave bits and pieces of me around," he told Evie.

"That's part of the problem. Sounds like Vanessa Milanos wanted you in the worst way, and she admitted to her mother that since she couldn't have you, she'd settle for a piece of you. She sabotaged your efforts at protection. Take a look at the picture in the e-mail. Same shaggy blond hair. Same baby blues. Same killer dimples. Plus Parker, being Parker, had a rush DNA test done." Evie paused. "It's a match, *padre*. He's your son."

Hatch's throat constricted, and he stretched his neck, trying to ease the way for words. As a crisis negotiator, words were his tools, his constant companions, always at the ready.

"There's more, Hatch," Evie added. "The granny needs you in Cypress Bend *pronto*. It appears your son has gotten himself into trouble. He's in jail."

* * *

Grace needed a bomb. Nothing fancy. Nothing complicated. Just something with the ability to blow up the attitudinal Ford compact she now called her own. She unbuckled her seatbelt, reached across her car, and took a hammer from the glove compartment. Hitting something sounded good.

"'Nother dead battery, Miss Courtemanche?" The security guard that prowled the government buildings clucked his tongue as he walked up beside her.

"This month it's the starter."

"Man, you didn't have problems like this when you owned that fine Mercedes. Now there was a car. You need some help, counselor?"

Help me!

Then call me! Grace shot a look at her phone on the dash. Ringer on. Fully charged. And painfully silent. No more calls from Lia Grant. And no update yet from the deputy at the sheriff's department who promised to look into the calls immediately.

"Thanks, Armand, but I can take care of it myself."

An hour later and with Lia Grant's voice still echoing through her head, Grace turned onto a rutted road winding into the swamp and drove to a one-bedroom shack with a sagging front porch and rusted metal roof. Feathery cypress branches filtered the retreating sun, but even the seductive cover of lacy shade couldn't soften the wretchedness of her new home. She climbed the rickety porch steps and tripped over a knobby column of white. Another bone, this one a grisly joint speckled with bits of dried flesh.

"Dammit, Allegheny Blue, how many of these do you have?" An ancient blue tick hound sprawled in front of the door opened a cloudy eye. He heaved himself up and rested his head against her thigh. She nudged him away with her knee. "Don't even pretend we're friends."

She tossed the bone into a trashcan on the porch, where it clunked and rattled among the dozen already there. "No more bones."

Her new *housemate* licked his lips, sending a line of drool across the hem of her skirt, and followed her inside where she reset the alarm, not that the shack held anything of value. Most of her furniture and home electronics were in storage. But her boss was right; her new place was remote, a good half mile from her closest neighbor, hence the security system.

With Blue at her heels, she filled the dog's food dish with dry chow, softened with warm water. When he looked at her with drooping eyes that had seen way too many doggy years, she said, "You're going to die of clogged arteries. You know that, don't you?"

He licked his lips.

She sighed and opened the refrigerator.

It's cold... Help me!

"I did!" Grace grabbed a piece of cooked bacon and slammed the door. Another wave of frosted air prickled her skin. "Okay, after the *ninth* call." She tore the bacon into bits and threw them in Blue's bowl. "What more am I supposed to do?"

Winners do, Gracie, and doers win. Not Lia's words. Her daddy's.

She breathed in his calm and confidence. "You need *my* help, Lia? Fine. You got me." She set Blue's bowl on the floor with a clank. The old dog thumped his tail against her leg and dug his nose into his dinner.

Grace dug out her phone and called Jim Breck, the internal security chief and her go-to guy with a local wireless phone company. The SA's office regularly turned to him for wiretaps and call records.

"Counselor Courtemanche, why does it not surprise me that you're working after hours?" Jim said. "Haven't you heard there's life beyond the office? Things like families and hobbies."

She laughed. "Not for souls like you and me, Jim. Now, did someone from the sheriff's department contact you this afternoon for a call search?"

"Not yet."

Probably because the deputy didn't have Lia Grant screaming in his ear. "I need to know the subscriber's name and contact information on a series of calls I received."

"Got the paperwork?"

No, and she wasn't likely to get a subpoena, not while on *vacation*. "This isn't an official investigation," she said.

"Sorry. Can't move forward without a subpoena."

Sometimes you had to bulldoze past a few roadblocks. "I received nine calls from a stranger begging for my help. This whole thing could be a series of crank calls from associates of a convicted felon who's been harassing me. Or it could be a young woman in danger and running out of time. I'm seriously leaning toward the latter."

Jim said nothing. She said nothing, letting her track record speak.

"Let me see what I can do," he finally said. An excruciating two minutes later he came back on the line. "Interesting."

Without a subpoena, they were walking a fine line. "Can you verify the subscriber's name?" Grace asked.

"No."

"Can you verify the subscriber's address?"

"No."

No surprise there. "Can you verify it was a prepaid phone?"

"Yes."

"And let me guess, the subscriber is listed as Mickey Mouse."

Jim cleared his throat and said with a cough, "Clark Kent."

Much like Allegheny Blue and his search for bones, Grace couldn't let go. "Where was the phone purchased?"

"Retailer in Port St. Joe."

"If I give you the time of the calls, can you tell me the location?" She rolled her shoulders and flexed her wrists, a warm-up of sorts, like in tennis.

"Caller didn't activate GPS functionality, but according to the Call Data Record, the call came off the Cypress Point cell tower. It's an OmniSite covering a three-mile section. Topo map shows dense swamp, a handful of high-end resort properties, and a few residences."

Her wrists stilled mid-circle as she peered at the shades of gray outside her kitchen window. Lia Grant's calls had been made within three miles of her home. Creepy coincidence? She gave both hands a shake. Even more reason to keep digging.

After thanking Jim, she called up a search engine and searched for "Lia Grant" and "Florida." A dozen hits turned up, including one about a young woman who lived in nearby Carrabelle. Within fifteen minutes Grace had a full page of notes on the nineteen-year-old nursing student, including a current address and—she grabbed her cell—a phone number.

After eight rings, a groggy voice came on the line. "'lo."

"Lia Grant, please."

"Lia's not here." *Yawn.* "Who's this?"

"Grace Courtemanche. She called me this afternoon." *Nine* times. "I'm returning her call."

"You spoke to Lia today?" Something rustled, and when the voice spoke again, all fuzziness was gone. "I've been trying to reach her all day. Last night she had a volunteer shift at the hospital, and she borrowed my car but hasn't returned it. If you talk to her, tell her to get her ass and my wheels home."

"I'll be sure to relay the message." Because Grace was going to find this girl. She phoned the Cypress Bend Medical Center, and the woman manning the welcome desk said Lia had not shown for her volunteer shift.

"Quite odd for Lia," the chatty woman said. "Although she's young, she's a responsible little thing, a real good girl."

Tell Momma I tried to be a good girl.

Grace hung up and reached for her purse. "No, Lia, I'm not going to talk to your mother because you're going to tell her yourself." The lump of dog struggled to his feet. "You're not going with me. You shed and drool, and you stink." She opened the front door and Blue lumbered past her, a slow-moving avalanche. "Dammit, Blue! Get back here." He plodded across the drive and planted his butt near her car. Tonight she didn't have time to fight. She opened the passenger door. "The vet said you're supposed to be dead by now."

This time her car started on the first crank, and Grace took the route from Lia's apartment—the place she was last seen—to the medical center—the place where she never showed. She crept along the two-lane highway bordered by swamp, pine forests, and a deserted oyster processing plant that reeked of long-dead fish. No stalled vehicles. No signs of foul play.

The employee section of the hospital parking lot had two security lights, both burned out. She aimed her headlights at the rows of cars, slamming on the brake when she spotted a blue hybrid. She checked the license plate number Lia's roommate had given her. A match.

"This is too easy," Grace said to Allegheny Blue as they got out of the car.

The hybrid was locked. No obvious damage, but between the front tires, Grace spotted something white and knobby, like one of Allegheny Blue's bones. She dropped to her knees, gravel digging into her shins, and pulled out a white purse. Sitting on the backs of her heels, she dug out a wallet with a driver's license and held it up to her car's headlight beam. Blunt bangs and a toothy grin with a slight overbite. Grace ran a trembling finger over the name.

Lia Marie Grant.

* * *

"Get prints off each door, the steering wheel, and passenger seat," Grace told the evidence tech from the Franklin County Sheriff's Office. "Also, get some more lights out here. There's blood on the asphalt we need to get typed."

"Yes, ma'am." The tech rushed to his van.

"My people know how to do their jobs, *counselor.*"

Grace spun and found Lieutenant Isabel Lang, the head of the FCSO's Criminal Division, standing behind her with her arms crossed. Grace wasn't a law enforcement officer, but thanks to the personal invitation from Lia Grant, she was on the hunt. "This is a priority case, lieutenant. We have a young woman missing and probably endangered."

Lieutenant Lang slipped her phone from the holster at her belt. "Which is why I'm taking the lead."

Excellent. The lieutenant had been with the department only a year, but Grace had worked with her on two cases. Lang had been rock solid, both in the field and on the stand.

Surround yourself with the best, and you'll become the best. Daddy.

"You know this girl?" Lieutenant Lang asked as she scrolled through notes on her phone.

Grace had wracked her brain, recalling names at work, in the news, even at her former racquet club. "Never heard of her. She called me by name, but she could have gotten that off my voicemail. No connections that I know of."

"I'll have the boys hunt down the girl's family and friends and get a search crew on Cypress Point. I want you to forward me her phone messages. Then I want you at home with doors locked."

"I'll be more use to you in the field. I know that area better than most of your men."

"All well and fine, but you're my only link to this girl. I need you safe and ready to answer your phone if she calls again."

Grace gave a single nod. No time for counter arguments. And no worries about missing any calls. She had excellent coverage throughout Cypress Point. She pushed slow-moving Blue onto the passenger side seat and turned to the darkened swamp. "Keep breathing, Lia. Keep breathing."

CHAPTER THREE

Grace nosed her car to the edge of a bayou spiked with branches that reminded her of bony fingers clawing out of the water. Lifting the binoculars from her chest, she searched the shore for the tip of a wooden box, disturbed earth, footprints, any sign of Lia Grant. Next to her in the passenger seat Blue lifted his head. His nose twitched.

"Must be bacon out there." The dog—allegedly one of the best hunting hounds in the Southeast—had been snoring like an airboat at full throttle for the past hour.

His ears perked, and he jumped to his feet, aiming a low growl out the driver's side window. She followed his gaze, squinting through spirals of fog to a stand of shivering shrubs. She tapped her brakes. The headlights flickered. "Don't you even think about dying on me," she warned her car.

The dog leaned across her, his growl deepening. The shrubs shook. Leaves tumbled to the earth. Blue bared his teeth. His body convulsed.

"Take it easy, old man." She dug her fingers into the folds

of his neck and scrubbed. "I can't handle you *and* the car dying on me out here."

Blue stretched his neck and let loose a long, low bellow. A branch snapped, and a dark, lean shape darted on two legs from the shrub toward a stand of pines. She shoved aside Blue to get a better look. The moon glinted off a piece of shiny metal. A belt buckle? The blade of a shovel? Her heart hammered the pearls dangling from her neck.

Blue planted his front paws in her lap and leaped out the window, a narrow missile of muscle and gnashing teeth. He bayed, the rumble rattling the night, as he chased the shadowy figure up a tree. Grace jammed the car in reverse and aimed the fading headlights at the stand of pines. The lights flashed off the silver.

She banged her fists on the steering wheel. "Congratulations, Blue. You just busted a garbage-loving bear for possession of a can of baked beans." Grace shoved open the door and slogged through decaying leaves and twigs to the pines. She grabbed the dog by the collar. His tail thumped her leg. "Glad one of us had fun."

She dragged him toward her car when a shrill noise cut the night. Bull frogs and crickets silenced. The bear stopped rooting in the can.

"Was that a pho—"

Rrrrrring!

The back of her neck prickled. Blue growled. She spun toward the ringing sound, which came from an ancient cypress tree with buttress roots the size of her shack. "Who's there?" Grace demanded.

Rrrrrring!

Every muscle in her legs tightened. "Lia? Is that you?" Someone could be calling the young woman's phone, which meant the girl and the box that held her could be nearby, just inches below her feet. Grace ran toward the tree. "Lia! It's Grace. I'm here to help. If you can't talk, make some kind of noise."

Grace tucked back the sides of her hair, praying for a bang or clatter or even a whisper of breath. Blue stood at her side, his head jerking from side to side as he sniffed the air.

Rrrrrring!

Grace and Blue jumped in tandem. This time the sound came from behind them.

"What the—" Grace turned and squinted.

Rrrrrring!

Dampness slicked her palms. The sound came from a group of saw palmettos thirty feet up the bayou. Was it a searcher? Someone out frog gigging or poaching game?

She wiped her palms on the front of her trousers. "I'm with the Franklin County State Attorney's office. Indentify yourself." Grace's words were steady, her tone calm but commanding. *Never show your fear.* More solid advice from her daddy.

Every sense on overdrive, she waited. Blue jabbed his nose in the air, here and there and everywhere, like he was searching but couldn't find a scent.

Seconds ticked. She scoured the area for shifting fronds, listened for slurping mud. A minute dragged by. Two.

Rrrrrring!

The ringtone shot up her spine like a ramrod. Blue yelped at the sound, now coming from a tangle of bushes behind her.

Rrrrrring!

Enough of this twisted version of phone tag. She ran to her car, grabbed her phone from the dash, and punched in Lieutenant Lang's direct number. "Get your people on the Gilbert Bayou road, third turnoff, ASAP," Grace said. "I found something." Keeping her eyes on the tangle of bushes, she inched to the back of her car and squatted near the trunk, the bayou eerily silent.

The silence was wrong. Death and decay filled the bayou, but it was still a living, breathing world of creatures of the land and sea and air. She should be hearing *something*.

Next to her, Blue's nose stilled, and his ears perked.

Then came the words, soft and at the back of her neck. "Quiet as a cat. Into the black."

Grace spun. The bayou spilled out behind her, puddles of blue and black ink. She squinted through swirls of steam but saw no one.

* * *

"Try over here." Wiregrass stabbed at Grace's ankles as she poked her way along the shore to the saw palmettos.

Lieutenant Lang swept the high-powered spotlight across the slick mud and rotting leaves. "No footprints, no flattened grass, no broken branches." Which had been the pronouncement for the past fifteen minutes, ever since Lieutenant Lang and two deputies had arrived in search of a fast-moving phone.

Grace studied the blue-black bayou. "Then he must have been on the water."

Lieutenant Lang swept the light in a low, slow arc, illuminating bony turtle heads and flesh-colored salamanders. "No signs of a boat docking. So how did he get to your car and behind the Cypress tree? This isn't making sense."

No, nothing about this evening was making sense.

Quiet as a cat. Into the black.

What did those words mean, and how was the person with the phone moving through the area without leaving a trace? More importantly, did any of it have anything to do with Lia Grant?

"Hey!" A deputy near the ancient cypress tree waved both arms. "Found some freshly broken branches over here. Bring the big light."

Grace and the lieutenant ran to his side, the beam slicing at the inky shadows before landing on the ground in front of the deputy. He swatted at loose leaves near the buttress roots.

Grace dropped to a squat. "A big cat," she said on a rush of deflated air.

Lieutenant Lang pushed a handful of springy curls from her face. "Grace, it's possible a big cat made that sound. This section of the Point is full of them."

"It was a phone," Grace insisted.

"Or a wild hog."

"It was a phone."

"Or a bird or insect."

Grace slipped her hands behind her back and locked her fingers. "Fine. Let's call the sound an act of nature, but what about the voice?" *Quick as a cat. Into the black.* "An animal or the wind didn't say those words."

Lieutenant Lang swept the spotlight across the clearing. "Then where's the trace evidence? The footprints? The tire tracks? *Any* sign that a human has recently walked through this area? You're a prosecutor. You know the importance of evidence."

"You want to talk evidence? We have Lia's phone calls to me, the abandoned purse and car, and the call data report showing Lia's calls came off the Cypress Point cell tower. Except for this"—Grace jabbed her hand at the spot where she'd heard the voice—"no one has seen or heard anything unusual on the Point tonight. What else do we have?"

Lieutenant Lang paused a moment before nodding to the deputy. "Get some more lights on this place, and I'll get a man on the water. The person out here may or may not be

Lia's abductor, but he may have seen something." She turned to Grace. "And you, counselor, get home and rest. I have every available uniform searching for this girl."

Grace shook her head. Not until she heard for herself Lia Grant breathing. "I'm fine."

"Yes, counselor, we're aware of your superhuman abilities, but your dog could use a rest."

"He's not my dog." Grace glared at the dog then groaned. He sat at her side, his front right paw lifted off the ground. She inspected his foot. He hadn't torn off the pad, but he'd split it open.

Back at the shack, Allegheny Blue struggled up the porch steps, plopped onto his side, and closed his eyes. With a sigh, she sunk onto the swing and kicked off her sling backs, now caked with swamp mud and decayed leaves. She'd been in such a hurry to search for Lia, she hadn't changed out of her suit. After a little rest, she'd change clothes and grab something to eat. The sun would be up in a few hours.

She scrubbed at the ache in her neck. This wouldn't be the first all-nighter she'd logged in this week. Thanks to Morehouse, she already had clocked in two sleepless nights. She pushed off, and the swing's gray, weathered wood creaked like an old man's bones. Grace found comfort in the rattles and squeaks. In a psych class in college, she'd learned repetitive motions such as swaying or swinging released endorphins, which sent little shots of happy through a person's body. She tucked her legs under her and rested her head on the back of the swing.

When she was young, her daddy had hung a tire swing from a sturdy branch in the giant oak that stretched across most of the front yard of Gator Slide, her childhood home. With no brothers or sisters and few children in the upscale neighborhood, Grace usually played on the swing alone, and on good days, with her mother.

* * *

"Hey, Momma, give me a giant push," Grace remembered calling to her mother one evening as she swung from the arms of the giant oak.

Momma left the porch step where she'd been waiting for Daddy to come home from work. "Have you been a good girl today?" Momma asked with a big smile.

"The bestest!" Gracie said.

Momma grabbed the rope swing, dropped a kiss on Gracie's head, and pushed with all of her might.

"Wheeeee!" Gracie flew through the air, her ponytails flying behind her. "Higher. Push me higher!"

"You're already so high, Gracie, you can almost touch the stars."

"To the stars! Push me to the stars!"

"And what will you do when you reach them?" Momma asked around a laugh.

Gracie scrunched her face in deep concentration. Then she let out a happy squeal. "I shall pluck them from the sky and make a bright, shiny necklace for you, so you'll never be afraid of the dark again."

Her mother's smile slipped away. She clutched the rope, drawing Gracie to her chest as she darted a glance over each shoulder. "They're everywhere, Gracie. The bad people are on the streets, in our neighborhood, beneath our home." Her mother's delicate fingers clawed into Gracie's shoulders. "They're watching me, following me, touching me while I sleep. Make them go away, please, please make them go away."

Early on, Gracie learned it was the things unseen—the

*shapes shifting in the shadows and monsters under the bed—
that scared Momma. She hopped off the swing, too,
Momma's hand, and turned on the porch lights, the ligh
over the garage, and the bright tennis court lights. She set
tled both hands on Momma's cheeks. "The bad people aren'
here, Momma, not tonight. It's just me, and I'll protect you."*

*With Momma smiling again, they ran back to the gian
oak. When they reached the tire swing, Gracie balled he
hands on her hips. "Someone broke my swing!" One fraye
end of the rope dangled from the tree while the other wa
curled like a water moccasin on the ground next to the tire.*

*"Probably those Dickens boys two streets over. Little hea
thens." Momma patted Gracie's head. "But don't worr
Gracie, Daddy can fix it."*

*Gracie rolled her eyes at Momma's silliness. "I don
need any help, Momma. I can do it myself." With a huff, Gra
cie headed for the garage and a new rope.*

*That's when she heard a soft voice say, "Quiet as a ca
Into the black."*

* * *

Something hard and heavy and foul-smelling slammed ont
Grace's chest. Her nose wrinkled. Dog. *Wet* dog.

Her eyelids flew open and she pushed Allegheny Blu
off her chest. Beneath her, the porch swing lurched. Sh
blinked. The sun had peeked over the horizon and earl
morning rays glinted off Blue's sopping fur and the pool o
water seeping across her porch.

"Nooooo!" Darting from the swing, she fished out he
key and threw open the door. A wave of water rolled ove
her ankles. She splashed her way to the kitchen where wate
shot from one of the exposed pipes running up her kitche

wall. She grabbed the wrench on the windowsill and cranked the valve underneath the sink. The geyser tapered to a trickle and finally stopped, but the damage was done.

The plumber had warned her the first time that she needed to have the plastic pipe replaced with copper tubing, but she didn't have the money for new plumbing. Hell, she didn't have two spare copper pennies to rub together.

She squeezed the water out of her hair. This morning was not starting out well, but then again—she ran a flattened palm down the back of her neck—last night hadn't ended well.

Quick as a cat. Into the black.

She'd heard those strange words after hearing the ringing phone in the swamp. Then they invaded her dreams. She grabbed a dishtowel and swabbed the water from her face and hands. Dreams. Not reality. The conversation with her mother on the tire swing and the broken rope had been real, but she didn't remember anyone whispering anything about a cat and black.

She dropped the towel onto Blue and toweled his head and neck. This whole thing with Lia Grant was getting to her. She scrubbed his chest and back and all four legs. Which meant she needed to get back on the hunt.

Within twenty minutes, Grace fed Blue and got him settled on the front porch, set up fans to air out the shack, and put in a call to the sheriff's station. Still no sign of Lia Grant.

"Keep breathing, Lia. Keep breathing."

Her car started on the second crank. Just past the myrtles, she spotted a bright yellow truck with a grading blade and a tractor with a ditch digging arm. Construction equipment, AKA dream builders. Thanks to Lia, Grace had forgotten construction on her new home began today. But the dream would have to wait, because right now, Lia Grant could be living a nightmare. Emphasis on *living*. Lia said the box wasn't air tight, and Grace envisioned streams of air snaking through the seams and keeping her alive.

As she sped around a corner, she slammed on her brakes to avoid hitting a sheriff's department SUV parked in the middle of the road. Her ribs contracted, squeezing her heart. Lia. Something must have happened.

Grace jammed the car in park and dove out the door. No deputy. No construction workers. She followed a trail of fresh footprints along a patch of camellia bushes and spotted a man in a hard hat leaning against a ditch digger. She tapped his shoulder.

The construction worker jumped, letting out a breathy curse. "Whoa there, Miss Courtemanche! You scared the snot out of me."

"What's going on? Why is the sheriff's department here?"

"Delbert over on the back hoe found something. Has everyone a little spooked."

"Lia Grant? Did he find Lia Grant?"

"That little gal who's missing? Nah. Don't think it's her. Least I hope not."

Her chest tightened. "You don't think? What's going on?"

"Delbert was digging stumps and found some old bones in one of the sand hills."

Grace's ribcage let go of her heart. "Of course you're going to find bones around here. Lamar Giroux's hounds spent sixty years burying them."

"Not these kind of bones, least I hope not." He led her through the camellia patch to a shallow ditch where a half dozen construction workers and a sheriff's deputy stood in silence.

"What kind of bo..." Her voice trailed away as she studied the land where her new tennis court was scheduled to be built. Poking up from No Man's Land, the section between the baseline and service line, was a human skull.

CHAPTER FOUR

Excuse me, Agent Hatcher, but your son is ready for you."

Hatch's fingers froze midway through the inch-thick folder the Franklin County Sheriff's Department had gathered on thirteen-year-old Alex Milanos, his *son*.

"Normally we don't keep children overnight," the clerk continued. "Not for something like this, but his grandmother didn't know what to do."

And I do? Hatch ran a hand through his hair.

He'd docked *No Regrets* at the Cypress Point Marina in Apalachicola Bay early this morning and hitched a ride to the sheriff's station where he now sat in a small conference room wondering how the hell a thirteen-year-old kid could have amassed an inch-thick rap sheet. And not just any kid. His kid, one he didn't know existed until twenty-four hours ago. He ran his other hand through the other side of his hair. He was still getting his head wrapped around the idea of *being* a father, and here he was expected to *act* like one. Was he supposed to give the boy fatherly wisdom? Tough love? A boot in the ass? The floor shifted beneath his feet.

"Alex is in one of the holding rooms, Agent Hatcher. You can talk to him there."

He was supposed to *talk* with this boy. *That* he could do. He thumbed through the mountain of papers. Alex was his son, but he was also a kid in a crisis situation, and in those cases, Hatch had plenty of miles on his dock shoes.

Hatch took a final look at Alex's file. Truancy. Underage driving. Curfew violations. The latest infraction: The boy and two unknown accomplices broke into Buddy's Shrimp Shack and lifted forty bucks from the register. As they tried to escape, the manager nabbed Alex. The other two got away. The kicker was that the manager agreed not to press charges if Alex would ID his fellow delinquents. The kid refused. On top of that, Alex had taken a swing at the deputy bringing him in.

Hatch slapped shut the file folder. This kind of crisis he could handle. "Let's sail."

The clerk, a twenty-something named Susie who had a sunny smile to match her bright yellow heels, led him down the hall toward the holding area. "Are you really one of Parker Lord's guys?" When he nodded, she leaned toward him as if to tell a secret. "You know he's one of ours, a Florida legend. Agent Lord first worked human trafficking in Miami, but I hear he's become a real maverick, butts heads with FBI brass on a regular basis. Is it true he answers only to the president?"

Hatch scrubbed the stubble at his chin. Parker Lord was called many things: maverick, mad man, God. And although his boss worked for the FBI, he served justice, which could never be fully embodied in a single institution or one man with presidential powers, both of which had proven sorely fallible over the years.

"Parker Lord answers to his conscience," Hatch said. So did the entire SCIU. It was what set them apart. And it ruffled a whole hell of a lot of feathers. Not that any of his team cared much about pillow ticking.

Hatch followed the clerk through a keypad entry door when something crashed at the far end of the hall, followed by a shout. He ran down the hall, pulled up beside a holding room, and inched his head around the doorjamb to see a red-faced deputy standing in front of a kid with shaggy blond hair. The kid's lip curled in a snarl, and the chip on his shoulder was so big it cast a shadow over the entire room. Definitely Hatch's flesh and blood. And the kid apparently had the same teenage disposition Hatch once had.

God had one cruel sense of humor.

Alex's hand jerked, and he poked a jagged chunk of wood at the deputy. From the looks of the broken chair in the corner, Hatch had a damn good idea where the kid had found his improvised weapon.

The deputy, a bear of a man with two chins, pointed his index finger at the kid. "Put that down, boy, before someone gets hurt."

Alex's fingers tightened around the splintered chair leg. "Don't tell me what to do! I'm tired of everyone telling me what to do."

"Make a few good choices, and folks'll talk a might different to you." The deputy slid a club from his belt.

Hatch ground his back teeth. *Idiot.* And he wasn't talking about the boy.

"Fuck you, dickhead!"

The deputy tapped a club against his thigh. "I think someone needs to take soap to that mouth of yours or maybe a strap to your backside."

Wrong words. The whole thing was wrong. Hatch stepped into the center of the doorway. "Yea, fuck him, fuck the whole thing."

Alex looked up. The wood slipped from the boy's hand, but he grabbed it before it hit the ground. "Shut up! I don't need nothing from *you*."

Hatch needed coordinates. He needed to know exactly where this kid stood. "You know who I am, Alex?"

Those eyes narrowed into slits, as if trying to block out as much of Hatch as possible. "Granny told me she was going to call the old man. Said that since you were some high and mighty FBI guy, you'd take care of everything. I told her don't bother because you're nothing." He jabbed the splintered chair leg at Hatch. "You hear that? You're fucking nothing to me!"

The words crept past the badge and slammed into the center of Hatch's chest. He took a step back as Alex's anger, wave after wave of rippling heat, filled the room. The deputy lifted the club, and Hatch gave his head a shake. Words hurt, but they were also the most powerful weapon known to mankind.

"You're right." Hatch leaned against the door frame. First listen. Then empathize and build rapport. Finally exert positive influence. Hostage Negotiating 101. The kid needed to be in control, or more precisely, Alex Milanos needed to *think* he was in control.

Hatch tipped his head toward the deputy who wore a nametag that read W. FILLINGHAM. "You want Deputy Fillingham here to give you some room?"

The boy shrugged one shoulder then the other. "Uh, yeah, that's what I want, for Deputy Dickhead to get off my ass."

With a tilt of his head, he motioned the deputy to walk toward the door. The lawman trained narrow eyes first on Hatch then the kid. *Now*, Hatched mouthed the single word. The deputy backed out.

Now time to distract the boy from that giant pot of anger and resentment he was brewing. Hatch took a bright yellow scarf from his pocket and snapped it in the air. He made a fist with his other hand and tucked in the scarf. Waving his fist in the air, Hatch opened his fingers one by one and revealed an empty palm. The kid stared at his hand, which gave Hatch a moment to study this thirteen-year-old in crisis. Alex Milanos was no longer a boy, but not quite a man. He was in that awkward, in-between stage where nothing fit. Not his clothes, his words, his emotions. Everything was off kilter.

Hatch took a seat at the table centered in the room. He opened the fist of his other hand, and a royal blue silk scarf floated to the table.

Alex tapped the scarred wood against his leg. "This is bullshit."

Hatch flattened the scarf on the table.

"The break-in—hell, no one got hurt. We didn't even have a real weapon, just a little pocket knife." Alex swallowed hard. "A stupid one I used at Boy Scout camp, and the only time I had it out was to pick the lock."

Hatch folded the scarf three times and nodded thoughtfully.

Alex waved the stick around the holding room. "This is stupid. All this for forty bucks."

No, this wasn't about forty bucks. This was about one angry, screwed-up kid who just wanted to fit in.

Alex's hand shook, the stick bobbing. "It wasn't even my idea. I told the guys we wouldn't get anything. The shrimp shack doesn't keep much money in the cash register on a weeknight, but I went along, and I was the one who got caught. The deputy said he'd release me if I squealed, but I can't do that, can't rat on my guys."

"It's important to look out for your buddies. I don't blame you for keeping quiet."

The stick grew still. "You don't?"

"My guys, my team, I'd do anything for them." It was the dead truth. Hatch would put his life on the line for his teammates, and he had, many times, and they for him.

Alex slumped into the chair across from him. "I'm in big trouble, aren't I?"

Finally. An opening. "Depends on what you do from here."

The chair leg in Alex's hand clattered to the table. "Am...am I going to prison?"

"Nah, the state of Florida doesn't imprison thirteen-year-olds for taking forty bucks from a shrimp shack." Hatch casually reached across the table, palmed the chair leg, and slid it to his lap. "But you can do time in juvie for threatening a peace officer."

The boy's Adam's apple bobbed. "Oh shit."

"That about sums it up."

"Granny is going to kill me."

"Yep, pal, I'd be pretty concerned about that, too." Hatch waited. The kid's actions and the repercussions of those actions needed to pound his head, loud and painful, like the sound of the chair crashing into the wall.

Hatch fingered the scar on the right side his jaw. He'd weathered a few crashes, poundings, too, most of them of the self-destructive nature, but lucky for him, he also had a great aunt Piper Jane who'd hauled his sorry, fifteen-year-old ass out of juvenile detention and onto her thirty-five-foot

Tartan. Together, the two of them had sailed around the world.

Those first few months he pulled ropes until his palms bled, buffed teak until his shoulders flamed, and went hungry because he burned his dinner on the galley stove. For more than a year, his life was the sun and sea and sails. No time for stewing and brewing. Somewhere around the Canary Islands his blisters turned into calluses. At the Suez Canal he officially went from deck hand to first mate. And by the time they sailed past Bali, Hatch knew the secret to the perfect pan-seared grouper. Keep scales on one side. Baste with butter twice.

That sail and the sailor behind it had saved his life. Unfortunately, Great Aunt Jane Piper was docked in the Sydney Harbor, which left him holding the compass for Alex. God help them all.

Hatch cleared his throat. "Well?" He held his breath, surprised at how much he wanted the answer to that question.

Alex studied a scab on his elbow. "What would you do? Being FBI and all?"

The tightness stretched across Hatch's throat eased. Alex had made some piss-poor choices, but he wasn't dumb. "First I'd tell that deputy I made a bad choice and apologize for threatening to break a chair leg over his skull. Then I'd hand over the names of my two buddies. Then, pal, I'd get down on my knees and pray there's an organization in town that needs a whole hell of a lot of community service this summer."

The kid picked at the scab, and a dot of blood trickled down his elbow. Hatch handed him the blue scarf. Alex's lip curled, contorting his face. Hatch lifted both hands. Okay. He was backing off.

A minute ticked by. Another.

Time to close the deal. Hatch stuffed the scarf in his pocket.

"Fine." Alex swiped the blood on his jeans and looked Hatch in the eye. "I'll do it."

Hatch shot prayers of thanks to God, the boy's Granny, and anyone else who'd been guiding his son these past thirteen years. Alex was in choppy waters and rudderless, but he wasn't completely lost. Not yet.

"Hey, that magic trick with the scarf." Alex spat the words. "I know how you did it. It's fucking stupid."

* * *

Grace's construction crew had left, replaced by members of the county's forensic unit who'd roped off a section of the construction site with crime scene tape and colored flags. With tiny shovels and feathery brushes, they sifted through sandy soil, unearthing bones.

Old bones, Grace assured herself as she paced along the crime scene tape. Denuded of all flesh and gray in color, these bones could not belong to Lia Grant, who was still missing. She'd wanted to head into the swamp at sunup to continue the hunt for the girl, but the detective investigating the grave demanded she stay put until he had a chance to question her about the bones.

Not bones, but a human being. The person cradled in the earth where her dream home would be built had once been a living, breathing human being. Until now. Until her. Her feet stilled, sinking into the damp earth. In the courtroom she was no stranger to uncovering old skeletons rattling in defendants' pasts, but there was something disturbing about putting down roots over someone's grave.

A siren wailed and lights flashed as Lieutenant Lang

pulled up to the excavation site. She hopped out of the SUV and jogged to Grace's side. "Any ties to Lia Grant?"

Grace shook her head. "Not that I'm aware of. Still no news on Lia?"

The lieutenant wore wrinkles, swamp mud, and grim lines around her mouth. "Not a damn thing. I stopped by to see if this buried body might shed light on the one I'm looking for." Lieutenant Lang ducked under the crime scene tape. "Pretty desperate, huh?"

Because Lia Grant may be running out of air. Grace followed the lieutenant. "With the sun up, we can get more searches on the Point."

"Absolutely." Lieutenant Lang picked her way through the camellia bushes.

"And we can get some deputies over to the medical center where Lia's car was found."

"That's the plan, but first, the bones." The lieutenant stopped at the depression and nodded at the tech from the forensics team. "What do you have?"

The man in the pit dusted the sand from his hands. "Given cranial development and femur length, definitely an adult. Pelvic tilt and girth suggest a female."

Like Lia. Grace knotted her fingers behind her back.

"How long has she been here?" Lieutenant Lang continued.

"Hard to determine at this point. Years, probably at least a decade."

"Anything unusual found with the body, like a phone?" Grace asked. If that was the case, they could be looking at a serial offender. A shiver rocked her spine at the thought of madness multiplied.

He shook his head. "Nothing yet, but we still have a lot more dirt to move."

"Any religious symbols or markings?" Lieutenant Lang studied the surrounding area, which consisted mostly of camellia bushes and a few sycamores. "It's possible Grace's crew stumbled on the Giroux family cemetery."

"Not likely," Grace said, even though she would prefer her crew had discovered a family's burial plot, a place where the dead rested peacefully amid flowers, shade trees, and prayers of the living. "Lamar Giroux lived here for more than sixty years. No wife, no kids."

"But we did find this." Another forensic tech held up what looked like a small black pebble. "Bullet slug. Discovered it lodged in the back of the skull."

Lieutenant Lang raised her weary face to the sky and let out a tired laugh. "You're doing wonders for my job security, Grace. Got any other buried bodies I need to know about?"

Grace was about to laugh—because with all she'd been slammed with in the past twenty-four hours, she needed to laugh—when she sucked in a gasp. "The bones."

With a tight knot in her stomach, she led the lieutenant from the construction site, past the black gum and myrtles, and to her shack, the one with the sagging front porch and a dented metal garbage can. She lifted the lid with one hand and pointed to Allegheny Blue with the other. "He's been digging them up and dragging them home for months now."

The lieutenant took a step back. "What kind of place is this?"

This was the land coveted by developers and half the town, the earth she'd paid for with every dollar she could scrape together, the place where she wanted to put down roots. Her home.

"You should probably head into town for a few days," Lieutenant Lang said. "Until we find out what's going on here."

Were there other human skeletons on the property, literally under her feet? Did any of this have to do with Lia Grant? The idea shook her to the bone. The brutal reality was Grace had nowhere to go. Her parents and grandparents were long gone, and she had no brothers or sisters. She had colleagues at work and tennis partners at the club, but not the kind she could phone and ask to crash in their spare bedrooms. She spent most nights with case files and her computer, which led to limited romantic entanglements. And she had no money to rent a hotel room.

She settled the lid on the garbage can with barely a clank. "I'll be fine, Lieutenant, right here." For now she had no choice but to stay on her land amid the garden of bones.

* * *

As Hatch and Alex walked out of the sheriff's station, the boy was quiet, but his gait, the set of his face, spoke volumes. Correction. Only three words.

Fuck you, world!

Hatch knew that hateful glare, the swagger, the attitude, and the words. Hell, he'd shouted them on a regular basis when he'd been Alex's age, and his old man had answered with the back of his hand. A ghost of pain rammed his jaw.

But Hatch would never raise his hand to his child, any child. He had other resources. "You want to stop and get some lunch before we go to the cemetery."

Alex kicked at an empty soda can that went flying across the parking lot, nearly missing a small blue Ford pulling into a space near the front door. "I want you to go to hell."

Hatch jammed his hand into his pocket and took out the keys to the SUV he'd sweet-talked out of the front desk clerk. Welcome to a whole new generation of father-son dysfunction. "Fine, we'll meet with Black Jack and—"

A woman in matched pearls the color of frosted ocean swells stepped out of the blue car, and Hatch forgot what he was going to say. Hell, he forgot to breathe. The edges of the world blurred and dimmed. His heart slammed his chest, rattling his ribs.

He opened his mouth. No words, except for the tiny voice in the back of his head.

Back away from the pearls, and no one gets hurt.

He wanted to laugh. He should have laughed, but he couldn't. His throat was too dry, too tight. The woman tugged at the pearls, as if she, too, couldn't breathe. At last she cleared her throat and managed to say on a breathy rush, "Theodore."

The boy at his side asked, "Who the hell is Theodore?"

The blonde didn't move. Hatch didn't breathe.

Alex stabbed his elbow into Hatch's gut. "And who the hell's the hot chick in pearls?"

Hatch focused on the jab, on the pain, on the distraction. After removing Alex's elbow from his ribcage, he winked at Grace Courtemanche. "I'm Theodore, and this is Grace, my wife."

CHAPTER FIVE

Ex-wife." The single word rushed over Grace's lips as she steadied herself against the side of her car. She hadn't seen Theodore "Hatch" Hatcher for more than ten years, not since the day he'd sailed out of Apalachicola Bay with the wind in his hair and her broken heart in his hand.

Hatch continued to stare at her with eyes the color of a steamy July sky. But then, Hatch *was* summer. Lazy days and lustful nights. Sun and sand. And heat. A heat so intense, even with a decade's distance, warmth crept along her cheeks, rushed down her neck, and pooled in her belly in a bubbly geyser.

Hatch's dimples deepened. God, she'd forgotten how easy it was to get lost in the depth of those creases, for a man like Hatch knew how to wear—and work—a smile.

She straightened the pearls at her neck.

"Yep, Alex, the lovely prosecutor is correct as usual. Tell me, Grace, do you ever get tired of being right?" He lowered his voice, his words pouring over her like honey, sweet and wild and golden.

For a moment she forgot everything and simply listened to his words, the words of a charmer. Grace tried to go to the calm, cool place in her head, but her heart slammed triple time, beating up a heat that left her dizzy. From the moment they met on St. George Island the summer after she graduated law school, Hatch Hatcher had left her off balance. She'd spent the summer teaching tennis at an exclusive children's camp, and he'd taught sailing. That hot, whirlwind summer led to a disastrously short marriage. It took them all of ten weeks to learn the universal truth: Mind-blowing sex does not a marriage make.

She'd come a long way since then. She was older now, stronger and harder. She straightened her pearls, centering the clasp at the back of her neck.

"What are you doing here?"

Hatch gave her a breezy shrug. "Just taking care of a little crisis situation."

The boy standing next to him, the one he called Alex and who was Hatch's spitting image, said something under his breath that sounded suspiciously like *asshole*.

Hatch's jaw flinched. The boy's nostrils flared.

"I see you ended up with the Bureau," she said to break the tension.

"Keeping tabs on me, Princess?" He waggled his eyebrows, the wicked grin back.

Hatch and his stupid nicknames. "It's hard not to. One of the country's premiere hostage negotiators receives a good deal of media attention." When she'd known him, he'd been a sun-soaked sailor without a paycheck or a plan, and she'd been shocked when she first heard he was working for Parker Lord's elite team of Apostles. "I saw the talk-down in

Atlanta last month of the high school boy with the bomb. It was all over the news. Good for you."

"Good for the twenty kids in that boy's science classroom." Hatch rested his backside against her car, crossing his legs at the ankles.

To any bystander, he was just a guy kickin' back and catching up with an old flame. But this man was an Apostle. He was one of the best crisis negotiators in the world. And she damn well knew every movement he made and every word he uttered served a purpose. She crossed her arms over her chest.

"And you?" Hatch said. "I hear you're working as an assistant state attorney and destroying bad guys with your lovely little hands."

"I've had a few successes."

"A few?" He laughed, but there was an edge to it. The edge surprised her. The old Hatch had been smooth, like the mirrored glass of a windless ocean. "You got what you always wanted, Princess, success so grand, so high no one can touch you. I bet your daddy's right proud."

Grace's back straightened. Hatch knew where to land a punch. "My daddy's dead."

Hatch's head dipped in a slow nod, and he remained conspicuously silent. He offered the respect the dead deserved but no condolences. No surprise there. Her daddy had despised Hatch. According to her father, Hatch was too light-hearted, lazy, and lethal to her future. Ultimately her father had been right. Marrying Theodore Hatcher had been a gargantuan mistake that had almost lost her not only her father, but her career.

"From what I've heard, you're on top of the world." Hatch uncrossed his arms and raised his palms to the sky. "And someday I bet you'll *own* it."

"And you'll simply *drift* through it."

The air grew still, and the afternoon clamor of the swamp silenced. It was like the heavy, pressurized seconds before a summer storm, before the swollen clouds and electric sky clashed in a thundering display of power.

He was the first to break. His mega-watt smile lit up his face, and he motioned to the building behind them. "And what brings you to the sheriff's office? Are you here for business or"—his dimples sharpened like tiny scythes—"pleasure?"

"Business." The short, tense word catapulted her to the present. She shouldn't be wasting precious time talking to Hatch. She'd spent the day in the swamp searching for Lia Grant, and with each passing hour, the girl's voice grew fainter.

It's cold. And dark. I can't breathe.

Hatch uncrossed his ankles and took a step toward her. She backpedaled. He'd always been so intuitive. He knew how to read people, especially her. This skill, coupled with his gift of words, gave him the power to unnerve her like few ever could.

She nodded at Hatch then the boy. "You'll need to excuse me."

"Of course. I'll leave you to your *business*." A light flecked in his eyes, like little whitecaps in a sea of blue. "But before you go, I have something for you."

Hatch fanned his fingers, reached behind her ear, and pulled out a small sprig with long, waxy leaves and tiny white flowers.

A gasp escaped the O of her lips.

"The sweetest flower of all." Hatch placed the small cluster of tupelo flowers on the hood of her car. "As always, Princess, seeing you has been an exquisite pleasure."

With those words, Hatch and the boy climbed in an SUV and disappeared. And so did her breath. With him out of sight, she leaned against her car, thankful for her temperamental Ford. How like Hatch. Waltz in. Send her world spinning. Waltz out.

She shook off the dizziness.

She had no time for dancing.

Lia Grant had been missing almost twenty-four hours, and finally, they'd gotten a break. One of the deputies had found a witness who saw Lia Grant last night in the hospital parking lot.

* * *

Greenup, Kentucky

Kentucky State Police Detective Tucker Holt heard bells, and not just any bells—giant church bells clanging right behind his eyes.

He grabbed the pillow and crammed it over his head, but the damn clanging wouldn't stop. His right hand snaked out, groping along the nightstand until he found his cell phone. He sent the call to voicemail and sunk deeper into the mattress, hoping he still had enough Wild Turkey left in him to burrow deeper into oblivion.

The giant bells clanged again.

He snatched the phone, ready to throw the thing across the room, when he saw the number. Damn. "Holt," he said around a tongue that was two sizes too big.

"Hey, Tuck," his boss, Henderson Rhodes, said. "We need you at Collier's Holler. Got a double."

Not only was his tongue too big, it was wearing a woolen sock that scratched the roof of his mouth. "A double?"

"Collier's bird dog found two bodies in the holler this evening."

Two bodies? He was too hung over to take on two bodies. Hell, he was too hung over to take to his own two feet. "Call Wilkinson."

"He's on vacation. Alaskan cruise with the missus."

"Greggs."

Henderson cleared his throat. "Tuck, I'm going to make this as clear as possible, because you need clarity in the form of a slap upside that head of yours. Get your nose out of the bottle and back into your work. You lost your house, your wife, and your kids. One more fucked-up case, and you'll lose your job. See you in the holler."

Tucker jammed his thumb against the side of the phone and the line went dead. For a moment he wished he could flick a similar switch on the side of his head. Tucker was a screwup and a drunk. The two were intertwined. He drank, he screwed up. He screwed up, he drank. He threw the phone on the nightstand where it slammed into a photo frame that toppled over and crashed to the floor. Dragging himself to the edge of the bed, he winced at the splintered glass spidering across Hannah's chubby cheeks and Jackson's toothless grin.

"Can you fix it, Daddy?" Hannah would have asked.

"Daddy can fix anything," Jackson would have said with the unwavering conviction of a six-year-old who hadn't yet learned how fucked up the world really was.

He picked up the photo, staring at the faces of his kids who, no matter how bad he screwed up, thought he could fix the world. Setting the photo on the nightstand, he dragged his hand across his face. Henderson was wrong. He hadn't lost his kids. Mara, his soon-to-be ex, had filed for full custody, but she hadn't won. Not yet.

With a groan, he dragged his ass out of bed, the bells clanging with every step he took toward an ice-cold shower.

Thirty minutes later the bells still clanged as he climbed out of his police cruiser, the one marked Detective Unit. He slipped on his aviator glasses, but they did little to block out the sharp lances of sun needling his pickled skull. An officer led him through the thick woodlands toward a ravine.

"Collier's dogs spotted up on 'em an hour ago," the patrol officer said. "Older couple, man and a woman, dressed in hiking gear. By the looks of the bodies, they've been here a few days."

"Any reports of missing tourists?" Tucker asked as he ducked under the crime scene tape.

"Nope, and no locals MIA, either."

Tucker grabbed a huckleberry branch and lowered himself into the holler. Already he could smell the obscene sweetness. He swatted a cloud of no-see-ums and picked his way through the steamy, tangled brush, hoping like hell this would be a simple tag and bag.

This time of year they got plenty of day hikers and bird watchers in the northern Kentucky woodlands. Beautiful country. Beautiful place to raise a family. He drew up before the first set of flags. Beautiful place to die.

Pushing aside a thistle bush, he spotted two legs with springy gray hair sticking out from khaki hiking shorts. The bloating body wore cross trainers and a fanny pack. He swatted at another branch, and a cloud of flies swarmed from the upper body. He swallowed a drunken chunkiness as he studied what was left of the old man's face, bone and cartilage bleached and dried by the sun. A grainy white powder clung to a few remaining strips of flesh hanging from the temples and neck. Likewise, the white, grainy powder had eaten away the flesh on the fingertips.

"The woman's over there." The officer pointed past a downed log where Tucker could make out a single white tennis shoe and veiny calf. The bells rang louder as he climbed over rocks and brambles to the second body. As on the male, the white powder had eaten away the female's face and hands.

He ground the palm of his hand into the center of his forehead in an attempt to stop the bells. No go. With the "Hallelujah Chorus" clanging in his head, he radioed the officer at the top of the holler. "Call in the crime scene boys."

CHAPTER SIX

Hatch had taken on machine-gun-packing bank robbers and bomb-toting terrorists. He'd talked hijackers out of the air and suicide jumpers off twenty-story ledges. But nothing ruffled him like Grace Courtemanche. His wife, even in the *ex* state, still had the power to slam him in the gut and get his adrenaline so pumped he thought he could fly.

It was a good thing Alex, who sat in the front seat next to him as they drove from the sheriff's station to the cemetery, wasn't in a chatty mood, because Hatch's head—check that, his entire body—was completely preoccupied with Grace.

She was still cool and classy, still breathtakingly beautiful. That soft flowery scent, so sweet it'd leave a grist of bees half drunk, still sent his pulse racing. Time and common sense hadn't dulled the old pleasures or pains. Which was why he needed to get him and his boat out of Florida bayou country. He'd lost too much blood, too much of his heart, last time he was in town.

However, he couldn't sail until he got wayward Alex on course, just like Great Aunt Piper Jane had done for him.

Hatch had worked a deal with the sheriff's office where his son would hand over the names of his delinquent friends, issue a formal apology to Deputy Fillingham, and work more than 250 community service hours at one of the local churches. The kid would be so busy this summer he wouldn't have time to get into trouble.

The old country road ended at the River of Peace Cemetery. Before them stood an ornate iron gate flanked by a pair of gnarled cypress trees reaching into the sky with bony hands. He wondered if Alex and his buddies ever pulled a prank or two around here on Halloween. It was something Hatch would have done as a kid.

"Hop out and open her up." Hatch dipped his head toward the gate.

Alex crossed his arms over his chest. "This is bullshit."

"Yep, but for the next two months, pal, it's *your* bullshit. Now open the gate."

Alex kicked open the car door and stormed out, adding over his shoulder, "Let's get something straight. I ain't your *pal*."

The kid was right. At this point, there wasn't anything between them but a few matching strands of DNA. With a sullen Alex inside the SUV, Hatch drove through the cemetery gate. A raven screeched. Alex jumped. The kid looked as white as the ghostly fog meandering through oaks and holly trees and headstones and crypts streaked with moss.

"You sure you want to do this?" Hatch asked. "Pastor Austin said you could also work your service hours at the church nursery."

"I ain't going to work with no snot-nosed brats. Get enough of that shit at home."

"If you change your mind, p—" Hatch shook his head. "That's right. We're not pals."

They drove over a rickety bridge where grave markers had sunk into the spongy earth and rust ate away at iron gates. The road ended at a small cottage with shuttered windows.

"Black Jack's probably not home." Alex waved a hand at the empty driveway. "We can come back in the morning."

"Pastor Austin said the caretaker would meet us this afternoon. We wait." Patience was a sorely overlooked virtue, something Hatch hadn't learned until well into adulthood.

Black Jack Trimble, the River of Peace Cemetery caretaker, would be in charge of monitoring Alex's community service, and that service was Alex's ticket to keeping his attitudinal little ass out of juvenile detention. Therefore, Hatch was not going to let the kid start off on the caretaker's bad side. As a crisis negotiator, he knew the importance of initial impressions.

Crushed oyster shells crunched under his feet as he walked with Alex up the drive to the cottage, a squat building of whitewashed wood with a corrugated metal roof. An alligator skull hung above the door, and a row of scarlet geraniums sat in a box below a window.

"Black Jack must be an interesting fellow," Hatch said.

Alex folded his arms across his chest. "Anyone who likes to hang out with dead bodies is a wack job."

"Sounds like Black Jack is pretty good at the job. He runs this whole place by himself." Not everyone could be a cemetery caretaker, just like not everyone could be a hostage negotiator. Or a father. Hatch jammed his fists into his low-riding khaki shorts. "Pastor Austin said he's been taking care of the cemetery grounds for almost thirty years."

"Probably 'cause he can't get work anywhere else. Not with his past."

Hatch sat on an old cypress stump near a woodpile. "Past?"

Alex flicked a glance over his shoulder and settled a serious gaze on Hatch. "Years ago big ol' Black Jack Trimble walked into Cypress Bend with no shirt, no shoes, and a fishing hook hanging from his back pocket. He had a bandage on his shoulder covered in blood. Some people said he got shot escaping from prison somewhere in Georgia." The kid's eyes widened. "Others said he was stabbed by a woman whose baby he was stealing for his dinner."

A storyteller. This boy was definitely from his loins. Great Aunt Piper Jane, who'd taught him the art and power of a good story, would love this kid.

"What about you?" Hatch tilted his head. "What do you believe is Black Jack's story?"

Alex scrunched his nose, as if surprised Hatch had asked him his opinion. And therein lay one of society's other problems. Not enough people listened. The boy's confused expression made him look oddly young, and for a moment, Hatch pictured Alex before the hard edge of adolescent rebellion had set in. Unruly, curly blond hair. Curious eyes. Sand-covered toes. Skinned knees. A mouth that never stopped. Hatch couldn't help but smile.

Alex scowled. "Don't know, don't care. So stop asking me all your stupid questions."

To their right, the bushes shivered, and a handful of leaves fell to the ground. The bushes parted, and a shadowy silhouette took shape. A bald man standing more than six and a half feet tall walked toward them, a stringer of fish across his broad back, the fish tails slapping his ebony skin. He wore no shoes.

Hatch introduced himself and Alex.

"I was 'specting you." Black Jack's southern drawl was deep, a tremor gripping the earth. Hatch handed the caretaker the paperwork from Pastor Austin. Without reading it, Black Jack put the papers in his back pocket.

"Six o'clock tomorrow morning, Alex. Bring gloves." The caretaker turned, and with the fish still flopping against his slick back, walked up the path to the cottage. "And a shovel."

"A shovel?" Alex's voice rivaled a whisper. "He's not going to make me bury no stinkin' bodies, is he?"

Black Jack stopped and turned only his head. The fishtails stopped flopping. "No, Alex, you will not touch the bodies. You have not yet earned that honor."

Hatch regularly stared death in the face, and more than once, he'd held it in his arms. At times his arms struggled under the weight of sorrow and injustice. Other times, he cradled joy and light. But there was one constant: Death was final. And that's why a soul needed to live life to the fullest, to pass from this world with no regrets.

The cottage door creaked open, and Black Jack and his stringer of fish ducked through the darkened doorway.

"See," Alex said under his breath. "He's a friggin' wack job." He stalked off toward the SUV and grabbed the passenger door handle. "You must be some piss-poor negotiator if this is the best you could do for me. Loser."

* * *

A baby screamed.

Excellent. The witness was here. Grace hurried down the hall toward Lieutenant Lang's office. Rhonda Belo had given birth two days ago at the Cypress Bend Medical Center where her second floor room overlooked the employee parking lot.

The screams sharpened and grew louder as Grace drew up in the doorway. Lieutenant Lang sat at her desk, and across from her sat a crying woman, two circles of dampness blooming across her swollen breasts. A man with rumpled hair, dark circles under his eyes, and a five-o'clock shadow circled the room like a marathon race-walker, a bundle of pink shrieking in his arms.

"Perhaps you can take the baby outside for a moment, Mr. Belo?" Lieutenant Lang suggested over the wails.

"No!" The mother knotted her hands beneath her breasts. "She's only two days old. I don't want her out of my sight. Walk faster, Greg. She likes movement."

"I'm practically running," the man said with a snap. "What more do you want me to do?"

"Something because I can't concentrate with this." She jabbed her hands at the front of her T-shirt, where the circles of dampness widened and a milky substance plopped onto the chair. Lieutenant Lang handed her a box of tissue.

Grace stepped into the room. "Give her to me."

The mother turned her head to the door. "Who are you?"

"Grace Courtemanche with the State Attorney's office," she said. "I'm working with Lieutenant Lang on the Lia Grant case."

"You know stuff about babies?" the new father asked.

Grace held out her hands and gave the man the comforting but assured smile she gave to nervous witnesses and grieving family members. "Yes." Clearly more than Mr. Belo.

He handed over the screaming bundle and eyed the doorway with longing. "Would you mind if I went out for a smoke?"

"No smoking around the baby," the mother said as she shoved tissue down the front of her T-shirt.

Grace tilted her chin toward the door. "Go get some fresh air, Mr. Belo. We'll be fine."

The bundle let out another wail, and the new mother glanced at her as if Grace were about to eat the child. Grace swayed. She knew nothing about babies, but she knew the soothing power of a good swing. She pictured her porch swing, old tire swing, and her daddy's arms. The screams softened to whimpers and finally to breathy hiccups.

Lieutenant Lang nodded at the mother. "Do you need any more tissues, Mrs. Belo?"

"I'm good as long as she doesn't start crying again. We've both been crying. Sleepless nights. Hormones." She pulled half a tissue from her bra and blew her nose. "Sorry I didn't come forth sooner, Lieutenant Lang. With Callie's birth, I've been out of it and Callie's been so fussy. When we got home this evening, she finally fell asleep, and Greg and I finally got a chance to relax. We turned on the TV and saw the news report about the missing girl."

"When did you see Lia Grant?" Lieutenant Lang asked.

"Two nights ago, the day Callie was born. It was around midnight. Callie was fussy. I'd fed her and changed her but she wouldn't stop screaming, so I started walking. It seemed to help." She smiled at Grace, who was still swaying.

"What did the woman look like?" Lieutenant Lang continued.

"Exactly like the picture on the news. Shoulder-length brown hair with bangs. Medium height and weight. She wore a purple volunteer smock and these cute white tennis shoes with purple laces."

"How can you be so sure of something so specific?"

Grace asked. "The lights in that section of the parking lot weren't working."

"It was dark, but I could clearly see her when the white truck pulled into the parking lot and parked next to her."

"What was she doing?" Lieutenant Lang asked.

"Locking her car. When she was done, she waved to the person in the white truck. I remember thinking how sweet she looked and that she was probably a great hospital volunteer. The person driving the truck must have said something to her because she walked to the passenger door and spoke to him."

"Him?" Grace asked.

"Did you see the driver?" Lieutenant Lang added.

"No, but the truck seemed like a guy's truck. Big, a lift kit, mud covered, and those oversized tires. Of course a girl could drive it. We're going to avoid all those gender stereotypes. Callie can play with trucks and play football."

Grace couldn't help but notice everything kept coming back to the baby. The young mother was consumed. And this was why Grace didn't have a family. There was no time in her life for a dog, let alone a child who deserved this kind of attention.

"Did you hear any of the conversation?" Lieutenant Lang asked.

"Nothing. My bedroom window was closed."

The baby kicked, and Grace rocked faster. "What happened next?"

"They talked for quite a while. I must have walked back and forth a hundred times. The girl was resting her arms on the truck windowsill. It looked like a pretty intense conversation. And then when I walked by and looked, the woman and the truck were gone."

"Did they leave together?"

"I kind of assumed they did."

"Can you tell us anything else about the truck? License plate number? Make? Model?"

The young mother shook her head. "I'm sorry. I had my hands pretty full that night."

Lieutenant Lang asked a dozen more questions and took the young mother's contact information. Grace made a mental note to see if the medical center or nearby businesses had any security cameras. Plus she needed to—

"Excuse me."

Grace turned to the young mother. "Yes?"

"Callie." She pointed to the bundle in Grace's arms. "I need my baby."

Grace stopped swaying and stared at the baby now sleeping deeply and peacefully in her arms. "She's sweet and beautiful." She handed the bundle to the new mother, her arms heavy despite the emptiness. She gave her arms a shake. "I'm sure she'll do great things."

With the witness gone, Lieutenant Lang picked up her phone. "I'll put a BOLO out on the truck. It's unique, and chances are someone will remember it. I'll also get CSU on the scene and check for tire tracks."

Grace nodded absently. All good, but they needed more. She looked out the window. "Clouds are coming in."

"And with the clouds come rain," Lieutenant Lang said.

Grace didn't say what they both were thinking. And with the rain would come mud which would seep into any cracks letting in air. "We need more help."

"We have more than a hundred searchers. Every news outlet within a hundred miles has given the story coverage. Even the Girl Scouts have joined the hunt. Lia Grant was a Girl Scout leader, and her troop is passing out flyers door to door."

"It's not enough." They needed manpower and resources and experts. Grace stopped pacing. "Have you called the FBI?"

"That first night. They're checking ViCAP for similar abductions and have offered tech support. Why?"

"Remember that stranger abduction last summer in Orlando?"

"Wasn't that the eight-year-old girl in the princess costume?"

Grace nodded. "Orlando police called in one of the FBI's foremost missing and endangered child specialists, an agent from Parker Lord's team. He wrapped up the case in sixteen hours. He was also involved in the hunt last month in northern Nevada for that old blind Vietnam veteran who was captured by the Broadcaster Butcher."

"Sounds like the kind of man we need on our side. If you can get him here, I'll make you friendship bracelets for life." The lieutenant tried to smile, but it came across as a grimace. "Do you know him?"

Grace took a deep breath. She could do this. For Lia. "I'm acquainted with one of Parker Lord's team members who is in town this week."

The lieutenant did an about-face. "You have an in with Parker Lord's team?"

And an out. Breathe in, two, three. Breathe out, two, three. Damn, she was never this agitated. "Yes."

CHAPTER SEVEN

"You really live on a stinkin' boat?"

Hatch ducked into the cabin and tossed the steaming, crumpled newspaper onto the galley table. "Yep," Hatch said to Alex, who filed in behind him.

On their way from the cemetery, Hatch had stopped at one of the oyster bars that squatted along the bay and picked up lunch: a dozen oysters, bakers with blue crab and artichokes, and a pair of fried amberjack filets. He'd told the waitress to throw in some fried greens. Kids needed vegetables, didn't they? Hatch swiped a hand down his face. He didn't know what the hell kids needed. He didn't know what the hell he was doing, other than keeping this kid, his kid, out of trouble. He owed that to Alex. Among other things. He'd help out with finances, Alex's education, and issues with the authorities. Maybe he'd drop by a few times a year and check up on the family. He could even take Alex and his kid brothers out for a sail, maybe drop a few lines and snag a few fish, like a favorite uncle.

As for the day-to-day stuff, it wasn't going to happen. It couldn't. Hatch had a job that kept him on the road ninety percent of the time. More than that, in his job he worked with some severely broken people, and many of them had grown up with mothers and fathers lacking serious parenting skills. Alex was screwed up enough without adding a father who knew nothing about raising a kid.

Hatch opened the fridge. Damn, he could go for a long-neck. He grabbed two bottled waters and tossed them on the galley table.

Behind him, Alex jumped and stumbled back from the shelf near the top berth. "It's alive!"

Hatch pointed to the shelf and then to Alex. "Alex, Herman. Herman, Alex," he said by way of introduction.

The kid poked at a crab scooting across a knobby sea sponge. "Herman is such a lame name for a hermit crab. Really original."

"His full name is Herman Melville, The Fourth."

Alex squatted so he was eye level with the crab. "Like the whale dick writer dude?"

Hatch swallowed a chuckle. "That's one way to look at Herman Melville." Hatch pointed to the dozens of books behind the glass case, which included *Moby Dick*. "You know about Captain Ahab's epic sea voyage?"

Alex shrugged.

"Feel free to take the book with you."

"Feel free to shut the fuck up."

Hatch's fist tightened. If he'd said that to his old man, he would have been knocked across the cabin. He shook his fingers. Nope, not going to happen in his world.

He sat at the table and tore open the newspaper. Buttery, garlicky steam poured out. Alex slumped onto the bench across from him and dug into the pile of seafood. Hatch had gained ten pounds during his last stint in Apalachicola. Oysters and shrimp. Biscuits slathered in honey. Fish so fresh it jumped in the frying pan. A decade ago when *No Regrets* had been anchored in the bay, he'd drop a line, snagging snappers and flounder the minute his hook hit the water. Within fifteen minutes he'd have them in a pan on his galley stove sizzling with butter. Grace would be at the table with two glasses of wine. And a smile.

At one point that was all he'd needed to live. A few fish, wine, and Grace.

He wondered what "business" she had at the sheriff's station. To the untrained eye, she looked calm and in control, classic Grace, but Hatch was a student of faces, of minute movements, of words not spoken. Earlier today Grace Courtemanche had been anything but calm. She'd smoothed the pearls at her neck one too many times, and if he hadn't been so slammed by the sight of her, he would have taken great delight in watching Grace be anything but graceful. But this little side trip to Cypress Bend wasn't about Grace. He had enough on his plate with his son.

He tapped a fisted hand against his chin, wondering what families talked about at the kitchen table. "You like to fish?" Hatch asked.

"Nope."

"Play video games?"

"Nope."

"What do you and your buddies do?"

"Hang out." Alex continued to inhale food.

Boys ate a lot. What else did they do? Hatch recalled his early teens. Back then he had one thing on his mind. "You got a girl?"

Alex snorted. "Like I'd tell you."

Hatch turned in the direction of Sydney Harbor. *Do you*

see me, Great Aunt Piper Jane? I'm trying. I'm really, really trying.

Hatch and Alex finished the meal in silence, and when Hatch went topside with the keys to the borrowed SUV, Alex followed. Instead of stomping down the dock, the boy plopped onto a deck chair. He toed a coiled rope.

"You and the hot chick in the pearls, were you really married?" Alex asked.

Hatch knew the boy was stalling for time, not because he wanted to spend time with his father but because he wanted to avoid going home to a granny who was tired and cranky and two twin brothers who terrorized him. "Ten weeks." Hatch sunk onto a bait bucket. He'd give the boy a few more minutes' break.

"What happened?"

"Respiratory problems. She couldn't breathe in my world. I couldn't breathe in hers."

"So why'd you marry her?"

Because when you were having the best sex of your life, who cared about respiratory failure? But he and the spawn were hardly ready for a father-son chat about birds and bees. Hatch leaned on the bucket and grinned. "I love girls in pearls."

Alex's forehead creased and he nodded slowly. What was going on in his crazy teenage head? Was he thinking about Grace? About his own hot chick?

Alex dug his toe into the coil of rope. "I had a boat once. Little dory skiff. Found it swamped out near Alligator Point."

Finally, something they could talk about. "You have to do much work to her?"

"Little bit of splintering on the bow. Borrowed a sander from a neighbor and got it sealed. Wasn't pretty, but she was great on the water."

"Get in any good fishing?"

"A few nice redfish. Did some oyster tonging, too. Used to take her all around the bay until Granny found out. Took it from me. Said it was too dangerous. Pissed me off."

"Your granny worries about you." Hatch was no profiler like his teammate Hayden Reed, but Hatch had had no trouble reading Alex's Granny. When he met with her earlier in the day, it was clear she was a tired old woman single-handedly raising a set of rambunctious twins and a thirteen-year-old boy who was mad at the world.

Alex kicked at the rope. "What the fuck do you know?"

Hatch jabbed at the flop of hair hanging across his forehead. "Apparently not a whole hell of a lot." Which meant it was time to go, but he owed this kid the truth. He leaned toward the boy and rested his elbows on his knees. "I'm not going to bullshit you, Alex. I haven't been around a single day in your thirteen years on this planet. As a matter of fact, until yesterday, I never knew you existed."

"Don't you go bad-mouthing my momma."

Hatch raised both hands. "I'm not blaming your momma for anything. She had reasons for what she did and didn't do, and it's not my place to pass judgment on her, but I am going to come clean with you, because you deserve it."

Alex's lip curled.

"I'm not father material, Alex. The truth is I'm not even family material. Just ask the hot chick in pearls." Hatch stood. He needed to move, to get the wind in his hair. "But your granny called me in here because she needed help. She said you needed help. And I want to help. I owe it to you, today and in the future."

"We don't need nothing from you." The chip on Alex's shoulder was back, blocking out the sun. "So why don't you take your stinkin' boat and your stinkin' crab and stinkin' leave." Alex kicked the rope and stormed off the boat toward the parking lot.

"That's the goal, pal, that's the goal," Hatch said to the wind. He'd come clean with the kid. His work, his lifestyle—hell, his history—were not conducive to caring for a teenage boy. And this boy had rightly recognized he'd be better off without Hatch. Smart, smart kid.

In the borrowed SUV, Hatch took Alex home, and by the time he got back to *No Regrets*, he was ready for that icy cold beer. The all-night sail had left him tired. Bullshit. The one-two punch of Alex and Grace had knocked the wind from his sails.

He grabbed a longneck from the galley, paused, and grabbed another. Topside, a briny breeze skipped across the deck while he polished off the first beer. Clouds were moving in, taking off the sharp edge of the late afternoon sun. He tucked the beer in a cup holder, settled back for a nap, and threw a cap over his face. Before he could start counting sheep, footsteps clattered on the dock, and his boat dipped.

"Beer's in the fridge below," Hatch said to his cap.

"I'm afraid I'll have to pass."

He bolted up. The glass bottle slipped from the cup holder, hit the deck and shattered. Another mess. Kind of par for the course with him and Grace. He couldn't force a smile. Alex had tested him and taken his last thread of patience. "What are you doing here, Grace?"

"I need an Apostle."

CHAPTER EIGHT

The first drop splattered Grace's right shoulder. Another hit her left cheek. Thunder rolled across the sky, shoving the clouds—and rain—closer to Cypress Point.

"We're on our way, Lia, and we're going to find you." Grace threaded her way through dozens of cars pulling into the parking lot of Don and Dar's Bait Shop. A news crew from a Tallahassee television station was preparing for a live feed, and volunteers outfitted with swamp waders, lights, and shovels were checking in and picking up maps. Thanks to Hatch's teammate Agent Jon MacGregor, a full-scale, state-of-the-art, best-of-the-best search-and-rescue effort was underway.

At the command station she found Lieutenant Lang, who handed her a sheet of paper with cross-hatch marks. "CSU found these tracks in an old oil spill in the parking lot where Rhonda Belo saw Lia Grant talking to the person driving the white truck."

Grace grabbed it, thrusting the paper in the air like a trophy. Finally, they had something.

Her smile faltered as Hatch hopped out of an SUV. She had no problem with him being here. He was responsible for getting Agent MacGregor on board and was certainly good in crisis situations, but she took issue with the hard glare he leveled at her.

His fingers clawed around her upper arm. "Don't you dare move until we talk."

"I don't need to take orders from you, as this is not your jurisdiction or your case." She tried to jerk away, but his grip tightened.

"'Fraid it is, Princess. You asked for help from the SCIU."

"Which would be Agent Jon MacGregor. I do believe that's the person I'll be answering to."

Hatch held up his cell phone. "Grace meet Jonny Mac. Jonny Mac meet Grace."

"Afternoon, Grace," a deep voice came from the cell phone's speaker. "I'll need to talk with you in a minute, but Hatch and I need to get the ground crew rolling. He's my eyes and ears and hands and feet."

And one of those golden hands was on her arm. "Of course," she said. "Let me know what you need me to do."

Hatch turned the phone off speaker, but before he spoke to Agent MacGregor, he mouthed, *Don't move.* With the phone at his ear, he plowed through the growing crowd of searchers.

There were times Grace felt Hatch wasn't of this world. He was a free spirit moving in a universe not of man. He was air and light, sun and heat. This afternoon was not one of those times. Today Hatch was solid, steely, in command. And he was an FBI agent from a renowned special unit with a vast number of resources at his golden fingertips. Grace might not need Hatch in her life, but until Agent MacGregor arrived, Lia did.

Another raindrop plopped onto her head. Wind tugged at her hair.

Hatch stepped onto a stump, and the crowd fell silent. "We're concentrating the search in a three-mile square area covering all of Cypress Point. We'll divide and conquer by land and waterways. In teams of two you will..."

Grace shook her head in amazement. Hatch was no longer the lazy, sun-baked sailing instructor who'd charmed his way into her bed and heart. Right now he was action and power.

When Hatch finished giving orders, he handed her his phone and she gave Agent MacGregor a rundown of the past twenty-four hours. When she finished, she joined Hatch and Lieutenant Lang at the check-in station where Hatch was asking, "Did you get the helicopter?"

"I made the request," Lieutenant Lang answered. "But I'm still waiting on the authorization."

"No worries," Hatch said. "I see something better has arrived."

Before Hatch could explain, a battered gold pick-up truck pulled into the parking lot, accompanied by annoyingly familiar bellows. Behind the truck on a flatbed trailer squatted a four-wheeled ATV, and in the truck bed were dogs, at least a half dozen of them: blue speckled ones, red speckled ones, black and tans, solid reds, all with thumping tails and enormous, droopy ears.

Grace pictured Allegheny Blue at the shack. Probably dreaming of bacon.

The driver, an older man with a long, grizzled beard, unloaded the quad from the trailer. He tipped his cap. "Hey there, Agent Hatcher. You got the little gal's scent ready? We need to get the old girl on the ground before the rain moves in."

Hatch picked up a T-shirt sealed in a plastic bag from the check-in table. "The roommate said Lia Grant always slept in it."

"Should do right fine." The hunter took the T-shirt and held it under the nose of one of the brownish-red dogs. "Here you go, Ida Red. Time to hunt."

The red bone hound's ears curled up and forward. Her nose flared and quivered, a shiver shaking her head and body. This was an animal doing what it was born to do, lived to do, loved to do. The hunter lowered the tailgate with a clank. Ida Red's nose hit the ground before her feet, and the other dogs followed.

Grace wanted to raise her hands in the air and shout, *Finally!* They were doing something to find Lia Grant.

A burst of wind sliced through the parking lot, rattling the tent. As the bay of hounds tapered off, the huddle of men and women in the parking lot broke, moving swiftly. Hatch, on the other hand, moseyed to her side, his gait slow and easy, but there was nothing conciliatory in his eyes. "You should have told me." His mouth and jaw barely moved as he spoke.

She tried to ease away, but he moved with her. "Told you what?"

"Hmmmmm, where should I start?" With his free hand, he jammed a finger in the air. "One, you received threats from a convicted felon. Two, you received nine phone calls from a girl presumably buried alive. And three, as we speak, a forensic team is sifting through dirt in your backyard looking for human bones."

"It's none of your business."

"Oh, Princess. Dear, dear Princess." He moved closer, a big, graceful, golden cat. He stopped a hairsbreadth from touching her, but the heat of his skin warmed her, nipping at the chill that had set in yesterday with Lia's phone calls.

When he spoke, his breath fanned her face in a low, rumbling half-purr, half-growl. "You have been and always will be my business."

The words, the closeness, so Hatch. For a moment, she considered sinking into his strength and warmth, which proved how deeply rattled she was by the past twenty-four hours.

Hatch didn't seem to notice the crazy thoughts flitting around her brain. He grabbed her elbow and led her toward a sheriff's department SUV.

"I'm not going home." Her boots dug into the damp earth.

Hatch opened the SUV's passenger door. "I wouldn't dare suggest it."

"I'm involved in this."

"That's obvious." He pointed to the seat. "Hop in."

"Where are we going?"

"Into the swamp. We're searching for Lia Grant. *Together*."

The humid air had left her hair a riot of waves, and she jammed a wayward curl behind her right ear. Together wasn't hard for her. She was a team player when she had to be, and Lia Grant needed the biggest team they could muster, and frankly, Hatch was on a winning team. She'd be an idiot not to ally herself with him. She hopped in the SUV. "Where to?"

He reached into his pocket and took out a coin. "Call it in the air?"

"Wait! You're going to let a coin toss determine our course of direction, which could very well determine if a girl lives or dies?"

Hatch fingered the coin. "Do you have a better plan?"

"Surely there's a more logical way to handle this. What does Agent MacGregor recommend?"

An enigmatic smile tugged at Hatch's mouth. "Like all of us on Park's team, Jonny Mac understands the value of a good coin toss." Hatch tossed the coin in the air. "Heads we go right, tails, left."

She snatched the coin in mid-air. Decades of tennis had done wonders for her hand/eye coordination. "I don't think so."

Hatch swept his hands at the dense forest stretching out behind the bait shop. "Fine, Princess. Lead and I shall follow."

Grace cradled the coin in her palm. She'd already played the phone messages from Lia, listening for ambient sounds, ideally something like a jet plane, which could be tracked. But in all of the voicemails, she'd heard nothing but Lia's increasingly desperate words.

I'm in a bad place, a really bad place.

A hand settled on her knee. Golden and steady. This was not her ex-husband but Hatch the Apostle. Hatch who was a master in a crisis situation. She ran her thumb over the face of the coin, and with quirked lips tossed it in the air. The coin spun and fell on the ground between them.

"Left." Hatch pocketed the coin and with a seriousness she'd never seen from him, climbed into the SUV and drove into the swamp.

Grace rolled down her window and leaned out, squinting through the graying afternoon at the road and searching for wide tire tracks with a deep cross-hatch pattern. They inched along a road following a twisting creek lined with reeds and cattails. Raindrops pinged the roof and splattered her arms and hands. A wind blew across the reeds, whisking them in a symphony of brushes and hushes.

"Liiiiia!" Hatch called. They waited. For a muffled cry. A tapping SOS. A low groan.

Hush, hush, whispered the reeds.

"Keep breathing, Lia, keep breathing."

Raindrops turned into a drizzle. Hatch flipped on the windshield wipers. Water puddled in the gutters on either side of the road.

"Keep your head up, Lia. You're strong, and you can beat this...this thing."

At a hairpin turn, Hatch slowed. "What's that?" He pointed to a section of flattened reeds.

Grace leaned out the window, shielding her eyes from the rain. "Gator slide. Too smooth to be man-made."

This land was filled with dangerous animals like gators and water moccasins and treacherous waterways.

"What does she need to do to survive?" Hatch asked.

Grace blinked then noticed a pain in her right fingertips. She'd wound them in the chain of her scattered pearl necklace. "If she runs into an alligator she needs to make noise. Same thing with a water moccasin."

"And..." The single word was low and slow.

She loosed her fingers. "If she has to cross water, she needs to do it midday when the alligators aren't as active. She can cover her exposed skin with mud to keep off ticks and jiggers. She needs to stay hydrated, drinking water from vines or collecting rainwater in leaves or her shirt."

"And..."

"If she finds a beer can, she's struck gold. It can be used to make noise and scare off predators, collect and boil water, and cut fronds for shelter."

His fingers intertwined with hers. A touch from the living. From the here and now. Damn he was good. She squeezed back.

Hatch nudged the car down the road, calling, "Liiiiiia!"

They followed winding side roads until blocked by bogs or creeks or stands of pines or cypress. All the while, Hatch scoured the slow-moving countryside, every muscle in his arms tensed. Just as the sun dipped, her phone dinged, signaling an incoming text. Grace grabbed her phone. Letters and words scrolled across the screen.

"Ida Red just found Lia Grant."

* * *

Grace ducked under the crime scene tape stretched across a wedge of earth near an old apiary, Hatch at her side, his hand at the small of her back. Here, among stands of tupelo trees and bee boxes, a hound named Ida Red had spotted up on a freshly turned pile of soil, and below that soil, searchers uncovered a wooden box.

An angry buzz rose from the bees as Grace and Hatch hurried past the boxes, the din much like the thrum building in Grace's chest. When they reached the lip of a gaping hole in the earth, Hatch tried to shield her from the sight, but she sidestepped his hands. She needed to see for herself.

Below her in a wooden box that reeked of urine and swamp water was a young woman. She wore a pair of navy blue pants, a white shirt, a purple smock, white sneakers, and a large button that read: *How Can I help YOU?*

Breathe in, two, three. Breathe out, two, three.

With the exhale, Grace tried to push out the anger. She tried to relieve the weight of injustice and atrocity pressing down on her lungs.

Lia Grant was dead.

Outrage rushed through her veins and capillaries, heated her limbs.

Why, Grace, why didn't you answer your phone?

Something hotter and thicker expanded, threatening to melt her from the inside out. This was the wrong ending.

She was supposed to find the girl. Lia Grant was supposed to win. Hatch's hand curled around her waist. Was he holding her steady? Himself? The entire world, which was spinning in insanity?

Lieutenant Lang joined them. She shifted from one foot to another, bits of earth falling into that gaping hole, which felt as big as the wound in Grace's chest.

"What is it, Lieutenant Lang?" Hatch asked, not releasing his hold on her.

"Lia's parents just arrived." A grimace twisted her mouth. "How the hell am I going to explain...this?"

"I'll do it," Hatch said.

Gone was the golden glow of his skin and amused glint in his eyes. No flash of dimple, no cocky set to his jaw. She couldn't imagine what he would say to Lia's parents. Not only was the Grants' daughter dead, she'd died a painful, gruesome death. What would he say if the parents asked to see their daughter's body? What if they wanted to know about their daughter's final words, her final moments on this earth? Would Hatch tell them about the phone calls to Grace? Of Lia's pleading, of her desperation and terror?

Hatch gave her waist a squeeze. "I got this one."

Lieutenant Lang didn't argue because Hatch's tone wouldn't let her. In the fight against evil, everyone had a role. Hatch, with his honeyed voice and sweet words, was meant to talk and comfort, and for that she was grateful.

As for her role?

Help me, Grace. Help me...

Grief and horror collided with anger so hard, a physical jolt rocked Grace's chest. She smoothed the string of pearls at her neck. When they found the evil that did this, she'd make sure the only phones he'd ever touch again would be the ones behind the bars of a maximum security prison.

All around her, the machine of death investigation buzzed. The rain continued to pour. Sheriff's deputies set up tents and lights to combat the approaching night. A photographer snapped photos. Crime scene techs measured and took samples. The medical examiner took field stats on Lia Grant's lifeless body.

Grace continued to stand at the lip of the grave. She'd been a part of Lia's final moments, and there was something she needed to know. "Conclusive cause of death?" Grace asked the M.E.

"We'll know more after the autopsy, but given the retinal hemorrhaging along with lack of ligature marks and no apparent bruising around the mouth, I'd say asphyxiation brought on by entrapment suffocation." The weight of those words pulled at the corners of his mouth.

Grace stared at the wooden lid, at the tracks of blood and crescent-shaped gouges no bigger than a young woman's fingernails.

Lieutenant Lang pointed to Lia's right hand. "But with a lifeline." Lia still gripped the cell phone, its face darkened with blood.

The steamy swamp spun. Grace tightened her stomach muscles and fought the nausea. Lia had used that phone to reach out in a final cry of help, but Grace hadn't found her soon enough.

The M.E. placed the phone in an evidence box, and Lieutenant Lang pointed to one of the crime scene techs. "Get that to the station ASAP. I have a tech specialist on his way."

After the M.E. finished with the body, he climbed out of the hole, and two techs spread a tarp on the ground before placing a body bag on top. She'd seen death's gruesome face but only in photos within the antiseptic halls and walls of a courthouse building. Up close, the girl looked smaller, younger. Beyond the smell of sweat and urine was a faint hint of strawberries. Was it her shampoo? Perfume? Favorite bubblegum? Grace knew nothing about this young woman being tucked into the body bag. Except for her final plea.

Help me, Grace. Help me...

Grace's entire upper body rocked in a silent sob.

A hand landed on her shoulder. Hatch. Who still moved as silently as the wind.

"It's not your fault," Hatch said.

"She called me." Nine times.

"With a call any sane human being would have thought was a crank, especially given the previous disturbing messages from Morehouse. Unlike most people in that situation, you reported it to the proper authorities, kept on those authorities, and even did investigative work on your own."

"I could have helped her."

He put a hand on either shoulder and turned her so she faced him. "Did you or did you not call the sheriff's department and report the call?"

"Yes, but—"

"And were you not the one who went out at midnight and found the girl's abandoned car, who got the lieutenant on the investigation?" He slid his palms along her arms, along her neck, and cradled her face.

"Yes, but—"

"Grace, you're not a law enforcement officer. You're not called on to investigate or protect." He drew his face within inches of hers until they shared the same breath. "You did everything you needed to do."

Ziiiiip. Lia Grant was gone.

Grace shoved his hands from her shoulders and jabbed her fingertips at her chest. "I let her down, Hatch. I failed Lia Grant."

CHAPTER NINE

Grace knew how to rock a set of pearls. She looked sexy as hell in a short tennis skirt. And when draped in only the soft glow of the moon, she literally stole Hatch's breath. But tonight she wore guilt so thick and heavy it threatened to smother her and everyone else in the conference room at the sheriff's station.

Lia Grant was dead, and Grace shouldered the blame. Because she hadn't answered her phone. Because she hadn't done enough.

Hatch settled his hip against a windowsill and crossed his ankles. He'd offered to take Grace home, but she refused to call it a night until she heard the report from the tech investigating Lia's phone. She was obsessed with the phone, with the fact that Lia had called her again and again. Latent had checked the phone for prints and swabbed for DNA. So far no leads.

When the tech finally set down the phone, Grace asked, "Well?"

"Pre-paid with five hundred minutes. Domestic calls only," the tech said. "Phone history shows only nine calls, all made to the same phone number."

"Mine," Grace said with a snag in her voice.

Hatch left the windowsill and stood behind her chair. He didn't touch her but was ready to catch her in case she cracked. Her face was the color of ancient marble.

"Why did Lia call *me*?"

"Because it's the only number she could dial," the tech said. "This phone was altered to dial only one number, relatively simple technology sometimes used with parent-controlled phones." With the tip of his index finger, he pushed send. Seconds later, a soft chirping sounded from Grace's purse. "The bottom line is anyone using this phone can dial for a month of Sundays and never get anyone but Ms. Courtemanche."

"So Lia didn't necessarily want to contact me, but who-ever gave her this phone did." Grace's words were as hard as the set of her jaw.

"What kind of sick SOB are we dealing with?" Lieuten-ant Lang asked.

In his hostage negotiation training days at Quantico he'd studied abnormal psychology. "It all comes down to wants and fulfillment," Hatch said. "Our bad guy wants something, he perpetuates the crime, and he gets his payoff. Sometimes it's external: money or sexual gratification. Other times the gain is more primal: revenge, hate, fear."

"No." Grace stood, a rush of color heating her cheeks. "I won't give that bastard anything."

"He got your attention," Hatch said.

Grace shoved in the chair. "And he's going to regret the day he did."

* * *

Hatch pulled the SUV into her driveway, turned off the ignition, and pocketed the keys.

"You can go now," Grace said. She had too much on her mind tonight to deal with Hatch. Lia Grant had died, and she'd been dragged into a murder by a madman with a phone. "I'm fine."

Hatch grabbed a flashlight, hopped out of the car, and poked the light beam through the darkness hanging over her shack. "I know."

Grace slammed the SUV door. "The lieutenant has drive-bys planned for the next twenty-four hours."

"Know that, too."

"Dammit, Hatch, would you just leave?" Her words came out in a tangled rush, but that was nothing new. With Hatch, her well-ordered, carefully planned life got tangled.

Hatch reached out with his free hand and cupped the side of her face. "After I get you inside, but first I want to make sure everything's okay."

No, everything is not okay, she wanted to scream. They'd just unearthed a nineteen-year-old girl who'd been buried with a phone programmed to call only Grace. For the second crazy moment in this crazy day, she thought of leaning into Hatch's big, callused hand. Which would only add to the crazy.

She took a step back and hurried up the steps but drew up short when she spotted the big, circular red splotch. She closed her eyes. Breathe in, two, three. Breathe out, two, three. When she opened her eyes, she still saw red.

Hatch was at her side in seconds. "What the hell happened here?"

She pointed to Allegheny Blue, who limped from a shadowy corner of the porch. "*He* happened."

Blue plunked down at her side and rested his bony head

against her thigh. She nudged him away, but he leaned harder. Good, she could deal with this type of trouble because unlike the killer who murdered Lia, the human skeleton unearthed on her property, or the reappearance of her ex-husband—she knew how to handle the stupid dog.

She squatted and checked the dog's right paw. "You went carousing again, didn't you? And look here, you split it open."

Hatch scratched at the stubble along his cheek. "You have a dog?"

"He's not my dog. He came with the house."

A laugh rumbled from Hatch's direction. "Now there's a marketing tool. Buy a shanty, get a free hound."

She let go of Blue's paw and stood, an unexpected smile curving her lips. She appreciated Hatch's attempt at levity, at anything to lighten the heaviness weighing on her chest. "The dog wasn't in the contract, and if he had been, I would have had the clause removed."

She unlocked the door and walked into the living room, the steamy mildew rolling over her like an ocean wave.

"Good Lord," Hatch said with a wave of his hand. "What died in here?"

"My central plumbing." She opened the windows in the living room, and Hatch unlatched the panes in the small dining area and over the kitchen sink.

In the kitchen she took a plastic bag from the refrigerator. "You know I don't have time for this," she said to Allegheny Blue, who hobbled behind her as she opened the back door, the molding shifting from the doorframe so it tilted like a fun-house door. The old dog had dislodged it two days ago chasing after a big cat caterwauling by the creek. Outside she fired up a propane stove on the porch. Setting a small, dented pot on a burner, she dumped a dollop of chunky liquid from the bag into the pot and tried not to gag.

Hatch joined her, sniffing the air. "Remind me to say no next time you invite me to dinner."

She stirred the offensive liquid. "It's for his foot."

"What is it?"

"Bear grease, pitch, and kerosene. Hunters have used the stinking concoction for years to treat the pads of their hounds' feet. I refuse to heat it inside."

Hatch's dimples carved slashes on either side of his face, and he laughed.

"It's not funny," she said as Blue plunked down beside her. "This is my second batch."

Hatch gave the old dog's ears a ruffle. "He seems to like you."

"The feeling is not mutual."

Hatch hopped up on the porch railing, the old wood straining and groaning. She waited for the decrepit railing to break, but it held, as did Hatch's gaze.

"I'm fine, Hatch," she said again. "I'm rattled and mad as hell, but I'm fine."

Hatch finally relinquished his eagle-eye stare and pointed to Allegheny Blue. "So what's the story?"

She gave the pot another stir. Hatch loved a good story, and he'd told so many that summer as they walked the white sand beaches of St. George Island and glided along Apalachicola Bay tonging for oysters. He told tales of hunting for treasure in three-hundred-year-old Spanish ships shipwrecked in the Florida Keys and adventurous yarns about his 'round-the-world trip with his great aunt Piper Jane. It was so easy to get lost in the music and magic of a good story. And maybe that was what she needed tonight, a good story to get her mind off Lia.

With most of the fat melted, she took the pot off the stove. "Once upon a time there was a really, really stupid dog." A rumble sounded from Hatch's chest, and she rested her butt against the table holding the stove. "Said dog belonged to the former owner of this place, Lamar Giroux, an eighty-four-year-old hunter who never married and spent most of his waking moments in the company of dogs and critters they chased. Earlier this year, Lamar broke his hip and moved to his sister's place in Tallahassee. He sold off all of his canine companions except his favorite, Allegheny Blue, who got a nice new cushy dog bed at Lamar's sister's two-bedroom patio home, complete with central air and a therapeutic Jacuzzi. But the canine hero of this tale did not buy into the new living arrangements. The really, really stupid dog walked from Tallahassee to Cypress Bend. Took him three days, and by the time he landed on my front porch, he'd torn the pads from his feet and was nothing but skin and bones."

"That's almost a hundred miles. He walked it all?"

"Twice."

"Huh?"

"I told you, he's double the stupid." She dropped a dollop of the bear fat mixture on her wrist. Still too hot. "After Allegheny Blue's first trek, Giroux's nephew drove down, got the dog, and took him back to Tallahassee, but Blue took off the next day. A week later he arrived on my front porch, this time in worse shape. I called the vet, who made a house call and said Blue wouldn't make it through the night. The vet offered to take him to his office and put him down, but it didn't seem right, taking the old dog away from a place he so clearly longed to be. Long story short, I offered to let him stay, and the vet gave him some pain meds. Why not let him die in the place he loved?"

"But he didn't die."

She grabbed the wooden spoon and gave the mixture

two more turns. "Not yet." Dipping the spoon into the bear grease concoction, she dribbled another spoonful onto her wrist. Just right. With an ease from way too much practice, she slathered the mixture on the old dog's front right paw.

"Hold still," she told the dog. "You need your stupid sock." She dressed the wound with one of her old tennis anklets and first-aid tape.

With the dog no longer bleeding all over the place, she walked into the kitchen where the dank smell had dissipated. Hatch, stickier than a jar of tupelo honey, parked his backside at the kitchen table where he thumbed through her mail. She should ask him to leave. Her life would be less complicated that way. But during this hellish day, he'd found a way to make her smile, and for the few moments when she'd been telling Blue's story, she'd forgotten about Lia Grant and that bloody phone. But now it all came back to her, especially the desperate cries of the girl she'd failed.

Hatch set down the mail and reached for her hand, his fingers curving around hers.

He'd always been so good at reading her.

She stared at his hand. Everything about Hatch was smooth, except for his hands. The ropes of his sailboat had rubbed permanent calluses along his palms and fingers, and tonight she took a strange comfort in the rough edges that took her to a different place, a place filled with sun and light, a place of wind and billowy sails. A place that had almost destroyed her.

She shrugged off his touch and bent to check on Allegheny Blue's sock. Good. No more blood. "You can go now," she said.

Hatch didn't move. He was worse than the mildew smell that refused to let go. Mildew? No. Hatch smelled of the sea and sun. And salt, for he was a man who spent his days bare-chested and sweating on the deck of a boat called *No Regrets*. She breathed through her mouth and looked at Hatch out of the corner of her eyes.

To her surprise, he wasn't giving her a sugary grin but frowning at her back porch. "I'll go as soon as I fix that door."

She shook her head in amazement. Evidence of the newly responsible Hatch. If she hadn't heard it with her own ears, she wouldn't have believed it. "I can take care of it."

"I know. You can take care of everything. Now where can I find a hammer?"

She pictured him shirtless and working on the deck, sweat trickling down the planes of his back to the slow-slung waistband of his swimming trunks. A man who lived alone, often away from the civilized world, needed to be handy. And what hands he had, she remembered. An unexpected heat crept along her face, and she jumped up and rummaged through a drawer near the sink until she found a small tool kit. "Here," she said. She had no doubt she could win this argument with Hatch, but in the long run it would be quicker to let him fix the door.

He squared up the door and began hammering nails, the mounds and valleys of his arms bunched and tightened, and waves of sun-kissed hair flopped over his forehead. Hatch had always been easy on the eye and fascinating to watch. He was always moving, his eyes, his mouth, his long bronze limbs. Now, like then, he proved to be a major distraction.

She grabbed the stack of mail, anything to keep from looking at Hatch. She thumbed through a catalog from a local tupelo honey co-op and opened another bill from the vet. With a glare at Blue, she reached for the final two pieces of mail, both small envelopes, the type that carried invitations to parties. Inside the first envelope was indeed an invitation from the couple who'd purchased her parents' house. They invited her to come for tea any time this week to pick up a few things that belonged to her father. Inside the second was a single piece of glossy paper. She flipped it over, a breath catching in her throat. It was a picture of Lia Grant, a red X slashed across her face.

"What is it?" Hatch asked from across the kitchen.

She checked the envelope. No return address. No postage meter mark. Her hands shaking, she squinted at the hand-written notation along the bottom of the photo:

Me: 1

You: 0

Lia's smiling, buck-toothed face slipped from her hands.

"Grace?" Hatch was at her side in less than a second, looking over her shoulder. "What the hell?"

"It's a game," she said. Hatch settled his hands on her shoulders, and for the first time she realized her entire body shook. She pointed to the jagged red X, horror sending tremor after tremor through her fingers. "It's a game, Hatch. Someone abducted Lia and gave her a phone programmed to call only me. Then it was my turn. I was supposed to find her, but I struck out."

Hatch stared at the photo and envelope, and slowly, his face twisted with a sickness Grace felt to her core.

The lack of oxygen was making her head dizzy. Names, hundreds of names, spun through her head—she had so many enemies. She'd spent the past decade putting bad people behind bars, most recently whorehouse king Larry Morehouse.

Hatch dug out his phone and called the lieutenant. Good. They needed to have the photo and envelope checked for trace. Her mailbox, too, as it appeared the message was hand delivered.

All day Grace had struggled with anger and shock and profound sadness, so much sadness as she looked at Lia's tear-streaked face and shredded fingertips.

Breathe in, two, three. Breathe out, two, three.

But now a warm wave of powerful relief surged through her. If someone was indeed playing a game with her, bring it on.

CHAPTER TEN

"Get your hands in the air, stranger, or I'll zap you with my super-charged titanium brain blaster." A child in dinosaur pajamas pointed a wooden spoon at Hatch.

An identical child aimed a spatula at Hatch's midsection. "He's a secret agent for the Axis of Evil. Get back, Agent Evil, or I'll turn you into a block of ice with my Freeze-All Vision."

Hatch raised his hands in defeat, covertly checking his watch. He had twenty minutes to get Alex to the cemetery for his first day of community service and then to Grace's. "Alas, I have been bested by Superheroes Ricky and Raymond, and I surrender." The boys circled closer. When they reached for his legs, Hatch lunged, scooping a boy in each arm and crying, "Into my evil clutches you go!" He spun until squeals and giggles filled the room.

"Losers," Alex said as shuffled past them and into the kitchen.

"Don't mind Alex. He's a grump in the mornings," one of the upside-down twins said.

"Alex is always grumpy," the other twin added.

With a sigh, Hatch settled the two boys on the floor.

One of the twins tugged at Hatch's shorts. "Granny says you're a real FBI agent. What's your superpower?"

"Superpower?" Hatch asked.

"You know, the special power good guys use to fight all those bad guys."

He'd love to have a superpower to deal not with bad guys but with a kid with a bad attitude. With lightning speed, Hatch grabbed the spatula and wooden spoon. "I have the power to turn little boys who should still be in bed into sea cucumbers."

The twins squealed and ran down the hall. This was the type of kid interaction he could deal with, like a favorite uncle who sailed into town for holidays. Now it was time to be a *father*. He stepped over blocks and Matchbox cars as he followed Alex into the kitchen.

Alex's grandmother stood in the back doorway puffing on a cigarette. "I know." She raised the cigarette to her lips. "It's bad for me and the boys, but sometimes you just need 'em."

"No need to explain yourself to me, ma'am," Hatch said.

Alex grabbed a jug of orange juice from the refrigerator and yanked off the cap.

"Get a glass," Mrs. Milanos said, "and don't spill on the fl—" Bright orange liquid trickled down Alex's chin and onto the cracked linoleum. "Come on, Alex, wipe it up."

Alex slammed the juice on the counter, a stream of orange pooling on the countertop.

Hatch grabbed the boy's arm. "Your grandmother told you to wipe up the juice you spilled."

"And who's gonna make me?" Alex asked with a curl of his lip.

Hatch's hand twitched. *I suggest you knock that smirk off*

your face, Son, *or I'll do it myself. Smack.* The twenty-five-year-old memory sent a tremor along his jaw and burned the backs of his eyelids. Hatch released Alex's arm. He used words, not fists, to resolve problems. "You need to take responsibility for your actions," Hatch said.

"Responsibility? That's too funny, someone like you lecturing me about *responsibility.*" He jerked out of Hatch's grip and stormed out of the kitchen.

Every muscle in Hatch's legs tensed. Should he run after the kid and drag his butt in here to apologize and clean the mess? He ran a hand through the waves along the side of his head. Or should he just plain run?

Alex's granny lit another cigarette and hauled in a long draw. "I'm too damned old to be raising three boys on my own. Don't have the patience. Don't have the energy. Don't have the strength. But when Vanessa left, it was me or foster care. The twins' father, he isn't in the picture, either. So what's a granny to do when her heart won't let go?"

Heart holds on, Hatch commiserated, *even when every other part of your body and brain tells you to set sail.* For almost a year after Grace sent him packing, he didn't have a woman in his bed. Hell, he didn't even look at another woman because his heart hadn't let go of hope that Grace would realize her epic mistake and come running into his arms. But this wasn't about him and Grace. Three little hurricanes were bearing down on Trina Milanos, including his disrespectful son. "There are people who can help, Mrs. Milanos. Social service agencies, boys' clubs, and school personnel."

Outside, a horn blared. Through the window, Hatch spotted Alex leaning on the SUV's horn. Hatch shot him a warning look. His son scratched his nose with his middle finger. Hatch tried one of Grace's deep breathing moves. Grandma took an extra long puff.

The horn blared again.

"I'll make some phone calls today," Hatch said.

Alex didn't say a word as they drove through town to the cemetery, which was fine, because Hatch had no idea what to say.

They found Black Jack in the far north section of the cemetery at a patch of land with no marble headstones or fancy sprays of flowers. Simple brass discs marked graves along with a few worn, wooden crosses. The caretaker stood next to a hole in the earth, turning a hand crank to lower a plain wooden box into the ground. He steadied the box, never allowing it to brush against the earthen sides of the grave. Alex shuffled next to him, kicking up dirt. Hatch stilled him with a single look. His son would respect the bodies *and* the process.

At last the gravedigger turned to Alex. "Time to work." Black Jack led them past the newly dug grave to a twelve-foot pile of crushed oyster shells. "Two inches thick. On the path only." He pointed to a freshly graded footpath winding through the paupers' graves.

Alex stared at the shells in disgust. "You mean I gotta spend all day shoveling shells?"

Black Jack walked to the hole, picked up a shovel, and hummed an old spiritual as he tucked earth around the wooden box.

When Alex turned to Hatch, clearly ready to complain, Hatch handed him the shovel Alex brought from home. "You got your ass into this situation, Alex, and you're going to shovel your way out." He thumped Alex on the back and tapped his fingers on his forehead in farewell to Black Jack. Shoveling two tons of oyster shells was going to be a hell of a lot easier than what he'd be up against today with Grace.

* * *

Grace poked pearl studs through both ears. Straightening the pearls at her neck, she grabbed her purse and phone from the nightstand. Last night Lia's killer had sent her an invitation to a deadly game of murder, and she was suited up and ready to play.

Allegheny Blue heaved himself from the rag rug in front of her bed, his old bones creaking.

"You need to take it easy today. No more treks through the swamp. No more digging." She pictured his latest bone, the knobby joint with dried bits of flesh, and shivered despite the steamy morning. The forensic team was still digging, searching for more bodies. She ran her knuckles over Blue's head. "Just stay on the porch today, okay?"

Blue plodded behind her to the front door. When she reached for the handle, his ears curled forward. A low growl rumbled in his throat, setting the hairs on the back of her neck upright. She checked the security system. Still red. She peered out the peephole. Nothing. As she reached for the door, Blue lunged, heaving his body between her and the door.

"For heaven's sake." She nudged him aside. "There's nothing out there." She threw open the door and rushed out, slamming into a rock-solid wall of flesh and bone.

A scream tore up her throat but sputtered on her lips when she recognized the shaggy, golden head crouched in front of her doorbell. She flattened her palm on her chest. "Theodore!"

Hatch stood and pointed at the little box on the door frame. "Your doorbell's broken."

"I know. The entire shack is broken." She hitched her bag up to her shoulder. "What are you doing here?"

"I've come to take you to breakfast."

Dining with Hatch was the last thing she wanted to do. "I ate."

"How about a game of tennis? I've been working on my serve." Hatch tossed an imaginary ball in the air and swung.

"I can't deal with you today." She held open the door and waited as Blue, now calm and slow as swamp sludge, hobbled across the porch and settled on a rag rug in a patch of sunshine.

Hatch rested his shoulder against the door frame. "Or we can play catch with your dog."

"He's not my dog." Grace set the alarm, locked the door, and barreled past Hatch to her car. Hatch and his team had done their duty. They'd helped find Lia Grant, and he'd soon set sail. Because that's what Hatch did.

She jammed her keys into the ignition and cranked. *No, not today. Please, please, not today.* Again she turned the keys, but the car remained deathly silent.

"How about a lift?" Hatch asked.

"No, thank you."

"I can call you a cab."

Grace popped open her glove compartment. "Dammit, Hatch! Go away!"

He leaned his hip against the fender of her car. "You are so damn beautiful when you're angry."

Grace closed her eyes. Breathe in, two, three. Breathe out, two, three. "What do you want?"

She expected a wink, a sugary comment about morning delight, but Hatch's face grew uncharacteristically serious. "You safe."

"I can take care of myself." She pulled out the hammer.

"And most of the free world, I know, but this isn't just about your safety. There's a crazy person playing a sick game, and you're the only one who's been invited. Someone needs to keep an eye on you for the next few days, and more than the few drive-bys the lieutenant scheduled last night."

"I hardly need a babysitter."

"If you refuse my company, the lieutenant will assign deputies to watch over you, which is essentially pulling man-hours from the investigation." Hatch pressed a palm to his chest. "And I can assure you those deputies won't have my charm and sunny disposition." He aimed his pointed fingertips to the borrowed SUV. "Your carriage awaits, Princess."

Yesterday she'd welcomed Hatch's support as they searched for Lia, but she had serious work today, and Hatch was clearly in a far-from-serious mood. But he was right about one thing: She didn't want resources pulled from the hunt for Lia's killer. She tossed the hammer in the glove box and climbed into the SUV. "We're going to Port St. Joe. I want to talk to the manager of the store where the cell phone found in Lia's hand was purchased. I'm looking for a paper trail, surveillance video, anything to link us to the person who bought the phone."

He turned his face to the SUV's headliner. "You can't stand by and let others do the work, can you?"

"It's not who I am. You of all people know that."

He jammed the keys in the ignition. "Yeah, I know."

They barreled along the highway, Hatch's right hand loped casually over the wheel, his right leg jiggling. She'd forgotten how he was always moving when something was on his mind. For not the first time in the past two days she pictured that blue-eyed, blond-haired boy who'd most likely brought Hatch to Cypress Bend and kept him anchored.

"You have a son," she said.

"You always go for the jugular, don't you?" A lopsided smile slid across his face, but it didn't meet his eyes. "I can see you in court, counselor, going at your prey. Sometimes you sneak up on them from the rear, other times you go straight for the kill."

"What's his name?"

Hatch scrubbed the stubble at his jaw. "I could never bull-shit you, could I?"

"Not in this lifetime." She knew Hatch, and she knew what he was doing, or at least trying to do, divert her attention to keep from talking about anything serious, including his son. "What's his name?" Grace asked again.

The jaunty grin slipped away. "Alex Milanos, and until two days ago, I didn't know he existed." He told her about Vanessa Milanos, a woman he'd met the summer before they were married who had admittedly sabotaged a condom because she'd wanted his child.

Hatch had a *child*, which meant he was a father. If Grace hadn't seen the boy with her own eyes, she would not have believed it. She knew firsthand Hatch took birth control seriously. On the other hand, she could picture a woman being so smitten, so charmed, that she'd take any piece of Hatch she could get.

"And you're here to negotiate peace?" Grace asked after he told her about the boy's trouble with the law.

Hatch's leg jiggled faster. "I'm doing what I can."

"Which is what?"

"Holding him accountable for the shrimp shack break-in and helping his grandma find some tools to deal with him and his twin hurricane brothers. And eventually help him unearth a bit of respect for himself and those around him."

"And how do you plan to do that?"

Hatch's entire body stilled, and the playful glint in his eyes faded. A moment later he winked. "Guess I'll have to buy him a bigger shovel."

Typical Hatch, backing off when the discussion got too deep. *Because I'm not a deep kind of guy*, Hatch had told her more than a decade ago. *I keep life simple. No baggage. No regrets. What you see is what you get.* Her ex-husband never pretended to be anything else. He lived big and loved hard, and the entire world adored him, including at one point in her life, her.

Grace dug out the address of the phone retailer from her purse and called up a map on her phone. "Take the next exit and go right," she said. "The phone store will be the fourth storefront on the north side." She looked at her watch. "They don't open for an hour, but I have the store manager's cell phone number."

A slow smile spread across Hatch's lips.

"What?" Grace asked.

"Just thinking that if I ever needed to move a mountain, I know who to call."

She slipped her phone in her purse. "You have a problem with strong, decisive women?"

"As you know, I adore strong, decisive women." He waggled both eyebrows.

Although his words came out with a charming tease, what he said was unarguably true. Unlike some men, Hatch had never seemed intimidated by her power and ambition. He had no need to compete against her and certainly never belittled her. A decade ago, she would have said it was just his laid-back, devil-may-care attitude, but now into her thirties and having studied human nature in and out of the courtroom, she recognized why Hatch had never been intimidated by her. Men comfortable with their own strength didn't fear powerful women. "You adore *all* women," she added with a laugh.

"True." He aimed the SUV off the highway and rested his fingers—all ring-less—on the top of the steering wheel.

"Did you ever remarry?" Grace couldn't help but ask. A charmer like Hatch had to have had more than a few women clamoring to get in his bed long-term.

"After you, Princess, all women paled by comparison." He gave her his bullshitting smile. "My wounded heart sought solace in the sea, and that there's my bride." He motioned out the front window where the waters of St. Joseph Bay stretched out before them in a deep, dark blue teardrop. And beyond that, the endless sea and whispering wind.

A shiver swept across her skin. "Must get cold and lonely," she said.

Hatch shrugged, feigning nonchalance, but the lift of those broad shoulders was anything but light and breezy. "And you?" His grin gone. "Has there ever been a Mr. Courtemanche?"

Over the past decade she'd been courted by a few men at work and her racquet and golf club. Most didn't understand her dedication to her career and the pursuit of justice, of her calling to put bad people behind bars. A few who were patient and persistent made it into her bed, but no one got close to her heart. She'd put it under lock and key after the summer of Hatch. Plus there was the issue that every man paled in comparison to Hatch, who had been a blazing golden sun that was the center of her universe.

She blinked away the brightness. "No husband."

"Must get cold and lonely." There was no snark, no biting edge to the echo of her words.

At times she was lonely, achingly so, but never, ever cold. Not with the fire burning in her chest to battle evil like Lia Grant's killer. She pointed to a highway exit. "Turn there."

When they arrived at the phone store, Grace cupped the sides of her face and peered into the storefront glass, spotting boxes, half-assembled displays, and wadded shrink wrap. She banged on the locked door until a woman with a pinched face walked out from a back room, a box cutter in her hand.

We're closed, the woman mouthed.

Grace was about to bang again when Hatch reached into his wallet, took out his badge, and tapped it on the glass, tossing in a brilliant white smile. The woman tossed aside her box cutter, smoothed the sides of her hair, and hurried to the door.

Hatch leaned so close his lips brushed the hair curved about her ear. "Can't say I'm just another pretty face."

Grace didn't bother with a response as the woman unlocked the door and pulled up the security grate. Hatch's ego was big enough already.

"I'm Grace Courtemanche from the State Attorney's office, and I need to talk to you about a recent purchase made in this store."

The manager, who was ogling Hatch, shooed away Grace's words with the back of her hand. "All that stuff's handled by my district manager."

"I have a call in to your corporate office already, but we need to move quickly. A phone purchased from this store was used in the murder of a nineteen-year-old woman."

The woman stopped ogling Hatch long enough to frown. "That's terrible." A buzzer ripped through the air. "I'm sorry to hear about the girl's death, but you'll still need to talk to the DM. They handle everything with the cops and press." Another buzz. "Listen, I need to get that delivery. Call the DM." The manager hurried through a door at the back of the store.

Grace checked her watch. The corporate office didn't open for another hour, and she'd already left a message. She could get some muscle and speed behind her request with a subpoena, but getting a judge out of bed could take precious time. However, she had something better than a court order. Grace couldn't imagine anyone listening to Lia's voice and not feeling the fear and desperation of the young woman's final, horrifying moments.

Next to her, Hatch picked up a cardboard cutout of a three-foot cell phone and began folding flaps. He hummed a soft, lilting song that reminded her of the sea.

As Grace retrieved her voicemail messages, the store manager dragged in a cart with a load of boxed phone accessories. When she saw Hatch, who had assembled the giant cardboard cell phone cover display, the lines across her forehead smoothed.

"Any chance you'll work for minimum wage?" the store manager asked with a flip of her hair. "I have three more of those that need assembly."

"My pleasure, ma'am." Hatch winked. "I'm a man with fast hands."

The woman almost swooned. "You're serious?"

Hatch took her hand in his and placed it on his chest. "As a heartbeat."

With a flustered smile, she rushed into the stock room.

"A man with fast hands?" Grace asked, not bothering to hide her censure.

"I seem to recall you liked my hands." He slid a thumb along the curve of her elbow. She'd forgotten how Hatch was always touching her. He was a man comfortable in his own skin and with others'. "The faster the better."

A rush of heat fired along her skin, and she swatted away his hand. This was not the time to be remembering the havoc his touch wreaked on many and varied body parts. "You were flirting with a potential witness."

"You catch more bees with honey." His tongue lingered

on the last word. Honey and Hatch. The two would always be intertwined in her mind.

"We're not catching bees, Hatch, but a killer."

"Tell me something I don't know, Princess." He rested his hand on his hip, and for the first time she noticed the bulge under his breezy cotton shirt. His gun.

The store manager reappeared with three display boxes and plopped them at Hatch's feet. Then she looked at Grace. "I can spare fifteen minutes."

Hatch grabbed a box and hummed another sea ditty.

Grace handed the store manager the information on the phone found in Lia's lifeless hand. "Two days ago I talked with someone in your operations department, and he told me this pre-paid phone was purchased from your store two weeks ago. I need to find the buyer."

"Easiest thing will be to check batch records and find out if the buyer used a credit card." The manager booted up a computer at the checkout desk while Hatch tackled another giant cardboard cell phone, still humming. Grace tapped the pearls at her neck.

"Here we go," the manager announced. "Found the buyer of the phones. Unfortunately, it was a cash deal, so I can't give you a name."

Grace heard the word cash, but she was focused on another word. "Phones?"

"Three pre-paids. Same model."

"Three?" Grace pictured the large red X across Lia Grant's face. "He bought three phones?"

At some point Hatch must have stopped humming. He stood silently next to her, his fast hands still. There was nothing relaxed and easygoing about him now. He, too, knew what three phones meant.

They were looking at two more victims.

CHAPTER ELEVEN

Hatch's fingers tightened around the SUV's steering wheel as they pulled out of the phone store parking lot. In the passenger seat next to him, Grace stared at her cell phone as if expecting it to grow razor sharp teeth.

Three phones. Three victims.

"The store manager is reviewing security tapes," Hatch told Grace. "And the lieutenant and her team are processing the crime scene. It's possible we'll nab this guy before he can put those other two phones into play."

"But what if we don't? What if another terrified girl calls me from the grave?"

"If that happens, we'll get every dog in the county and track him down. And this time we have the advantage. We know he's playing a game. We know to take the first call seriously. We'll have techs on standby and searchers ready to hit the ground running."

"What if he changes the rules? What—"

He reached across the front seats and placed his hand

on her thigh. "At Quantico we're taught that crisis situations aren't about the future. They are about the here and now, the things we know and the things we can control. We can't waste time and energy on monsters of our own making."

Grace did one of those deep breathing moves and slipped her phone into her purse.

He pressed on the accelerator and sped toward Cypress Bend and a game-playing monster. Grace was no longer his wife, and this wasn't his gig, but he had no plans on backing down from this monster. He made his living talking to people in crisis situations. He knew the tone to use and questions to ask, and he wanted to be the one on the phone if and when the next victim called.

When he turned onto the dirt road leading to Cypress Point, they passed Grace's construction site where earth movers sat deathly still, like giant yellow insects with spindly arms and huge glassy eyes. Hatch waved at the forensic team buzzing around in bright orange jackets and boots. Grace had a hell of a lot on her plate.

When he pulled into the driveway, Grace pulled in a fast breath. "The front door. It's wide open. I know I locked it this morning and set the alarm. Oh, God. Where's Blue?" Before he stopped, she yanked open the door and dove out. "Blue!"

He slipped the keys in his pocket and grabbed his cell phone from the charger. Grace may have noticed the wide open front door, but she'd failed to see the phone company truck parked at the far end of the drive, probably because she'd been preoccupied with thoughts of two more voices from the grave. "Grace!" he called out.

She waved him off and darted around the side of the house.

When he reached the porch, he jogged up the steps.

"What are you doing?" Grace said as she ran toward the porch. "You can't walk in there without a gun or back-up."

"Aw, shucks. Nice to know you care about my old hide."

"Hatch, this is serious."

"Indeed it is." He pointed to the utility truck. "Which is why the phone company is putting a trace on your home phone." He turned her toward the door just as a man from the phone company walked out. Hatch nodded. "Morning, Doyle. I'm Hatch. We spoke on the phone earlier."

"Hey, there, Agent Hatcher," the technician said. "Got the trap and trace feature installed on Ms. Courtemanche's land line. Also have her cell phone and work phone on watch. You should be good to go."

"You?" Grace extricated herself from his hands. "*You* ordered this?"

He'd been on the phone twice with the phone tech this morning while Grace had been getting information from the store manager. "If we're looking at two more potential victims," Hatch said, "we need to be ready for additional calls on any phones associated with you."

She slid her palms along the pressed creases of her trousers, leaving a pair of damp spots. "Of course."

Another shape shifted in the doorway, and Allegheny Blue ambled out.

"Blue here didn't give you any trouble, did he?" Hatch asked the technician.

"Nah, I just gave him a piece of bacon like you suggested." The tech rubbed the dog's floppy ears. "We're good buddies now." With a wave, he hopped off the porch and walked to his truck.

"Wait!" Graced balled a fist on her hip. "Exactly how did you get in my house?"

"Agent Hatcher had a locksmith out, and he got me in without a problem."

"And the security code?"

"Agent Hatcher gave it to me." With a tip of his ball cap, the phone tech drove away.

"So you just had someone break into my house without my permission?" A vibrant pink splashed across her cheeks. Good; no more pasty white.

"Yup."

"And it never occurred to you I would mind?"

"Do you?"

"Of course not. It's a matter of principle."

Hatch just smiled.

"And my security system? How did you get the code?"

"From watching you. You're a beautiful woman, Princess. Sometimes I can't take my eyes off you." And last night, he dragged his attention from that angelic face and devilishly hot body to watch her punch in her security code. His teammate Finn Brannigan was fond of saying, *Chance favors the prepared*.

Grace opened her mouth, but no sound came out. She finally flung her hands in the air. "How can I fight with someone on the same team?" Spinning on her polished pumps, she whistled at Blue. "Get in here, Blue. I want to check your stupid foot."

While Grace and the dog went inside, Hatch sat on the bottom step and took out his phone.

Parker answered on the sixth ring, his breathing winded. Must have been swimming. Every day of the year, even on days when the frigid Maine air was barely above zero, Parker Lord swam a hundred laps in the heated lap pool situated on the thin strip of cliff between the ocean and the Box. His boss was a man of discipline and endurance, and lucky for Hatch, Parker Lord was good at adjusting his sails when needed.

"I need to stick around Cypress Bend a few more days," Hatch said. "Can you see if Hayden will suit up for the Big Easy?" Hayden Reed was the SCIU's criminal profiler who'd last month collared a serial killer in northern Nevada called the Broadcaster Butcher. The Butcher case had snagged a great deal of attention, fascinating a nation and showcasing Hayden's world-renowned profiling skills. In New Orleans, Hatch had been scheduled to give a workshop on crisis negotiation, but the event organizers would probably jump at the chance to have Hayden speak. They'd probably make him a keynoter.

"I'll take care of New Orleans," Parker said. "You ready to talk?"

This was one of the reasons he liked working for Parker. His boss didn't require daily status updates or reports in triplicate. "Don't have much so far." Hatch ground his dock shoe into the wet loam, bits and pieces of this place clinging to the sole of his shoe. "We just learned Lia Grant's killer bought three phones, so it's likely he's planning two more abductions."

"Need anything?"

"Have Hayden give me a call. I want him to create a profile on this guy, and get Jonny Mac out here. If another person goes missing, I'll want him on site." Hatch would be on that phone, and he wanted a teammate in the field.

"Will do," Parker said. Hatch was about to say good-bye when Parker added, "And Alex? Everything okay with your son?"

Hatch could not and would not bullshit his boss. "No."

* * *

Greenup, Kentucky

"Excuse me, Detective Holt, the press are getting antsy." A Kentucky state trooper charged with crowd control at Collier's Holler jabbed his thumb at the news vans gathered along the old country road. "Are you ready to make a statement?"

"No." Tucker Holt, who'd rather see a few shots of Wild Turkey than a few worked-up reporters, watched the crime scene boys pack their last CSU-labeled suitcase into their van and pull away from the holler.

"And old man Collier," the trooper added. "He's wondering when he can let the dogs out of their pens. You ready to release the scene?"

"No."

This case was full of no's. Twenty-four hours ago Collier's bird dogs spotted up on Grandpa and Grandma Doe sprawled in the holler. His team found no ID, no wallets, no jewelry, and no artifacts that would aid in identifying the victims. An acidic substance confirmed to be pool acid had been poured on their faces, the flesh eaten away so he had no shot at a facial ID. The same substance devoured their hands. No fingers meant no prints. A five-mile radial search turned up no abandoned cars or campsites.

And on top of that, he had no shot of Wild Turkey.

Calvin Tanner, a fellow detective and his favorite drinking buddy, joined him at the top of the holler. "Ready to call it quits, Tuck?" He fanned the air between them. "Man, you smell like you could use a break."

Tucker ran a dirt-streaked palm down his face, breathing in decaying body, holler mud, and eau de dog. "No," Tucker told Calvin. "I'm gonna stick around a few more hours, talk to some of the regular hikers along this trail and find out if they noticed any suspicious characters or vehicles."

"Any word from the M.E.'s office?"

"No." Frustration tightened his lips. "I put a call in, asking for an escalation, but I probably won't hear anything until Monday. I'm shooting blanks on this one."

Calvin motioned with his chin at the crime scene tape. "Bullshit. A guy like you, you gotta have something. What's your gut telling you?"

For years, Tucker had relied on his gut, and more often than not, it paid off. But this case was different. His job was on the line, not to mention his kids. He needed to collar the asswipe who knocked off Grandpa and Grandma. Unfortunately, all he had was a shitload of *no*.

But Calvin was right; he had his gut.

Tucker pointed to a section of the path jutting out in a sharp point. "So I'm thinking Grandpa Joe, Grandma Jane, and Asswipe are standing here."

"Just one suspect?" Calvin asked.

"Hard to tell as Collier's dogs tracked all over the scene." Crucial point, because the scene had been so compromised he had no viable impression evidence. "At this point, I'm speculating only one. So Asswipe takes out a gun and shoots Grandpa. Dead shot straight to the brain. Grandpa falls into the holler."

"A sharpshooter?"

"Someone who knows his way around guns." Tucker walked along the lip of the ravine. "Grandma takes off to the east, justifiably worried she's his next target and gets about ten yards. Asswipe shoots a single bullet into the back of her skull. Down and dead in the holler."

"That's it?"

"CSU boys found no prints or trace on or near the bodies, and so far I have no witnesses."

"Man, Tuck, this is a tough one."

"No shit." And this case was the reason why he was going to have to cancel his plans tonight. After Calvin left to deal with the media, he took out his phone and checked the time. He'd better call Mara before she called him.

His soon-to-be-ex-wife answered the phone with a growl. "No, Tuck, no, no, *no*!"

"Let me talk to Jackson."

"You promised to be a dad tonight. I made plans."

Probably a date because, unlike him, his soon-to-be ex-wife had a life outside of her job. "My sister will take the kids," he said. "Now let me talk to Jackson."

"He's at the creek fishing. What do you want me to tell him this time?"

"Tell him the truth. Tell him I can't make it to his baseball game because I have a dead grandma and a dead grandpa, and I'm guessing they have some grandkids somewhere who are wondering where the fuck they are." Tucker rolled his head along his shoulders, the dried sweat on the back of his neck cracking, and he pictured that broken glass on the photo of his son and daughter. "Tell him, tell him I love him, and I'll see him next week."

"Sure, Tuck. Next week." A sigh—more sad than bitter or angry—rolled across the line. "It's always next week."

* * *

The minute they arrived at the crime scene where Lia Grant had been murdered, Grace headed to Lia Grant's grave while Hatch made his way down to the creek. He'd always been drawn to water. It was his thoughtful place, his happy place, but the hard set of his jaw as he squatted and studied the earth made it clear he was anything but happy. Nor was Grace. Lia Grant's killer had purchased three phones.

Grace found Lieutenant Lang near the gaping hole that had once held Lia Grant. "Any news on the other two phones?" Grace asked.

Lieutenant Lang shook her head. "Techs are monitoring, but so far they haven't been activated."

A pair of deputies attached ropes to the wooden prison that had become Lia Grant's deathbed. This spit of land was so dense with trees and vines, it was hard to get through on foot. They'd never get digging machinery back here. A perfect place to hide a body.

A deputy cranked the winch, and the ropes tightened and groaned, lifting the wooden box from the earth's clutches.

"Anything on the coffin?" Grace asked.

"No handy fingerprints or stray hairs," Lieutenant Lang said. "But it tells us something interesting about the killer. This box didn't come from an undertaker. Construction is crude. Uneven boards. Jagged cuts. The sides don't meet in a flush seam."

"Which means air can get in if the dirt's not packed too tightly."

The lieutenant looked grim. "Exactly. This coffin wasn't meant to suffocate, at least not right away, but to contain."

"Because the game clock needed to play out." Grace pressed at her temples. "Anything on the construction materials?"

"Commonplace, supplies that can be found at home improvement centers across the country."

"Not exactly a smoking gun, but another thread to follow." Grace momentarily closed her eyes, picturing those threads intertwining, growing longer and stronger. "And soon we'll have enough rope to hang Lia's murderer."

"That's the plan, counselor. Now let's see what your FBI guy is up to."

"Hatch is not my guy." But he was a member of an elite FBI team, and he'd been intently focused on the water.

"We're fairly certain our killer came by water," Lieutenant Lang said as they picked their way through tangles of vines and spiky grass toward Hatch. "Landed his boat here, unloaded the coffin, and dragged it to the burial site."

"Any accomplices?" Grace asked.

The lieutenant pointed to the footprints. "Only one set. Looks like he made two trips. One dragging the coffin, the other dragging the girl. He made no attempt to cover any impressions, so he could have been in a hurry or not worried about someone finding him because this place is so far off the beaten track."

"Or more likely, he wanted us to find the body," Grace said. "Because this is some kind of game." She still couldn't get her mind wrapped around such warped thinking, even though as a prosecutor she faced insanity and evil on a daily basis. But this was different. This insanity had become grossly personal.

Lieutenant Lang pointed to the footprints. "Techs already made casts. Appear to be some type of wading boot. Size eight."

Hatch didn't seem interested in the muddy prints. Instead he was gazing at the cattails and water lilies near a rock outcropping. No, not gazing, studying. Grace joined him on the rock, her shoulder brushing his tense, rock-hard arm. "What is it?"

Hatch pointed to the gouge in the earth, including a single silvery shaving next to a rock protruding from the riverbank. "He drove a flat-bottomed skiff with a boxed bow, aluminum, not too big. Probably a fourteen- or sixteen-footer. What do you think?"

Hatch rarely talked of his childhood, but she knew he'd

spent a year on a boat with his great aunt Piper Jane sailing around the world. She, on the other hand, knew swamp boats. "Fourteen footer tops."

The lieutenant took out her phone and made notes. "That fits the description of hundreds of boats around here."

Hatch hopped off the rock. Squatting, he whisked away slime and rotting leaves floating at the water's edge. He ran his finger along the still water and brought it to his nose. "No fuel residue. So we have two scenarios. One, we're looking at a hand-propelled craft, which given this remote location, would indicate someone nearby."

"Or, two, this boat had an electric motor," Grace offered.

Hatch nodded. "If that's the case, I assume we'll be looking at a considerably smaller pool of watercraft?"

"Definitely fewer electric motors around here," Grace said.

"I'll send a man to the harbor and rental boat places to poke around for fourteen footers with electric motors," Lieutenant Lang added.

Hatch stared at the grave where the deputies were shouldering the coffin and carrying it through the tangled brush, a perverted reversal of the burial process, Grace couldn't help but think.

"Any witnesses?" Hatch asked.

Grace had been waiting for this. Hatch was a people guy, one who talked.

"I've got guys going door-to-door, but no leads yet," Lieutenant Lang said.

"What about the owner of this place?" Hatch asked. Ida Red had tracked Lia's scent to land owned by Lou Poole, a woman who ran a small apiary. "Did she see or hear anything?"

Lieutenant Lang's lips flattened. "No."

"You think she was lying?"

"Not sure. She's old and half batty."

"But?" Hatch prompted.

"But someone who still runs an apiary and roadside honey stand has more than a few functioning brain cells. Her house is less than two hundred yards away, and her back porch hangs over the slough. It seems to me she would have seen or heard something."

Grace pictured the bloody tracks raked across the top of Lia's coffin and bruised flesh of the doomed woman's hands. She replayed the girl's screams captured on her phone. "Lia's death wasn't fast or quiet."

"When I pressed Ms. Poole," the lieutenant added, "she got agitated, and when I sent Deputy Fillingham for a separate interview, she threatened to send her bees after him."

Grace had seen the frazzled deputy in action. He was green and clearly rattled by this gruesome death. Perhaps someone with a bit more finesse, someone who knew how to talk to people, needed to question the old beekeeper. She turned to Hatch, but he was already heading down the path toward a rickety shack two hundred yards down river.

She caught up with him. "You're going to talk to Lou Poole."

"No, I'm going to build a bridge."

CHAPTER TWELVE

Okay, Princess, tell me what you know about the crazy old bee lady."

"She's old and crazy," Grace said as she walked alongside him on the path winding from Lia Grant's grave to a wooden house perched on stilts above the brackish green water.

Despite Grace's deadpan delivery, Hatch laughed. On some days, like today, he needed a good laugh. This morning he and Grace had learned Lia Grant's killer purchased three phones.

What happened if Grace struck out three times? Did the killer have plans for the *loser*? He walked faster. There were so many unknowns at this point.

"I'm serious," Grace said. "Lou Poole's probably close to eighty years old and talks to bees."

He had no problem with a woman who talked to bees. The question was, would the woman who talked to bees have a problem talking to him? Lia had been buried alive near the beekeeper's home. The old woman would have to be deaf, blind, or comatose not to have noticed anything. "Have you ever met her?"

Grace nodded. "Most everyone in Cypress Bend knows Lou. The Poole family has been making tupelo honey on this land for more than a hundred years." She motioned to the stacked bee boxes near a stand of tupelo trees. "When I was young, Momma and I would make a trip to Lou's honey stand at least once a year." A smile hovered on Grace's lips.

He stopped in the middle of the path. "You have a story on your mind, one about a crazy old beekeeper."

Grace walked past him but slowed and eventually turned. She was itching to go, to talk to the beekeeper, to make any kind of headway in the search for a killer, but his strong-willed, let's-get-the-job-done former wife also knew the power of stories. As a prosecutor she spent her days weaving tales and creating emotions and eventually desired responses from judges and juries.

"One year Momma and I went to Lou's roadside stand to pick out a jar of honey for Christmas for one of my school teachers. I took forever, poking through the display of mismatched jars. I'd hold a jar up to the sun and weigh it in my hand before moving on to another. I don't remember what I was looking for, but it was a big deal to me. As usual, Momma was anxious and worried about bad people following us and swore she'd seen someone with wild, dark hair ducking between the trees on the other side of the slough and watching us. But old Lou, she patted Momma's hand and reminded her the bees would let us know if anyone bad was lurking.

"When I finally selected my honey, Lou carefully took the jar from my hands and set it on her lap. Then she snapped a length of grass from the ground, tied a bow around the jar's neck, and tucked a dried twig between the loops. 'That thar's my de-lux gift wrap for special customers,' she'd said. I remember reverently taking the honey and thinking it was the most beautiful gift in the world."

"Nice memory," Hatch said. "Sounds like a nice lady."

"Nice." The creamy plane of Grace's forehead wrinkled. "But different. Lou comes from old-time swamp people. She rarely travels to town, pretty much lives off the land. As far as I know, she's the last of the Pooles."

"No husband? No kids?"

"Not that anyone knows of."

"Friends?"

"Just the bees."

"Just the bees," Hatch echoed softly.

With the story tucked in the back of his head, they continued down the path until they reached a fence made of hand-tied barbed wire and cypress sticks. A gate on the fence held a crooked black slate that read: *NO honey 2 Day—Go Away!*

The hinges creaked as Grace opened the gate. The ground beneath their feet grew damp and more uneven, but Grace trudged on. Nothing could stop this woman when she set her mind to something. Hatch's feet slowed. Like her decision to divorce him. Grace had made up her mind and *wham*, done. But in this case, Grace was using her tenacity to track down a killer. A half smile settled on his lips. And that killer better be shaking in his size eight wading boots.

Hatch followed Grace along the slough under the dappled shade of tupelo trees until they reached a raised wooden walkway hugging the water's edge. A dozen more boxes squatted on the weathered boards, the air above peppered with bees.

A sun-dried woman hobbled along the walkway, a smoking stick in her hand. When Grace stepped onto the walkway, the old woman called over her shoulder, "No honey today!" She jabbed the smoking stick at them then waved it over a bee box.

"Yes, ma'am," he said. "I saw the sign on the fence. We're not here for honey. My name's Hatch, and I'm a friend of Grace's."

The old woman squinted. "Little Gracie?"

"Yes, Miss Poole," Grace said. "We'd like to talk to you about the girl they found up river."

"We're trying to find whoever hurt that girl," Hatch added.

"No honey today. No honey today. Take Little Gracie and go away." Her voice was as soft and gritty as the curls of ashy black snaking from the stick. She went from box to box, releasing waves of smoke.

Hatch leaned against the walkway post. "Something wrong with the bees?"

"Yep, they're mad and sad." Lou sent another wave of smoke over the bees.

"The smoke helps?" Hatch asked.

"Smoke soothes the bees. Makes them eat. A tummy full of honey calms 'em down."

A gray haze hung over the area, and a sweet, charred odor wafted on the wind rustling through the trees. Grace angled her body toward the slough and squinted. "Water's high this year. That's good, right?"

Lou Poole nodded enthusiastically. "Good for the trees. Good for the bees."

"And the bees are happy now," Hatch said. Building bridges between people was a simple matter of joining bits and pieces of building materials, and there were so many different types of building materials: words, silence, memories, shared looks, shared friends, even if they were of the insect variety.

"They're happy now," Lou said with a toothless grin.

"But the bees weren't happy before?" Hatch asked.

"Nope." Lou's lips smacked off toothless gums. "They was spooked."

"Because of the girl in the ground?" Grace pressed.

"Of course not," Lou said. She crooked her finger at them, inviting them closer. "Because of the ghost."

Grace's shoulder, pressed against his, slumped.

Hatch kept building the bridge, hoping to get past the crazy. "Did the ghost hurt the bees?"

"Nah, just spooked 'em." The old woman's eyes widened. "Ain't every day they see someone back from the dead."

Grace shifted, her pumps snapping a branch while he remained still.

"Nope, doesn't happen often," he said. "Was the ghost here with the bees?"

"'Course not. The ghost was burying the dead girl."

Grace stopped fidgeting. "Dead girl?"

Lou jutted her dried apple chin in the direction of Lia Grant's grave. "Yep, a dead girl floated down the river. We saw her face, still and white as a salt lick. And we saw that button pinned to her shirt, *How Can I help you?* So sad. Nothing could help that sweet-looking little girl. Me and the bees said a prayer for her."

Hatch caught Grace's gaze over the smoke. The old woman clearly had seen Lia Grant if she knew about the button. But the girl couldn't have been dead, given the phone calls to Grace. Probably drugged.

"Can you tell us more about the ghost who frightened the bees?" Grace asked. "What did it look like?"

Lou scratched at the wild wisps of snowy white hair escaping a dirty bandana tied around her forehead. "Wrong, it looked wrong. After being dead so long, it should have been bones, just bones."

"The ghost was more than bones?" A sharp buzz shot up his spine. "Was the ghost big or little, old or young, man or woman?"

"Bodies buried in the ground should rot after all those years. They give back to the earth because earth gave them life. That's the way of the land." Lou waved the stick in faster, longer arcs, as if hoping the smoke would bring more calm, but the stick flew from her hand and fell into the water, hissing and sputtering before finally extinguishing. She looked up from the stick and glared. "No honey today. No honey today!"

Hatch dropped his chin to his chest so the old woman couldn't see him swallowing a curse. He'd lost her, and there was no way he'd get her back, not today. He raised his face and nodded at her. "Yes, ma'am. No honey today, but maybe tomorrow."

Lou Poole hobbled down the walkway, muttering something to the bees. Hatch tucked one hand in his pocket and slipped the other hand around Grace's waist as he pulled her along the path.

Grace dug in her heels and forcibly removed his hand from her waist. "That's it?" Grace asked. "Did you not hear her? She saw Lia Grant. She saw the killer. And you're leaving. Are you crazy?"

"The bridge collapsed. We aren't going any further today." He walked down the path.

"Lives are at stake here."

He stopped and turned. "Yeah, Grace, including yours. Tell me something I don't know." At her booming silence he jabbed a hand toward Lou Poole's home. "Yes, that woman saw something, and I could drag her into the sheriff's station and grill her. Hell, I could even threaten to take away her beloved bees, but that's going to get us nowhere."

"It could get us one step closer to a killer. Dammit, Hatch. We need to do everything we can to prevent a second abduction, and that means pressing harder, not giving up."

"And that's where you're wrong. I am not giving up. I'm simply giving an old, frightened woman the time she needs to process the fact that she witnessed a murder." He took a step toward Grace. "Do you doubt me?"

She opened her mouth to argue, to build her case like the successful prosecuting attorney she was, but her hard face softened. "Okay," she said.

Grace, soft? Not in this decade. "Okay, what?"

"You"—she straightened the already straight pearls at her neck—"win."

He tucked his hand in the crook of her arm and escorted her down the path. "It's not about winning or losing. The goal is simply to keep everyone alive. But rest assured, I'll be back here tomorrow and the day after until I get Lou Poole's story." Because Grace was right; lives were at stake.

When they left the canopy of oak and sycamore, Hatch squinted at the sky and let out a curse. Dusk had slipped in on him. He checked his watch and grabbed Grace's hand.

"You have a watch?" Grace asked with a puzzled frown. "You swore you'd never wear a watch."

He pulled her along the path to the main road where he'd parked the SUV. "We need to go."

"When did you start wearing a watch?"

"We're late."

"For what?"

He dragged her through a tangle of creeping nettles and grinned.

CHAPTER THIRTEEN

This is it?" Grace raised her hands and motioned to the blood-red sky above Hatch's thirty-five-foot sailboat anchored in the Cypress Bend Marina. "This is why we left the crime scene? This is why you drove across town like a maniac?"

Hatch tossed her an icy bottle of beer before he rested his elbows on the deck rail. A pop and a soft hiss sounded as he opened his own bottle. He tossed the cap in a bait bucket and stared at the sun setting across Apalachicola Bay. "Beautiful, isn't it?"

Grace slammed the beer on the railing. A pair of gulls perched on a weathered dock post screeched and took off. Hatch, on the other hand, continued to watch the sun say good-bye to the day. She ran the icy beer along the heat brewing at her temples. Why did this not surprise her? They were in the middle of a murder investigation and attempting to thwart two other murders, and Hatch wanted to watch the sun set.

She pointed her longneck at him. "Do you ever take anything seriously?"

Hatch aimed his beer at the western sky. "That's one serious piece of art."

She opened her mouth but couldn't argue. The sun hovered on the horizon, a giant peach against fiery streaks of red and orange. The bay shared the same color, as if someone had poured melted red and orange crayons into the waters. The last of the oyster boats had tucked in for the night, bobbing black silhouettes against the fiery palette. She'd spent her entire life in this town and had enjoyed thousands of sunsets. There was no more beautiful place on earth, no other place she ever wanted to call home. She pictured herself growing old here in her house on a hill.

Hatch, on the other hand, would never settle down. He'd initially come to town to get his son straightened out, and he was taking a detour with her to catch a killer. But through it all, he remained Hatch to the core, a man who took time to enjoy the journey.

With her bare palm, she uncapped her beer and rested her elbows on the railing. The evening was warm, the beer cold, and if she was honest with herself, the man at her side welcome. Despite Hatch's laid-back appearance, he'd contributed significantly to the investigation today. He'd sweet-talked the phone store manager into talking to her, identified the boat the killer most likely used, and made inroads with Lou Poole. She toasted him. "You're good."

He smiled around his longneck. "So I've been told."

She chased her groan with a frosty swig. No, Hatch would never change, and with the chaos and uncertainty of her life, she welcomed the familiar. How ironic. His laid-back attitude had frustrated her, like the times he forgot to pay the bill at the marina and they lost power and all those times she made appointments to house hunt with a real estate agent and he forgot. But tonight she found comfort in his insouciance.

Somewhere down the dock, country music played, the melody slow and soulful, speaking of loss and sorrow, and today she'd felt it to her bones. An innocent girl had died because of her, and it was possible two more would follow. The question was where and when? And of course, why? Why her? She took another swallow.

Lieutenant Lang had asked her to put together a list of people who may have a grudge against her, and in her work, the list was long. Already she'd given the lieutenant a dozen names off the top of her head of hostile, hateful individuals she'd helped convict, and tomorrow, she planned to get into her work files to search for more. But this grudge match may have nothing to do with her work. The idea that this could be someone from her personal past or present sickened her. A disgruntled lover? Someone she once beat out for a job? Heck, why not someone she beat on the tennis courts? Crazy, but as Hatch said, they were dealing with a crazy individual.

As a darker shade of red slid across the sky, Hatch tossed his empty bottle in the bait bucket. Quiet as a big golden cat, he slipped behind her, lifting his hands to her neck where his fingers performed an old, familiar magic. She'd once called him Magic Man. He had a pocket full of silly magic tricks, not to mention magic fingers. More than once in their short, fiery time together, he'd rubbed away the tension of a work headache or pains from shoulders that had seen decades of tennis.

"You're tense," Hatch said.

"Murder in my backyard does that to me." Her head lolled forward, giving him access to the full curve of her neck.

His fingers dug into the coiled muscles. "Tension's in your neck. That says a lot."

Her skin heated and muscles softened. "What is my neck telling you?"

His fingers fanned out and up to the base of her head, where he scrubbed. "That you have a lot on your mind."

"Hmmmmm." She closed her eyes. Her mind was blessedly chaos-free, filled only with a good-night sky and lullaby of the bay, and Hatch's magic fingers. She practically purred.

His fingers stilled.

She bit on her lower lip. Had she purred? She'd done that plenty of times as his hands—fast and slow and every speed in between—ran along her body. And she'd moaned and laughed and screamed in a pleasure so strong it was painful. She stood. No need to think about that brand of chaos. "I need to go. I have work to do."

Hatch dropped his hands, tore himself from the railing, and turned his back on the fiery sky. "Me too."

A twinge of disappointment shot through her. The old Hatch would have slid a lingering finger along her neck while he smiled and cajoled, asking for five more minutes, five more strokes, five more kisses. He took her empty beer and dropped the bottle in the bucket. As she hunted around the deck for her purse, he slipped a phone from his pocket and leaped to the slip housing *No Regrets*, but she could hear his voice. He was checking on his son, Alex.

She wondered about the boy's mom. Hatch collected women like other people collected baseball cards or coins. And like most avid collectors, he took great delight in his hobby. Did he rub her neck? Show her silly magic tricks? Make her purr? And was that a lance of jealousy stabbing at Grace's chest? She found her purse and flung it onto her shoulder with a half laugh.

How could she be jealous of something that was never hers? Hatch had sworn his love to her on a rocking boat under a melon moon. In the presence of bees and a justice of the peace, he'd signed a paper that made him her husband. But Hatch was and always would be his own man.

When he finished his phone call, she joined him on the dock. "Everything okay with Alex?" She was curious about Hatch's son. Cypress Bend was a small town, and she'd heard about the shrimp shack B&E. She knew of the Milanos family, had seen the grandmother chasing the hell-raising twins around town.

"After a day of shoveling shells, Alex showered, ate, and is in bed and snoring loud enough to wake the dead in Black Jack's backyard."

"Sounds like he's headed in the right direction."

"You think?" An uncustomary line of worry divided Hatch's forehead. He could bring comfort to parents who had just lost their daughter and get crazy old women to talk about murder suspects, but when it came to this thirteen-year-old boy, Hatch was out of his element. Her ex claimed he wasn't a family man and never would be. True.

Twenty minutes later, Hatch parked in front of Grace's shack. Much to her chagrin, he hopped out and escorted her up the steps. As she dug into her bag for her keys, she waved him off. "I don't need you to walk me to the door."

Hatch slid a hand along her spine, the column tightening and tingling. His fingers stopped at the base of her neck where he pressed softly.

"What are you doing?" Grace asked.

"Looking for the off switch," Hatch said. "I'm tired of hearing that same old song."

She probably did sound like a broken record. Even as a kid she'd been fiercely independent. Much to her mother's horror, she began taking the family skiff out on her own at age nine. She'd tried doubles tennis, but excelled in singles, winning the state championship her senior year of high school. And after her divorce from Hatch, she'd thrown herself into her work, handling most of the casework on her own because at that time in her life, she wanted to be so busy she wouldn't have time to think about how much her heart ached.

Hatch rubbed his knuckles across the top of Blue's head. The old dog had been waiting on the top step for her. "Since your watchdog has a weakness for bacon, I want to poke around, make sure no bogeymen are hiding under your bed."

Arguing with him would only prolong the moment, so she opened the door. A wave of hot air that reeked of musty wood and wet dog rolled over them. Wrinkling her nose, she threw open the windows and cracked the back door, hoping not too many bugs would sneak in. Or bad guys with pre-paid phones and blood red markers. She peered into the darkness stretching beyond her back porch but saw nothing.

In full FBI mode, Hatch searched the living room and kitchen area, and she could hear him checking her bedroom and bathroom. "No bogeymen," he announced as he sauntered into the kitchen.

"Thank you, I was worried." She dug through a drawer and took out a vanilla-scented candle, lit it, and placed it in the middle of her kitchen table.

"Planning a candlelit dinner with yours truly?"

"Planning to get rid of the Eau de Blue."

Hatch sniffed and grimaced. "You might be better off getting a hotel room for a few days. I'm sure you can find a place that'll take both you and your dog."

"He's not my dog." Grace yanked the lid off an airtight container and dug out a giant scoop of dog chow. Hatch didn't need to know she'd almost zeroed out her checking account to pay the next installment to her general contractor. "A breeze is picking up. It'll be fine in a few minutes."

She added warm water to the chow and sprinkled cooked bacon on top. The dog padded across the room to the bowl but raised his head and looked at her with big, droopy eyes.

"You are *not* getting two slices of bacon."

With a chuckle, Hatch opened the refrigerator and poked around a half dozen cartons of takeout. "You do realize you talk to that dog all the time," he said.

"I do not."

He lifted his eyebrows, and she ducked under his arm, grabbing a carton of grilled grouper and hushpuppies. "I appreciate everything you've done, Hatch, really I do, but you can go now."

Hatch handed her a bottle of her favorite hot sauce and grabbed a takeout box for himself. "Now, Counselor Courtemanche, you're a lot smarter than that." He set the carton on the table and dug into the drawer near her sink, which irritated her, that he knew where she kept her silverware. "I'm not going to leave you in this house alone with all the doors and windows open."

Breathe in, two, three. Breathe out, two, three. "I don't have an extra bed."

"We can share."

She shoved her takeout box in the microwave and jabbed the reheat button.

"Fine, Grace, I'll crash there." He aimed a bottle of tartar sauce at the small settee in the front room.

She pictured those long, golden limbs spilled across the tiny sofa. Hatch had a way of taking up space, in any room, and in her head. Today he'd been everywhere as they worked the case. Impressive. And effective. But that didn't mean she needed him on her settee. "You're too big for that thing. You'll wake up with a backache."

"Nice to know you still care."

"I don't c..." But she couldn't finish. Less than an hour ago, they'd sat under a good-bye sun, and he'd run his magic fingers along her neck, chasing away hell. Hatch was one of the good guys. He was on her side, Lia's side, and at one point in her life, he'd been her world. At some level, she'd always care about him.

"If I have to, I'll stretch out on Blue's rug on the porch." The veins along his forearm thickened, and he set the sauce on the table so hard, the candle flame flickered and jumped. A similar fire flickered in his eyes, one that had warmed her after Lia Grant's chilling phone calls and horrific death. The man was dead serious.

Ten years ago Hatch hadn't believed in serious. He'd sworn he'd never own a watch, have children, or be tied down by anyone or anything. But something had changed. He was here to help straighten out his son and determined to make sure she was safe. He committed himself and his team's vast resources to a small-county sheriff's department in need of big-time help. Somewhere along the way Hatch had grown up.

"I'm not leaving you alone with this place wide open." He crossed his arms over his chest, a golden guardian angel with a halo of blond hair. He filled her tiny kitchen, the smell that was uniquely Hatch conjuring memories of sunny days and sensuous nights.

And somehow he'd grown even more irresistible.

The microwave dinged and she pulled out the steamy carton of grouper. She'd spent years repairing the damage to her heart after that summer. Scar tissue appeared rougher, thicker, but was in actuality much weaker. She grabbed a fork and napkin and headed down the hall, calling over her shoulder, "Extra sheets and a pillow are in the cupboard in the bathroom. Sweet dreams."

* * *

Hatch plopped onto Grace's little blue sofa with his carton of takeout and took out his phone. He wouldn't be dreaming anytime soon. He checked his messages and frowned. No word yet from his teammate Hayden.

As Hatch had stood at the edge of Lia Grant's grave, the severity and sickness of what they were dealing with almost brought him to his knees. The individual behind Lia Grant's murder and this game had a twisted mind, one that he wanted his teammate to get into ASAP. Hatch dialed Hayden's number.

"G-man's phone," a scratchy old voice said.

"Hey there, Smokey Joe," Hatch said. Joseph "Smokey Joe" Bernard was a friend of Hayden's fiancée, Kate Johnson. Hatch had met the blind Vietnam vet last month when Hatch joined Hayden's hunt in northern Nevada for the Broadcaster Butcher, another twisted mind. "Parker got you on payroll these days?"

"Nope. G-man and Katy-lady are coming to blows outside. G-man got himself so rattled, he forgot his phone, so I decided to take care of FBI business for him."

Hatch swallowed a laugh. And woe to anyone who told old Smokey Joe he couldn't take on whatever he damned well pleased. "Coming to blows?" Hatch asked.

"Something about my new aide. The crotchety old woman bailed on me last week. Got Kate in a snit, which got G-man in a snit. They didn't want me listening, so they went outside and are having a loud discussion in the car."

"How loud?" Hatch asked with a smile. He loved seeing his formerly buttoned-up teammate get riled because it showed Hayden was deeply in love with a woman who loved him enough to give it back with equal passion. The opposite of love wasn't hate; it was indifference. Hatch poked his fork into the shrimp fettuccini. That had been part of the problem with Grace. She'd announced they were getting a divorce and said good-bye. He'd wanted to argue and fight, but she disappeared, like she no longer cared.

"Loud enough for me to hear words like 'assisted living'." Smokey snorted. "Now tell me about what's going on down at the swamp. I heard about that little gal buried alive. Got another sicko on the loose. You need me out there to give you a hand? You know I got experience in stuff like this, taking on serial killers and all. Jist say the word, and I'll be there. Hang tight, G-man's walking up the driveway. Nope. They stopped. And they're yammering again. Katy-lady just stomped her foot." Smokey chuckled. "Man, she's fit to be tied."

Smokey Joe was legally blind but had incredible hearing. Hatch would have loved to have had the old man in the swamp when Grace heard that ringing phone and voice. Old Smokey might have been able to hear footsteps or a boat with an electric motor gliding through the water. At first Lieutenant Lang had thought they might be looking at a potential witness, but with the game-like quality of the exchange, Hatch had other ideas.

"Actually, Smokey, I have a question for you. You spent some time dodging through the jungles of Vietnam. How does a guy move around without being heard?" Hatch told him about the ringing phone and voice Grace heard in the swamp.

"You say she heard the voice only once, right behind her?"

"Yes, coming from the water."

"And the old dog didn't pick up a scent?"

"Didn't seem to."

"I'd put my money on a water entry. If a body's under-water, you can't smell or see him. As for that ringing phone, a guy in the know can do some fancy-pants stuff with audio software, stuff like making sounds appear in places where he ain't." Smokey Joe chuckled.

Hatch had a feeling Smokey was speaking from experience, and it most likely involved pranks on an aide or two. "You can tell me that story later. Right now I want to hear about this manipulation of sound."

"So if I was wanting to make a phone sound like it was coming from different places I'd apply some low-pass filters and adjust the slider. Then I'd drop out most of the high end here and add some reverb over there. Boom. Got it. A phone that sounds like it's moving around. Hey, here's G-man. Now, don't forgit. You give me a call if you need anything else."

"Smokey talk your ear off?" Hayden asked.

"He actually gave me some useful information." Hatch told him about the ringing phone.

"So we're looking at someone or multiple someones with considerable technical skill, physical agility, and knowledge of the area."

"That's why I called. We don't know what we have. I need you to get in this guy's head."

"Send me everything you have. Crime scene photos. Witness accounts. Victim profile. Given the method of kill, we're clearly chasing a sociopath."

One who was fixated on Grace.

CHAPTER FOURTEEN

Grace curled her fingers around the window latch and slammed. The moulding shook and the pane rattled, but the man on her settee didn't bat a golden eyelash.

Her ex-husband could sleep through a class-five hurricane. Hatch had spent the night on her settee, and right now one leg was flung over the arm, the other stretched out across the floor, a white sheet draped across his lap and torso. She picked up his shirt and pants and flung them onto his chest. Still no movement.

Her fingers pressed at the ache between her eyes. The dull ache had worsened, as if she, not Hatch, had spent an uncomfortable night tossing and turning on a too-small bed. The problem was that her bed, while large, had been too crowded, thanks to the questions crowding around her most of the night. Why bury Lia Grant alive with a phone programmed to call only her? Who killed the girl? Someone Grace helped put behind bars? Someone who harbored a serious grudge? But most importantly, when would he strike again? She'd taken a steamy shower this morning, trying to wash away the questions along with the accompanying angst and uncertainty, but the tiny jets of hot water hadn't helped.

Her mind momentarily wandered to Hatch's magic fingers. No, she didn't want to go there. She bent, her hand ready to thwack Hatch on the shoulder, when his right eye popped open.

"Hey, Princess," he said around a yawning grin. "What a beautiful sight to wake up to."

She ignored the swirl of heat that megawatt smile sent throughout her shack. She poked him in the shoulder. "Up. My car won't start and I need a ride." She'd banged on the starter for fifteen minutes without luck.

He rolled to his side, pulled a pillow over his head, and held out his hand, the fingers stretched wide. "Five more minutes."

She yanked the pillow off his head. "I don't have five minutes. We need to get moving, I want to go to the phone store and see the security files."

"Files?" Hatch stretched his arms over his head in a lazy arc, and on the down slope he ran a finger along the crease of her trousers.

She side-stepped his hand, remembering such casual touches were second nature to him. "From the security cameras. The manager said her people would pull up both the indoor and outdoor security images for the day the phones were purchased." She threw the pillow at his chest.

"Okay, I'm up." Hatch blinked and inched to an upright position. He scrubbed the side of his hand against his stubbled jaw, his hair falling in messy waves across his forehead. Morning always looked good on Hatch, all crumpled and tumbled.

She walked into the kitchen, and when she turned around Hatch had slumped back down and closed his eyes. Over the past few days she'd seen flashes of brilliance that made him worthy of Parker Lord's team, but not now. She hurried to the settee, pulled off the sheet, and opened her mouth to help him rearrange his priorities but drew up short, his naked lap giving her a good idea of what he'd been thinking.

Hatch's devilish chuckle chased her into the kitchen. She didn't turn as he padded on bare feet—and bare everything else—into the bathroom where the pipes groaned and rattled and where water would soon be sliding over every inch of his wide-awake body.

"I never thought I'd admit this, Blue." For the second time that morning she emptied and filled the dog's water bowl. "But there are worse roommates than you." She reached for the food bowl to wash it, but it was still half full. "What's wrong? You're usually an eating machine." She took off the anklet and checked his foot. No signs of infection. "It's probably all that bacon."

Fifteen minutes later Hatch appeared, fully clothed and with his hair slicked back. He grabbed a loaf of bread from the counter and dropped two pieces into the toaster. "Did the store manager call and say the video was ready?"

"No, but you saw her yesterday. She's overworked and harried." Grace reached into the cupboard and set a jar of peanut butter on the counter.

"And what are you going to do, go through the records yourself?"

"If need be."

"The store's not even open." The toast popped, and he slathered on peanut butter.

She handed him a banana. "Then you can flash your shiny badge or perhaps do something with your fast hands."

Hatch peeled the banana. "You know what your problem is, Grace?"

She handed him a knife. "I'm sure you can't wait to tell me."

"You need to be more patient." He sliced the bananas and placed them in neat rows on the peanut butter.

"And you need to check your fishing line more often."

For a moment, their gazes locked. Shortly after they were married, they took a sail past the barrier islands where Hatch dropped anchor and a fishing line to catch dinner. For hours they sat side by side, she with case notes from work, Hatch with a book of Longfellow's poems. As the sun dipped and there was still no nibble, Grace pointed out that boats around them were reeling in line after line of Spanish mackerel.

"Why don't you check your line?" Grace had suggested.

"Why don't you be more patient?" he'd countered with a slow grin.

When he finally reeled in his line, he discovered he'd lost his bait and his hook. Who knew how long he'd been fishing with nothing?

Hatch tossed the banana peel in the trashcan, threw back his head, and laughed. "Touché, Princess, touché."

She grabbed the other piece of toast, smashed it on the bananas, and spun out of the kitchen, Hatch and his breakfast on her heels.

When they reached his borrowed SUV, he opened the door for her and lingered as she buckled her seat belt. "I want you to stay close to me today."

"Hatch, I'm a big girl who—"

"Who's playing a game with a sociopath." His morning cheer had faded, replaced by a grim seriousness she found even more disturbing. "Our team's criminal profiler sent me some notes this morning. Grace, the person playing this game with you is twisted. He plays by a different set of rules. He's the type who isn't going to play fair."

She placed her fingertips on his chest and pushed him away. "Then we'll just have to play dirty."

They reached Port St. Joe, and the phone store manager unlocked the door the minute she spotted Hatch. "Tired of the FBI and itching to work retail?"

"Itching for something," Hatch said with a wink.

Grace tried not to roll her eyes. "Are the security recordings ready for viewing?" One camera. One clear face shot. That's all they needed. Would it be someone from the Morehouse camp? Another low-life lawbreaker? Someone from Grace's past? This was about her, and she, more than anyone else, should be able to identify the buyer of those phones.

"Didn't the district manager call you? Our security guys called up the files for the day the phones were purchased, but everything had been wiped. No files from any cameras on that day, interior or exterior."

"Did you have a system-wide malfunction?" Grace asked.

"Nope. It's a relatively new system. Never had a problem with anything getting wiped."

"How about the day before and after?"

"Both okay. Not a single minute missing."

"Is it possible you or your staff could have accidentally erased it?" Grace asked.

"We don't touch the stuff. The file archive dumps are automated."

"Any break-ins?"

"No."

"Who has access to this office?"

"Just me and my assistant manager."

"What about staff or corporate personnel?"

"I guess they could, but they'd need the key."

"And where's the key?"

The manager reached into her pocket and pulled out a packet of gum and an Exact-O knife. With a frown, she hurried to the offices behind the sales floor and found the key in the door, the door wide open. "Oh, man, I can't believe I did that. With inventory and new hires not showing, it's been crazy around here."

This kind of crazy Grace could deal with. "I need a list of all of your employees and any district or corporate personnel who have had access to this room and the security recordings."

The store manager gnawed on her lower lip as she stared at the key she'd left in a door. "Are you thinking some of my people tampered with the security tape?"

Hatch set his hand on her shoulder and spun her from the dangling keys. "At this point all we're thinking about is saving another life."

The store manager disappeared into the office and returned with a list of names of people who had access to the store's back end. "I also included the cleaning crew and temps we used during inventory two weeks ago." The manager grabbed the key from the door, the sharp edges biting into her fingers. "Let me know if there's anything else I can do. Anything."

Grace took the papers, and Hatch took the woman's hand. "We will," he said with a squeeze.

As they walked to the SUV, Hatch draped an arm over her shoulders. "Well done, Princess, well, well done. If you ever decide to retire from law, Parker could use you on the team."

Grace couldn't tell if Hatch was joking, offering genuine praise, or slipping her a thinly veiled criticism. Despite Hatch's teasing as he got out of bed and his saucy banter with the store manager, there was an edge to him this morning, and she wasn't sure if it was because of a bad night's sleep on her settee or his escalating concern about catching a killer. Or it could just be he was getting anxious to set sail.

Once in the SUV she hauled out her phone. Next to her, Hatch dug out his.

"I'll get these names to the Box," he said. "We have access to databases filled with millions of names and phone numbers and addresses. It's possible we'll get a hit."

Exactly her thoughts. Bad guys tended to leave slimy trails. "Go ahead, but we'll have a better chance with me putting out feelers."

Hatch's thumb froze mid-dial. "Excuse me?"

"Your people could miss something."

"You do realize I work for Parker Lord and one of the world's most effective and efficient crime-fighting units, don't you?"

Again, she felt an edge, sharp and shiny, and she realized he thought she'd just insulted his team. "Of course," she said. "It's not about how well they do their jobs. The issue is not one of your team members is a player." Grace settled her fingers on her chest. "The killer chose me, Hatch, me. It's possible someone on this list is somehow connected to me, to my work, to my past, and if that's the case, won't I be the best person to track him down?"

Without waiting for an answer, she turned on her phone and unlocked the screen saver. As she dialed up her contact list, Hatch said something under his breath, something that sounded a little like, "Ready, set, go!"

* * *

Greenup, Kentucky

Detective Tucker Holt pulled the stool next to the lab table holding the body with no face. "Who are you, Grandpa? Who the hell are you?"

"Detective Holt, you've worked homicide long enough to know dead men make for poor conversationalists."

Tucker looked over his shoulder to find Dr. Ray Thorpe, the medical examiner, standing in the doorway with a large manila envelope in his hand. Tucker had begged for a push on the autopsy, and Ray must have sensed his desperation.

"Someone needs to tell me something," Tucker said, "because I don't have much in the tank on this one. Thanks for doing this over the weekend, Ray. I'm hoping you'll wow me with evidence that will help us identify Grandpa and Grandma here and their killer." He pulled in a long breath to fan the tiny ember of hope in his gut. "Let's hear it."

The M.E. sat on the stool next to him and opened one of the folders. "Male between the ages of sixty and seventy. Multiple posterior sliding abrasions, blunt force trauma to head, all postmortem. Cause of death was GSW to the head. Given the charring and stellate pattern of the entry wound, the gun muzzle was pressed against the victim's forehead at the time of shooting."

So Asswipe got up close and personal, which means Grandpa could have made contact with the killer. It's possible Grandpa fought back or grabbed Asswipe before falling into the ravine. Unfortunately, Grandpa had no hands left, so no scraping under the fingernails.

The M.E. went on to detail other findings and estimated death occurred on Monday afternoon. Then he set aside the folder.

"That's it?" Tucker asked. "No artificial body parts with

serial numbers? No unique scars or birthmarks? Hell, I'll even take the name of his mother tattooed on his big toe."

Ray scanned another folder. "Got some interesting stomach contents." He flipped through the pages. "Half-pound bacon cheddar burger, sweet potato fries, and a slice of huckleberry pie. From the rate of gastric content digestion, he ate about two to three hours before death."

Tucker ran a hand down his face. "That's it?"

"He also ate vanilla ice cream. Probably three scoops. Your Grandpa Doe had a sweet tooth."

"Unless Grandpa has a set of dentures engraved with his name, I'm not impressed."

The medical examiner grinned and pushed off the table, rolling his stool toward the table on the other side of the room, which held Grandma Doe. He opened another folder and read the findings. As with the first report, there wasn't a damn thing that would help Tucker ID Grandma or her killer.

Tucker rested a fisted hand on the autopsy table. "Anything else?"

"More pie." Ray ran his finger down a column in the report. "Stomach contents for her include Caesar salad with chicken, bread stick, and pie. Best guess is white chocolate mousse with pomegranate seeds."

"I want a smoking gun, Ray, and you give me pie?"

The M.E. rested a hand on his arm, which was streaked with holler mud and dried sweat. He probably stunk to high heaven.

"You're good at what you do, Tucker, because you care," Ray said. "Or you wouldn't be in here on a Saturday afternoon. I gave you more than you had walking in. Now it's your turn. Go find the *wow*."

He left the medical examiner's office thinking if he couldn't have *wow*, he'd settle for Wild Turkey. He checked his watch. Choir practice would just be starting at R.C.'s

Tavern, and most of his drinking buddies from the station would be warming up to sing the night away.

But the M.E. was right. He cared about Grandpa and Grandma Doe. Tucker slipped into his cruiser and looked at the splintered photo frame he'd clipped to the visor. And he cared about his kids, a daughter who thought he could fix anything and a son who believed he was a hero.

So far, this case had a whole lot of *nos*, but as of fifteen minutes ago, he had something besides a *no*.

He had pie.

Back at the station Tucker tied ten equidistant knots in a string, each knot representing ten miles. Then he tied the string to a pencil. He placed the knotted end of the string on the bright red dot that represented Collier's Holler on the map on his desk. There was probably some computer app that could do this for him, but he needed to keep his hands busy. Busy hands were less likely to grab the whiskey behind desk drawer number two.

Given the M.E.'s report, Grandma and Grandpa Doe ate between two and three hours before they were murdered, and chances were they ate in a restaurant. His job was to find a restaurant that served huckleberry pie and white chocolate mousse pie. He'd start with a hundred-mile radius.

Tucker eyed the circle, which encompassed cities in Northeastern Kentucky, Southern Ohio, and Western West Virginia. He poked his head into the squad room. "Hey Carl, get in here." Carl was one of the greenhorns. Plenty of enthusiasm and a good head on his shoulders. The kid seemed keen on making detective one day, so Tucker threw him an occasional bone.

"Got something new on Grandma and Grandpa?" Carl asked.

Tucker tore the map in half. "Not yet. But I want you to get on the computer and find out if there are any diners, restaurants, or roadside stands in the towns within this half circle that sell huckleberry pie and white chocolate mousse pie."

"White chocolate mousse?"

"With pomegranates."

* * *

Grace dropped her phone onto the beachside picnic table and raised both hands. "Ronnie Alderman."

Hatch took a bite of his grilled shrimp po' boy. He and Grace had spent the past two hours using their respective sources to glean information on individuals who had access to the security equipment in the phone store. He'd joked with Grace that this was some kind of race, which it was, because with Grace everything was a competition.

By the smile on her face, looked like she'd won.

He recognized the name Ronnie Alderman from the store manager's list of people who had access to the office where the store kept its security equipment. "He was a member of the store's cleaning crew, right?"

"Yes and no." The green in Grace's eyes brightened.

"I sense a story." He took another bite of sandwich. He could spend hours watching Grace smile and listening to her talk. She had a strong, confident jaw softened by full lips, chiseled cheeks flushed by an inner fire, and those eyes...

"Ronnie was listed as a member of the cleaning crew." She brought her fingertips together under her chin, then pointed them at him. "He's dead."

Hatch dropped the sandwich into the basket, shrimp scattering across the table. One landed on his whirring laptop. "He got another—"

"It's not what you think." Grace scrolled through a message on her phone. "He died eight years ago. Coronary failure. He's buried in the Twin Buttes cemetery in Southern Utah. Son of Ronald and Ruth Alderman of Salt Lake City. He went to BYU where he studied English Literature. He taught high school English for forty-two years and is survived by nine children and forty-one grandchildren. At the time of his death he was eighty-five."

Eighty-five-year-old grandfathers, especially those who've been dead eight years, don't work nights on cleaning crews. "Most likely a classic case of stolen identity," Hatch said.

"That's what I was thinking. Someone manipulated something somewhere and used Ronnie's name and social security number to get a part-time job on the cleaning crew. It's a serious red flag."

"One worth looking into. This person stealing a dead man's identity could be an accomplice or even the killer. We may have a fake name, but we also have a—"

"—face," Grace finished for him. "The other cleaning crew members must have seen this version of Ronnie Alderman." She dangled her phone before him, a smile lighting her face. "We're getting closer, Hatch. We're going to catch this sick killer before he strikes again. Whoever started this game is going down."

If Hatch could have any superpower, he'd have the ability to stop time. That way he could hold onto those moments in his life that left him awed.

A perfect day of sailing.

A night of love and laughter with a woman dressed only in moonlight and pearls.

And moments like this when the criminals of this world, the men and women who perpetrated wrongs against humanity, had no chance of winning, not when people like Grace Courtemanche were on the other side.

CHAPTER FIFTEEN

Hatch pulled a pan of golden biscuits from Grace's oven and fanned the steam her way. "What do you think?"

Grace breathed in the buttery air and sighed. "Perfect."

He set the pan on the counter. "Let's hope Lou Poole thinks so."

She shook her head, not in disagreement, but in amusement and with a touch of admiration. She'd finally accepted this new version of Hatch. He was a successful, creative crisis negotiator, a master of building bridges, as he called it. This evening he planned on constructing bridges with biscuits. "So you're just going to show up at Lou's place bearing biscuits and a smile?"

"Yep. Then she will do her neighborly part, haul out a jar of honey, and invite me onto her porch, where she'll tell me the latest bee gossip and I'll give her great aunt Piper Jane's recipe for exploded biscuits with eggs and sausage gravy." He dug around the drawer and pulled out a spatula. "Then she'll tell me more about the flesh-and-blood person she saw with Lia Grant. And then we'll catch a killer."

"And all this starts with biscuits."

"Food is universal. It hits a primal chord with most people. Some foods invite closeness." He slid the steamy, golden circles of bread onto a tea towel. "Like biscuits."

She laughed at him and herself, because she actually thought this plan could work. "They taught you this kind of stuff at Quantico?"

"My hostage negotiation and crisis training instructors taught me about connections. It's all about connecting in ways people in crisis can understand and deal with, like Big Willie Walberg."

"Big Willie? That name rings a bell."

"He's the disgruntled warehouse worker in Galveston who stormed into his former place of employment and held his boss and five co-workers at gunpoint two years ago. He claimed he wanted to get media and government attention on alleged safety violations at the warehouse, but in the end all it took to establish a connection with him was a donut." Hatch grinned and handed her a biscuit.

With the tips of her fingers, she split the biscuit in two and watched as steam rose in gauzy curls. "I'm sure there's a point to this."

"Big Willie was mad at his supervisor at the warehouse for firing him, the electric company for turning off his power, and his girlfriend for leaving him. Big Willie got slammed with some big stuff in a small amount of time. He decided to take punches at the people who started the downhill slide, his former employers. Parker sent me over, and in less than two hours Big Willie and I were sharing a dozen chocolate-glazed donuts—mind you, with a parking lot separating us. Over coffee and donuts, Big Willie told me his troubles, and I listened. And that was the key. All he wanted was for someone to hear his story, to commiserate with him, and in the end to help him find a way out of that misery."

"He surrendered with no injuries to anyone, right?"

Hatch grinned. "Before the last donut was gone."

She took a bite of the biscuit. "Amazing."

"I do have my moments." Hatch knotted the ends of the towel. "Now I'm heading to the Poole place. You stay here. And you," he pointed to Blue, "don't leave her side."

"Don't encourage him, Hatch. He's annoying enough as it is."

"I'm serious, Grace." He placed a hand on either side of her face and forced her to look into his eyes. The blue was warm and steamy, like the air in her kitchen, and it left her more than a little breathy. "There's a killer out there."

Which was why Hatch was here, to catch a killer.

"I know, and Lou Poole may have seen him." She placed both hands on his shoulders and pushed him away, acutely aware of the retreating heat. "So go. Go and build your biscuit bridge."

With Hatch gone, she cleaned the kitchen, washing a sink full of dishes and sweeping spilled flour from the floor. In Blue's dog dish she found a bone-shaped biscuit. Grace laughed. Vintage Hatch. Blow in, make a mess, but leave her smiling.

After cleaning the kitchen, she checked her phone and e-mail. No news from Lieutenant Lang. No calls from the cleaning company that employed the long-dead Ronnie Alderman. She changed Blue's water and re-applied the bear grease ointment.

As she slipped a new anklet on Blue's front paw, something splashed in the creek winding along the back side of her property. Could be a gator, an osprey catching his dinner, or a killer. She taped the anklet in place.

Hatch had been confident the killer traveled to and from the crime scene in a fourteen-foot aluminum skiff, propelled by hand or an electric motor, and he suggested the killer had been relatively close to the burial site. It was also likely the person with the ringing phone came by water in a silent boat. So far, the sheriff's investigators had drummed up no leads on the boat.

She eyed the path leading down to the creek where Lamar Giroux's boat was tethered to an old, splintered dock.

She flexed her fingers and rolled her wrists. She knew this area. She knew of dozens of nooks and crannies around Cypress Point, perfect places to hide a boat. Hatch would have a fit if she went out on her own, but she'd be safe. She had no plans to gun down a killer, and at this point in the game, she was certain the killer wasn't gunning for her. He was too busy playing games and keeping score.

Me: 1

You: 0

Grace didn't fear for her own life, only the lives of two others.

And Hatch was right, she sorely lacked patience.

With Blue at her side, she hurried to her bedroom, slid open her nightstand drawer, and took out her mother's gun, a Smith & Wesson Airweight. She opened the chamber. Loaded. She couldn't remember a time when this gun hadn't been loaded.

One of her earliest memories came from her preschool days. She'd been looking through her mother's nightstand drawer for paper to color on and found the gun.

* * *

"Don't touch, Gracie, it's baaaaaad," her mother had warned.

"If it's bad, Momma, why do you have it?"

"For when the bad people come." Her mother's face, pale and creamy as a proper southern woman's face should be, turned a sickly shade of gray.

* * *

Her mother always believed people were following her, tip-toeing through the house, and taking her things. She'd point out a fruit bowl with a pear missing or an empty hook in the garage where her mother had supposedly hung her gardening hat. Neither Grace nor her father noticed anything missing, but her mother insisted someone slipped in and out of the house, and she always had the gun close by. Grace's mother was terrified the bad person who took her things would hurt her family, and she needed to protect them.

In the end, a fully loaded .38 Special would not have prevented her mother's death. Her mother's own body had turned on her. Stomach cancer—the family euphemism for liver cancer caused by her mother's excessive drinking— took her life.

"A couple drinks a night relaxes her," her dad had said. "Takes off the edge."

Grace didn't understand that thinking as a child, nor did it make sense when at age thirteen she stood at her mother's grave. On the day they laid her mother to rest, Grace planned to take a hammer to every last bottle of Scotch in the house. But as she and her father pulled into the drive, she swore she'd seen the curtains in her mother's room move. Maybe it was her mother's ghost. Maybe it was a bad guy. Or maybe her mother's paranoia had rubbed off on her. Whatever the reason, when Grace ran to her mother's room, she took out the gun and slipped it into her own nightstand. Then she smashed every bottle of Scotch.

Tucking her mother's gun in her purse, she grabbed an old set of keys from a nail in the kitchen. Even though a damp mustiness still clung to her shack, she locked up tightly. As she made her way to the creek, Allegheny Blue followed, like she knew he would. This time, she didn't force him to stay home. After all, she'd promised Hatch she'd keep him at her side.

Grace and Blue reached the creek and the rickety dock where Lamar Giroux kept his fishing boat, a sixteen-foot aluminum dory with more dents than Blue had speckles. But it was water-worthy, and it had a relatively new motor.

Blue hopped in and clomped his way to the bow, his nose in the air. She yanked the motor string, and a belch of gray, gassy air sent her reeling backward. She grabbed the string and yanked again. On the sixth tug, the motor roared and she sunk onto the back bench.

Blue thumped his tail.

"So glad you approve." She tossed off the tether rope and aimed the boat down river.

Mosquitoes heading out for their pre-dusk meanderings dove at her head as she aimed the boat in and out of brackish creeks, looking for a fourteen-foot skiff with an electric motor. Lieutenant Lang was correct in pointing out they didn't have many electric motors in this neck of the woods. Fishermen and people who lived along the river needed the power of big motors, and many tourists preferred big, noisy fan boats that flew across the watery marshes.

Sweat trickled down her back, and low-hanging branches scraped at the sides of the boat, sending out banshee-like wails that made her cringe. At a bend in the river, she spotted a flash of something at the end of a long but shallow inlet. Ducking the oak branches lacing above her head, she aimed the boat along the narrow waterway. She squinted through the tangled branches. Metal, definitely a curving piece of silver. Her hand tightened around the throttle, and she inched forward. A branch scraped at her shoulder, another at her hair. This was a private place, a good place to hide something.

A tremor that had nothing to do with the vibrating motor raced through her hand.

She pushed aside an oak branch and frowned at the metal bobbing in the water. Not a boat, but an old oil drum. She plunked onto the bench and raised her face to the sky.

Her blood froze.

Above her two slitted eyes bore into hers. Curled in a slice of sunlight cutting through the branches was a water moccasin. Six inches above her nose.

A scream lodged in her throat. Blue growled. The snake blinked then uncoiled and headed up the tree branch.

She settled a hand on her racing heart.

Breathe in, two, three. Breathe out, two, three.

She settled her other hand on the throttle and backed far, far away from the snake.

Once out of the inlet and once she caught her breath, she checked her watch. Hatch should be heading back to her house soon. On the way to her shack, she took a shortcut through a tiny creek cutting through Brittlebush Island. As she came out the back side, Blue jabbed his nose in the air. She darted a glance to the leafy trees, searching for water moccasins but seeing none. They passed an inlet with cypress knobs poking out of the water like tiny brown headstones.

The dog's ears perked, and his nose quivered.

"You smell something, Blue?"

She spotted no boats, no structures, and thankfully, no snakes, but as she poked the nose of the boat around a bend in the inlet, she spotted a small houseboat.

Blue heaved himself to his feet.

"Don't even think about chasing garbage-picking bears." She cranked the throttle and backed away from the floating house. Blue lunged onto the houseboat deck. "Get back here!"

The dog scrambled across the deck and pawed at the door until it swung open. Grace growled and grabbed a pole on the deck, steadying the little dory. "Blue!"

He feigned deafness. And dumbness. No. The latter wasn't fake.

She tied off the boat. Taking out her mother's gun, she climbed onto the deck and craned her neck to see in the door. Streaks of light slipped through the dirty windows, illuminating a broken rocking chair, a three-legged table, and Blue, who was nosing around a corner piled with wooden crates partially-covered with a tarp. "Come. Now!"

He continued to sniff.

Stepping gingerly on the rotting floorboards, she crossed the tiny hut and reached for his collar. The dog stopped sniffing and stiffened. The scruff of hair on the back of his neck bristled like a saw blade. The boat dipped and swayed as if weighted at the far end. Steps sounded on the deck. Grace ducked behind a stack of crates, her mother's gun still held tightly in her hand.

A shadow crossed the doorway. Blue howled and lunged.

* * *

Alex pulled the blanket over the two pillows he'd centered lengthwise on his bed. It didn't look like a sleeping body. It looked like two stupid pillows, but his Granny was watching that TV show about the old fart private detectives. She wouldn't know he was gone, which was good, because if she did she'd probably call that asshole Hatch again.

He climbed out the window and inched along the side of the house. A pain shot along his back and his shoulder. Doing community service hours at the cemetery was killing him, and it pissed him off that Hatch arranged the whole thing, like that loser was the boss of him. When he reached the twins' bedroom window, he ducked. Ricky and Raymond regularly snuck out their bedroom window at night to go chase fireflies, and he didn't need the little brats tagging along. He forced his aching body to move faster, and he finally reached the mini-mart where he spotted Gabe and Linc leaning on a blue convertible and drinking Cokes.

After Alex had given their names to the cops for the shrimp shack robbery, he'd thought his friends would dis him, but Gabe had called tonight wanting to hang out.

"Hey, great wheels," Alex said. "Where'd you get them?"

"Granddaddy over in Panama City," Gabe said. "He's on vacation for a few weeks. Didn't think he'd mind if I borrowed it."

Linc snickered.

"No one knows you took it?" Alex asked.

"Of course not, dumb shit," Linc said. "Gabe doesn't have a license."

They piled into the convertible and cruised through the downtown area, all ten blocks of it. Alex couldn't wait to get out of this place. Maybe he'd get a hot set of wheels like this or better yet, a sweet boat, something like Hatch's.

On the second loop, Gabe slowed the car in front of a haircut place—not a barbershop, but one of them old lady shops like his granny went to. The big sign read CLIP &

CURL. Gabe stopped the car at the corner and took a right, making a quick turn into the alley. "The old lady who runs this place doesn't go to the bank on Saturday because she has a bowling league. Should be a couple hundred in the till. Tonight we're going to hit it."

Alex jammed a hand under his thigh, wincing as a blister snagged against the rough fabric of the seat. The last time they'd "hit" something, he'd been the one who landed in jail. Alex untucked his hand and stared at the ooze running along his palm.

"You want in?" Gabe asked, waving a Coke at the back seat.

Linc, sitting in the front seat and sucking on a Coke of his own, smirked. *Wuss*, his look screamed.

Gabe and Linc had bailed on him, but only at first. When that asshole Hatch made him come clean with the sheriff's office, his buddies hadn't abandoned him. He wiped his hand on his shorts and took the Coke. "I'm in."

"Good." Gabe continued down the alley. "Here's the plan..."

* * *

Grace ducked deeper into the corner as a figure, backlit by the setting sun, slipped into the doorway of the small houseboat.

"Whoa there, big guy, what are you doing here?" Hatch bent and rubbed Blue's floppy ears.

Grace forced her heart back into her chest and stepped out of the shadows. "He's with me."

"No." Hatch pressed his fingers into his eyes. "No, tell me I'm not seeing this."

"Hatch—"

"Tell me you did not come out here on your own after I told you expressly to stay put."

"I had a gun and Blue."

"Of course. Who the hell needs anything else if you have a hound dog at your side? Dammit, Grace, there's a killer out there. Do you hear me?" He grabbed her wrists. "Do you!"

Fascination rooted her in place. A vein at Hatch's temple bulged. His knuckles grew white. He was usually so easy-going, rolling with the punches. "Yes, Hatch, I'm fully aware of what we're dealing with."

"Then why are you putting yourself in danger? You shouldn't be out here alone."

"I'm not in danger."

He released her wrists and stepped back as if affronted. "I thought you were a smart woman."

"It's true, Hatch," she insisted with a steely calm. "Lia's killer isn't going to hurt me. He's having too much fun toying with me. Think about it. I'm not a victim, not a pawn. I'm a player. The *only* other player in the game. He's not going to kill me, at least not at this point in the game."

Hatch stared out the window.

"Get your team's profiler on the line, and if Hayden says I'm in danger, that the killer's after me, I'll lock myself in my shack. I swear I will; just tell me I'm wrong."

Hatch's look said it all. He knew she was right. "You're safe," he said. "That's the important thing. Now let's get out of here."

He cupped her elbow and walked her toward the door where she grabbed the doorframe. "Wait a minute," she said. "Why are you here? How did you find me?"

"Lou Poole," Hatch said. "She said the bees at the hives in this area told her something was going on up here. I drove over here to see what was bothering the bees."

Grace knew from years spent in the courtroom that people communicated without saying a word, so why not bees? "Did you find anything?"

"Some tire tracks off the road. Big cross-hatch pattern. They led me here. I was poking around when I heard him growl." Hatch pointed to Blue, who'd clawed the tarp to the ground and now was curled in a ball and snoring.

Grace opened her mouth, but words wouldn't trickle out. Behind Blue was a crude wooden box, with jagged cuts and uneven seams, a perfect match for the one that had held Lia Grant.

She grabbed Hatch's arm. "We found the killer's hiding place." Grace's excitement was short-lived. "But there's only one coffin."

Next to her, Hatch crouched and pointed to a wide scrape gouging the wooden floor. He brushed away a whorl of dust. "But it had some recent company."

They followed the drag marks to the door and outside. Here the gouge marks dug deeper, tearing bits of splintered board.

"Something was definitely dragged *away* from the storage area," Grace noted.

The marks ended at the far side of the houseboat. "And most likely loaded onto a watercraft here."

"The next move in the game has started," Grace said, a tremor rattling her voice.

CHAPTER SIXTEEN

Alex grabbed the edge of the garbage Dumpster behind the Clip & Curl, his fingers sliding over a clump of fuzzy hair and slimy gel.

"This shit is gross," he said to Gabe and Linc, who stood next to him in the dark alley. "Why am I the one who has to climb up there?" He pointed to a small window above the Dumpster.

"Because you're the best lock picker," Gabe said with a huff of exasperation.

"And because you screwed up the last job," Linc added.

Linc was right. Alex had panicked during the shrimp shack break-in. He'd picked the lock in record time, but inside he'd knocked over a table with bottles of hot sauce and a million packages of crackers, which woke the manager who lived next door. He'd let down his guys, and he made things worse when he ratted them out. This was his chance to prove he wasn't a rat. Alex pulled himself to the window.

"Can you see the cash register?" Gabe asked.

Alex rubbed the dirt from the window with the hem of his shirt—he didn't want to leave any fingerprints—and squinted. "Nah. Too dark. I can't even see the window lock."

"Here," Gabe said.

A beam of light swept across the window until Alex raised his hand. "There! Keep it there."

"Shut up!" Linc said with a hiss.

Alex took a small culling iron, screwdriver, and a paperclip from his back pocket and worked the lock. He'd first learned to pick locks three years ago because the twins thought it was funny to lock themselves in the bathroom. Within two minutes, the lock popped open. Alex shoved. A screech tore through the air.

"Hell, Alex, are you trying to wake the fucking dead?" Linc asked.

"It's not like I carry WD-40 in my pocket," Alex said on a huff.

"Well, move your ass so I can squeeze through the window," Linc said.

"Would you two shut the fuck up?" Gabe warned. "Let's get moving, just like we planned."

The plan was for Alex to pick the lock and Linc, the smallest, to crawl through the window and open the door so all three of them could hit the cash register. Gabe, on a recon trip when his mom got her hair cut last weekend, had already determined the Clip & Curl didn't have a security system and the owner who drove a brand-new Lexus wouldn't miss a few hundred bucks.

Alex could use the money, maybe for a new pair of shoes when school started. Maybe he'd even take the twins to the movies and get his granny some of those chocolate-covered cherries she liked so much. He pushed on the window again. It squealed, moving another six inches, and then lodged.

Alex tapped at the bottom with the culling iron. The pane moved an inch. He tapped harder.

"Why don't you get out a jackhammer?" Linc said in a pissed-off whisper.

"I'm doing my best."

"Well, do it quieter. And faster," Gabe said. "Linc should be inside by now."

Alex rested both hands on the bottom of the window and tugged. The window shot up and shattered. Glass rained down on him and the Dumpster. He reeled back, his foot slipping on the slick goo. He lost his balance and crashed to the ground. Linc and Gabe bolted down the alley. Two buildings down, a door opened.

A woman in a dirty apron poked her head out the door and asked, "What the hell's going on back here?"

* * *

"Johnson, you and Marquez take Arrowhead Creek," Lieutenant Lang said. "And Dominguez, I want you and Hubert to circle Brittlebush Island."

Moonlight sliced the water as more deputies cut a path down the river in search of a fourteen-foot aluminum skiff hauling one six-foot-by-two-foot wooden coffin. That made eighteen boats on the water, thirty-six searchers hunting for a killer who might be on the move.

The lieutenant stopped in front of Grace. "Got your phone?"

"On and fully charged." Because the second coffin was most likely in play. And this time Grace was going to pick up on the first ring.

With the lieutenant leading the charge, Grace went in search of Hatch. She found him pacing along and glaring at a set of tire tracks marked off by a set of flags.

"You're good, Hatch, but not that good," Grace said. "You'll never get those tire tracks to talk."

He ran his hands through both sides of his hair, his forearms ropy with tension. "Can't blame a guy for trying." And Hatch was trying. He'd been moving like a giant golden cat all evening, crawling on his hands and knees in the houseboat and trekking through the forest, desperately searching for bits and pieces a killer might have left behind. She still wasn't used to this tense and intense version of Theodore Hatcher. Tonight she appreciated the sweat at his neck, the mud on his shoes, and the intensity in his eyes as he sought to keep a second victim from being buried alive.

"So far this is the only impression evidence," he added. "No handy footprints to match those at Lia Grant's grave, no fingerprints. I'd give anything to see what these tire tracks saw."

And it looked like he'd spend the night trying, but he'd be doing it alone. She held out her hand. "I need your SUV keys. One of the searchers borrowed my boat." She needed to get her car fixed for good. She didn't like relying on Hatch for rides. "I'm going home for the night."

For the first time since they'd found the coffin, the dogged sharpness left Hatch's face. He tugged at his ear. "What? I must have misunderstood you. Surely you didn't say you're ready to knock off for the night?"

"I'm not." Grace frowned at Blue, who'd spent the past three hours limping at her side, nosing around vehicles and crime scene equipment from the sheriff's department. "But he is. He broke open his foot again, and he won't rest with all these people around. Too much to see and smell."

Hatch scrubbed the dog's head. "I'm telling you, old man, she likes you."

"Hardly. I just don't want him bleeding all over a crime scene."

Hatch took out his keys but didn't hand them to her. "Okay, let's sail."

"You're coming with us?"

"Yep."

"There's work to be done here. You yourself said the goal is to catch the killer before he abducts the second victim."

"True, but I specialize in talking, and since the tire tracks aren't saying much tonight, I'll best serve the investigation by sticking at your side. Chances are you're going to get another call, and that's a conversation I plan on being in on."

Grace's phone sat heavy and silent in her purse. She'd probably checked it a hundred times tonight, waiting and dreading that call. But Hatch was right; she wanted him at her side if another terrified victim reached out to her from the grave.

On the way to her shack, Hatch stopped at the marina for a clean set of clothes as once again he planned to spend the night on her settee.

"I'll wait in the SUV," Grace said. "I don't want Blue to do any more walking than necessary."

"No, Grace. You and ol' Blue, if he so chooses, will come with me to the boat."

"You're being silly."

"And you're being stubborn."

She aimed a finger at the watch on her wrist. "It'll take you how long to get a fresh set of clothes? Five minutes?"

"Probably."

"I'll be fine."

"Yes, Grace, you are a fine, fine woman." He held open the door and winked.

She crossed her arms over her chest, the seat belt biting into her arm. This wasn't about five minutes. It was about the past forty-eight hours. Two days ago Hatch had slipped into her life

like the sun slid into the day, warm and effortless, just as nature intended. At times being with Hatch was infuriating. His
teasing and taunting and silly nicknames drove her nuts, but
increasingly, she was finding comfort in his presence. It would
be so easy to fall into his arms. Her fingers clawed around the
seat belt. But ten years ago she had learned in the end there
was nothing effortless about falling apart. She needed time and
space away from this man.

Blue hobbled from the back seat, clomped across her lap,
and loped to the ground, plopping his butt next to Hatch.

"See? Even your dog agrees," Hatch said.

But she had to look beyond her own needs. She needed
Hatch at her side for when the next call came through. "I dis-
like you both." She snapped off her seat belt and slid out the
door. "And he's *not* my dog."

Hatch grinned, cupped his hand under her elbow, and escorted her across the parking lot, Blue at their heels. The
boards creaked and groaned as they walked along the dock,
Hatch's deck shoes shuffling alongside the tap of her sandals. A sliver of moon sliced the night sky, but she could
see Hatch's face, the lines somewhat softened. Hatch needed
the salty sea air moving through his hair like most people
needed oxygen.

In front of her, Hatch stopped so abruptly she ran into
him. "What..." she started to ask but stopped when he squatted to the ground, pulled a pen out of his pocket, and clicked
it. A sharp beam of light swept across the dock, highlighting
a series of shiny dots. She bent next to him as his finger slid
over one of the dots, and he brought it to his nose.

"Blood?" Grace asked.

Hatch nodded and pointed the penlight along an uneven
trail of red. "From the direction of the splatter marks, I'd say
something heading toward the boats."

They followed the trail, the drops getting bigger and closer together until they ended at the slip holding *No Regrets*. Hatch reached behind him and pulled his gun from the back of his waistband.

The door leading to the galley was open, and light spilled out. Leading with his service revolver, he slipped onto the boat, motioning her to get behind him. They crouched next to the door and Grace grabbed the dog's collar and pulled him to her side.

"Theodore Hatcher, FBI," he said. "ID yourself." His voice and gun were rock steady.

Silent light continued to pour from the door. Hatch waited, looking like he had all the time in the world. At last a shadow split the pale light.

"Ah, shit," Hatch said as he jammed his gun in the holster at the back of his waist.

* * *

"What the hell happened to your arm?" Hatch asked with a roar echoing in his head.

Alex's upper lip curled. "Ain't none of your business."

"You're bleeding all over my teakwood deck, and that sure as hell makes it my business."

"I needed to get some stupid towels." Alex held up his left arm, which was wrapped in a wad of paper towels. "But now that I got 'em, I'll get off your damned *teakwood deck*." The boy took a step toward the door but swayed. Hatch grabbed his arm. Clammy skin. Trembling flesh. He pointed to the bench seat at the galley table. "Sit. I want to take a look at that arm."

"Well, you ain't gonna." Alex lifted his hand, smacking Hatch's arm.

Hatch froze at the sound of skin against skin.

Sit down, boy! And you'll stay there until I say you can drag your sorry ass off.

I don't need to take any more of this shit.

Shit? You think I'm giving you shit. Hot breath and the stink of sweat and automotive grease swelled and gagged him. *Well, boy, let me give you some real shit.*

Smack. Smack. Smack!

Hatch slid a finger under his nose, half expecting to feel warm blood.

"You're bleeding, Alex," Grace said, "and not a small amount. Let me take a look at it."

"I don't think so. I'm outta here." On unsteady feet, Alex walked to the door.

Grace centered her body in the doorway, her arms over her chest. "Sit down, Alex, and take off those paper towels. I need to see your arm."

The boy didn't move. Grace put one manicured fingertip on the boy's shoulder and pushed him onto the bench seat. A few times over the past two days, most recently during their standoff in the SUV just moments ago, an unexpected vulnerability had softened Grace. But she was in charge and invincible. Hatch dropped his hand to his side. Thank God one of them was.

Grace, her eyebrows raised, bent over Alex's arm and carefully unwrapped the paper towels. "He needs stitches."

Alex snatched his arm away. "You got a fucking medical degree on your wall?"

Hatch grabbed the kid by the collar and dragged him from the bench. His other hand knotted in a fist at his side. "You mouthy little punk."

A soft gasp sounded behind him, followed by fingers brushing his arm. Hatch stared at that hand, Grace's hand, calm and steady. Then he stared in horror at the fisted curl of his hand. His gut churned. Hatch took a step back, but only one.

"Apologize to the lady," Hatch said. Alex may not respect himself or even Hatch, but he sure as hell wasn't going to talk to Grace that way.

Alex dropped his gaze to his sneakers. "Sorry."

Grace nodded and tapped her toe until Alex finally took a seat on the bench. "I don't have a medical degree, Alex. I have a BA in political science and a Juris Doctorate from Harvard. However, throughout high school and college I worked summers as a tennis camp instructor and am Red Cross certified in both CPR and first aid. I have bandaged more than a hundred skinned knees and split lips, but nothing like this. This is the type of stuff people with medical degrees need to stitch up." She turned from the boy. "Hatch, please bring the SUV to the end of the dock, and we'll get him to the emergency room."

Alex sunk into the cushions. "No. No hospital." His teeth dug into his lower lip as he looked at Grace. "Please."

Hatch slipped his hands behind his neck, intertwining his fingers and staring at the ceiling, hoping someone far wiser than him had scrawled a note or two there on how the hell to parent this kid.

What had the kid been up to tonight? Hatch pressed his fingertips into the base of his neck. Something bad enough that Alex would rather bleed to death than go to the ER. Hatch unlatched his fingers. That wasn't going to happen, because that was the one thing in this messy situation he could handle.

Hatch reached into a cupboard in the galley and took out a large first-aid kit. He poured a dollop of antiseptic on his hands and opened the suture kit.

"What the hell are you doing?" Alex asked, his eyes growing wide.

"Playing doctor."

"Not on me."

"Would you prefer to go to the emergency room?"

Alex gave his head a frantic shake. Yeah, because then the kid would have to answer a lot of questions. Hatch grabbed Alex's hand, and he didn't feel one damn bit guilty when the boy winced.

Alex swallowed. "You, uh, know what you're doing?"

Hatch lifted his pant leg, displaying a neat, inch-long scar on the side of his knee. "When you live by yourself on a boat in the middle of nowhere and spend a good deal of your time with knives, hooks, and boat engines, you learn a thing or two about first-aid." He knelt in front of the trembling boy and added in a softer tone, "Like Grace, I have a few certifications in stuff like this, but if you prefer, I can take you to the emergency room."

Alex gnawed on his lower lip. "Just do it."

Hatch picked up the needle, and Alex gripped the seat cushion with his free hand.

Grace sat on the other side of the table. "See the old dog in the corner? His name's Allegheny Blue. He's famous."

"Famous?" Alex jerked as the needle bit into his skin.

"He was the hound who nosed his way all the way from Tallahassee to Cypress Bend a few months ago. But even before that, he was in the news. Five or six years ago he tracked and treed the black bear in Eastpoint that had mauled two hunters and left one without an eye. Even aired on the national news."

Alex studied the dog snoring in the corner. "That's cool."

"Apparently many people thought so. His former owner had hunters in the tri-state area offering stud fees as high as a thousand dollars, and someone even offered $10,000 for him."

"Wow. You gonna sell?"

"No, he's too old now. He just sits around and eats and sleeps. And drools."

Alex scrunched his forehead. "Ten thou? That's a nice chunk of change. I'd like to get my hands on that kind of money."

"What would you do with it?" Grace asked.

Alex pressed his lips together, which Hatch noted were no longer quivering. "I'd buy a boat, 'course nothing as fancy as this." He waved his good arm around the cabin. "Something small, but big enough to take out on the open water. I'd take it through the gulf, maybe all the way to Mexico and..."

By the time Hatch tied off the final stitch, a smiling Alex was telling Grace about his plans to go gator hunting with his buddies Gabe and Linc.

"Okay." Hatch tossed the needle in a trashcan and gathered the rest of the supplies. "We're done." If he'd pulled something like this, his father would have beaten the shit out of him. "Now it's time to talk."

"I don't think so." Alex jumped up and wobbled past him. He reached for Alex but slipped his fist in his pocket.

"If you don't talk to Hatch," Grace said, "you'll need to talk to someone at the sheriff's station."

Grace, as usual, delivered. One more reason for wanting to throw his arms around her and land a kiss squarely on those lips he'd been fantasizing about this morning when she woke him up on that damn little sofa. She got his son, and she was clearly getting the boy's attention.

The blood drained from Alex's face. The kid tried so hard to be tough, but tonight he looked so damned young and scared. Hatch ran a hand along his face. Maybe that was what the kid needed, to have the shit scared out of him so he'd turn his life around. With an encouraging nod from Grace, Alex reluctantly told them about trying to break into the Clip & Curl and breaking only the window.

"So what do you need to do now?" Grace asked.

Alex shrugged. "Don't know. Don't care." Boom. The attitude was back.

"Dammit, Alex," Hatch started, but Grace's fingers dug into his thigh.

"Alex, you better care or you and your dad are headed to the sheriff's station first thing in the morning."

Alex toed the floorboard. "I guess I should contact the hairdresser lady and offer to pay for the window."

"That sounds quite appropriate. Hatch, what do you think?"

Hatch had no idea what the hell he was doing, but he was grateful Grace seemed to have a game plan. "Sure."

"Excellent," Grace said. "Tomorrow you two will contact the owner of the Clip & Curl and talk about making restitution."

They drove Alex to his house, and as the boy got out of the car, he looked like a kid walking to the principal's office. He and Grace followed. The minute Alex walked through the front door Trina Milanos hollered, which woke the twins, who thought midnight was a great time to play.

"Pillow fight!" Raymond cried as he grabbed a pillow from the sofa.

"Prepare to be conquered, wench!" Ricky grabbed another pillow and threw it at Grace's head.

Grace ducked. "I don't think so." With her customary agility and grace, she grabbed a pillow of her own. "Prepare to go back to bed!" She chased them out of the room amidst peals of little-boy laughter.

Hatch rubbed at his forehead, wishing he could join in the sweet laughter. Alex shot him a final glare and stomped to his room where he fell onto his bed fully clothed. Hatch talked to the grandmother while Grace corralled the twins and got them in bed.

As they walked to the SUV, Grace picked feathers out of her hair. "Alex needs rules and consistency."

"And you know this because?"

"Because what he has isn't working." Grace placed her hand on the SUV's door handle but didn't pull. "Hatch, the boy needs a man in his life. Even I, with my limited knowledge of small people, can see that. He needs someone besides a tired grandmother with health issues to help him navigate the waters of his teenage years."

"And you think he can get that from me?"

"Can he?"

"No."

"Why not?"

He began pacing in front of the SUV. "Did I ever tell you about my old man?" That was a rhetorical question because he never talked to anyone about his dad, other than to say he died when Hatch was in high school. "All Pops ever wanted was to race cars. At age twelve he started pumping gas at the local station just so he could be around them. No big career plans, no dreams of going to college. He just wanted to drive fast cars, but at age sixteen, his world and dreams came to a screeching halt. He became a father. Hard to grow a racing career when you have a wife and kid and a minimum-wage job pumping gas. Pops spent most of his life frustrated and mad at the world, but mostly, Grace, he was mad at me, and he wasn't shy about letting me know. I was the reason he worked sixty hours a week behind the counter of a tiny auto parts store where he died before age forty."

"You're not your father."

"Exactly, and I have no plans to step into his shoes. I'm not going to die an angry, bitter man with a laundry list of regrets."

"But you're nothing like him. You don't have a temper. You love your job. You're happy with your life. And you can be a good father to that boy."

He stopped pacing and reached for the passenger car door.

She slipped between him and the door. "You need to trust you can do some good for Alex."

He tried to nudge her aside.

She wouldn't budge. "That boy needs you."

"Dammit, Grace!" He grabbed her arms and yanked her away from the door. "Drop it!"

Blue growled.

Hatch stared in horror at his fingers, digging into the creamy flesh of her arms, fueled by too much anger, too much heat, and too much past. Grace must have felt it, for she stood with her mouth open and eyes wide, an unnatural sight from a woman with a marble resolve.

"Oh hell, I'm sorry." He jammed a hand through his hair. "You see why I'm not meant to be a father? I've got too much of my old man in me. Alex will be much better off without me. Hop in the car, and I'll take you home."

Grace remained stone still. Under the soft glow of the moon, she looked like a marble statue. At last she moved, just her mouth, and just a fraction. "No, Hatch. You're taking me sailing."

His fingers slid down the ropy tendons of his neck. "Not tonight, Grace. Did you forget we're waiting on a call from someone buried alive?"

Grace shook her head and held up her cell phone. "I have bars throughout the bay."

CHAPTER SEVENTEEN

Grace loosed the tether and hopped from the slip to the deck, her sandaled feet barely making a sound. So graceful and beautiful, and, as usual, so right.

Hatch needed to sail, to feel the wind on his face and the salty sea spray against his skin. He gunned the motor, and like a well-trained horse, *No Regrets* slid out of the gate straight and hard, away from the town where his son had once again attempted a B&E with his two best *friends*. Alex frustrated him, angered him, but more than anything else, the kid confused him. He was trying to help get his son straightened out, but he didn't have a ruler or even a straight edge.

Grace pulled on the rope, unfurling the mainsail.

But he had Grace, and that counted for a whole hell of a lot. Despite him losing his temper over Alex, she was still at his side.

Although it was past midnight, the bay was far from quiet. Trawlers with their bright lights and big booms headed out to rake for shrimp, frogs bellowed, and owls tore the black sky with razor-sharp screeches. With his eye on his depth gauge and a flashing thought that he was so out of his depth with Alex, he slipped through the night, the wind in his face and the bay beneath his feet.

Sometime later, when the moon had shifted in a night dance to the ballad of the bay, he realized the heaviness tugging at his shoulders and the fog clouding his vision were gone, thanks to Grace. She knew him, and she knew he needed to sail.

He rolled his head from side to side then took a seat on the bench next to her and stretched out his legs. Grace sat with her chin on her knees and her cell phone on the seat next to her thigh. The sail had clearly not been a catharsis for her. She looked thoughtful but far from peaceful. Maybe she was thinking about the minefield that was his son. Maybe she was thinking about a game-playing killer. Or maybe, after he'd manhandled her in front of Alex's house, she was once again thinking about ways to get his sorry ass out of her life. Knowing Grace, she was pondering a little bit of everything and creating a plan to fix the world, because unlike him, she didn't know how to unwind.

He reached into his pocket and took out a set of small silver rings. One by one he dropped the circles on his palm, the metal clinking softly and her cool green gaze following. He took the final ring, tapped it onto the top ring, and the rings linked. He spun the next ring on his palm, and it, too, joined the chain. He slid the rings in and out and up and down, eventually adding all the rings. As the chain grew, the lines along her forehead softened.

Some nights, especially a night like tonight, called for a little magic.

When the last ring clinked onto his palm, she smiled.

"The rings were always my favorite." She took one and slid her finger along the curve. "A perfect circle of seemingly unbroken steel. Simple but solid and strong."

"But under the right hands"—he swirled his hands in the air—"capable of such incredible feats."

Grace threw back her head, a soft laugh falling from her mouth. "Your good humor's back. We should call it a night."

Hatch slipped the rings in his pocket and dipped his chin toward Blue, who was snoring in the galley doorway. "He looks too peaceful to be disturbed."

* * *

"Come on, Hatch." She nudged his shoulder with hers. "We both have a lot going on. You have to get up early and meet with Alex and the hair salon owner, and I need to..." Grace couldn't say the words, but they were in her head. *Wait around for a call from someone in box number two.*

He gazed at her with half-lidded eyes. "Do you remember the first time you were on this boat?"

"Hatch—"

"Do you?"

She pulled in a deep breath and counted to three before releasing. She'd dragged Hatch out on the ocean to clear his mind of his troubles with Alex. Mission accomplished, but now he'd turned the tables with his clinking rings and this little walk down memory lane.

"Well?" Hatch asked.

"I won't insult either one of us by saying *no*," Grace said. To say it was a memorable night was the understatement of the decade. That entire summer, the summer when Hatch sailed into her world, had knocked her senseless. Literally.

"You couldn't resist me," he said.

Grace laughed. "Technically, I couldn't resist the chance to kick Victoria Jensen's ass."

"Victoria Jensen?"

"The lead swim instructor at camp. Black and red razorback swimsuit. Nicely filled out."

A puzzled look twisted Hatch's face. "I don't remember a Victoria or the swimsuit."

"You made quite the impression on her. That first week of camp she talked about you every night. She told us about the book of poetry you carried in your knapsack, Longfellow, and about sailing around the barrier islands and skinny dipping at midnight. With a lascivious grin she assured us you didn't have a single tan line anywhere on your body. She was smitten, and if it weren't for Victoria and the other dozen girls who were half in love with you that summer, I don't think I would have bothered with the contest."

"Contest?"

"You never knew?"

"I wasn't one for gossip around the water cooler, remember?"

He might not gossip, but he'd been the subject of most of the gossip that summer ten long years ago. "That first week of camp the female staffers decided to have a contest to see who could snag you. The first one to get you to commit to a summer exclusive got the room with its own bathtub."

"The prize was a *bathtub*?"

"A *private* bathtub. One with claw feet and its own water heater."

"This is so not good for my ego."

She popped him on the arm, her fingers lingering over the swell of his bicep. "But I didn't go after you for the bathtub. In the beginning I pursued you because I didn't want to lose to Victoria."

"And you won."

"Yes and no," Grace said.

His brows lifted in a curious tilt.

"I won the contest but lost my heart." He opened his mouth, but she waved off his words. "And more importantly, I lost my way." A decade's distance didn't take the edge off the raw truth. "I'd created this grand plan for my life, clearly defining what I wanted to accomplish and where I wanted to go, and I was well on my way." Her hand fell into her lap. "Until that first night on this boat. Until you."

"That's not a bad thing, Princess." He inched closer, his thigh pressing against hers, his deck shoe sliding along her sandal. He rested his hand on her knee. "It's okay to ramble and roam, to be without purpose or a plan."

"For you, Hatch." The Hatch she knew ten years ago had lived without a compass, without a care, and he still did to some degree. He'd come to town to get Alex straightened out with the law, and he'd certainly thrown himself into the hunt for Lia and her killer. But his time in Cypress Bend was just another layover on Hatch's never-ending journey.

"That's the fundamental difference between you and me," Grace continued. "It's not okay, not for me. You're content to sail under sunny skies wherever the winds may take you. I need something more, something solid and lasting."

His brow furrowed, more contemplative than contentious.

She slid his hand from her knee, her skin growing oddly cold in the steamy night. "You never understood my need to sink my feet into the earth and put down roots. You expected me to give up everything—my job, my family, my dreams— and sail with you into the sunset."

"Whoa there, Princess. I never asked you to give up your life. If I recall, I was the one who changed course. Without a second thought, I docked ship so you could work at the prosecutor's office, so you could be close to your daddy, so we could live out *your* dreams." He pointed a sharp finger at the water. "I dropped anchor."

"You were there in body, Hatch, but not in spirit, at least not fully," Grace said gently. "Every time we visited Daddy, you looked like a man walking to the gallows."

"Your daddy hated me. The first time I visited him, he threw a punch at me and called me a loser."

"Because he didn't know you or understand the depth of my feelings for you, but if you would have given him time, he would have come around. He wanted me to be happy, and there's no doubt in my mind I could have been happy—deliriously happy—with you. But this isn't just about Daddy. You hated my job. You hated that I had to work nights and weekends and that we couldn't take off for a week when the weather was good. And you resented being dragged to social functions with my workmates or community fundraisers I supported."

"I never complained, and if you recall, I managed to be quite charming and entertaining."

"Exactly, Hatch. You *managed*. You didn't want to be there in a banquet room crowded with people in suits and ties. You were counting the days, the hours, the minutes until you could set sail for another adventure. You were doing time."

He slid his fingers along the captain's wheel. "I gave you what I could, Princess. I'm not going to apologize for who I am."

"I know. I passionately believe with one hundred percent of my entire being that you gave me everything you could."

His knuckles whitened. "And it wasn't enough."

"Oh, it was. It was very much enough for me."

"Says the woman who demanded a divorce." The words were sharp and brittle.

She slipped her hand over his and didn't move until he looked her in the eye. "Says the woman who was deeply and madly in love with you." The pulse at his wrist spiked under her fingertips. Somewhere nearby a fish jumped, sending a soft, chiming tinkle of water through the air. Inland, a bird squawked. But the loudest sound was the pounding of her heart. "I could live on a boat. I could work long days during the week so we could have weekends together. And I accepted the idea of not having kids because you were so against it." She released his hand. "But the problem wasn't me."

"I gave you more than I'd ever given anyone. Hell, I put my heart on a silver platter and handed it to you." He thumped the sides of his hands on his chest, an eerily hollow sound echoing through the now quiet night.

"Yes, you did. I never doubted your love." She saw it now. Hot and passionate, sweet and golden. She'd also seen his pain. She still did. She smoothed a lock of hair from his forehead. "What I doubted was your ability to survive. You hated being tied down. You hated this town, and in time, you would have hated me." He shook his head, but she placed a hand on either side of his face and forced his gaze on hers. "You could never give up that restless part of your soul, and it was killing you, Hatch. God, I hated sitting on the sidelines and watching your head and heart do battle. With the passing of every day, every week you were getting bloodier and bloodier."

"I was coping."

"You were dying!" A shudder wracked her body as she pictured him as summer slid into fall. "You stopped humming sea songs, and you stopped doing silly magic tricks." Her shoulders dipped in a bone-weary shrug at the weight of the memory. "And watching you was killing me." She tried to clear her throat but the jagged lump wouldn't budge. "So I sent you away."

It had been the hardest thing she'd ever done. She may as well have reached into her chest and pulled out her own heart, leaving a gaping, bleeding hole. After Hatch left, he'd called—ten times.

And not once had she picked up the phone.

Why didn't you pick up the phone, Grace, why?

On the eleventh call, she threw her cell phone in the sea and holed up in a motel room, where she tore the landline from the wall to keep from calling him. Nor did she contact her father or her boss. For five days it was just her and a searing pain that left her a molten puddle on the floor, like an addict going cold turkey. On day five, the motel manager knocked on her door with a message from her boss: *You're fired*.

Those two words had been the wake-up call she'd needed.

With Hatch out of her life, she needed something to fill the hours, the days, the years ahead. She scraped herself off that stained motel floor carpet and poured what was left of her into getting her life back on track. She fought like she'd never fought before, and when Travis gave her her job back, she vowed never to let anyone bring her that low again.

Hatch inched closer, his knee pressing into her thigh. "Princess, do you—"

She pressed her fingers against his lips. She didn't want to hear his words. Oh, Lord, she didn't want to hear, because she knew Hatch. She knew his heart, and she knew what he was about to ask.

"Do you still love me?" His words pressed softly against the quivering flesh of her fingers.

She knew there was only one way to answer. "Yes." She

loved Hatch—everyone she'd dated, everyone she'd slept with left her wanting more. No, not wanting more. Wanting Hatch. "I love you, Hatch, and I will always love you." She kept her words matter of fact because facts and evidence were so much easier to deal with than the chaotic emotion swirling through her body. "But I can't *have* you. No one can. You're too much of a free spirit. In a few months, the box will close in on you again, and regardless of me or Alex, you'll take off."

His fingers slid through hers, and the long-buried desire burst from a cold, dark place deep in her chest. His eyes, so blue and earnest, bore into hers. "And after I take off, I'll come back. I have to, I *want* to, because of Alex. As long as you'll take me, I'll always come back."

She'd hoped he'd tell her she was wrong, that he didn't need the wind and sea. Hatch had changed so much. He wore a watch and carried a gun. He was trying to be a good father to Alex. But he still couldn't wrap his head around her need for something solid and constant, a house on a hill and roots to dig into that soil. "And I'm supposed to be happy with that?"

"Why not? You're married to your job, and I'm shacked up with the sea. Neither one of us has found happiness with anyone else. I'm not going to lie to you. I'm not the kind of man who'll be happy with nine-to-five and two-point-five kids. But I can be happy with you. I love you more than any human being on this earth, and I'm giving you part of me."

"Part is not what I want, not what I *need*."

"But it could be." With their fingers clasped, he drew her closer. "Tell me you don't need this." He lowered his face and brushed his lips against her temple, her cheek, her jaw, a tiny trickle of kisses but with the power of a tidal wave, drowning her and taking away her breath. "And tell me you don't need this." His lips trailed along her neck and shoulder, and the fingers of his free hand glided down her back and pulled. And like the tug of the moon on the tide, she moved closer. "Tell me, Grace. Tell me, and I'll stop."

Hot desire rippled her flesh, heating her blood and sending swirls of steam fogging her brain and blurring the line between want and need. His lips slid along hers. Sweet, so sweet. A wave of golden warmth, like a jar of honey sitting under a July sun.

She slipped her fingers through the sides of his silken hair, pulling his lips from hers. "You're right. I want this, even *need* this." Because what she felt for Hatch was a gut-deep need. "But I deserve *more* than this."

Hatch's fingers stilled along her ribcage. "Do you need me to tell you again and again that I love you?"

Her heart hammered against his hands. "I deserve more than words, Hatch. I deserve a man who can commit."

"I'm committing to now."

She ripped his hands from her skin. "But what about next week or next month?"

"We'll deal with them next week and next month."

"And there's the crux." She brought her knees to her chest and wrapped her arms about her legs, holding them tightly against her chest so her heart, her aching, bleeding heart, wouldn't jump out of her body and into his hands. "I don't want just next week and next month. You of all people know me. I want the win and the grand prize that comes with it. If I give you my love this time, Hatch, I want forever. I *deserve* forever."

Hatch frowned at his empty hands, as if genuinely unable to comprehend why they no longer slid across her skin, wreaking havoc and bringing up emotions she long ago buried. Seeing his confusion and hurt wasn't any easier the second time around.

"My phone battery is getting low," she said. "We need to get back."

They could work a case together, but they could never work.

Hatch remained silent. Because there were no more words. He stood at the wheel in shadows, and she couldn't read his face. Did he regret coming back? Admitting he loved her and always would? The marker lights of the marina drew close, and she took her position at the sails, the wind snapping the canvas and stinging her eyes. Hatch didn't believe in regrets, and that would be a healthy attitude to adopt. Her relationship with Hatch had been intense and incredible but in the end, impossible. Even though she loved him and always would, they had no future. Her fingers curled around a rope. The decade-old realization still rocked the deck beneath her feet.

When they reached the dock, Hatch turned off the motor, and *No Regrets* slid silently into the slip. She tied off while Hatch secured the boat for the night, his deck shoes padding over the deck. Without a word, he ducked below to gather his things. She sat on one of the bench seats and ran her toe along Blue's belly. The dog cracked one eye, shifted so she could reach more of his belly, and fell asleep, oblivious to her pitching world.

A soft, chiming ring broke the quiet. She dug her phone from her pocket as Hatch popped his head out of the doorway. "Alex?" he asked.

The ID on the screen showed *Restricted Number*. She sucked in a fast breath.

Hatch flew to her side.

"Hello," Grace said.

"H...h...lo? Wh...who...who is this?"

Grace's skin grew stone cold. "My name is Grace Courtemanche."

"H...help...m...me, Grace." A scream ripped from the phone and tore at the night sky.

CHAPTER EIGHTEEN

I'm here." Grace clutched the phone as if it were a lifeline. "Do you hear me? I'm here!"

Another high-pitched scream pierced Grace's ear. She held the phone closer, tighter. "Tell me where you are. Tell me, and I will get you out of there."

Sob after sob poured out of the phone.

"It's going to be okay, but you first need to calm down."

Hatch dropped to her side and handed her his phone. "Call Lieutenant Lang. Have her come down to the marina. I don't want to move and risk a dropped call." One by one he pried her fingers from her phone and said to the caller, "Hey there. My name's Hatch, and we're going to get you out of there."

Grace stared at her empty hand, now ice cold. She curled her chilled fingers into her palm and brought her hand to her chest, where her heart was beating in a heated frenzy. She wanted to be on the line with that girl, to do something, anything, to help. Next to her Hatch continued to talk, his voice steady, his words soothing. He was doing what he did best.

She gave her hand a shake, getting the blood flowing again. They had a game plan in place. The minute the phone activated, the phone company would triangulate the call to determine the location, Lieutenant Lang would mobilize searchers, and Hatch would talk. This time she had her team in place. This time there would be no strike.

Grace hopped onto the dock, and with steady fingers dialed the lieutenant, who answered on the third ring, her greeting fuzzy with sleep.

"Second victim," Grace said. "Hatch and I are at the Cypress Bend Marina, middle dock. Hatch is on the phone with her."

The lieutenant swore with sudden clarity and volume. "Location?"

Behind Grace screams still poured from the phone. "Hatch is working on it."

"On my way."

Grace joined Hatch, who'd put the girl on speaker phone. The screams had faded to choky sobs. "Good, that's good, sweetheart," he was saying. "What's your name?"

"J...j...janis," she said with a raspy cough. "Janis J...J...Jaffee."

Grace snatched her purse and dug out a pen. Where the hell was a piece of paper? If Hatch was going to do the talking, the least she could do was take notes. She found a takeout menu and jotted the girl's name in the margin.

"You're doing great, Janis," Hatch said. "Can you tell me where you are?"

"N...n...no. Can't see. Too dark. Can't see." A sob tumbled from the phone.

"Are you in some kind of box?" Hatch asked.

"Y...y...yes." A jarring pounding sounded as if Janis were banging the phone against the lid of a wooden coffin.

Grace pictured Lia's hands, black with bruises, the fingertips shredded. "Get me out. Get me out now!"

"We're doing just that, darlin'."

"C...can't breathe. I...I'm gonna die."

"You can breathe, Janis. The box isn't air tight. Lift your hands. Find one of the joints. Find the air. Then breathe. Just breathe."

Grace pulled in a long draw of air, her own breathing steadying and evening out along with the woman on the phone.

"Good girl," Hatch said. "Now I need you to pretend your phone is my hand. Can you do that?"

"Y...yes."

"Good, now wrap your fingers around the phone. Are you doing that?"

"Yes."

"I'm at your side, Janis, holding your hand. When you get scared, you give my hand a squeeze. Okay?"

"Okay."

"Do you know where you are?" Hatch asked, his free hand fisted and white-knuckled on his thigh.

"No."

"How did you get in the box?"

"Running on beach. Carrabelle Beach. By my house. Always run. Years and years of running. But..." She choked out another sob.

"And you're going to run again. What happened while you were on the beach?"

"Hit me from behind, knocked me out. Next thing I know I'm in the bottom of a boat."

"Did you see your attacker?"

"No. But I heard her voice."

"Her?" Hatch and Grace said in unison.

"Your attacker was a woman?" For the first time since taking the phone call, Hatch's voice was anything but calm.

"I . . . I think . . . so. I remember her hands. Small and soft."

"What did she say?"

"Crazy. Something crazy." Another sob. "Something like . . . like . . . level two. Must have been the hit to my head. Doesn't make sense."

But it made perfect sense. "Lia Grant was Level One," Grace said under her breath, and Hatch nodded.

"Are you on or near Carrabelle Beach?" Hatch asked.

"No. Swamp. I think I'm in the swamp."

Grace jotted the name of the beach and texted the abduction location to the lieutenant.

"What makes you think you're in the swamp?" Hatch asked.

"I woke up in the boat. Smelled swamp water, not seawater."

"Did you see anything? Landmarks? Buildings?"

"Blindfold. Hands and feet tied." Another sob.

"Do you know how long you were out?"

"No idea. God help me. Someone help me!"

"Squeeze my hand, Janis." When the girl's scream faded to a whimper, Hatch asked, "How about sounds? Do you hear any sounds now? Running water or animal sounds or cars?"

"Quiet. So quiet. Alone. All alone." A scream tried to tear from Janis, but it came out as a strangled gasp.

"You're not alone, Janis. I'm holding your hand."

"Yes. Okay. I remember."

"When you were on the boat, did you hear anything? Anything like a train or cars or people?"

"No . . . nothing like that. But I heard dogs once. Lots of dogs."

This county was full of hunters, much like Lamar Giroux. Grace grabbed Hatch's arm and pulled the phone to her chin. "Did you hear any rattling, like metal jostling, when you heard the dogs?"

Long breath. "Yes, clanking. I heard barking and clanking and metal against metal."

Grace's fingers dug into Hatch's arm. "I know of a few hunters who keep their dogs on floating pens."

"Anything on Cypress Point?"

"No, further west toward Apalach." She searched her memory, visualizing the pens. The hunters built floating docks and piled on large crates in game-rich areas. In less than a minute, she jotted down the names of four creeks, all further from her home. But that made sense. Level Two would be more challenging.

"Any other sounds?" Hatch continued. "How about smells? Do you remember anything else?"

"No. Nothing." Janis coughed then sputtered. "Can't talk. Getting harder to talk."

"Okay, Janis. You just keep hold of that phone and keep squeezing my hand, and I'll do the talking. You're a strong woman, a smart woman, and pretty soon we'll have you out of there. You know, my great aunt Piper Jane is smart and strong like you. Five months ago she took off on her sixth trip around the world. Sixty-two years old and..."

A siren wailed, and Grace ran up the dock. A sheriff's SUV with flashing lights pulled into the parking lot followed by four other vehicles. Lieutenant Lang ran toward her. "The phone guys are on it," the lieutenant said. "GPS wasn't activated, so they're tracking down the cell sites and sectors. Anything specific from the girl?"

"She's in the swamp, possibly near Apalachicola and near a group of dogs." Grace drew a map on the takeout menu, showing the four areas she knew housed dogs as she brought them up to speed. "I'm going to start here near Nettle Creek."

The lieutenant took the paper, and together they hurried to Hatch's boat, where a small group had gathered. Hatch climbed off the boat, his hands empty but for the keys to the SUV.

Her heart lodged in her throat. "Did we lose Janis?"

He shook his head and stepped to the side, revealing a tall, lean man in black pants and a black knit shirt. He stood in the shadowy stern, Grace's phone to his ear. He was as dark as Hatch was light, with trimmed midnight black hair and intense charcoal eyes. "Jonny Mac's here."

The raven man dipped his head in a slight bow. This was Hatch's teammate, the Apostle who specialized in finding lost souls.

* * *

Lamar Giroux's fishing boat wasn't fast or big, and it smelled like Allegheny Blue, but it did a hell of a job winding through twisting sloughs and creeks. Hatch had spoken to Jonny Mac minutes ago. Janis was no longer talking, but his teammate could still make out low, shallow breaths. Hatch ran the spotlight along the shore of Nettle Creek and peered through the dense shrubbery for any sign of a young woman buried alive. Downriver a pack of dogs barked.

"Shine the light to the right near the lilies," Grace said as she squinted through the blackness, softened only by a sliver of moon. "Something's been there."

The spotlight cut across the lilies and landed on a flattened patch of broken reeds. His pulse spiking, he grabbed a low-hanging cypress branch and pulled them closer.

Damn. Too narrow for a boat, even a fourteen footer. "Another gator slide," he said. Another dead end.

Grace maneuvered the boat out of the tiny creek, gliding to a set of yellow-slitted eyes poking out of the water. Hatch stared down the gator until it blinked and spun away. He'd take on every gator in Florida if it meant getting to Janis Jaffee in time. Although time was key, Grace continued to boat slowly down the river as he searched the banks, looking for any signs of human disturbance. Hatch ground his back teeth. Make that any signs of a disturbed human. They were dealing with a twisted and dangerous mind.

Once on the Apalachicola River, Hatch's phone vibrated with a text from Lieutenant Lang. "Cell phone company just identified two towers picking up signals," he told Grace. "Cross section of the towers is some place called Bremen's Bayou. Name ring a bell?"

"Northwest of here," Grace called out over the gun of the motor.

"Big area?" Hatch asked.

"Couple hundred acres."

Even with the roar of the outboard, he heard the excitement in her voice. "What?"

"One of Lamar's old hunting buddies keeps his dogs on a floating pen in that area. Janis heard the dogs right before she was dragged from the boat. We find the dogs, we'll find the girl."

Within fifteen minutes, Grace had them racing down the Apalachicola River and onto Bremen's Bayou, a slow-moving waterway surrounded by cypress and oak dripping with Spanish moss. His light glided over cypress roots reaching up from the water like fingerless hands. The trees hung low over the water, and branches scratched the side of the boat. And some of the branches—

"Broken!" Grace said on a fast breath. "The wood's still damp at the break. Someone's had a boat back in here recently."

She inched the boat through the tangle of branches. His light landed on a flattened bush and a pair of crushed white trumpet-like flowers. He fanned the light higher. "Drag marks. Too wide for a gator."

Grace jammed the boat into the bank. He launched himself over the side, his feet sinking into swampy earth. Swatting brush, he chased the drag marks into the knot of blue-black shrubs and trees. Vines reached for his hands and legs. A ropy length of moss wrapped around his neck, and he yanked. Something snarled. Something else hissed. And still he ran.

The brush gave way to marsh. Mud sucked at his feet. His shins. His knees.

On the other side of the bog, he spotted the earthen mound.

He tore up the rise. Something sharp sliced into his right foot. Shoe. He'd lost a shoe.

At the mound, he fell to his knees and clawed the earth. "Janis!" he called. "It's Hatch. I'm here."

No banging. No choking gasp.

He scraped harder, faster, sandy soil flying. His finger scraped against something flat and cold. He tugged, and a rock came free. With the flat rock he shoveled earth.

Something crashed through the marshy grass and fell next to him. Another set of hands.

"Spotted three boats coming this way." Grace jammed her hands in the dirt and shoveled.

His rock hit wood. Someone let loose a cry. Grace? Him? Janis?

More sandy soil flew through the air. He unearthed one corner. Another. With two feet of wood exposed, he banged the rock at the joint along the top. The wood split. He grabbed the broken lengths of wood and yanked, every muscle in his body straining. Nails screeched, the wood splintered, and half of the top board broke off, exposing a pale, dark-haired young woman.

In the weak glow of the moon, the young woman was stone still. Not even her chest moved. Grace jammed her fingers against her neck. "No pulse, but she's still warm."

Hatch reached under the woman's shoulders and heaved her from the grave. He dropped to his knees beside the girl, settled his mouth on hers, and breathed.

* * *

Allegheny Blue hobbled down the porch steps and rested his head on Grace's thigh, a line of drool sliding onto her mud-caked sandal. She scrubbed the old dog's head and matched her breathing to his, slow and steady.

Breathing. An act so mundane and engrained that most people weren't aware of doing it until they couldn't.

Janis Jaffee, a twenty-three-year-old jogger from Carrabelle, was breathing, but not on her own. She was surrounded by a team of doctors and machines at the Cypress Bend Medical Center helping her fight for her life. Relief mingled with joy and exhaustion as Grace walked up the porch steps.

Hatch locked the SUV, but instead of climbing the steps he walked to the side of her shack, his movements slow and labored, as if weighed down by the mud caking his body. He toed off one shoe and peeled off his shirt. He slipped the gun from the holster at his back and set it on the porch along with his long shorts. Standing only in a pair of boxers, Hatch reached for the hose bib.

"You can shower inside," Grace said. "A little bit of mud won't hurt this place."

Hatch cranked the spigot, and a frothy arc burst from the hose. Hatch stared, as if mesmerized by the rushing water. Was he thinking of the inky waters they'd traveled in their hunt for a girl buried alive? The sweat running down his face as he pulled the girl from her grave? Or other waters that would take him away from the horror of the night? He lifted the hose over his head and closed his eyes, sighing as a river of mud sluiced down his chest and legs to the pebbly ground. Or maybe he was just a tired, dirty guy who wanted to clean up after a long day's work.

At one time she'd accused Hatch of being a lazy, sun-loving drifter. Never again. Tonight she'd seen a man so intense, so consumed with his work, that at one point she was sure that all that existed in his world was one young woman. And now he needed to scrub his mind and body of the ordeal. She didn't blame him. He'd been in deep.

She slipped out of her muddy flats, went inside for a bar of soap and towel, and joined him on the side of the house. She reached for the hose. His eyes flew open, but he didn't object. Time to help Hatch wash away the mud and horror.

She handed him the soap and ran the water along his back.

In the halo of the porch light, Hatch lathered up, scrubbing his head and torso so hard his golden skin turned pink. She ran the arc of water along the hills and valleys of his body. And still he scrubbed.

At last she took the soap from his hand. "It's gone, Hatch. All gone." Dirt and sand had sunk back into the earth. His chest rose and fell in a long, soundless sigh, and a tremor rocked his body.

"Now go inside and warm up under the shower," she said.

"Your turn." Hatch reached for the hose, but she held it out of his reach.

"I can do it."

Hatch laughed. "Yep, Grace, we've already determined you're capable of single-handedly taking over the world." He unclenched the hose from her hand and took the soap. "But I've had a hell of a night. Humor a guy, okay?"

She slipped out of her linen shell and trousers and tossed them on the porch.

Hatch lifted the hose, and cool water poured over her shoulders and neck. The dried mud and sweat pinching her skin softened and disappeared. The steady stream massaged the stiffness between her shoulder blades and soothed the scratches on her arms and legs. Hatch slid the soap along her arms and back, chasing away the stench of the swamp clogging her nose and thickening in her throat. When there was nothing left, she raised her face to the sky and breathed deeply.

Hatch turned off the water and she opened her eyes. He stood before her, his breath as slow and steady as her own. A few hours ago he'd sent her heart thundering and breath racing on a boat called *No Regrets*. And she'd ended it. This time she wanted forever, a concept well off his navigational charts.

His arm loped around her shoulder. "Come on, Grace. You're beat, I'm beat, and ol' Blue looks pretty beat, too." The dog had lumped their clothes into a single pile on the porch and curled on top in a ball.

Inside the house, she filled Blue's water bowl and food dish, including his customary slice of crumbled bacon. When she set the bowl on the floor, he nosed it and looked up at her. "You are not getting another slice of bacon."

He yawned and rested his head on her foot. The old dog

was exhausted. So was she. The roller coaster that had taken her from terror to bone-deep fear to guarded relief had left her physically spent. She wanted nothing more than to sink into a warm, clean bed and wake up to sunshine and news that Janis was breathing on her own.

In the bedroom she found Hatch sprawled across her bed, his face smashed into a pillow and not a stitch of clothing on. Still no tan lines, she noticed with a tired smile.

She toweled her hair, slipped out of her wet bra and panties, and pulled a worn pair of boxers and a T-shirt from her dresser.

"I'm not sleeping on the settee tonight," he told the pillow.

She sunk on the bed. "I know."

"And I'm not going to ravish your exquisite body."

She stretched out next to him, close but not touching. "I know that, too."

A few miles away Janis Jaffee lay in a hospital bed, air moving in and out of her lungs. Thanks to Hatch. Thanks to her. She just needed to be next to him, close enough to hear him breathe.

CHAPTER NINETEEN

Portsmouth, Ohio

The handwritten sign in the front window of Florie's Café read: *Pie today! Chocolate Silk, Banana Coconut Cream, Triple Berry.* On this sunny Sunday morning, Tucker hoped someone at the diner would also serve him the names of two dead bodies found in Collier's Holler.

Tucker had called the diner owner yesterday, who confirmed that last Monday the diner had served plenty of huckleberry pie and white chocolate mousse pie with pomegranates. Finding the restaurant where his victims had eaten their last meal was a long shot, and finding a waitress who remembered them and their order was an even longer shot, but it was his only shot.

"Let me get Linda for you," the owner said when he introduced himself. "She works the morning and lunch shifts on Mondays. She's a real people person, never forgets a face."

Unfortunately, the bodies found in Collier's Holler had *no* faces. Grandpa and Grandma's killer had purposefully destroyed their faces and fingertips because he didn't want them identified. Logic told him once he discovered the victims' names, the killer wouldn't be far behind.

"What can I do to help?" Linda asked when he told her about his investigation.

"We're looking for an older couple in their sixties. He's five foot ten, and she's five two." Tucker went on to describe their weight, hair, and clothes.

"That describes half my customers." The waitress tapped her pen against her cheek. "You don't have a picture, do you?"

"Not that you'd want to see, I'm afraid."

"We're right off the main highway," the waitress continued. "And we get so many people through here, families on vacation, truckers, salesmen. It's possible they came through here, and if they did, I waited on them."

"He ordered a half-pound bacon cheddar burger and sweet potato fries. She had Caesar salad with chicken, bread stick. Both had pie." He didn't bother checking his notes. Given the dearth of information and evidence, he'd memorized what little he had. "She had the white chocolate mousse with pomegranates, and he had the huckleberry—"

Linda's finger shot through the air in an excited jab. "—with a triple scoop of vanilla."

He held his breath. Come on, universe, give him a *yes*, even one measly *maybe*.

"Sure, I remember them now. First-time customers. He had quite the sweet tooth and the belly to prove it. His wife tried to talk him out of the ice cream, and he patted his stomach, saying there'd just be more of him to love. Cutest little couple. They had these little matching fanny packs. Does it sound like the people you're looking for?"

"Yes." Yes. *Yes.* Finally. "Do you remember their names, maybe from a credit card or personal check?"

She tapped faster. "I think they paid with cash. Yes, I'm sure they did because as he was paying, he ordered a chocolate cream pie to go, and she put up a bit of a fuss about it. Worried about his cholesterol."

"Anything memorable about them? Accents? Jewelry? Sports teams on T-shirts?" Questions of a man desperate enough to turn to pie to jumpstart this investigation.

"Nothing stands out."

Windows ran across the front of the diner, overlooking the angled parking spaces. "Did you by any chance notice what kind of car they drove?"

"No."

"Did they mention why they were in town or where they were going?"

"I'm pretty sure they were just passing through. I think they were on vacation."

"Did they say where they were headed?"

"South, I think. He said it had been a cold winter and he was looking forward to sunshine."

"Do you remember a city or state? Where they came from or where they were going?"

Her mouth puckered in concentration. "Honestly, they talked mostly about their grandkids. Real proud of them. She said one of the granddaughters was heading off to some dolphin camp this summer. The kid was gaga over dolphins and wanted to be a marine biologist. He talked about his grandson, the star player on his high school's baseball team. The boy got a scholarship to some community college."

"Did you get a school name, camp name, even a city?" Anything.

"No."

The two letters connected with a one-two punch.

The waitress must have noticed his distress. She chewed the tip of her pen. "I'm sorry, detective."

"Me too." He'd had high hopes for pie. Hell, pie had been his only hope. He handed her his business card and told her to call him at anytime, day or night, if she remembered anything.

Back in his cruiser, he jammed his keys in the ignition but didn't start the car. What now? Would he be forced to wait until someone reported the couple missing? Would his boss put the hammer on him for coming up with a whole hell of a lot of nothing? He turned the key. There was a grocery store on the corner, and he hoped they had a few Wild Turkeys in stock.

He was backing out of the parking space when he heard, "Wait, Detective Holt! Wait!" The waitress ran, waving at him. "I have something for you." She reached the window and handed him a flat box. "It's triple berry. You look like you could use a good pie."

Pie. He wanted a killer, and she gave him pie. His chest jiggled. His job was in the crapper, and his ex was trying to take his kids. He wanted Wild Turkey. And he got pie. Hilarious. So fucking hilarious. He laughed so hard, his hands shook too hard to take the pie. The waitress stared at him and swatted at a pair of bees who were clearly more interested than him in triple berry pie.

He finally calmed down enough to thank her and take the pie. The waitress stood rooted at his window, staring. Yeah, he was fucked up. He opened his mouth to apologize, but she held up her hand, her eyes growing wide. "A name," she said around a toothy smile. "I have a name. The Hornets!"

"Excuse me?"

She motioned to the bees buzzing around the pie. "The name of their grandson's high school baseball team. I specifically remember him saying they were called the Hornets and his grandson, the boy who received the baseball scholarship to a community college, was called the Stinger."

* * *

Grace lay on her side, her head resting on the palm of her bent arm. Mid-morning sun sifted through the muslin curtains of her bedroom and set Hatch's golden hair on fire. He was magnificent, like one of the nude bronzes from the Renaissance. And last night he'd been magnificent, too. With words and then his bare hands, he'd lifted a terrified woman from her grave.

Last night they'd won.

See that, Daddy? Another win.

And this one counted like no other. Unlike Lia Grant, they'd saved Janis Jaffee. A feather-light joy fanned out from her chest and danced its way to the tips of her toes. Not only had they saved the young woman, they'd learned from Janis Jaffee that the abductor had been a woman. Grace still couldn't get her mind wrapped around that.

Next to her, Hatch stretched his arms over his head, smacked his lips, and creaked open one eye. He blinked and groaned. "Please tell me I didn't sleep through the best night of sex of my life," he said around a yawn.

She laughed. "There was no sex."

He ran a finger along her arm, a grin sliding onto his lips. "We can change that if you like."

She gave his finger a playful smack. Hatch loved to tease and play, and after last night's triumphant search for Janis, she didn't begrudge him his good mood.

"I don't like," she said, although the thought of spending the morning in bed with Hatch would bring her to a whole new level of happy. He loved just like he lived, full out with a dash of mirth, mischief, and magic. Like she'd ever forget the magic of those hands. She cleared her throat and prayed she wasn't blushing. "And neither do you." She rolled off her side of the bed, the air cooling her heated skin. "Because this morning you need to call the owner of the Clip & Curl and set a time to meet about Alex."

Hatch sunk onto his pillow. The easygoing grin gave way to a scowl, and anything sweet and fun about the morning slid away on golden dust motes. Cramming both hands into the sides of his hair, he scrubbed, as if coaxing his brain cells to rise and shine.

It was disconcerting, seeing Hatch, who oozed with so much easy confidence it bordered on cockiness, struggle with anything, especially a person. He knew he needed to help his son, but he was at a loss at how to do it, which floored her. The answer was so easy for her to see and, in theory, easy for a man of Hatch's skill. He needed to do what he did best: talk. Last night Hatch's words had pulled a girl from death's door, and within minutes he'd managed to build a bridge strong enough and long enough for them to rescue her. This morning Hatch needed to talk with the shop owner and Alex, and they needed to come up with a plan to hold Alex accountable for his actions and to keep him from making more bad choices.

A cloudy mixture of dread and resignation darkened Hatch's summer blue eyes as he grabbed his phone from the nightstand. She settled a hand on his arm and squeezed.

Like Hatch, she didn't have the luxury of lying in bed. She had too much to do. She dressed, set a pot of coffee brewing, and opened the back door to let out Blue.

The dog poked his nose out the door, sniffed, and plunked onto the floor.

"What?" Grace ran a bare toe along his back. "No morning dig?" Every morning for the past three months the dog had plodded off the porch, sometimes digging in her yard and other times heading deeper into the woods, but always digging.

Blue lowered his huge head onto his paws.

"Are you okay?" She bent and looked at his paws. No swelling. No new split pads. His tail gave a happy thump as he drooled on her hand. She flung off the slime. "I have more important things to worry about today."

She grabbed her phone and called the Cypress Bend Medical Center. The good news: Janis was still breathing. The bad news: Janis was still not breathing on her own. Still hooked up to a respirator and surrounded by family and friends, Janis would be undergoing further tests and observation that morning.

Next, Grace called Lieutenant Lang and confirmed that a guard had been posted at Janis's door. The killer had struck out, and Grace had no idea if she'd make another move. No one knew the rules of this game.

Last night the momentum had swung in Grace's favor, but she had no plans to rest. Janis said her attacker was a woman. This morning she was heading into the office. She wanted to dig through past cases to see if she could spot a particularly despicable female who had a grudge against her and who knew her way around the waters of Franklin County. Plus she still needed to track down the person impersonating Ronnie Alderman from the cleaning crew at the phone store.

When the coffee finished brewing, she poured two cups—one black, the other with three sugars and two dollops of cream, Hatch's morning dessert, which always brought a smile to his face. When he walked into the kitchen a few minutes later, she held out the cup.

"No thanks," he said.

Blue rolled to his back, offering Hatch his belly. Hatch stepped over the dog and reached for the keys on the kitchen table. Grace almost laughed at the affronted look on Blue's face, but bit back her amusement when she noticed the tight lines around Hatch's mouth.

As he tried to leave the kitchen, she snatched the keys from his hand. "Let's play a game," Grace said.

"This isn't time for games." He reached for the keys.

She whipped them out of his reach. "If you win the game, I give you your keys."

"Grace..." He closed his eyes and pressed his lips together, holding back words he clearly didn't want to say. This was Hatch at war. In his head he was already doing battle with Alex, and he didn't want to start on another front with her. She'd seen plenty of these battles toward the end of their marriage.

"The game is called, What's the Worst Thing That Can Happen? I used to play it with my mother on the days when her paranoia was so bad she couldn't get out of bed." She placed her fingertips on Hatch's shoulders.

His muscles tightened, as if ready for mutiny, but he slumped into the kitchen chair.

"For example, when Momma was worried about the bad man in the closet, I'd say, 'Momma, what's the worst thing that could happen?' She'd answer with something like, 'The bad man could come out of the closet and hurt you.' Then we'd go another round and another round until the entire world ceased to exist because of nuclear annihilation. Sometimes I'd get her to smile, but most of the time the game just got her mind off her immediate concerns."

Hatch ran a hand down his face, worry leaching the gold from his skin. "You don't need to do this."

"I know I don't, but you're going to let me." She made a silly dinging sound, sending a reluctant smile onto Hatch's face. God, she loved that smile. "You take Alex to meet the hair salon owner. What's the worst thing that could happen?"

Hatch placed both hands behind his neck and rubbed. "The owner presses charges."

"Then what's the worst thing that could happen?"

"Alex would be locked up in juvie until he was eighteen."

"And then..."

"And then he'd fall under the influence of kids destined to be career criminals and druggies."

"And then..."

"He'd get out, rob a bank to pay for his new drug habit, and kill someone."

"And then..."

"He'd get life in prison or worse"—Hatch blanched— "the death penalty."

"And then..."

Hatch shook his head as a slow grin slid onto his mouth. "He wouldn't be able to get his degree in nuclear physics and save the world from nuclear annihilation."

"All because he broke a window at the Clip & Curl." She sat on the edge of the table and dangled the SUV keys in his face. "You win."

Hatch ignored the keys and gazed at her, an overly long lock of sunshine spilling across his forehead. "I'm being an ass."

"No, Hatch, you're being a *parent*."

He shook his head. "I'm no parent. I have no idea what the hell to do."

"Your heart will tell you." Growing up with a mother

who in later years acted more like a frightened, confused child, Grace had received an early lesson in parenting. When she found her mother cowering in the corner because she thought someone was after her, Grace instinctively knew to join her in the corner and wrap her own body around her mother's, providing warmth and protection. Within minutes the bad guys were chased from her mother's mind.

She opened up Hatch's clenched fist, dropped the keys on his palm, and closed his fingers.

Hatch pulled himself from the table. "Sure you don't want to come? You and Alex seemed to have bonded."

"I think this is one you need to handle on your own." She walked him to the door.

"You will stay put. You will not leave this house."

Hatch knew her well. She wanted to go into work and visit the site where Janis was buried, but that wasn't going to happen this morning. "That's the plan," she said with an irritated sigh. She aimed her chin at Blue, who was still sprawled in the middle of the kitchen floor. Not only had he missed his morning dig, he hadn't eaten a bite of bacon, and he hadn't taken a drink of water. "I need to keep an eye on him. Something's wrong." She opened the door. "Now stop stalling and get the Clip & Curl issue straightened out with your son."

CHAPTER TWENTY

Alex scooped the tangled pile of hair with the dustpan and dumped it in the trashcan, banging until every hair was gone. With a determined face, he headed for the next pile.

"He's not a bad kid," DeeDee told Hatch as she motioned to the hydraulic chair. DeeDee, the owner of the Clip & Curl, had agreed to let Alex clean the shop every Sunday until he earned enough money to pay for the broken window, and to his credit, Alex was taking the cleaning job seriously. Maybe because DeeDee had gray hair and a few wrinkles, much like the boy's granny. Or maybe the kid was finally beginning to realize these guys he called friends were anything but, because they'd bailed on him again. Or maybe the boy had played one of Grace's *what if* games and was picturing nuclear annihilation.

Hatch sunk into the chair. "If he's a good kid, why's he habitually doing bad things?"

DeeDee chuckled as she snapped a pink plastic cape and

settled it around his neck. "Growing pains. I know. I raised four boys."

"Four boys?" Hatch squinted into the mirror in front of him. "Where are your battle wounds?"

DeeDee ran a comb through his damp hair. "I got a few, the boys, too, but they all turned out all right. Two are doctors, one's a college professor, and the baby runs a bunch of vacation rentals over on St. George Island."

"What's your secret?"

DeeDee picked up her scissors and snipped at the back of Hatch's head. "Horses."

Hatch laughed.

"If I'm lying, I'm dying." DeeDee continued to snip his hair. "My boys raised and showed horses. They were too busy mucking stalls and combing horse tails to get in trouble." She pointed the scissors at Alex, who was now cleaning the front glass window with a wad of paper towels. "I'm guessing your boy has too much time on his hands. A bored kid is a kid who spends too much time in his head, and sometimes that place leads to trouble."

Between working at the cemetery and cleaning the Clip & Curl, Alex was going to be one busy boy over the next few months. Not much time to hang out and cause trouble with rowdy friends. But what about after this summer, long after Hatch left? Alex would go to school and do what? Hang out with other bored kids?

Hatch couldn't let that happen, not as long as he breathed the good air on this earth. He would talk to Alex's granny about sports and clubs, maybe even suggest a part-time job. He could put some feelers out and talk to Grace. She knew this town, loved this town, and she seemed to have a soft spot for Alex. He'd been surprised at how good she was with the kid until he remembered much of her childhood had been spent taking care of her mother. DeeDee continued to cut, and the heaviness weighing on Hatch's shoulders fell away. He could rely on Grace to help with Alex.

By the time Alex emptied the final garbage can and put away his cleaning bucket, DeeDee had finished Hatch's long overdue haircut. He ran a hand through his hair and squinted at himself in the mirror. "You didn't take off much."

"Cuttin' off liquid sunshine like that would make this world a much darker place," she said as she took off the cape and gave it a shake. "The woman you share a pillow with would kill me."

That would be Grace. Waking up and finding her looking into his eyes was like waking up in heaven. Most folks saw Grace as cool, maybe even a little steely, but that was just the by-product of her drive and determination, which both came back to heart. And boy had he seen Grace's heart, with Alex the past few days and during the hunt for a sadistic killer. He jammed both hands through his damp hair. And he'd seen it last night on his boat.

Grace's bold admission of love had tangled his tongue, along with her motive for divorcing him. She'd severed their marriage with a swiftness and sharpness that had left him bloody and flat on his ass, all because she'd wanted to save him from himself. As usual, she'd been right. He loved Grace—hell, still did— but couldn't live in her world. After they married, he'd taken a few charter fishing jobs to keep him at sea, but still, he was restless. However, he'd been unable to leave Grace. Leaving her would've meant leaving his heart, and that would've been suicide.

As he'd grown more bored and restless, he'd gone deeper into his head. And like father like son, that's where the trouble had started. Deep in his head, he saw his father, tied to a life he never asked for and dying before age forty behind a counter in a tiny auto parts store with a heart full of regrets. Hatch swore he'd never be that man. He swore he'd never be a parent. And he swore he'd never give his heart to another woman. Grace had hurt him too much the first time.

But the truth was he didn't have any choice about giving his heart to another woman. Grace still held his heart, and he had no idea how to get it back. And after sharing a pillow with her and waking up in heaven, he wasn't sure he wanted it back.

* * *

"One, two, heave!"

The veterinarian, Grace, and twins Ricky and Raymond lifted Allegheny Blue onto the exam table. Blue licked her elbow.

"Yaaay!" cried Ricky. "Mission accomplished!"

Raymond tugged at the hem of Grace's linen tank and looked at her through a fan of dark brown lashes. "Is Blue gonna die?"

She settled her hand on the boy's head. She hadn't planned on bringing the twins to the vet, but their grandmother, who'd given Grace and Blue a ride when Grace's car had once again refused to start, needed to stop by the sheriff's station and talk with a deputy about Alex, and the twins didn't need to be there for that. "Blue's a tough old guy," she said. But this morning he hadn't eaten, gone outside to dig, or moved from the kitchen floor. She settled her other hand on the dog's head and scrubbed his floppy ear. "Let's see what the vet has to say. Now you two have a seat."

The boys scrambled onto the bench seat across from the exam table while the vet scratched the dog's belly. "How's the old guy's pads?"

"A few days ago he broke open the front right again, and I administered the bear grease ointment."

The vet studied Blue's paws. "You're looking good, old man, and I'm glad to see you stopped those long treks along Highway 319." The vet lifted the saggy skin around the dog's mouth, checked his teeth, throat, and ears. Then he poked around the dog's belly. At last he sat on the swivel stool next to the exam table.

Grace sat between the boys on the bench, where hundreds of worried pet owners had sat before her. Not that she was his owner. "Well?" Grace asked.

The vet put away his clipboard. "He's old."

"That's it? He's *old*?" She hated not knowing what was going on, of being in the dark.

"Pretty much sums up his problems. His teeth and gums are in relatively good shape given his age. Coat, ears, and nose indicate general good health. Of course I could do imaging to check for internal issues, take some blood, and put him through additional tests." The vet dug his hand into the saggy skin around Allegheny Blue's neck and scrubbed. The dog purred. "But at this point I don't recommend an invasive course of treatment. He's content and not in pain." The vet took a small pad of paper from his coat pocket. "If you feel a need to do something, get this prescription filled and give him vitamins. In the meantime, rub his belly and scratch behind his ears. If he seems to be in distress, bring him in."

"But he's not eating."

"Make his meals more appealing. Soften his dog food with warm milk. Add a special treat, like a scrambled egg."

"Bacon," she said with a sigh. "He likes bacon."

"So give him bacon."

"I already give him a slice with every meal."

"Give him two."

"That can't be good for him."

"Grace, your dog is old."

"He's not my dog."

Blue thumped his tail.

The vet chuckled. "Blue's time is limited. In my professional opinion, I suggest you let him enjoy what time he has left. Let him have another slice of bacon."

A warm, tiny hand slipped into hers. Raymond's head dipped in a serious nod. "Or two."

CHAPTER TWENTY-ONE

Hatch hopped onto the gunwale and tied off Lamar Giroux's boat to the temporary dock set up in a tiny inlet along the northern end of Bremen's Bayou. A portside seam in the boat had buckled, letting in a tiny puddle of dark, brackish water. The water sloshed over Grace's shoes, but she didn't seem to notice.

"You're quiet," he said.

She stood. "I've been thinking."

He grabbed the dock post with one hand and offered her the other. "About?"

She took his hand and steadied herself as she stepped onto the dock. "Bacon."

The boat rocked, but Hatch didn't move. He wasn't sure what surprised him more, Grace accepting his assistance or her answer to his question. "Did you say *bacon*?"

As if sensing his profound confusion, she shrugged. "It's complicated." Straightening the pearls at her neck, she headed down the dock toward the crime scene tape.

Welcome to his world.

In the bright light of day, the swampland looked no less menacing. He and Grace picked their way along sickly brown marsh grass and through noxious-smelling mud. Tangles of vines and branches clawed at his legs as they climbed the rise to where more than a dozen men and women in uniform worked the crime scene. The team included Jonny Mac, who along with three other men was helping wrangle Janis Jaffee's wooden coffin from the earth.

"Nice of you to finally drag your ass out of bed," his teammate said as he yanked on a rope. The coffin lurched from the mud.

Hatch shoved aside a rock wedged against the wood. "You know us pretty boys. We need our beauty sleep. Even took some PTO to get a haircut this morning." He gave his head a waggy shake. "What do you think?"

Jon shifted his eyes from the coffin. "Everything go okay?"

Jon, like the rest of his team, knew about Alex and his latest transgression. "No blood."

"Glad to hear." Jon and the others yanked again. Hatch lifted, mud slurped, and the earth finally relinquished the coffin. Once they got the box settled on a tarp, Jon stepped away and smiled at Grace. "Good afternoon, Grace."

"Is it good?" Grace held her arms close to her chest, her hands rubbing her skin as if to ward off the cold. Heat rose from the earth in steamy waves, but the gaping hole in the earth was chilling.

"Still working on that," Jon said.

"What'd you all find?" Hatch asked.

"No surprises," Jon said. "Same MO as the first victim. Crudely built coffin, phone restricted to call only Grace, size eight wader prints."

"Witnesses?"

"Two alligators and a bobcat, and none of them are talking."

"What about on Carrabelle beach?" Grace asked.

"No signs of struggle in the sand or shoreline. It looks like Janis was running along the water's edge, rendered unconscious, and dragged to a boat. Tide washed away all prints."

"Level Two." Hatch rubbed at the back of his neck. "Higher level of difficulty."

"But how can someone abduct a grown woman from a public beach and boat through the bay and river with no one noticing anything?" Grace asked.

"Someone using a boat with no lights and an electric motor," Hatch said. "Given the clouds last night, she'd be all but invisible."

Grace toed a chunk of caked mud. "Exactly. We're running through the dark, not quite sure of what we're chasing."

Hatch worked best with people. He could touch people with his hands and words. Other than Lou Poole, they had no witnesses. Grace had compiled a list of people who may want to start a grudge match against her, but so far, they had no suspects. He paced from one end of the tarp to the other. Their unsub wasn't invisible, just good at maneuvering through the dark. "We need light," Hatch said.

"And since it's not coming from the outside..." Jon started.

"We turn inward." With a smile, Hatch reached for his phone.

Grace looked from one to the other, her forehead creased. "What are you two talking about?"

Hatch and his SCIU teammates at times spoke a language only they understood. At other times, they didn't need words. "I'm bringing in The Professor."

"Hayden Reed," Jon added. "He's our team's criminal profiler. He'll walk the places where our unsub's walked, get in her head and—"

"—once in her head, Hayden can tell us an uncanny amount about her processes and motivations and history," Hatch added.

"And the good news is Hayden's nearby in New Orleans to give a talk tomorrow. Looks like he'll need to make a little detour."

"Which reminds me, after you talk to Hayden, we need to head out of the swamp for a detour of our own," Grace told Hatch. "I tracked down the cleaning crew that employed the man posing as the long-dead Ronnie Alderman."

* * *

Hatch flashed his badge, and a middle-aged man pushing a vacuum across the entryway of an insurance office rushed to the door and opened it. Once again, Grace marveled at the doors so readily opened by Parker Lord's famed Apostles.

After meeting with the vet, she got hold of the owner of the property management company responsible for cleaning the phone retail store where Lia Grant's killer had purchased the phones, the same store where the security images, both inside and outside, had been conveniently wiped for the day of purchase. She then tracked down the cleaning crew who'd worked with the person posing as the long-dead Ronnie Alderman.

"Thanks for seeing us, Mr. Montoya," Grace said as she shook the burly man's hand. "About the crew member you worked with, the one called Ronnie Alderman—"

"I already told my boss, I don't remember working with a Ronnie Alderman. We get a lot of college kids in and out of here during the summer, and all the faces and names run together."

"Maybe it was that weird chick." A younger man pushing a cart with a squeaky wheel stopped near the receptionist's desk and picked up a trashcan. "You know, the one who liked to vacuum in the dark."

The older man scratched the side of his head. "That was a guy, wasn't it?"

"Nah, she was pretty small, wasn't she?"

"Okay, might have been a woman. Her name was Ronnie, huh?" He shrugged. "She wasn't with our crew but for a day or two."

"Did she get fired?" Grace asked.

"No, she just didn't show up."

"What did she look like?" Hatch asked.

The man rested his hands on the vacuum cleaner handle. "Smallish. Youngish. Hard to tell because like Caleb said, she liked to work in the dark. Kind of weird, now that I think about it, cleaning in the dark. But I didn't say anything because she did a damn good job. Must have had eyes like an owl. Caleb, here, may have a better idea than me. He worked with her."

"Dark hair." The young man dumped the trash into his cart. "I think."

"Long? Short? Straight? Curly?"

"Not sure."

"How about her face?"

"Nothing stands out. Kind of average. Kind of pale. Maybe."

"Physique?"

"Maybe skinny, but she wore baggy clothes. All black, by the way. I think. Or maybe they just looked black because she kind of lurked in the shadows."

"Any distinguishing characteristics like tattoos, scars, or jewelry?"

"Not that I remember."

More unknowns. More dark. More shovelfuls of nothing.

"Would you be willing to work with a forensic sketch artist from my team?"

"Sure, I'll talk to your sketch artist," the burly cleaning guy said. "But I'm not too sure how much it would help. Seriously, I don't remember much about this Ronnie Alderman."

"You'd be surprised what you'll remember when asked by a person trained to dig deep into your head."

"I can try, Agent Hatcher, but don't hold your breath."

On the way back to Cypress Bend, Grace drove while Hatch dialed his team's forensic artist. The phone rang thirteen times. Grace would have hung up, but Hatch leaned back in the seat and watched the countryside rush by.

"Peace and goodwill," said a woman with winded breath.

"Peace and goodwill back at you, Berk," Hatch said with a smile that reached his eyes. "Did I catch you chasing the sun again?"

"Chasing, but not catching." A chiming laugh tinkled. "I went through half a tube of cadmium yellow and six different brushes. Maybe I'll have better luck tomorrow."

"The sun will have to wait. I need you."

And like that, one of the finest forensic artists in the country was making arrangements to hop aboard a private jet and make her way to the Florida panhandle. Parker Lord's team featured the best of the best, including the man sitting next to her.

Hatch had grown up, but he'd grown in other ways. Although still restless, he'd grown more patient. Although still the laid-back charmer, he'd grown a more serious side, and she had a feeling Parker Lord had a great deal to do with that.

"You're being quiet again," Hatch said long after he hung up.

"Still thinking," she said.

"About bacon?"

"About you."

He settled his fingertips on his chest and dipped in a half bow. "I'm flattered."

"Don't be. I'm thinking about what a liar you are."

"Excuse me?"

"You said you wouldn't make a good family man, but you're a part of a family. You and Agent MacGregor are like brothers, and the minute you need something, *boom*, your teammates Hayden and Berkley are there. Sounds suspiciously like a family to me."

"You must be hearing things, Princess, because I don't do family."

She just smiled.

With a frown he rolled down the window and rested his arm on the frame, his thumb tapping a steady beat on the metal. He said nothing on the remainder of the drive to Cypress Bend, and she wondered if he was thinking about his dad. Her family hadn't been perfect—a paranoid mother and a father who spent long days and sometimes nights in the office—but she loved them and couldn't imagine growing up alone and lonely as had been the case with Hatch. No wonder he was a hell-raiser. He desperately wanted the attention of a disconnected father.

When they reached Cypress Bend, she pulled into the sheriff's station to update the lieutenant about their interviews with the cleaning crew.

On their way to the lieutenant's private office, Deputy

Fillingham waved them down. "Hey there, counselor. I was going to call you today. The forensic team working on your property wrapped up their investigation. I just received the paperwork releasing the site. Your construction crew can start digging tomorrow."

In light of more recently dug graves, Grace had forgotten about the old bones. She'd even tucked away her need to push forward with construction of her dream home, a longing that had driven her the past six months. Crazy didn't begin to describe the past few days.

"And while you're here," the deputy continued, "I'll need to get an official statement from you."

"I already talked to the lieutenant. I know nothing about the remains of the woman."

"I know, but the forensic team found more than one set of remains."

* * *

"Holy shit," Hatch said under his breath.

Grace shared Hatch's sentiment but couldn't utter a word, her throat thick and tight as she stared at the two skeletons stretched out on the steel table in the county morgue, one full size and the other so tiny it would fit in a shoe box.

"Newborn?" Hatch asked on a ragged rush of air.

The M.E. nodded. "Skull shows signs of passing through the birth canal. Live birth. Cause of death is severed spinal cord."

Hatch shook his head. "Such a violent way to die."

"After only barely living." Grace finally found her voice. She pointed to the full-size skeleton. "And this one?"

"Given the circular pelvic inlet and broad sciatic notch, definitely female. She's of European ancestry, and the clo-

sure in the cranial sutures and rib ends show she was between the age of thirty and forty."

A woman and child. As far as Grace knew, Lamar
Giroux, who'd lived on her land for more than sixty years,
had never married. He had one sister with kids, all who lived
in Tallahassee. The old hunter had seemed content to live
out his life with his dogs on twenty acres of secluded land.
"Have your people talked with Giroux yet?" Grace asked
Deputy Fillingham.

"Not yet," the deputy said. "But I'll be heading to Tallahassee when we get the Gravedigger off the streets."

"What about the woman?" Grace asked the coroner. "She
was shot, right?"

The coroner ran her finger along a jagged hole in the
skull. "Single GSW to the head. Bullet entered right temple.
No exit wound."

"Self-inflicted or homicide?" Hatch asked.

"Given the slight upward trajectory, I'm leaning toward
self-inflicted."

There was so much story in these old bones, and each
bone was a chapter. The woman could have killed her baby
then killed herself. Or perhaps someone else killed the baby,
and in her grief, she took her own life. Had the baby been
nestled against her chest at the time she killed herself? Had
the babe been buried in her arms?

"The arm," Grace said with a start. "What happened to
the infant's arm?"

"The skeleton indicates normal bone and skeletal growth.
Appears to be a recovery issue. The team in the field
widened the search area and never found the arm."

"But they found some other stuff," Hatch said, motioning
to a small tray at the head of the table. "These the artifacts?"

Artifacts, such a cold, hard word for the bits and pieces of what had once been part of a human being. On the tray was a synthetic woman's slipper, a strip of wide ribbon attached to a square of nubby fabric with pink bunnies, a silver coin, and a large silver filigree barrette.

Grace slid her finger along the barrette. "She must have had long hair." Was it blond, brown, or black? And what about her eyes and the color of her skin? If only these artifacts could talk and tell of the secrets buried here.

"What's that?" Hatch asked, pointing at a pile of red dirt.

"An anomaly," the M.E. said. "The earth at the exhumation point had a large concentration of sand. This loamy, red earth was clumped around the infant bones."

"Which means the baby was most likely buried in a different location, unearthed, and placed with the mother for communal burial," Hatch said. "Could be the reason for the missing arm."

Grace pictured the baby nestled in its mother's arms, and for the first time since she'd seen the skull poking up from her construction site, the situation felt a little less gruesome. This mother and child belonged together.

Hatch studied the artifacts while she gave a formal statement to Deputy Fillingham. No, she had no knowledge of either set of remains, nothing about the artifacts looked familiar, and Lamar Giroux had never said or done anything that led her to believe he knew anything about this lone grave on his property.

When she finished with the deputy, she turned to Hatch, who was still standing at the table over the bones. His fingers traced, but didn't touch, the curve of the woman's skull. She settled her hand on the hard curve of his shoulder. "What are you doing?"

"Listening to the bones."

Bees and bridges and talking bones. Her world was much

less drab with Hatch back in her life. She slid her hand down his back. And right. "Bones don't talk."

"Not to people like us." A fire glinted in his eyes. "When Berkley's done with the Ronnie Alderman sketch, I want her to find out what these bones have to say."

CHAPTER TWENTY-TWO

Greenup, Kentucky

The cop shows got it all wrong. Detective work wasn't about car chases or dodging bullets while tailing bad guys in souped-up sports cars. Detective work meant planting your ass in a chair, jamming a phone to your ear, and plastering your eyeballs to a computer screen.

Detective Tucker Holt squeezed eye drops into both eyes, the liquid burning, but after ten seconds his eyeballs no longer felt as if they'd met up with a few sheets of coarse grit sandpaper. He'd spent all day searching the Internet for high schools in the contiguous United States with mascots called Hornets. He found more than seventy and had spent the past three hours tracking down high school athletic directors to find out if they had any star pitchers called the Stinger. So far he'd racked up twenty-two *nos*.

His phone rang, and he grabbed it, hoping it was a call-back from one of the coaches he'd left messages with. Caller ID showed no such luck. For a moment he thought about sending Mara, his soon-to-be ex, straight to voice mail. It wouldn't be the first time a case kept him from personal calls, but this late on a Sunday evening, it was probably something about the kids.

"Hey, Daddy!" came the bubbly voice of his four-year-old, Hannah. "I'm a bumblebee, Daddy, a bumblebee."

A smile settled on his face even though he needed a damned hornet, not a bee. "That's nice, Hannah-Banana. I'll bring you a bouquet of flowers and you can make honey."

Hannah giggled. "Not a real one, silly, a dancing one. You'll come watch me dance, right?"

"Of course I'll watch you dance."

"Promise?"

"Promise."

Hannah made a slurping kiss sound, and the phone rattled, as if dropped.

After squeals and scuffles, Mara came on the line. "We'll see you Thursday at seven o'clock. Make sure you're on time because the bumblebees go first."

Bumblebees? His head was still wrapped around hornets and stingers.

"Tuck, you didn't forget Hannah's year-end dance recital, did you?"

Like last year. Mara had always complained about him being disconnected from the kids, but two days ago, he'd taken the time to record all of Jackson's and Hannah's summer activities on his phone. He called up his calendar and scrolled through the week ahead. "'Course not. Seven o'clock at the Center for the Arts."

"And this time you'll bring the flowers?"

It was a long-standing tradition at the dance studio for fathers to bring flowers to the dancers, and only slacker dads forgot. Like him last year when Hannah had dressed up as an itty-bitty sugar plum fairy. Thankfully, one of the dance teachers had plucked a pair of roses from her bouquet and tucked them in Hannah's hands before the tears started. "I'll bring the flowers." He wasn't a monster, just distracted by monsters. He was getting his shit together for his kids, Hannah the bumble bee and Jackson the fisherman. "Is Jackson still awake?"

Muted voices sounded on the other end of the line. "He doesn't want to talk," Mara said. "He's playing a computer game."

"Tell him to get off."

"Tuck, he's busy."

"And I'm busy, but I'm making time for him. You see that, don't you?" She needed to because he didn't want her convincing some judge he was a shit of a father.

Mara let loose a sigh, and Jackson finally got on the phone. "Hey."

"Hey buddy, I thought maybe you and I could go fishin' sometime this week."

"Sure."

"We'll pick up some night crawlers, the big, fat juicy ones."

"Sure."

"Everything okay?"

"Yep."

"Anything you want to talk about?"

"Nope. Now can I go? I wanna get back to my game."

Mara got back on the line, and Tucker said, "He didn't sound too enthusiastic."

"What do you expect, Tuck? You talk about fishing all the time, but it's all talk."

"Because of work."

"Exactly, Tuck, because of work. See you at the dance recital. And in case you forgot, Hannah's favorite flower is—"

"—daisies," Tucker finished for his ex. "I'm not a total fuckup."

When the phone went dead, he stared at the photo of faceless Grandpa Doe. According to the waitress, he was a guy who spent a lot of time with his grandkids. Did he take them fishing? Go to their dance recitals? Buy them daises or pie with three scoops of vanilla ice cream?

He picked up the phone and continued to look for a Hornet called the Stinger. Up next, a high school in St. Paul, Minnesota. It was late, past the decent hour for phone calls from strangers. Fuck decency.

"Coach Lancaster, please," Tuck said.

"You got him."

"This is Detective Tucker Holt with the Kentucky State Police. I'm investigating a situation here and am trying to track down an older couple who may live in your neck of the woods. You coach high school baseball, correct?"

"Yep."

"Ever hear of a player called the Stinger?"

"The Stinger? Sure. He's our boy. One of the best shortstops I've ever seen. Devan Lassen."

The palms of Tuck's hands prickled. "Do you by any chance know if he has a set of grandparents who came out and watched him play?"

"Sure does. Never missed a home game. Real nice couple."

The prickle moved down his arms and across his chest, kicking up his heart rate. "Can you describe them for me?"

"She's tiny, gray hair. Looks like a typical grandma. He's

a big guy, probably played football in his day but has a gut on him now. Likes the sweets. Is everything okay?"

Now it was Tucker's turn for the word that had haunted him for days. "No."

* * *

The Game had changed.

Someone had discovered her secret hiding place. No one was supposed to know about the floating cabin. It was her secret, and secrets, like bones, should stay buried forever. But now everyone knew about the hiding place, and she couldn't use the third wooden box. Someone had taken it away. None of this was supposed to happen. It wasn't a part of The Game.

Tiny worms skittered across her arms, and she brushed her hands along her skin, trying to push them away. They burrowed deeper, crawling toward her insides. She pushed harder, pushing away the flesh-eaters, and finally her skin smoothed. They were gone.

Good. She had work to do.

The pawn from Level Two dangled by a handful of tiny tubes and wires. Soon they would break, and soon she would be out of The Game. Then they could all move on to Level Three. Unfortunately, they couldn't go to the next level without a box. She wasn't about to go to the home improvement store in Tallahassee and purchase more lumber. That FBI agent, the one the color of the sun and sky, was smart, and so was Grace. But none were as smart as her.

She smiled. Definitely not as smart as her.

She parked her truck in the far corner of the Walmart parking lot where the light couldn't reach and grabbed a cart from the cart corral. Inside, the bright light seared her eyes.

She ducked her head, letting her hair fall across her face. Walmart had security cameras, although anyone with computer skills like hers could figure out how to break into a system and corrupt the video.

Under the glare of lights, she went on the hunt. The store had plenty of storage chests and boxes, but nothing large enough to fit an entire body and light enough that she could put it in play by herself. A sweet surge of satisfaction swelled in her chest. Grace had dozens, no hundreds, of people on her side, and she, all by her lonesome, was winning.

At last she stopped in front of a plastic tote and pushed her glasses to the bridge of her nose. About three feet by two feet. Not large enough for a jogger running along the beach or a girl walking to her late-night volunteer shift at the hospital. And certainly not big enough for the third pawn, the overweight waitress from the oyster bar who walked home alone every night after her shift ended at eleven.

Think. Think.

Simple. If The Game had changed, she needed to change pawns.

She squinted at the tote. A smaller person could fit inside, not stretched out but curled into a ball, but not too tight of a ball. The small person inside would have to be able to move around, find the phone, and dial Grace's number. That was part of The Game. She studied the lid, the snap-on kind that fit tightly. No air flow. Not good. The small person would be out of The Game in just a few minutes. Not fair. Not fair at all. Grace needed a fighting chance or it wouldn't be any fun for anyone.

She put the plastic tote in her shopping cart, making a note to punch a few holes in the top so air could reach the small person.

* * *

Hatch slipped his gun into the holster at his back and walked up the steps of Grace's back porch. Instead of going inside, he settled his elbows on the rickety railing and stared out at the black. Like the young women buried in those wooden coffins, he and the others trying to crack this case were in the dark. The splintered wood dug into his elbows.

But his team was at his back. Jon was in the middle of the hunt. Hayden, a world-renowned criminal profiler, was walking in a killer's shoes and getting into the twisted place that was this unsub's head, and Berkley was giving the killer a face. He smiled. And maybe he'd call Evie, the SCIU's bombs and weapons specialist. His fiery little teammate had a way of lighting things up. Grace had called the group he worked with his family. He'd always called them his team. They were the men and women he'd fight for and put his life on the line for. Wasn't that what one did for family? Wasn't that what he was doing for Alex? For Grace?

His head lolled forward and hung between his forearms. The steamy swamp was clouding his brain again, blurring and tumbling his truths. The first time here the fog had been so thick he couldn't see anything beyond Grace.

A wedge of light cut across the porch, and Grace's bare feet padded across the rough boards. She joined him at the railing but said nothing.

He aimed his interlaced hands at the pitch black night. "No bogeymen."

More silence. She was probably thinking again. About Janis's fight for her life, about the killer's next move, about old bones. Grace didn't know how to unwind and shut down, something that usually came as natural as breathing to him.

He sucked in a long breath of warm, soupy night air clogging his throat.

Grace raised an arm, her fingertips sliding down his back, the touch so light it may have been more about him wanting her touch than her actual touch. Shifting so she stood behind him, she ran her other hand down his back. He pulled in a breath, the air sliding through his lungs now lighter and sweeter and cooler. Her fingers brushed along his waist and slipped under his shirt, skin settling on skin.

Every muscle in his torso tightened, trapping the sweet breath in his lungs. And still her fingers traveled, gliding along his ribs, across his chest. His lower body stirred. She pressed against his back, her thighs and midsection molding to his. This time his lower body quaked, sending a tremor to his brain.

He settled his hands over hers. "Whoa there, Princess." He spun so they were shadowy face to shadowy face. "What's this all about?"

Grace's tongue darted over her lips, more nervous than naughty. "Bacon."

He blinked. "Bacon?"

She knotted her fingers in the bottom of his shirt. "Bacon, Theodore. I am bacon. You are bacon." With each line, she drew him closer. Her teeth dug into her bottom lip. "You do like bacon, don't you?"

"It's...uh...nice. I'm partial to hickory smoked. With grits. And eggs. Over easy." Easy. Yeah, it would be so damned easy to pull Grace into his arms. He jammed his hands in his pockets because letting them slip across Grace's skin would take them to a place neither one of them needed to go.

Grace's lips curved in a soft smile. She rose on her toes, her breath fanning his neck, his jaw. Her hands, her mouth, her words, everything about Grace was so soft and easy. The fog. Must be the fog. A gauzy steam blurred everything but the woman before him. Too close. She was way too close.

He unclenched his hands and settled them on her arms. "I'm not sure what this is all about, but last time we talked about this, about us, forever wasn't on the table, at least not for me, and that's still the case."

"I know." Her sweet breath danced across his skin.

"Dammit." He pushed her away, out of arm's reach. He needed space between them. An ocean would be nice. "Then why are you doing this?"

She closed the space between them in half a heartbeat but didn't touch him. "Because old dogs die and newborn babies never get a chance to live." Her lips trembled. "And because someday soon you'll sail off into the sunset." She lifted her hands in surrender. "And there isn't a damn thing I can do about it, any of it. So until then, Hatch, I'm going to make the most of every moment I have with you, and according to Allegheny Blue's vet, that means having an extra slice or two of bacon."

Hatch breathed in her soft, summery scent and her words. No demands. No promises. "Just here? Just now?" His heart threatened to leap out of his chest and close the distance between them.

"Here. Now. The future doesn't exist."

The groan ripped over his lips as he pulled her to his chest and pressed his lips against hers.

Sweet. So sweet. Like summer peaches and honeyed iced tea. His tongue dug deeper. And warm and soft. A sunsoaked sail. Baked silky sand. His hands slid down her back and around the curve of her butt.

"Uh, Hatch." Her hands slipped between them.

He pulled her closer. "Here and now." He pressed the words against her lips.

She flattened her hands on his chest and pushed. "Not here." She yanked her mouth from his. "I can't do this in front of him."

Hatch fumbled for his bearings, for words. "Him?"

She pointed to her right foot, where Allegheny Blue had rested his head.

Hatch grabbed her hand and pulled her into the shack, Blue plodding behind them. "You stay here," he told the dog, "and there's an entire pig in your future."

Blue yawned and settled onto the rag rug in the middle of the kitchen.

Grace laughed. "Look who's talking to the dog now."

With her hand in his, he nudged her down the narrow hall to the bedroom. Grace moved like an angel sent to earth. Graceful arms. Heavenly face. And legs that went on for eternity.

Once in the bedroom he clicked shut the door and slipped his hands over her hips and down her thighs. "You know I still dream about you." He trailed his fingers up her belly and through the valley of her breasts. "About this spot here."

One by one he unbuttoned the silk-covered buttons of her blouse, his lips following the trail blazed by his fingers. And Grace, being Grace, didn't back away from the fire. She dug her fingers into his hair and drew him closer.

"I dream about you standing before me wearing moon-light and pearls." Her shirt floated to the ground followed by her slacks, the whoosh of air fanning the heat firing through his body.

Ten years' worth of want and need tugged at him, but he forced himself to step back. In the moonlight streaming through the window, her skin was smooth and pearly white but far from cold. "I dream about sliding my hands through your hair, feeling your breath against my skin."

She reached for him, her fingers tracing his lips. A tremor rocked her hand and his lips. No fear. Not tonight. Anticipation rippled because they knew what lay ahead.

He dipped his head into the curve of her neck and trailed kisses along the smooth, delicious column. "And those legs, Grace, I dream about those legs wrapped around my waist."

"Hatch?" She pulled back until he looked up at her.

"Yes, Grace?"

"Can you please stop talking?" Settling her fingertips on his chest, she pushed him across the room until his knees hit the bed. "I have something else in mind."

He laughed, falling onto the bed and bringing her with him. Words turned into kisses that rained along her neck, across her breasts, and down the center of her belly. She melted into him, and he into her.

CHAPTER TWENTY-THREE

Y ou know if you get bored during the service," Hatch said against the side of her neck as he escorted her across the cemetery parking lot, "we can take off and get a BLT or something."

Given his total lack of reverence, she should have swatted him away. After all, they were going to a funeral, but she couldn't bring herself to do anything but smile. She had no regrets about throwing herself at him last night with silly talk of bacon and hated having to drag herself out of his arms this morning. Ten years ago, sex with Hatch had been explosive and fiery, and at times the fire had consumed her, leaving her body spent. But last night's lovemaking had a different fire, the steady, red-hot glow of long-banked coals. Even now, it warmed her from the inside out as she walked to Lia Grant's final resting place.

Her silk pumps slowed.

"You don't have to go." Hatch squeezed her hand. "Lia's killer is not going to be at the funeral."

Grace knew some killers attended their victims' funerals to celebrate their success and flaunt their power, but according to Hayden's profile, Lia's killer only played in the dark. "It's not about the case," Grace said. "It's about the girl." She hadn't been there for Lia Grant in life, but she would be there for her in death.

They walked along the path to the plot where Black Jack was preparing for the funeral. Hatch stopped to talk to one of the deputies on duty. Steam hung in wisps above the cemetery, like ghosts caught between heaven and the earth, and she couldn't help but think of another young woman. She slipped into a gazebo where she took out her phone, sat on a quiet, shady bench, and dialed the number she'd called twice this morning.

"No change in Janis's condition," the nurse on duty reported. "And no news yet on the new round of tests the doctor ordered."

"And the guard is still at Janis's door."

"Yes, Grace."

"And only authorized personnel and immediate family members are entering her room."

"Yes, Grace."

"Thanks, Brenda." Grace was on a first-name basis with all of the nurses manning the floor where Janis Jaffee was fighting for her life. She was attending the funeral for a girl who'd called her from the grave, and the thought of attending another left her boneless. When she finally hung up, Hatch dropped an arm over her shoulders and guided her to a large awning.

Grace had attended two funerals in her life. Her mother's had taken place on a sunny day in April the year she'd turned thirteen. She'd stood at her father's side, holding his hand while he wept unabashedly for the love of his life. Although she'd refused to cry—she'd needed to be strong for her father—Grace had felt the sting of loss, grieving the death of her mother and the death of what she later learned was a little part of her father. Her father never remarried because in his world marriage was forever, which no doubt colored her own thoughts of marriage. Given all the ill-fated dates and lackluster relationships post-Hatch, at a subconscious level Grace must have been still holding on to the love of her own life. She brought Hatch's hand to her lips and kissed his knuckles. He squeezed her fingers.

As they neared the awning, Hatch's hand tensed in hers. On the far side of the green Alex shouldered a stack of chairs from a cart and hauled them to the aisle, where he aligned them in a razor-straight row. Sweat circled the boy's neck and arms, and a black line of grease marked his cheek.

"How's he doing?" Hatch asked Black Jack, who was hauling two large urns of flowers toward the rectangular hole in the earth.

"Working hard this morning," Black Jack said.

"He's not complaining or giving you a hard time, is he?"

Black Jack set the urns on either side of the hole. "No."

Alex hauled another armful of chairs from the cart, and Hatch scrubbed his index finger across his chin. "How's his arm this morning? Is it giving him any trouble?"

"Mr. Hatcher," Black Jack dusted the dirt from his palms, "your son is fine."

Hatch took in a long, deep breath, as if trying to take in the caretaker's words. Grace knew he desperately wanted to believe Alex was fine, he'd learned his lesson, and would never make another bad choice. But when it came to his son, Hatch had some kind of mental roadblock, most likely constructed by his own father. Despite his bridge-building skills, Hatch hadn't figured out a way to get through to his son. Nor did he realize he had serious feelings about the boy, feelings even Black Jack could see. She took Hatch's hand, gave it a squeeze, and led him to a pair of chairs in the back row.

A sweaty Alex finished setting up the final row of chairs and disappeared with the cart just as mourners trickled in. With the boy out of sight, Hatch slipped his arm along the back of her chair and casually looked about. She caught him nodding at Lieutenant Lang, who stood near the fountain, and at a pair of fidgeting men who looked like they'd be more at home in cop uniforms than their ill-fitting suits. Hatch said they didn't expect the killer to show, but no one was taking chances.

The crowd swelled, and the service began. Six suited men carried a casket of shiny cherry wood with brass handles up the aisle, so different from the uneven sheets of stained plywood that had housed Lia's lifeless body last week. Behind the casket came a middle-aged couple with red-rimmed eyes. The woman clutched a worn stuffed cat to her chest, her gaze never leaving the casket, while the man acknowledged the sea of mourners with a somber resolve. When he spotted Grace, the steely strength that held him faltered. For a flash of a moment, his stoic face crumbled. He knew who she was and what she'd done, or rather hadn't done.

Why, Grace, why didn't you answer your phone?

She dug her nails into her skirt. *I'm sorry I didn't do more. I'm sorry I didn't act faster. I'm sorry I failed to save your daughter's life.*

Hatch's hand covered hers.

After worship songs and the eulogy, Hatch slid back his jacket and slipped out his phone. It was on silent, but she could see the light flashing. He scrolled through a text, and the arm over her shoulder grew rock hard.

"What?" Grace whispered.

"It's Berkley," he said against her neck. "The sketch of the woman posing as Ronnie Alderman is ready." He tucked his phone in his pocket. "I need to slip out a few minutes early. Do you want to come?"

"No, I need to see this through." Because she didn't do anything halfway—not growing up, not in her work, and not with her relationships. *If you do something, Gracie, give it your all or don't do it at all.*

Hatch slipped his lips along her ear. "Wait for me. I'll be right back."

* * *

"You okay?"

The soft voice surprised Grace, as did the young man standing before her. Alex had slicked back his hair, tucked in his shirt, and donned a tie.

"Tough day," she said. "Actually, it's been a tough week." Lia's funeral had wrapped up two hours ago, and the last of the girl's family and friends were long gone. Only Alex, a pair of sheriff's deputies, and Black Jack remained. She stood, knowing Alex needed to pack up the chairs, but he waved her back into her seat.

"I hear you on that tough week stuff." The boy sat next to her, his sneaker tracing a line in the crushed oyster shell path. "You, uh, want to talk about it? This counselor my Granny's making me see says it's supposed to help, you know, talking about stuff."

She pointed at the hole in the ground that now held Lia Grant. "A girl with a big heart and a bright future died because I didn't get to her soon enough." Her hand plopped into her lap. "Another girl who reached out to me is in the hospital, and on top of that, my dog's sick."

"You're right. That's a bad week."

"Yeah."

Alex scraped the oyster shells into a pile. "Last week I saw a grave of an entire family who died the same week from swamp fever in the 1800s. A mom, dad, and six kids."

"That's a bad week," she said.

"And I saw another headstone of a man who died when he fell in a pit of water moccasins."

"Seriously?"

"Nah." Alex looked at her out of the corner of his eye. "I made up the last one so you'd stop thinking about all that other stuff."

A tiny laugh trembled and fell over her lips. Hatch might think the kid was bound for trouble because Hatch had been full of trouble as a teen and he had no faith in his own parenting skills, but the young man had displayed a number of redeeming qualities, including this sweet, charming side. "How's the arm?" Grace asked.

"Don't tell *him*, but it's killing me."

"Maybe after you get off work, you and I can get away from this really, really bad week and go out for a boat ride. I don't have a fancy sailboat like Hatch, just a little skiff. Allegheny Blue loves to ride. He'll come with us."

Alex scraped more oyster shells into a pile. "Can't. Granny grounded me for the hair salon break-in."

"When you're ungrounded, let me know. I'll even let you drive."

Alex smoothed out the oyster shells. "That would be great. Now I gotta get back to work."

Once again Grace checked her watch. Where was Hatch? His teammate Berkley had finished the sketch, and she figured he was working to disseminate the drawing of the woman calling herself Ronnie Alderman to law enforcement and the media. But that shouldn't take more than two hours. She checked her phone. Still no call from the nurses at Janis's bedside. What now?

Doers win and winners do, Gracie.

Patience, Princess, patience.

This time she listened to Hatch, not her daddy.

* * *

An angry buzz shook the air near Lou Poole's bee boxes.

Hatch slipped through the gate and along the wooden walkway to the house on stilts where Lou sat on the front porch in an ancient rocking chair.

"She died," Lou said, her gnarled hands curling around the carved knobs of the groaning chair.

The media had been at the funeral in full force. Lia Grant's death had rocked this community. "Yes, Miz Poole, I was at the funeral earlier this morning."

"Funeral?" Lou swatted a veiny hand at her face. "And people call me batty?"

"Begging your pardon, ma'am?"

The beekeeper tilted her head toward the bee boxes. "The queen, she died. Found her this morning on the ground. Bad time to die. Bad for the hive." She rocked faster, the groan getting louder. "Bad time to die."

The beekeeper had lost an old friend, but also a business partner of sorts. A hive needed its queen. "I'm sorry." He should say something more, but he didn't have time. The funeral was long over, and he didn't want Grace alone too long. "I was hoping we could talk some more." He took the sketch from Berkley out of his pocket. "About the ghost who buried the girl."

"Dead. Like the queen, the ghost is dead."

"Yes, but I need to know if your dead ghost is the same ghost I'm looking for." He unfolded the paper and held it in front of the old woman.

"Unless they make a new queen, the hive will die."

"Miz Poole, do you recognize this woman?"

At the rustling paper, she turned to him. "Dead. She's dead." Lou picked at a tiny scab on her arm. "The queen is dead. The ghost is dead. The hive..."

He needed a way to get this woman out of her head. "The hive's not dead yet, Miz Poole. The bees are working hard. They're making a new queen. And while they are, please tell me." He squatted in front of her, taking both of the rocking chair arms in his hands and stopping the frantic movement. "Is this the ghost you saw with the girl in the boat?"

Lou Poole finally stared at the paper and nodded.

"What's her name, Miz Poole? Does the ghost have a name?"

She ran her hand along the narrow face but said nothing.

Bridge. He needed a bridge. "You knew this woman before she was a ghost, right?"

Nod.

"She had a name then. What was her name?"

Lou turned from the sketch to the bees, her gaze beseeching, as if they had the answers.

"Was she a friend? A relative? Did she have something to do with the bees?"

Lou sprung from the chair, her eyes wide and wild. "She's dead. The queen is dead!" With a sob, she hobbled into her house.

Wave after wave of frustration swarmed through Hatch's head as he drove to the cemetery. Inside Lou Poole's head was the name of a killer. He knew he'd reach it, but she wasn't giving up anything today, not with the death of the queen bee.

When he reached the highway, he called Lieutenant Lang. "Poole confirmed the sketch of the woman posing as Ronnie Alderman on the cleaning crew is the woman she saw with Lia Grant's body."

"Did she give you a name this time?"

"Nope. And I tried." Damn, did he try.

"We can nail her for obstruction of justice."

"And where will that get us?"

"A whole hell of a lot of nowhere," the lieutenant said.

CHAPTER TWENTY-FOUR

Time had stopped. Literally. Grace, still sitting on one of the chairs near Lia Grant's grave, tapped her finger on the face of her watch, but the second hand didn't budge.

She checked the clock on her phone. Hatch had been gone almost three hours, and all that time she waited.

I'll be back.

She'd heard those words before, more than a decade ago, on the night she'd been invited to an oyster roast at her boss's house. It had been her first casual get-together with the SA staff, and she'd wanted to make a good impression. She'd asked Hatch to run out and pick up a bottle of wine. He'd planted a long, passionate kiss on her lips and grinned. "I'll be back." In town he'd run into an old college friend from Savannah, and the two had knocked back a half dozen beers together.

He'd traipsed back to the boat past midnight, a smile on his face but no wine bottle in his hand.

"It was an *old* friend," Hatch explained.

"And I was trying to impress a *new* boss."

Hatch simply hadn't understood her anger and hurt. He hadn't even bothered to call. He was too busy living in the moment.

She checked her voicemail. No call from Hatch. Fine, she'd give him fifteen more minutes and if he didn't show, she'd...She picked at a nub on her raw silk skirt. Hatch had driven, so she didn't have keys or her car. Over the past few days, she'd relied more and more on Hatch. She slid her fingers along her pearls. But this was a different version of Hatch she was dealing with, the grown-up version.

Ten minutes later, Hatch sauntered down the path, his tie and jacket gone, his face lined. "Got it," he said, taking a paper from his pocket. "Berk dug deep and got us a face. I stopped off at the Poole place, and Lou confirmed this is the woman she saw with Lia Grant's body."

Grace hopped from the chair and reached for the paper that could lead them to a killer. "Did Lou give you a name?"

Hatch shook his head. "Today wasn't a good day for her or the bees." He told her about his failed bridge-building attempt. "But the lieutenant distributed the sketch to the law enforcement community and is holding a press conference to update the media. Someone somewhere knows this woman."

Grace studied the woman's sharp features. Narrow face with a long, thin nose, strong chin, and angular cheekbones. Even the lips were sharp, two thin lines of barely-there pink. Amid so many razor-sharp planes and angles, the big, wide eyes with lush lashes and irises the color of dark melted chocolate looked oddly out of place.

"Do you recognize her?" Hatch asked.

This woman had hand-picked Grace to play this game, so it would make sense that they knew each other. She ran her

finger along the thick, black eyebrows. Grace would have remembered seeing eyes like those, especially across from her
at the defense table or on the witness stand. "No. I'm sure I
never faced her in a courtroom, but there's something familiar about her. I'm wondering..."

Hatch stood quietly.

"I'm wondering if maybe she's related to one of the defendants I prosecuted. Maybe she sat in the courtroom or
gallery and watched a trial day after day. There's something
about her." Grace continued to study those sharp features.

On the way to the SUV, Hatch drew up short. "Is that
Alex?" The boy, still dressed in the tie and dress shirt, was
stacking chairs.

"Respect looks good on your son," she said.

Hatch studied the boy, a strange half smile tugging at his
lips. He picked up a chair and folded it.

Grace grabbed his elbow. "What are you doing?"

"Helping. It'll take the two of us fifteen minutes to get the
rest of these chairs put away."

Hatch claimed all that connected him to Alex Milanos
were a few matching strands of DNA, but that was a crock.
Hatch cared about this boy, which wasn't a surprise. Hatch
had a huge capacity to care. He cared about this boy's
health, his safety, and his future. She motioned to the chair
in his hands. "I think it would be best if you let Alex take
care of the chairs."

"His arm probably hurts like hell."

"It does, but his fragile ego will hurt more if anyone in-
tervenes, especially you. This is his job, his responsibility."

She tried to take the chair from him, but he wouldn't let
go. Time for a story. "When I was young, probably five or
six," Grace said, "I got a new tennis racquet for Christmas. I
was so excited, I hopped around the house swinging the rac-

quet. Daddy warned me to settle down, but I didn't. Not two minutes later, I swung so hard I knocked down the Christmas tree, a ten-footer crammed full of ornaments. I didn't get hurt, but Daddy made sure I spent the next two hours picking up the mess I'd made. And you know what?" She didn't wait for him to answer. "I never swung my racquet in the house again."

Hatch set down the chair and looped an arm over her shoulder. "As usual, you're right. You're a freak of nature, Princess. You realize that, don't you?"

"With the week I've had, I'll take that as a compliment."

"You should because it was." He pecked her on the forehead, a kiss so light she should have barely felt it, but a tingly warmth rushed from her head to her toes.

Side by side they walked away from the gravesite, passing Black Jack, who stood at the grave, a shovel on his shoulder, his face solemn. With the ceremony over, now it was time for the practical side of burial, for those who tended the dead to do their part.

A part of Grace wanted to turn away, but another part of her, a part that longed for a world of decency and respect, stood rooted in the middle of the road as the caretaker bowed his head, his lips moving. This far away, Grace couldn't tell if he sang or prayed. When he finished, he reached into his pocket and threw something small and shiny into the grave. Then he picked up his shovel and tucked dirt around Lia's casket like a parent settling a blanket around a child.

* * *

Grace wanted to dig through her work files and see if she could find a name to go with the face Berkley Rowe had sketched. Unfortunately, Hatch had other ideas.

"This will only take a few minutes." Hatch dragged her through the parking lot of the sheriff's station at a near-run.

"The lieutenant isn't here. She and most everyone else are either at the press conference or the cemetery."

"That's what I'm counting on." Hatch winked and pulled her into the reception area.

"Why, Agent Hatcher!" The front desk clerk leaned forward, offering him a rounded display of cleavage.

"Boy, did I need to see a bit of sunshine," Hatch said. "Too much gloom today." He rested his elbow on the counter and said something low enough for only the desk clerk to hear. She giggled. Reaching behind the woman's ear, he pulled out a creamy camellia blossom that matched the ones on the bushes flanking the entrance door. Grace tapped her foot while the two chatted. She wasn't jealous of the clerk. Hatch was and always would be a flirt. She just wanted to get moving, to do something.

When Hatch finally extricated himself from the clerk, he walked with Grace down a hallway to a room marked *Evidence*.

"What are we doing here?" Grace asked.

"Looking for evidence." He grabbed the knob. Locked.

"The evidence tech must be at lunch," Grace said.

"That's what the receptionist said."

"We can come back later."

Hatch dug into his pocket and pulled out a key. "Or not."

"How did you get..." She shook her head, not bothering to finish the question. Hatch would charm the keys off clerks until he was old and gray.

He unlocked the door, flipped on the light, and walked through the rows of shelves, stopping in front of a large box with the case number 11672. Inside, she recognized the artifacts from the pair of skeletons found on her property.

"What are you doing?" Grace asked.

"I told you, looking for evidence." Hatch grinned.

"And when you get it?"

"I'm going to steal it."

She pressed her lips together, not sure if she was biting back an admonition or a laugh. "You're a sworn agent of the federal government, and I'm a prosecutor bound to uphold the U.S. constitution and laws of my state while maintaining respect due to the judicial system." She rested her head against the shelving unit holding hundreds of evidence boxes. "And here I am helping you steal evidence. What's crazy is I'm not at all concerned." A manic giggle escaped her lips. "Do you hear that, Hatch? I don't care, because while you may be unconventional and at times exasperating, you're one of the good guys."

He unearthed the silver coin found with the remains of the mother and child. "That I am." He kissed the tip of her nose. "Now let's get to the cemetery. We need to talk to Black Jack."

"Why?"

"Because he knows something about the woman found on your property." He held the silver coin to the light. "Black Jack tossed a silver coin like this in Lia Grant's grave, and I'll bet the bank he slipped this one into the grave on your property."

Her pulse stuttered. "You don't think Black Jack has anything to do with all of this, do you?" Grace had known the cemetery caretaker most of her life. He'd helped bury her mother and her father, and she'd always found him a quiet, thoughtful giant of a man.

Hatch tucked the coin in his pocket. "I have no idea, but he has some explaining to do."

Twenty minutes later, they found Black Jack at the caretaker's cottage standing near a water spigot and hosing off a shovel. Hatch leaned against the SUV's hood and flipped the silver coin in the air. Two silver coins. Two dead women. Grace wondered if it could all be connected.

When Black Jack rested the shovel against the cottage, Hatch held up the coin, the mid-day sun glinting off the circle of silver. "Why the coins?"

Black Jack rinsed his hands and arms and turned off the water. "It is of no import to the likes of you."

Hatch aimed the coin at the corner of the cemetery where Lia had recently been laid to rest. "The girl you buried this morning matters to me and so does another young woman who is barely hanging on to life and a third I'm desperately trying to keep from ending up here." Hatch rolled the coin over and under his knuckles. "Today you threw a coin much like this one into Lia Grant's grave. I'm guessing ten or twenty years ago you tossed this coin into another grave on the old Giroux property."

Black Jack took the coin and cradled it in his palm. "It is one of mine."

"So ten to twenty years ago you buried a woman and her infant child on Cypress Point."

The cemetery caretaker remained as still and cool as a marble headstone while Grace held her breath. Did he know about the woman and child? And more importantly, did they have anything to do with a game-playing killer?

"We can talk here," Hatch said. "Or you can join me for a chat at the sheriff's station."

The muscles along the big man's arms tensed into ropy cords of burnt bronze. Grace had never seen the cemetery caretaker strolling through town or sitting down to lunch at one of the oyster bars or shrimp shacks. She couldn't see the giant man sitting in a folding chair behind a table in an interrogation room. He was at home here with the crypts and graves.

"Or you can fling your fishing line over your shoulder and walk out of town on bare feet, never to be seen again." Hatch held out his hand, palm-side up. "Which would be unfortunate because you have much work to do here, work no one else can do."

Black Jack uncurled his fingers and gave Hatch the coin. "Come with me."

They followed Black Jack into the stand of oaks and ivy where the spongy ground sucked at her dress shoes. In the near distance water rushed, and they finally drew up to a gray-green, sluggish river.

"Coins have long been used to pay the ferryman," Black Jack started in his soft, rumbling voice. "A coin gets some across the River Styx into Hades and others through the gates of heaven." He reached into his pocket and took out another coin. "And sometimes souls need coins to pay the porter."

The river swished and churned as Black Jack fell silent. Hatch's jaw grew hard and tense, and Grace could tell he was fighting for patience. Like her, he wanted to know the story behind the bones and if they were by some crazy stretch connected with a deadly game.

"Some souls have so much baggage here on earth," Black Jack went on, "that they need to pay someone to take it from them. Only then will their loads be light enough to move on. The young miss we buried today, her final load was heavy. I figured she may need to pay a porter."

Lia Grant had been buried alive and greatly suffered. If that didn't account for baggage, Grace didn't know what did. The sliver of fear itching at Grace's back slipped away. Black Jack was no killer. "You and the coins help lighten the load," she said.

"We try."

Black Jack had a broad, strong back, and Grace wondered at the burdens he carried, both for himself and others. "And the woman and child found on my land, the old Giroux place, you buried them, didn't you?"

Black Jack plucked a lily from a bush huddled on the riverbank, his leathery hands spinning the fragile bloom.

Hatch walked to the edge of the river. "Most people think the law is black and white. You break the law, you pay the price. The truth is, life isn't always black and white." Hatch motioned to the silty river. "There are so many shades of gray, so many stops between right and wrong, between good and bad."

Black Jack stopped twirling the flower. "Her burdens were many."

"Who was she?" Grace asked.

"Her name I do not know. Her face I'd never seen. I knew nothing of her life, but I'd held her after her death. She took her own life. Shot herself in the head."

"Yes, that's what the forensic scientist's report indicates."

"Science?" Black Jack scoffed. "Save your science for the living. There is little place in death for science."

"Was there anything about her that reminded you of the girl we buried this morning?" Hatch asked. "Any damage to her hands, as if she'd been trapped and was trying to escape?"

Black Jack shook his head.

"How about a phone? Did she have a cell phone?"

Another somber shake.

Hatch was reaching for connections. They all were, because they had so little to go on. "How did the body find its way to you?" Grace asked.

Black Jack tossed the bloom in the slow-moving water,

the lily long out of sight before he spoke again. "A dark angel brought her."

"Dark angel?"

"A dark-haired angel with skin so white it glowed. She floated down the river in a boat with the bodies draped in a white sheet."

"What kind of boat?" Hatch asked.

"I do not remember," Black Jack said. "I was more concerned with tending to the bodies."

"And the infant?" Hatch asked. "Was there anything unusual or telling about the infant?"

"The babe, it had died years before the woman, and it had been disturbed." The veins on his neck thickened in anger Grace could feel.

"In other words, someone dug it from its initial grave," Hatch said, his words rough. "Did you recognize the angel, the person who brought you the bodies?"

"No. Nor did I know her name or how she came across the woman's body or that of the babe. She left the bodies with me and asked that I give them a proper burial on the highest point in Cypress Bend. That is all I know, and now I am done talking." Black Jack turned from the water and slipped into the woods.

The SUV bounced along the rutted road as Hatch drove away from the cemetery, but the low rumble of Black Jack's words still echoed through her head. *The highest point in Cypress Bend*. She'd heard that phrase often from her father and watched his eyes light with fire as he talked about a house on the hill he'd sketched on the back of a napkin before she was born. At times the fire was so intense, it frightened her. When she was six or seven, she'd finally asked him why the land was so important.

Her father had squatted before her and took her hands,

holding so tightly her bones bit into her skin. "Unlike your momma, Gracie, I came from the dirt, from the lowest of the low where people around me told me I'd never amount to nothing, that my feet would always be stuck in the swamp. I'm not ashamed of where I started out, but I'm not going back. I clawed my way out of the muck, and I'm headed for that house on the hill. *We're* headed for that house on the hill, because that house wouldn't mean a thing without my family."

"He's telling the truth," Hatch said.

Grace snapped her head from the past and flexed her fingers, shaking off the ache. "What?"

"Black Jack," Hatch said with a hint of exasperation. He must have been talking while she'd been thinking about that sketch on the back of that napkin, the one of the two-story house with tennis courts and a tire swing. "He's telling the truth. He buried that woman's body but doesn't know who she is."

"I agree," Grace said. "I've seen thousands of people on the witness stand, and ninety-nine times out of a hundred, I can spot the liars. Black Jack's not lying."

Hatch's right leg jiggled, rattling the key chain hanging from the ignition. "What do you make of the angel bit? From my limited knowledge of angels, their preferred conveyance is not swamp boats."

Surrounded by death, Grace couldn't smile. "The angel could be metaphorical, an angel of death. Maybe the mother shot herself in the head on the boat and floated Black Jack's way, knowing he'd take care of the body. Or maybe someone put her on the boat. In some cultures, suicide is shameful, and in some religions, an egregious sin."

"Or the angel could be someone who simply looked angelic," Hatch said. "But at this point, it doesn't matter, does it?" He swung the SUV onto the highway and floored the accelerator. "This is essentially a cold case of a missing person no one's missing."

"You don't know that. Someone, somewhere is probably missing her, wondering where she disappeared to all those years ago."

"You sound like you care."

"The woman found on my construction site was someone's daughter, someone's lover, maybe even someone's best friend or sister. Somewhere she has a family, and she belongs with them. As soon as we get Lia's killer tracked down, I'm going to hound the sheriff's department to find this woman's family or do it myself."

For the first time that day, Hatch laughed. "Some things will never change, will they, Princess?"

"Nope. Now let's stop by the hospital and check on Janis. We should have heard something by now."

CHAPTER TWENTY-FIVE

The automatic doors of the Cypress Bend Medical Center swung open, letting out a belch of cold, antiseptic air. The air didn't chill Grace as much as the volunteer at the visitor's desk. She wore a large button with the words *How Can I help YOU?*

Grace pictured another button on another volunteer, one who would never smile again, never offer a kind word to visitors walking through hospital doors. Lia Grant was dead and, as of this morning, buried, and now another girl was barely hanging on to life.

"Good afternoon," the volunteer said with a shot of cheer that felt at odds with Grace's world. "Here to see a friend or a relative today?"

"Janis Jaffee," Grace said softly.

The chipper smile faded. "I'm afraid they're not allowing her any visitors. She's part of that nasty situation with the uh...Gravedigger."

"We know." Hatch took out his badge. "We're part of the nasty."

Poor you, the clerk's face seemed to say as she gave them a room number on the third floor. As they made their way through the main entrance, Hatch nudged her and pointed to a television screen in the corner. The local midday news rolled, and the screen was filled with the image of an anchorman at a news desk. Superimposed on a scrolling bar along the bottom of the screen was the type: THE GRAVEDIGGER.

"The Franklin County sheriff's office released a sketch of a person of interest in the grisly murder last week of local nursing student Lia Grant," the news anchor said as Berkley's sketch popped onto the left-hand side of the screen. "Authorities are looking for this woman, last seen in Port St. Joe two weeks ago, where she'd been working on a commercial cleaning crew.

"The woman is described as thin and about five feet tall. She has large brown eyes and dark hair, possibly long and curly. She has a tattoo on her wrist, maybe a butterfly. She may be wearing a thin gold chain with a gold key around her neck.

"Authorities said the woman, who is also wanted in conjunction with the attack and abduction of a jogger from Carrabelle, should be considered armed and dangerous. Anyone with information should contact the sheriff's office…"

They walked to the elevator, and Grace pushed the up button. "Incredible," Grace said. "Yesterday those two men on the cleaning crew struggled to remember if Ronnie Alderman had been a man or a woman. Then along comes Berkley, and she gets them to remember that the woman wore a gold necklace and had a tattoo."

"I told you Berk's good."

Grace jabbed the elevator button again. "And she's going to take a look at the bones, right?"

He pushed the elevator button, and seconds later, it dinged open. He placed a kiss in the middle of her forehead. "Berkley's listening to the bones as we speak. Now let's go see what Janis's doctors have to say."

On the third floor the nurse told them there'd been no new developments, but she reported Janis's mother had left her vigil at her daughter's bedside an hour ago to meet with doctors.

The machines surrounding Janis Jaffee, with their arms and tiny lines of blood and other life-giving liquids, wheezed and beeped and blinked. They looked more alive than the still, pale-faced girl. Grace reached out and took Janis's hand in hers. Still warm. Still alive.

"Hold on, Janis. You need to keep holding on," Grace said. "Because someday you're going to run on that white sand beach you love so much. Picture it, Janis, picture Carrabelle beach. Hear the ocean. Feel the sand between your toes. If you believe something long enough and hard enough, it's going to happen."

"Spoken like a true champion," Hatch said from where he was peering out the window.

"Spoken like my daddy. Winning starts up here." She ran her fingers along Janis's temple. She'd do anything to give some of her daddy's fighting strength to this girl. "You're going to fight this, Janis, and you're going to win."

Footsteps sounded in the hallway, and a man in a white coat walked in. "There you are, Agent Hatcher. I was hoping to talk to you or the lieutenant in person." He hoisted a thick stack of papers. "We completed our extended clinical watch on Ms. Jaffee and received a second determination from the neurologist. Unfortunately, we have the same results." He flipped through the papers while Grace gripped Janis's hand. "The long and short of it is we've had two rounds of testing and prolonged clinical observation, and there has been no brain activity since she arrived."

"Brain death?" Grace asked, the two words razor-sharp barbs digging into her throat. No, that couldn't be right. Janis was going to breathe on her own and dig her toes into a white sand beach.

"Conclusive," the doctor said. "I spoke to the family. The mother is talking with a minister, and we're waiting on word as to how she would like to move forward with organ donation."

"Organ donation?" Grace's fingers tightened around Janis's wrist. "But part of her is still alive." Warmth radiated from Janis's skin. The pulse at her wrist beat weak but steady against Grace's fingertips. That counted for something. "Miracles happen all the time."

"They do, but—"

"I'm sure someone was given up for dead but came back to life right here in this hospital. Right here on this floor. In this room."

"Yes, of course, but—"

"Medical advances happen, too. If she holds on long enough, it's possible some procedure or drug could rebuild her brain."

The doctor tucked the folder under his arm. "Perhaps I'm not making myself clear, Counselor Courtemanche, so let me try again. Due to sustained oxygen deprivation, Janis Jaffee suffered irreversible cessation of the functioning of the entire brain. Her brain stem is dead. All cognitive and life support functions have irreversibly stopped. I know you're personally involved in this, and I'm terribly sorry for your loss."

* * *

Hatch pulled off his shirt and yanked the holster from behind his back. His fingers clawed around his gun. He hated violence, rarely pulled his service revolver while on duty, but he sure as hell wouldn't mind using his gun.

He tossed the gun on Grace's dresser and sat on the bed. He kicked off one shoe, which shot across the room and crashed into the closet door. The other shoe bulleted into the hallway. The crash and thud brought no satisfaction. Another girl had died, which meant their unsub would move on to Level Three.

And then what? What if another victim died? Grace would be the loser? He cradled his head in his hands. If she survived that long, because she was beating up herself.

In her mind, Grace had failed Janis. With her overblown sense of responsibility and self-reliance, she insisted she alone was responsible for the young woman's death. Hatch tugged off his belt and unfastened the button of his dress pants. Guilt was a vicious beast. It devoured some people, destroying them from the inside out. With others, guilt simply held them hostage, keeping them forever fixed and unable to move on with their lives. But with some people, guilt snuck in and took over, controlling their thoughts and actions and lives. He unbuttoned his shirt. With Grace, he suspected the latter. After learning of Janis's death, she'd spent the next six hours at her office going through past cases and work files, looking for a different kind of beast that had a face but no name.

The beast remained nameless.

Something whizzed by his ear and landed with a thud on the bed.

Grace stood in the bedroom doorway in her tennis whites, a racquet in her hand. "Let's play."

God, he loved this woman. Her drive. Her tenacity. Her fight. And he loved that she knew him inside out. Physical sounded damned good. He'd love to get on his boat, pulling ropes, fighting with sails, and battling the wind. He needed the wind pounding him, shoving away the anger and fear. He slipped off his shirt and let it fall to the floor. But that was hardly the responsible thing to do. For now, slamming a few tennis balls would work.

With a quarter moon lighting the way, Grace took him to a large area surrounded by a chain link fence, Blue lumbering after them. She flicked a switch on the gate, and a pair of overhead lights hummed, flickered, and brightened. "It's Giroux's old dog run, not quite regulation. The lighting is awful, and you'll need to watch for holes."

With no more words and no warm-up, Grace pounded the ball past the net, and he slammed back. Over and over they rifled shots at each other. Sweat dripped into his eyes. Heat and dust swirled up from the baked, hard-packed earth.

Grace won the first set, and he snuck in a final ace to take the second. He almost laughed at the outrage flashing across her face. During the third set, more than an hour later, sweat drenched his body and he was at one with the sticky night air. At match point, she slammed a shot that caught the outer edge of the baseline. He dove for it and scooped it back. She reached the ball and set up her shot, her pearly skin aglow, her long, lean limbs stretched out like a sleek missile. Sweat curled her hair and glued her white tennis tank to her breasts. She slammed, and the ball probably whizzed past him.

He couldn't tell because he was so focused on the woman he loved.

Her eyes flashed hot and steamier than the night. "You

missed that last shot on purpose." She gripped the racquet like a club. "Dammit, Hatch, you let me win."

He wiped a towel along his face. "Now why would I do that?"

"Because you know I hate losing." She lowered the racquet and plucked her fingers at the sweet spot on the strings. "Because you wanted to make me happy."

He hopped the net, took the racquet from her, and tossed it on the bench next to his. Then he took her hand in his and laced their fingers. "I think we could both use a bit of happy."

* * *

She held her breath and pushed ENTER.

The computer on her right went blank for one heartbeat, two, three.

Swoosh.

The door burst open and line after line of pixilated characters chased each other across her screen—so much text, so much light, that she squinted her eyes and scrambled for the contrast control. The vicious bits of light dimmed, but not her glee. Computer systems like the one used at the Cypress Bend Medical Center were like twenty-story apartment buildings. You had to keep trying different levels, scamper along a few fire escapes, and dodge nosy residents. But if you kept knocking on doors and checking tiny windows, you'd find a way in.

She scrolled through the notes of the physician attending to the pawn from Level Two. Most of the report was in medical-speak, but a few key words jumped out at her.

...absence of brain waves...

...no breath activity...

...no blood traveling to the brain...

The pawn on Level Two was no longer a pawn but a potato. She clicked on a few more keys, and squinted at the lines of pixels. And as of five-sixteen this afternoon, the potato was officially mashed.

With a victorious grin, she flicked off the computer and turned to the one on her left. While waiting for news on the potato, she'd played a little side game with Grace, technically with Grace's checking account. Fun times for all.

But not as fun as Level Three.

With a red marker, she slashed a giant X on the Level Two pawn's face. Tonight she'd slip into the wonderful darkness and deliver the strike to her opponent. Poor Grace. She was going to lose. With a grin, she turned the photo over and with the marker penned Grace a little message.

The Game was heating up, and she was ready to win, but first, she needed to find a small person.

The problem with small people was that they were always surrounded by big people, she realized once she got to the park. She stood in the shadow of a cedar and watched the children on the playground at Harbor Park. Night had settled in, and most small people were already curled up in their beds fast asleep. However, a young couple with a double stroller holding an infant and toddler wheeled along the path circling the playground equipment. One of these two small people would fit nicely in the box but neither could use the phone and call Grace.

Bad move.

An older small person, maybe eleven or twelve, sat on a bench eating a double-scoop ice cream cone with a bored teenage girl talking on her phone next to him. The boy with the ice cream cone could use a phone, but parts of him were not small. Rolls of fat hung from his belly, and his legs reminded her of tree trunks. It would be a tight squeeze to get him in the box.

Small. She needed small.

The Game was in full swing, and she was winning. Grace had made a smart move at Level Two, nearly getting to the pawn in time, thanks to all of her allies. Although the formidable prosecutor was notoriously self-reliant, she'd mustered a team, including members of the sheriff's department, two local police forces, the Florida State Police, and the FBI.

She pictured the man the color of the despicable sun. Theodore Hatcher—"Hatch" was such a stupid name—was a part of some elite FBI team based out of Maine and run by a man named Parker Lord. She'd spent a good deal of time at her computers, digging up information on this team, because she'd learned at an early age it was easier to battle an enemy you knew. There was something strange about Hatch's boss. For fifteen years, Agent Lord had been an FBI hotshot, the shiniest of stars, who'd made a name for himself in the worldwide fight against human trafficking. Then, a decade ago, he'd disappeared. Not a hint of scandal. Not a clue as to motive or mission.

Poof. Gone.

Then all of sudden he was in the land of the living with a sparkly new FBI team, the Special Criminal Investigative Unit. If Theodore Hatcher was any measure, indeed, there was something special about Parker Lord's team. Unfortunately, Team Parker Lord was going down. They were on the wrong side.

Grace's allies had made it more difficult to move around. Local TV stations plastered her face on the nightly news and labeled her the Gravedigger. The likeness was surprisingly good, and she hadn't been surprised when she learned the artist was from Theodore's team, a former L.A. cop named

Berkley Rowe. Hundreds of people were looking for her, posting fliers, hunting the swamp. She fingered the chain at her neck. She didn't know the swamp well, not like Grace. Her *daddy* didn't take her out much. But she was good at being invisible, quiet, too.

Time to play the invisible game. We can't let anyone see us. Fun, huh?

She crouched, dashing behind the pine trees lining Harbor Park.

Look Momma. Quiet as a cat. Into the black.

As she slipped from tree to tree, she wondered where else she could find a small person. Maybe she'd try the ball field. So many bright field lights, but there were bound to be little ball players walking home from night games.

With a rush of excitement rising in her chest, she dashed through the pines, where something growled. She jumped back, using her hands to fend off a dog.

"It's okay," the man said as he rubbed the top of the dog's head. "Ramsey here won't bite, will you, old boy."

"Get it away!" She backpedaled until her heels hit the trunk of a pine tree. "Just get it away!"

"Seriously. It's okay. He's fourteen years old and half blind."

She knew she looked ridiculous. The dog weighed less than ten pounds. But it terrified her. "I...I'm allergic to dogs."

"Sorry." The man tugged the dog's leash, pulling him away from the tree. "Have a good night."

She nodded and ran deeper into the dark and away from the dog. Dogs weren't bad, not evil in the sense that humans were evil. Dogs were...dogs. They did dog things. They barked at mailmen. They chased their tails. They dug holes. They chewed bones.

CHAPTER TWENTY-SIX

Grace shook the rag rug and set it in a puddle of early morning sunshine. Allegheny Blue plodded across the porch and settled onto the circle of light. She checked the pads of all four feet and filled the water dish near the porch swing.

"Your dog's fine." Hatch slipped out the front door, kissed her cheek, and hurried down the steps to the dock.

She opened her mouth to remind him that technically Blue wasn't her dog, but she decided to save the fight for something that mattered.

Yesterday another young woman had died, and the killer would soon be looking for a third victim. For Grace, the face Berkley had sketched was key. Something about that face tugged at her. She'd been through her files at work and nothing stood out. She'd shown the sketch to her co-workers, and none of them recognized the woman. She planned to take the sketch to her old racquet club and condo complex and see if anyone there recognized the woman. She planned to dig into her storage unit and pull out old yearbooks and photo albums. But first she would spend the early morning boating with Hatch.

Last night as they lay in bed, spent after a round of lovemaking that picked up where their explosive tennis match left off, Hatch had grown uncharacteristically quiet. She figured like her, he was stewing over the horror of Janis Jaffee's death, maybe thinking about the young woman's hands growing cold. When she pressed him, he admitted his mind was on a boat.

"Both times the killer used a small aluminum boat not propelled by fuel," Hatch had said. "That boat can't be far away, and there can't be many of them. We find that boat, we find the killer."

When she reached the dirt path that led to Lamar's old dock, she stopped and listened for the rumble of earth movers. With clearance from the forensic crew, the construction crew was supposed to resume digging at sunrise. She tucked her hair behind her ears. Blue snored on the porch, two jays chattered in a pine at the head of the path, and down by the slough, Lamar Giroux's boat motor coughed and sputtered as Hatch tried to bring it to life.

No rumbles, rattles, or beeps from the construction site.

She'd left a message with her general contractor yesterday letting him know they had the green light from the authorities, and he told her they'd begin work at sunrise. Surely they hadn't found another reason to halt construction. Another body?

She rushed up the rise. When she reached the site she found the equipment but no workers. Taking out her phone, she called her contractor. "Are you aware your men haven't shown up?"

"They showed, but I had to call them off. I got an e-mail

from my bank this morning. I'm afraid the check you gave us, Miss Courtemanche, bounced."

"There must be a mistake. I had the money for the payment." She wouldn't commit to a project she didn't have the funds for. Hell, she'd sold most everything she had so she could make the payments.

"You might want to talk to your bank, ma'am, because the check came back to us marked 'insufficient funds.' I'm afraid until we get that check cleared, we aren't working on your house."

She clenched her teeth so hard her jaw ached. "Fine. I'll call the bank and get this cleared up. Just make sure your crew is ready to go."

Grace hung up just as Hatch walked up the rise. "Got the boat started," he said. "What are you doing here?"

"Trying to get a house built."

He ran both hands through the sides of his hair. "Now?"

She looked from her phone to the land. She should be helping track down a killer, looking for a boat or a face, but she was on the phone with a guy who was supposed to build her a spiral staircase, kitchen island, and a central vacuum system. Crazy. She jammed her phone in her pocket. At this moment, the house shouldn't matter.

She pulled in a deep breath of piney air. But it did. It mattered so much she felt the pull in her toes pressing into the earth, a pull that came from deep inside her, a pull that had nothing to do with the dreams of her long dead father. For the past few days, she and Hatch had been talking in a roundabout way about family. Her passion for this house had nothing to do with her father and a faded sketch on a yellowed cocktail napkin. She wanted five bedrooms and a tire swing. She wanted a dock where she could tie up a skiff like the one she and her mother used to take out and search for flowers for the dining room table. She wanted a tennis court like the one where her father had first showed her how to hold a racquet and be a winner. Even after she'd met Hatch, who told her upfront he'd never have kids, she didn't throw away that cocktail napkin because she'd always wanted a family. This wasn't about a house, but family.

She must have made some noise because Hatch settled a hand on her arm. "You okay?"

"I'm not too sure." She tucked the ends of her hair behind her ears. "But let me make one more call."

Grace called up her banking account on her phone and saw red. Her check to her general contractor had bounced because someone had emptied her account. Could this be slimy residue from Larry Morehouse? He'd manage to open a bank account in her name in Nevis. The slug, or more likely one of his bottom feeders, could have hacked into her bank account. With a growl, she clicked on the button for customer service and got canned music.

Hatch, who'd jogged to the mailbox, came back with a fist full of mail, including a small, familiar envelope.

The elevator music stopped. "Good morning. You've reached First Southern Bank customer service," a woman with a pleasant voice said.

With the tips of his fingers, Hatch slipped a photo of Janis Jaffee from the envelope, a scarlet X slashed across her face. Grace had been expecting this photo, but the shock of seeing that face made her fumble with her phone.

"My name's Miranda," the voice on the phone continued. "What can I do for you today?"

Hatch's eyebrows bunched as he looked at the back side. She grabbed his arm and turned the back side her way. In chunky red letters were the words: *Three strikes and Grace is out.* Next to the words was a stick person with two Xs for eyes and pearls around its neck.

"Hello? This is Miranda with First Southern Bank. Can I help you?"

"Son of a bitch!" Hatch said with a hissing breath.

The phone fell from Grace's hand.

* * *

Greenup, Kentucky

Teeth were amazing little body parts. When soft tissue decayed and bones broke and splintered and dissolved into dust, teeth held strong. And long after the heart stopped beating and brainwaves ceased crashing the skull, teeth could still tell a story.

Soft classical music rose from the phone speaker as Tucker took a long swig of coffee and waited for the dentist in St. Paul, Minnesota. After talking to the head coach of the Hornet high school baseball team last night, Tucker contacted Lawrence Lassen, father of the Stinger and possibly son of Grandpa and Grandma Doe who'd been found in Collier's Holler five days ago. Lawrence Lassen reported he hadn't heard from his parents in more than two weeks, but that wasn't anything out of the ordinary. His parents were healthy, wealthy, active sixty-somethings enjoying their retirement and prone to spur-of-the-moment road trips. His mother loved to hike and watch birds, and his father loved to eat. Dad's favorite food: pie. Last night Tucker had express-mailed dental x-rays of his two unidentified victims to the Lassen family's dentist.

"I looked at the films of both individuals, Detective Holt," the dentist said when he finally took up the line, "and they're consistent with the films we have on file for two of our long-time patients, Oliver and Emmaline Lassen."

Grandpa and Grandma Doe finally had names.

The simple fact left Tucker's knees weak with relief. After he thanked the dentist and offered his condolences, he studied the photo on Emmaline Lassen's Facebook page, the one of her and Oliver standing in front of a Christmas tree surrounded by five grandchildren. Smiling faces, whole faces, faces not eaten away by pool acid.

Why would Asswipe want to destroy these faces? Attacks to the face were common in personal grudges or between victims and perpetrators who had a history. Maybe someone feeling wronged by the Lassens wanted them dead. The couple had money. Maybe the homicides were the result of a simple robbery turned violent.

Tucker chugged the rest of his coffee. He'd dig into the couple's private and financial backgrounds, talk in depth with family members and former coworkers, but he wanted to unearth another name. For days he'd been itching to get his hands on Oliver and Emmaline's car, which had been noticeably absent from the parking lot at the trailhead. If he found the car, he might find Asswipe.

Because like teeth, cars could talk.

Tucker called his contact at the Motor Vehicle Division, who patched him through to an MVD contact in Minnesota. In one of her bitchier moods, his soon-to-be ex-wife had suggested he take his phone out for dinner on Valentine's Day because he spent more time with the thing than her. On some cases, like this one, the damn phone may as well be surgically attached to his right ear.

Within fifteen minutes, Tucker had the VIN and plate number to the Lassen's car, a late-model, champagne-colored Cadillac. He ran the car through the NCIC database of stolen vehicles and came up empty, but when he ran the make and model through a database of local law enforcement agencies in the Kentucky-Ohio-West Virginia area, he got a possible hit. A group of boys going dirt biking had found a champagne-colored Caddie down a secluded country road. The car had no plates, and the VIN had been destroyed.

Tucker followed the breadcrumbs and discovered the Caddie had been towed to an impound lot in southern Ohio. Within the hour, he was at the lot with the impound manager.

"Car came in unusually clean," the manager said. "No registration or insurance information. No personal items of identification. Cops found no fingerprints, not even on the steering wheel or door handle. Just a few pieces of trash."

One man's trash could be another man's case breaker. Tucker snapped on a pair of gloves. Time to dig in and get dirty. In the center console he found a box of tissues, a few loose coins, and a set of lightweight binoculars. Didn't the Lassens' son say his mother liked to bird watch? In the driver's door pocket, he found a handful of crumpled napkins, all from Peggy's Pie Palace. And Oliver Lassen loved pie.

Yes.

"Got someone who can start her up for me?" Tucker asked as his heart revved.

"Sure, but I can't release it yet."

"I won't be driving anywhere. I want to see the car's navigation system." If teeth and pie could talk, Tucker reasoned, imagine what a GPS could tell him.

While a mechanic poked around under the hood, Tucker checked his calendar. Jackson had a ball game tonight. He'd spend the rest of the day in the office, glued to his phone and computer as he dug up information on why someone would kill the Lassens, and then he'd go to Jackson's game. But that's where he usually ran into trouble. Days turned into nights, and he wouldn't even realize it. He set an alarm on his phone thirty minutes before game time.

When the mechanic finally got the Caddie purring, Tucker slipped into the passenger seat and turned on the navigation system, which showed a trip route in progress. He scrolled to the destination point. Cypress Bend, Florida.

He called up a map. Looked like a small town on the coast of the Florida panhandle. A long way and quite a few degrees from St. Paul, Minnesota. Florida? Why did that ring a bell? He went through his notes, now in the hundreds of pages. On one of the early pages he found the list of vehicles seen at the trailhead where the Lassens had been murdered. All from Kentucky and Ohio, but one of the hikers reported earlier in the day he'd seen an out-of-state pickup. He flipped through the pages.

Damn. Colorado, not Florida.

He continued to dig until he found his notes on the interview he'd had with Oliver and Emmaline Lassen's son. The son had told Tucker his parents had recently bought a new winter home in Florida, a town on Apalachicola Bay called Cypress Bend.

Something about that town nagged at his gut.

CHAPTER TWENTY-SEVEN

Lamar Giroux had built his shack for one man with a Spartan lifestyle. Two people would find the one-bedroom house cramped. Five people should have been tripping all over each other. But Hatch's team moved and worked like cogs in a wheel.

Grace marveled at the well-tuned machine that was focused on preventing the next abduction, which meant finding the Gravedigger. The killer had left a clear message. Grace was the grand prize. The Gravedigger wanted her dead. The idea terrified her, but more than that, it galvanized her. Bigger stakes meant a bigger effort on her part.

Berkley Rowe, the SCIU's forensic artist, sat on the back porch where "the light was good," smoothing clay strips along markers sticking out from a cast of the skull that had been found on Grace's construction site. The artist's long, nimble fingers, dry and chafed with bits of pigment hiding under nails, moved quickly and decisively, while a long blond braid poking out from a headband swayed along her back. She reminded Grace of a chic hippy, not a former L.A. cop.

No one had found any connection linking the bodies found on Grace's land to the Gravedigger murders, but Berkley, like Grace, had been drawn to the woman and child, and she'd spent all day working on a 3-D reconstruction that could help identify the woman.

Berkley wiped her hands on a towel around her waist. "Okay, I'm ready." She untucked the towel, set it on the table, and motioned to the clay bust. "Take me to her home."

Grace walked Berkley to the construction site, still temporarily on hold while the bank worked out where her money had gone. The artist trailed her fingers along a row of camellia bushes then sat cross-legged at the edge of the gaping hole. Her fingers dug into the ground, lifting and sifting through the sandy earth. Her eyelids lowered.

Grace waited because frankly, there was nothing else she could do. It was a good thing she'd been working on patience with Hatch.

"This is where your new home is going to be built," Berkley finally said.

"That's the plan." But not all plans worked out the way they are initially envisioned. She wanted a home filled with children's laughter and Hatch's silly sea songs. It wasn't about the land or fulfilling her daddy's long-time dream.

The artist tucked her legs against her chest, rested her chin on her knees, and stared out at the river. "It's beautiful here, Grace, and so peaceful. A good place to live"—her gaze slid to the excavation site—"and die. Whoever buried the mother and baby here loved them very much."

Despite the high sun, Grace shivered. "And then I had to bring out the bulldozers and rip them from the earth."

Berkley's braid dangled to the ground as she tilted her head in confusion. "And that upsets you?"

"I destroyed the peace."

Berkley brushed sand from her hands, unfolded her legs, and stood. "Or perhaps you're bringing peace."

"By disturbing a decade-old grave?"

She motioned to the hole. "We're looking at an isolated image. Sometimes we need to step back and look at the entire canvas. Perhaps that woman and her child have a different destiny. Perhaps this land has a different destiny. You have to be open to what the universe sends you." She tucked her hand through Grace's arm and strolled along the camellia bushes.

Grace pictured what the universe had sent her way: a sun-soaked sailor who would never put down roots and give her forever and a speckled hound with bleeding feet. She laughed. "The universe must have mixed up a few deliveries lately."

Berkley patted her arm. "The universe usually gets these things right."

So much about Hatch was right. She loved his passion for life, his dedication to fighting the evils of this world, and the way he made her feel like she wasn't alone anymore, like she was part of something bigger and better. Here she was walking arm and arm with one of Hatch's teammates. She'd held hands with Ricky and Raymond and invited Alex out for a boat ride. Her life was no longer all about whorehouse kings and baby killers named Helena Ring. And the crazy thing? It wasn't bothering her. Her father might be turning over in his grave, but she was the happiest she'd been in years, in a decade. She raised her face to the sky and laughed.

When she and Berkley reached the shack, the artist glided

on her beaded sandals to the back porch while Grace lingered in her kitchen, where Agent Jon MacGregor had set up a command center complete with three computers and four phones at her kitchen table.

"Anything yet from the final number?" Agent MacGregor asked the RF engineer from the phone company.

"Nothing, but the minute anyone turns on the phone, we'll jump on it. We're assuming that once again mobile positioning will be unavailable," the engineer said. "But we can begin triangulation of the signal as soon as the phone's turned on."

"And the cell sites on wheels?" Jon asked.

"We put four COWs in place, all in remote areas. Concentration of base station cells is low because the area's so desolate. The COWs should help us pinpoint location more accurately."

Grace didn't understand this language, but she was grateful for the crew at her kitchen table. She strolled into the living room and searched for Blue. With all the people, he must have slinked off to find a quiet place to nap.

She stepped onto the front porch and immediately her skin prickled. Someone was watching her. She spun and found Hayden Reed, the SCIU's criminal profiler, sitting in the corner on the porch swing.

Hayden motioned to Blue, who was stretched out on his back in the middle of the porch, showing his belly to the sun. The skin around the dog's mouth sagged, exposing his gums and teeth. "He looks like he's smiling," Hayden said.

Grace sat on the top porch step and rested her back against the post. "Most upside down dogs look like they're smiling." Blue had every reason to smile. He'd had a long life, a full life, a life doing what he loved on land he couldn't leave. Right now he was making the most of the time he had left. She stretched out her leg and rubbed her foot along his belly.

Hayden closed his laptop and Grace noticed a pair of wicked scratches down the back of his hand. "What happened?"

"Ellie the Devil Cat," he said. "She's not quite as docile as your friend Blue here. On my way to the airport, I dropped Ellie off at the boarding kennel because my fiancée is out of town helping an old friend who's having some problems, and the cat from hell let me know of her displeasure."

The screen door opened and Hatch stepped onto the front porch with Agent MacGregor. "The teams are heading out," Agent MacGregor said. "Lieutenant Lang is putting extra patrols on the rivers, local police departments are on high alert, and the media is working with us to alert the public to be ultra watchful, particularly young women walking alone. The sun's going down in a few hours, and I want everyone ready."

Because at night the Gravedigger comes out to play.

The peace she'd found at the grave of the mother and child flitted away on the wind. It could be tonight, tomorrow night, or a week from next Tuesday. The only thing they were sure of was that she'd strike at night.

Hatch took a seat on the step below her, his shoulder brushing against her knee. He might not be saying much, but she welcomed his solid, steady presence, two words she never thought she'd use to describe Theodore Hatcher.

"Professor, what do you have on our gal?" Jon asked.

Grace shook her head. "I still struggle with the idea of the killer being a woman. In general, men are much more competitive."

"Really?" Hatch asked with a lift of both brows. "You're the most competitive person I know."

Finally, Hatch said something. His absolute silence unnerved her, but the accusatory look on his face only made her smile. She had a deep, wide competitive streak that colored almost everything she did, and she'd never apologize about that.

Hayden straightened his cuffs. "Grace is right. Men are traditionally more competitive, but we have a victim who claimed to have heard a woman. The evidence backs that up. The wading boot prints found at the first victim's grave are size eight, too small for most men. Given the depth of the impression and the relatively constant moisture level, we're looking at an individual around one hundred pounds. As for the actual abductions, they were far from physical attacks. According to our second victim, she was hit with a stun gun and incapacitated long enough for the unsub to inject her with a substance to render her unconscious. A needle mark on the first victim's upper shoulder points to a similar situation. Our unsub is not a person with brute physical strength, but she is agile and in relatively good health."

Grace shuddered. No, the Gravedigger was sick, twisted sick. No one could do what she did and be called healthy.

"Good *physical* health," Hayden amended with a smile in her direction, as if he could read her mind.

"So we're looking at a woman," Hayden continued. "Age twenty to thirty-five, around five feet tall and one hundred pounds. She's local or has spent a considerable amount of time studying the area, but she doesn't like the water or the outdoors in general. As a child, she was a loner and never played team sports, but she's extremely competitive. She played computer games as a kid for hours on end, the kind with complex and fully-developed worlds. She isn't gainfully employed but has access to money, either family money or ill-gotten. She may be a computer hacker. She's not involved in any committed relationship and hated her mother."

While the men on the porch mulled Hayden's profile, Grace shook her head in awe. She'd worked with criminal profilers before, but never one who made such detailed claims with such confidence. "Amazing."

Before anyone could say anything, Berkley opened the screen door and popped her head out. "Camellia's ready."

While the woman found at her construction site had nothing to do with the Gravedigger, Grace was anxious to put a name to the mother's face. The bones were real and visible, unlike the invisible woman they were chasing.

On the back porch, late afternoon sun flooded the air, and Grace let her eyes adjust to the brightness. Once she did, her mouth fell open. "That can't be right," Grace said. Maybe the Apostles weren't miracle workers, or maybe Berkley Rowe was having a bad day.

"This is her," Berkley insisted. "This is Camellia."

The clay skull had a narrow face, thin lips, and big eyes with lush lashes that looked uncomfortably familiar. Berkley had outfitted her with a thick black-haired wig and chocolaty brown eyes. "She looks like your sketch of the Gravedigger," Grace said. "Are you sure you aren't getting the two projects confused?"

Shaking her head, Berkley packed clay and tools and slipped them into a large silver suitcase.

"I agree with Grace, Berk," Hatch said. "The two could pass for sisters. You haven't gotten any sleep in the past forty-eight hours. Maybe you're a little fuzzy."

Berkley shook her head as if she were dealing with young children. "*This* is Camellia."

"But—" Hatch started.

"What's wrong with you, Hatch?" Berkley asked. "You

know how this works. I relied on tissue depth markers tied to age, sex, and race. The bony substrate of the skull told me what kind of nose, mouth, and ears to make. This is science."

Maybe Black Jack was wrong. Maybe there was a place in death for science.

"She's beautiful, in a wild, earthy sort of way," Grace said. "Why did you give her dark, curly hair?"

"That was just a hunch. Same thing with the eye color. The blackish-brown felt right with a strong face like this."

"And the Ronnie Alderman/Gravedigger sketch?" Grace asked. The coincidences in appearance were too hard to swallow. "Were the dark curly hair and brown eyes just a hunch?"

"No. Direct observation. In separate interviews both members of the cleaning crew reported with a fair degree of certainty that the woman calling herself Ronnie had brown eyes and dark, curly hair."

Hayden, who'd joined them on the porch, crossed his arms over his chest. "I'd be shocked if they're not related."

Berkley shrugged. "Very well could be. They could be mother-daughter, aunt-niece, even sister-sister."

"That makes for quite a coincidence," Grace said.

"Or does it?" Hatch paced along the railing, his hands in the back pockets of his long shorts. "When did you talk to Lia Grant?"

Eons ago, long before Hatch and bacon and old buried bones, when all that mattered was putting a whorehouse king in jail and notching another win. "On Wednesday," Grace said. The day would be forever imprinted in her brain.

"And when was construction slated to begin?" Hatch continued, walking faster, so fast his hair fanned back from his forehead.

"Thursday."

"So maybe the Gravedigger wanted to distract you. Maybe she didn't want construction to begin because digging here would disturb what was essentially a sacred burial ground."

"I'm all for positive thinking, Hatch," Jon said. "But there are much easier ways to derail a construction project."

Grace turned to the land beyond the porch, to the construction site with the silent machines.

"What is it, Grace?"

"The land. When Lamar Giroux put this land up for sale, there were six initial bidders, including me. Four of them dropped out quickly, but one was a serious contender, beating my four initial offers. I had to scrape together every dollar I could find to make that final bid."

"But in the end you won," Hatch said in a tone that was anything but victorious.

Every hair on Grace's body stood on end. "And the other bidder lost."

"Get the name of the real estate agent who brokered the deal, Grace. We need to find out about the other person who desperately wanted this land."

* * *

Hayden tucked the name of the real estate agent into his jacket pocket and motioned Hatch to follow him to his rental car.

"Who is she?" Hayden asked when they reached the driveway.

Hatch slipped his hands through his hair. He could pretend he didn't know what his teammate was talking about, but it was hard to bullshit a man like Hayden who saw everything. "Nothing gets by you, does it?"

"Who is she?" Hayden asked again.

"An old girlfriend."

"And I love cats," Hayden deadpanned.

Hatch thwacked his teammate on the shoulder. "You know, I like this lighter side of you, Professor. I think you should have hooked up with Kate years ago."

"Who is she?" Hayden insisted.

Hatch stretched his neck. "My ex-wife."

Hayden, unshakable, solid Hayden, let loose a low whistle. "You were *married*?"

"I had a head injury at the time. The plates below my feet collided after a few nights of incredible sex."

"Does Parker know?" Hayden asked, then immediately waved off the words. Parker knew everything.

When they reached Hayden's rental car, Hatch handed him a sheet of paper. "Here are the questions I want you to ask the real estate agent."

Hayden ducked inside and laughed.

"What?" Hatch asked.

Hayden shook his head. "Nothing."

"Come on, Hayden, talk. Tell me what's going on in that head of yours because you see things no one else sees."

Hayden thumped Hatch on the shoulder and started the car. "I'm looking at you one year down the road, my friend, and I'm not seeing you on a boat."

CHAPTER TWENTY-EIGHT

Hatch stood on the front porch of Grace's house and waited for the green flash, that magical moment at sunset or sunrise when the sun slipped past the horizon line and an arc or ray of green slashed across the sky. According to an old Scottish sailing legend, the man who sees the green flash shall be blessed, for he shall be able to see closely into his own heart and within the hearts of other people.

In his ocean travels, Hatch had seen more than his fair share of green flashes, and he'd give anything to see one now and harness the power behind the legend, not because he wanted to see into his own heart, but because he desperately needed to get into a killer's heart, a killer who wanted, ultimately, to kill Grace.

He pictured that stick figure in pearls with crossed out eyes. Who the hell wanted Grace dead? Who would orchestrate an evil game like this? And when would she strike next?

"She's getting anxious," Hayden had said before he went

to track down the real estate agent who'd been representing a killer. "Our unsub's been out in the open, out of her comfort zone too long, and she needs this game to end. I wouldn't be surprised if she struck tonight."

Tonight. The single word pounded Hatch like gale force winds. Tonight the Gravedigger could abduct the third and final victim. And what's the worst thing that could happen?

The victim would die.

And then?

Grace would have three strikes.

And then?

Grace would die.

And then?

His own personal brand of nuclear annihilation.

He rested his knuckled hands on the porch railing with so much pressure, the gray, splintered wood creaked. He knew exactly what was in his own heart. He loved Grace and couldn't imagine a life without her. How they were to manage a life together still needed to be worked out. Grace had accused him of being a free spirit, but that was far from the case. He was chained to Grace, and he had no desire to break those bonds.

The door opened and Grace stepped out with Blue shuffling behind her. "Land or sea?" she asked.

With the dark of night sliding in, the goal was to get as many bodies out in the swamp and marshes and beaches as possible. Jon had commandeered a high-powered fan boat and was already out on the Cypress Bend river.

"Land," Hatch told Grace.

Blue hobbled behind them to the SUV. "Do you think we should make him stay home?"

"Do you think he'd let us?" Grace asked with a tilt of her eyebrow.

The old dog was like...like a dog with a bone. Hatch shook his head. Once he sunk his teeth into it, he wasn't giving up, much like Grace. After that first phone conversation with Lia Grant, she'd thrown herself into the investigation, committed to see it through to the end. She climbed into the SUV, and he shut the door tightly behind her. His job was to keep her alive.

They drove away from the shack and into the deepening dusk. Their unsub could be anywhere, including Grace's backyard. As they rounded the corner near the construction site, leaves on one of the camellia bushes rustled. Could be a deer, a black bear, or a killer.

He slowed, squinting into the graying night.

"What is it?" Grace asked.

"Not sure."

He parked the SUV, and he and Grace walked across the recently cleared earth, circling the hole where Camellia and her child had been buried. A flash of silver glinted behind one of the camellia bushes. He grabbed Grace and lunged behind a wide sycamore.

The leaves shivered, and Hatch raised his Glock.

The bushes parted, and a woman stepped into the clearing.

"Lou?" Grace asked with a sharp intake of breath.

The old beekeeper jumped, something sharp and shiny falling from one hand and a fistful of red falling from the other. "Saints alive!" Lou clasped her gnarled hands to her chest. "You scared the living daylights out of me."

Hatch lowered the gun but didn't put it away. He closed the distance between them and picked up the length of silver that had fallen to the ground. A knife. "What are you doing here?"

Lou whisked the dirt from her hands, stepped aside, and motioned to the bush. "Gathering flowers." She bent slowly, and he could almost hear the creaking of her old spine as she picked up a half-dozen lengths of camellia blooms scattered on the ground. "For CoraBeth."

"CoraBeth?"

"The one they're calling Camellia." Lou tottered to the edge of the hole. "I saw her picture on the news and heard she was buried here."

"You knew her?"

Lou tossed a single spray of camellias into the hole, the deep red blooms tumbling along the damp chunks of earth until they splashed into a shallow pool of water that had collected at the bottom. One by one, she tossed the flowers into the grave. Tears trailed down her lined cheeks and splashed into the water. "She was my daughter."

A whoosh of wind slipped across the swamp, silencing bullfrogs and crickets. According to Berkley, the Gravedigger and Camellia looked similar.

"Your daughter?" Grace asked. "I never knew you had a daughter."

"She was long gone by the time you came along, little Gracie." The old woman snipped another cluster of blooms from the camellia bush.

"Tell us about your daughter, Lou," Grace said.

The old beekeeper plucked a petal from a flower.

"Please, Miz Poole, little Gracie's life may be at stake."

Lou looked at Grace out of the corner of her eye and plucked faster. What did those old eyes see? Little Gracie picking out a jar of honey? A grown woman who was in danger? Hatch jammed his hands in his pockets so he didn't grab the old woman's shoulders and shake the words from her.

"CoraBeth was born more than fifty years ago," Lou finally said. "Her daddy was a farmhand who worked the cotton fields north of Apalach one summer. He was a wild one, but he had him a smooth way with words. Charmed me *and* the bees." Her cracked lips lifted in a faded smile. "Like her daddy, CoraBeth was a wild one. Didn't like staying cooped up inside. Didn't like goin' to school. Spent her days wandering the swamp and dreaming of the day when she could fly away."

"And?" Grace asked.

"And one day she got her wings. She came home all aflutter and said she'd found the man of her dreams, that he was going to pull her out of the swamp and build her a castle fit for a queen. I never heard from her again."

Grace placed her fingers on Lou's, and she stopped destroying the flower. "I'm sorry."

"I did my grieving sixteen years ago when CoraBeth died."

"Wait a minute," Hatch said. "How did you know she died sixteen years ago?"

The old beekeeper threw the mutilated flower on the ground. "The bees told me."

"The *bees* told you your daughter was dead?" Hatch asked with a rise in his voice.

"Yep, they told me she was buried in the ground, giving back to the earth because the earth gave her life. That's the way of the land."

"The woman you saw with Lia Grant, the one being buried near your place, she looked like your daughter, right?" Grace grabbed the old woman's trembling hand and held it between hers. "That's why you called her a ghost, because you thought she was CoraBeth, who had died a number of years ago."

"Wrong, it looked wrong. After being dead so long, she should have been bones, just bones."

"But she wasn't," Grace said with a calm she didn't feel. "The person with Lia Grant was a real person, someone who looked exactly like your daughter."

"Bones. She should have been bones," Lou said as she extricated her hand and plucked at the gray hair sticking out from the bandana across her forehead.

"Someone like—"

"A daughter," Hatch finished for her. "That's why Berkley's sketch and facial reconstruction look so much alike." He turned to Lou. "The woman buried on this property is your daughter, CoraBeth Poole, which means the young woman you saw in the boat with Lia Grant and who worked on the cleaning crew in Port St. Joe could be your granddaughter."

Lou tugged on the gray wisp of hair.

"Talk to me, Miz Poole. Did CoraBeth have a daughter?"

She pulled on the hair, as if trying to tug something from her brain. "I...I don't know." Her mouth trembled, the saggy skin of her neck quivering. "The bees never told me. Usually the bees tell me the important things. They should have told me. They *would* have told me."

He took her hands in his, their fingers interlaced. "Think, Lou, think back. Did you ever receive a call, a note, a visit from a young girl who looked like CoraBeth?"

Lou stared at the bridge of their arms with longing. She wanted to cross over, to admit she had a granddaughter. The old woman's thin arms grew as stiff and still as sun-brittled twigs before she threw off his hands. "She's dead. The queen is dead!" Tucking the wisp of gray under her bandana, Lou Poole stomped off into the swamp.

"It's her," Grace said. "The killer is Lou Poole's granddaughter. It's all connected and it starts with this land, the highest point on Cypress Bend."

Hatch turned his face to the night sky, which had slipped from plum to gray and was now bleeding to black. "The more important question isn't who she is but where she is."

* * *

Sometimes luck, not skill, separated the winners from the losers, and tonight she had both. She watched the two boys sneaking down the alley. The authorities were expecting the next pawn to be another young woman. Oh, this was good. Another game changer. One of these two noisy little boys would be just the right size. But two was one too many.

She pushed her glasses back up the bridge of her nose. *Think. Think. Think.*

Divide and conquer. That's what she needed to do. She searched around the alley and found an aluminum can on the ground. Extra points for picking up litter. She tossed the can at a metal trashcan, the clank jarring the night. The boys jumped and took off. At the mouth of the alley, the boys split.

Silent and invisible, she took off after the one who turned right.

When she reached the boy, she grabbed him and swung the stun gun at his neck. The boy, small and scrappy, like a vicious little dog, slipped out of her hands. She lunged, flying through the air and slamming into him.

He kicked, his small-person tennis shoes connecting with her side. The stun gun slipped from her hand, but she caught it. She blamed all those video games she played as a kid. Good for hand/eye coordination. Jamming the stun gun against the small person's neck, she watched as his body jerked and froze. At last she dug the needle from her front pocket—it was amazing what a person could buy off the Internet—slipped off the protective cap and jabbed it into his neck.

"*Aaargh*!" he cried.

"Final level," she said when the boy's eyes finally closed. She turned her face toward Cypress Point, where Grace and her pretty pearls lived and said, "And may the best sister win."

* * *

Something cold and wet nuzzled her hand. "Go away." A long, soggy piece of sandpaper licked her neck. "Not now, Blue. I'll get you some bacon later."

She reached for her pillow to throw at the dog, but her pillow wasn't beneath her head. Her fingers slid along something warm and firm but soft, something that smelled of salt and sun. Hatch. Her head was on Hatch's lap.

That's when she heard the ringing.

Her phone. Someone was calling her phone. She scrambled upright. She was in the SUV. Where was her phone? She'd been holding it and must have fallen asleep. Hatch, asleep in the driver's seat with his head against the window, didn't move.

She dug between the seats and under Hatch. The ringing continued.

"Where are you?" She fell to her knees and fumbled along the floorboard, banging her head on the console. "Dammit!"

"Who you talking to?" Hatch said with a yawn.

"My phone."

Hatch's eyes flew open. His seat squeaked as he lunged for the light switch on the dash. Light flooded the vehicle.

At last she found her phone. The display read RESTRICTED

NUMBER. "Hello!" Grace said, her hand shaking. Was this it? Level Three? "Hello!"

"Who the hell is this?" The voice was more than a little irritated.

"Grace. My name's Grace Courtemanche. Are you okay?"

"Not really." The bravado wrapped around the words faded away. "I kind of need some help."

"What's your name? Where are you?"

"My name's Linc." A quiver rocked the voice followed by a soft sob. "I was out messing around tonight with my buddy Gabe and got into a little trouble."

Sweat broke out along her neck. "Oh, God."

"What is it?" Hatch dropped to the floor next to her.

She handed him the phone. "Level Three. She has one of Alex's friends. The one called Linc."

Hatch took the phone. "Linc, my name is Agent Hatcher and I'm with the FBI. Where are you?"

"I'm in a hole in the ground in a stinkin' plastic tote, like the one my ma has in her laundry room to hold dirty laundry."

Good. This kid was a fighter, one clearly not immobilized by fear.

"I'm going to ask you a set of questions," Hatch said. "I need you to stay calm, and we're going to get you out of there. You ready, pal?"

CHAPTER TWENTY-NINE

Are you hurt or in any pain?" Hatch asked Linc, the Gravedigger's third victim. A boy. She'd abducted a thirteen-year-old boy. He swallowed the curse swelling in his throat and forced himself to remember what he was trained to do.

Stay calm. Keep others around him calm.

"I...I...passed out for a while." Linc's voice cracked, but he cleared his throat. "But I'm okay now. No bleeding or anything." The kid was holding it together, trying to be brave.

"Do you have fresh air?"

"Yeah. Got a few holes in the top of the plastic lid. I'm breathing good."

Excellent. Good mental and physical health. Jim Breck of the local phone company and Lieutenant Lang were both tapped into the line and ready to go. Breck and his team were triangulating the call, and the lieutenant's team was ready to dig as soon as they received coordinates. Grace and Allegheny Blue sat in the SUV with him on one of the many back roads snaking through Cypress Point.

"Be as still as you can, Linc. We don't need any dirt jostling and obstructing those holes. Do you know where you are?"

"No clue."

"Do you hear running water or cars or boats or birds?"

"It's quiet. Don't hear a thing."

"What about smells? Do you smell fish or car exhaust?"

"I smell dirt."

They weren't going to get a quick fix on him. Time to backpedal. "Where were you when you were taken?"

"The alley behind Robson's Grocery Store off Main Street."

"What time?"

"Midnight or so."

"How did you end up in the box?"

"A girl popped out of nowhere and came at me. A freakin' girl. I almost got away but she hit me with some kind of stun gun and jabbed a needle in my neck. That's when I passed out."

"When and where did you wake up?"

"Don't know how long I was out, but I woke up in this stupid laundry tote. I kind of went all sissy until I found the holes and realized I could breathe." A sob caught in Linc's throat.

Nope, he wasn't letting the boy slip into panic like Janis Jaffee had. "Then what did you do, Linc?"

"Then I screamed and punched the box. Really pissed me off."

Linc needed to hang on to that anger. That fighting-mad spirit would keep him in the game longer. "When you woke up, were you already in the ground?"

"No. I was outside and moving. I felt the wind kind of beating on the tote, and I could hear the road below."

If Linc felt the wind, he must have been in the bed of a truck. Most likely a white four by four with wide tires with a cross-hatch pattern. "Asphalt, like on a highway or city street?"

"First asphalt. Then we must have turned down a dirt road because it got bumpy."

"How long were you on the asphalt?"

"Don't have a clue. She took my cell phone. That pissed me off, too."

"Did you hear anything while you were on the asphalt? See anything through the holes?"

"Nah, nothing." The kid's voice wavered. "This... this isn't good, is it?"

"You're doin' great, pal. You need to just keep talking to me because my buddies at the phone company are figuring out where you're at."

"Yeah, that's right. They can do that, can't they?"

"You bet they can. So the truck turned onto a bumpy road. What happened next?"

Next to him, Grace wrapped her fingers around the pearls at her neck. She'd spent her childhood playing the What Happens Next Game, but never with these kinds of stakes.

"Made lots of turns," Linc continued. "Not sure how many, and I have no idea how long we were on the dirt road. Box slid around. Thought I was going to puke."

"And when you stopped?"

"She pulled the tote from the truck, right off the end, and I crashed to the ground. I bit my freakin' tongue."

"One person? Same person who nabbed you behind the grocery store?"

Pause. "Yeah, just one. Probably the same chick. I let

a stupid girl nab my ass. A stupid girl!" A series of sharp smacks sounded.

"And we're going to catch her." He needed to de-escalate the search. "Do you hear me, Linc? We're going to get you out and nab her ass."

"Yeah, that's what I want. Her ass in a box like this one."

"Okay, pal, so what happened next?"

"She dragged the box on the ground."

"Were you on pavement? Grass? Gravel? Shells?"

"Not gravel or shells, but there must have been some rocks. Tore a hole in the bottom of the tote. Small. Can fit two fingers through it."

"Did you see, smell or hear anything as you were being dragged?"

"Nothing."

"What happened next?"

"She slid me and the tote into a hole. Got banged around but landed upright. Then I heard and smelled dirt clods dumping on top of me."

"Think hard, Linc. During this time did you see anything through the holes?"

"No. Too dark."

"Hear anything? Dogs or birds or boats? How about smells? The ocean or fish or car exhaust?"

"No, noth—" He sucked in a fast breath. "Smoke. At one point I smelled smoke, the campfire kind. I swear at one point it smelled like roasting marshmallows. That's stupid, huh?"

"Marshmallows definitely aren't stupid." Lieutenant Lang was probably mobilizing one of her search teams to head into local campgrounds to scout around for marshmallow roasting sticks. "Anything else? Other smells or sounds? Maybe people talking or even singing?"

"Nothing."

He checked his watch. "What about your attacker, what do you remember about her?"

"Short. My size. Skinny, too. Dark, long hair. Curly."

"Anything else?"

"Big eyes. And she had a tattoo on her wrist. Saw that when she jammed the stun gun on my neck. A bee. A freakin' bumblebee. A pansy ass girl with a freakin' bumblebee."

"And we'll get her. Did she have—"

"Hang tight, Agent Hatcher. I think I got another hole." Shuffling sounded, along with a splash and a swear word.

Grace frowned. "Did he say hole?"

"Linc?" Hatch said. "What's going on?"

"Hey, sorry 'bout that. I'm back. Yep. Got two holes, not one. I tore my shirt and got the new one plugged. Not too much water's coming in."

"You have water coming into the tote?"

"Yeah, almost an inch now."

"Salt? Fresh?"

A soft swish sounded, and Linc said, "Salt, really muddy. But I don't need to be worried about the water because you're on your way, right? Your guys are triangulating the call, just like on all the cop shows on TV. You'll be here and—"

Silence stretched over the phone. "Linc?" More silence, not even a hint of breath. "Linc!"

The phone light died, the face blackening and becoming one with the night. "Dammit!" Hatch's hand tightened around the phone. "The call dropped."

"He'll call back." Grace pressed against his side, staring at the black, silent hunk of metal in his hand. "Lia called nine times. Linc will call."

Hatch willed the phone to ring. "Come on, pal. We're not done talking. Call me." When it remained silent, he shook it, as if trying to scare it into submission.

A phone rang, and Hatch's heart slammed against his ribcage. He went to push the call button, but the face was still black.

Grace nudged him in the chest. "Your phone. It's Jim Breck from the phone company."

He took his phone from Grace. "What the hell happened?"

"Signal's gone," Jim said. "We lost the control channel completely. We'll continue to monitor, but it looks like the battery may have died, the boy turned off the phone, or the phone malfunctioned."

"Or more likely our killer programmed the damn thing to cut off after five minutes because we're on Level Three." Hatch's hand shook as he handed Grace her phone. Linc wasn't calling back. But they hadn't lost him, not yet. This kid was strong and coherent. Hatch pulled solid information from him. "You got a location?"

"We've been on it since the boy turned on the phone," Jim said. "We're still working on coordinates, but we caught him roaming strongest on a tower near Tate's Hell."

He turned to Grace.

"A state forest with primitive campsites," she said. "More than 200,000 acres."

Hatch ran a hand along his face. That was some serious acreage. He cranked the motor. In the backseat of the SUV, Blue's tail thumped. Dogs, like bees, could sense things, and old Blue knew he was going on a hunt.

* * *

"A kid?" Agent MacGregor slammed a fisted hand onto the hood of Hatch's SUV, the bang echoing through the pre-dawn darkness. "I can't believe she got a kid."

"A thirteen-year-old boy named Lincoln Henderson," Grace said. For the past fifteen minutes searchers, including Special Agent Jon MacGregor, had been pouring into the south parking lot at Tate's Hell State Park.

"How'd the kid sound?" Agent MacGregor asked.

"I only had about five minutes with him before the call dropped, but he was in good shape. Unfortunately, I'm not sure how long that'll last." Hatch gave his teammate and the group of deputies and searchers a detailed description of his phone conversation with Linc ending with, "Water's rising. So on this level, the victim could suffocate or drown."

Level Three. Less time and more obstacles. The bitch. The sick, twisted, sadistic bitch. Allegheny Blue licked her hand, and she dug her fingers into the soft folds of skin at his neck.

Within thirty minutes, Agent MacGregor had a massive search underway. Dogs, a helicopter, searchers in boats and on wheels. The sun had broken the horizon, and deep plum with streaks of peach stretched across the sky.

"I want you and Hatch on the Cypress Bend River." Jon tapped a map spread out on the hood of the SUV. "Go ahead and start here."

Grace reached for Hatch's hand, but he no longer stood at her side. She found him standing at the river's edge, a tall, dark silhouette with rumpled hair, a man who couldn't resist the siren's song of moving water. Even now when minutes were crucial, Hatch needed a moment to find the strength that enabled him to do what he did so well.

Behind her, cars continued to roll in. Boats roared down the river. In front of her, Hatch watched the water, but as she got closer, she noticed he was far from still. His hands fisted and unfisted. She placed her hand on his arm. "What is it?"

He slipped away from her touch and paced along the riverbank.

"Tell me what's wrong," she insisted.

"You want to know?" The question was raw and sharp. "You *really* want to know what's wrong?" He spun toward her, his face twisted. "I'm feeling relief, Grace, a feeling so strong, it's wrong."

"Alex," she said on a soft breath.

"Yeah. That could have been *my son* buried alive in a plastic tote. *My son* battling for breath. *My son* trying to keep his head above water." Hatch jammed both hands through his hair. "But it's not my son who's in danger, and that makes me so damned relieved and so damned happy I can't stand myself." He kicked at the bank, and a chunk of mud flew. An osprey shot from a nearby tree.

Grace settled a hand on his shoulder. "Stop."

"Stop what?"

"Stop being an FBI agent, and for a moment allow yourself to just be a dad. Do what you need to do here," she tapped his chest, not surprised at the thundering beat against her fingertips. "And when you get all the parenting stuff taken care of, then you can go here," she tapped his forehead.

Hatch closed his eyes and brought his fist to his chest. He tapped. Was he beating back feelings? Assuring himself his heart wasn't about to leap from his chest?

At last he grabbed her hand. "How do you know so much about kids?"

"I don't." She placed her hands on each cheek. "I know you." She brought his face down to hers and pressed her lips against his, just long enough to share a slow, steady breath.

"Okay," he said. "Time to find a pissed off and frightened thirteen-year-old boy." Half running, he pulled her to the parking lot, where the number of cars had tripled. Dozens, maybe a hundred, gathered around the picnic tables where Jon had set up the command post, and cars continued to trickle in.

Her feet dug into the earth, and she pulled her hand from Hatch's.

"What are you doing?" Hatch asked.

Winners do and doers win.

Shut up, Daddy. She held out her hand to Hatch and wiggled her fingers. "Keys, please."

"Jon wants us on the river."

"I'm not going."

"This is Level Three, Grace, more challenging than the other two, and we both know how those levels played out."

"Linc is in grave danger, so you and everyone else need to get moving." The sun peeked over the horizon, and soon the town would be wide awake and getting on about their days. Oyster boats would head into the bay. Her coworkers would head to the courthouse. And a thirteen-year-old boy would ride his bike to the cemetery to do community service hours.

"Someone needs to be with Alex," she said. "Linc and Gabe may not be the best choice for friends, but they are your son's friends." She waved at the parking lot, which now included two television news crews. "Very soon Alex is going to find out about his friend, and when he does, someone needs to be there for him, someone besides a silent cemetery caretaker, his frazzled granny, and the twin terrors. This is your world, Hatch, your expertise. Linc needs you here. That leaves me to be with Alex."

Hatch slid a finger along her cheek, as if not quite sure

what he was touching. Then he settled his forehead against hers. "You, Grace Courtemanche, are beyond amazing."

"So I've been told." She stuck her hand in his shorts pocket and grabbed the keys. "Keep me posted, and you—" She waved a hand at Allegheny Blue, who'd been nervously pacing between the riverbank and busy parking lot. "Come on, you big lug. You're just going to get in everyone's way here."

CHAPTER THIRTY

Grace pulled up in front of Alex's house just as he was taking his bike out of the garage.

"Hey there, Grace." He pedaled to the passenger side of the SUV and scrubbed Allegheny Blue's floppy ears.

The muscle in the center of her chest lurched. He looked so happy, so normal, and she was going to crush it. "Hey, Alex."

"Guess what Black Jack's gonna have me do today? I'm going to build a bridge. A real bridge. There's this creek that runs across the southern part of the cemetery, and there's this old lady named Mrs. Rubidoux who's been visiting her husband's grave every week for the past twenty years. I guess she busted a hip or something and is having a hard time with the long walk through the cemetery, so Black Jack got this idea about building a bridge over the creek near her husband's grave so she doesn't have to walk so far. And he's going to let me do it. Nothing fancy. Just some boards and blocks, but I think I can do it."

"I'm sure you can, Alex," she assured him because the boy was like his father. Hatch was a master bridge builder, and she prayed he got enough information so someone could reach Linc before the water rose or the boy ran out of air and fight.

"Mrs. Rubidoux isn't due to visit until Monday, so I have five days to work on it. I should be able to do it in five days." A rosy pink that made him look even younger flushed the boy's cheeks. "Don't you think?"

Five days to build one bridge. Five minutes to build another. "I'm sure you can make it work."

"Hey, is something wrong? You don't look too good this morning. It's not Blue, is it?"

At the sound of his name, an extra long line of drool slid from the old dog's mouth.

"Blue's fine," she said, struggling to find the words.

"Is something wrong with Hatch?" Alex stopped scrubbing Blue's neck. "He bailed, didn't he?"

For someone called the Blond Bulldozer, she was stalling and sputtering. She straightened the pearls at her neck. "Hatch is fine, and he's still in town. Alex, late last night Linc and Gabe were downtown after midnight behind the grocery store and—"

"I wasn't there. I swear."

"I know."

"Idiots. I told them the locks on that grocery store couldn't be picked. The sheriff's guys busted 'em. Serves 'em right."

"No, Alex, the sheriff didn't find them. Someone else did. The person who buried those girls in the swamp took Linc."

Every bit of pink slid from Alex's cheeks.

"Don't worry. Linc is fine. Your dad talked to him just an hour ago, and he's alive and mouthing off about Gabe. And more important, hundreds of people are in the swamp looking for him."

Alex's chin quivered. "Linc's in one of them boxes? He's underground?"

She reached across the SUV and put her hand on his. "But he's going to be fine. He's a smart kid. He was able to give Hatch some useful information."

Alex fidgeted with the hand brake on his bike. "And Hatch, he's out there looking for Linc?"

A knot formed in Grace's throat. "Yes, Alex, Hatch is searching for your friend."

"Good. Hatch is a hot-shot FBI agent. He knows how to take care of stuff like this." Alex dug his hands into Blue's sagging neck and scrubbed. "Okay. Linc's going to be okay."

Alex was trying so hard to man-up, to keep it together. "I'm sure Black Jack and your granny will understand if you don't want to go in to work today."

Alex continued to stroke the underside of Blue's chin. "No. I need to go in to work. I uh...I need to build the bridge for Mrs. Rubidoux, make it easier for her to visit her husband. I promised Black Jack."

Grace understood. The boy needed to keep busy. "Put your bike in the garage and get in. I'll drive you to the cemetery." She tugged at Blue's collar and guided him into the backseat. "And believe it or not, I'm actually pretty good with a hammer. Kind of have to be when you have a car like mine. How about some help building that bridge?"

* * *

Tucker Holt liked this little town. Cypress Bend would be a great place to vacation with kids. Plenty of boat rentals, white sand beaches, bike trails, cheap places to eat, and even some nice-looking campgrounds. The one outside of town called Tate's Hell was hopping. Jackson and Hannah would love this place. He and Jackson could cast their lines on one of the rivers while Hannah built fairy houses out of daisies, bark, and grass. Maybe once Tucker got this double homicide in the bag, he'd bring the kids here for a little R&R. They hadn't vacationed much the past few years, not since he'd made detective.

Too many bodies, too much death.

He rolled down the window of his rental car as he continued along the highway. Even away from the holler, the stink of asswipes and the poison they left behind clogged his nostrils.

When Tucker pulled his rental car into the Franklin County Sheriff's station, he had his pick of parking spaces. Not a single car in the lot. Inside he discovered the lobby equally empty. And that's when he caught the first stench of asswipe.

He pushed the buzzer at the front desk. A door at the far right swung open, and a woman with lots of red lipstick poked her head through the doorway. "Be with you in a minute, sir," she said.

"No hurry." His flight to Kentucky didn't leave until three this afternoon. He had plenty of time to check out Oliver and Emmaline Lassen's new winter home and get home well before Hannah's ballet recital tonight.

When the woman came back, she gave him a frazzled smile, and he gave her his card.

"Sorry 'bout the wait, Detective Holt. We have a missing thirteen-year-old boy. Horrible situation. The Gravedigger's third victim." She showed him a photo of a boy with a cheesy smile, chipped front tooth, cowlick, and freckles. Looked like a little hell raiser. He frowned. Who was now in hell.

Tucker had heard about the Gravedigger on the news. He shuddered. That was one fucked-up asswipe.

"I'm investigating the deaths of a retired couple who have a winter home here," Tucker said. "Oliver and Emmaline Lassen of"—he checked his notepad—"Gator Slide."

"Names don't ring a bell, but I can have someone give you a call as soon as we get a deputy freed up, because unless your homicides have any connection to the Gravedigger and this missing boy, I'm afraid you're on your own for a while."

"Related to the Gravedigger? I seriously doubt that." The Lassens hadn't been buried alive, but dumped after being shot dead. The only reason he'd taken this detour was that nagging at his gut. "I'm going to head on over to the couple's new place and poke around a bit."

Once outside he thought about that missing boy's face, about his freckles so much like Jackson's and his chipped front tooth like little Hannah's. Tucker couldn't imagine what that boy's parents must be going through, but he had a damned good idea what the lead enforcement officer and the search team were going through—the toxic fires of hell.

Mara had often called his work toxic. *"It's poisoning you and our marriage,"* she had said the day she moved out. *"No more, Tuck. I'm not going to let the poison destroy me and the kids."*

And so Mara had moved out and moved on because of the poison, poison he felt in his nostrils, his throat, and his cottony mouth. It stung and burned his eyeballs. He ran the back of his hand over his eyes. Liquid glistened on his skin.

His knees buckled, and for a moment the earth shifted. He sunk to the top step, his ass hitting the pavement.

Mara was right. This job was toxic, killing him from the inside out because he lived it, breathed it. The poison ran through his blood, filled every inch of his skull. Sometimes he couldn't see anything but the job.

Again he pictured that missing thirteen-year-old with the freckles. In a few years, that could be Jackson, trapped, struggling to breathe, dying. His gut jackknifed. And where would Tuck be? On a case. Catching killers. Breathing poison.

He'd missed so much of Jackson and Hannah's short lives. An asswipe or accident or illness could take them away today. No more bumblebee ballet recitals. No more fishing trips.

He should have gotten out long ago, about the time he started to reach every night for a pint of Wild Turkey. Alcohol disinfected. It killed. Every night for the past two years he'd been trying to kill the poison taking over his body.

Made sense. He smacked his open palms against the sides of his head. So. Much. Fucking. Sense. *Smack. Smack. Smack. Smack.* Anyone passing must think him a lunatic or a drunk. But for the first time in years, his brain was crystal clear.

He needed to get rid of the poison. He needed to get out of police work.

Just yesterday that would have been unthinkable, but today and for every day and month and year ahead, it was the right thing. He hopped up from the steps.

This wasn't the end for him. Sure, it was an end to this chapter, but there were a whole lot more chapters ahead, chapters filled with Jackson and little Hannah and fishing. Lots of fishing.

As for work, there was plenty he could do. Private security work. A desk job with the state. Or maybe he'd teach. He spent a lot of time with the greenhorns. He loved teaching kids like Carl at the station, helping them ease from the classroom to the real world. Tuck had a BA in history. He could teach history, maybe even coach baseball. Teachers made shit for money, less than cops, but he didn't need much, just enough to pay rent on his trailer space and maybe buy a boat, something big enough for him and the kids. And if he took on a few side security jobs, once in a while he and Jackson and Hannah could vacation in a place like this.

Tucker Holt needed to get out of police work, but before did, he was going to find one final asswipe.

*　*　*

Jon MacGregor had a name for creatures who abducted children.

Worms. Mud-sucking lowlifes that didn't know their heads from their assholes.

And he had a place where he envisioned this most heinous of all criminals.

Hell. A place of fire and molten rock. A place where slimy, wormy bodies would curl and crisp. Of course that was after he crushed them with the heel of his boot.

Jon stopped the boat and killed the engine. "Liiiiinc!"

He checked the radio at his waist. Also silent. More than one hundred searchers had been canvassing the area for more than three hours.

Every minute, the same thing.

Nothing.

Hatch had called him Agent Optimist. Yeah, Jon had hope because worms who abducted children always left trails, and Jon wouldn't stop until he found the slime.

*　*　*

Hayden Reed crossed his arms and leveled a razor-sharp stare at Glenna Wheeler. He'd spent all night tracking down the real estate agent who'd brokered the land deal for the Giroux property. Turned out she had spent the night at Alligator Point visiting a "gentleman friend." He found her this morning when she arrived at her office. When he asked for information on the bidder who'd lost out to Grace, she refused to tell him, claiming she'd signed a confidentiality agreement.

She wrapped the cord of her office phone around her finger. "Please stop looking at me like that, Agent Reed."

"Like what?"

"Like you can see right through me." The phone cord was so tight, Glenna's finger turned a bright red.

"I see a woman who desperately wants to help Linc Henderson."

Glenna repositioned the picture frames on the credenza behind her and rearranged the bouquet of irises on the corner of her desk. "I can't give you the name. I'm bound by law to not disclose any information. You understand, don't you?"

"No, I don't understand, Glenna, nor does the thirteen-year-old boy who's been buried alive."

"Stop saying that!" She stared at the phone. "When is that damned judge going to get back with us on the court order?"

"Hopefully before the boy who's been buried alive runs out of air."

Glenna drummed her fingers on the desk, her gaze glued to the multi-line phone on her desk, every light dark. "I could lose my job over something like this."

Hayden laced his fingers, settling them on his tie.

She turned to him. "She got a kid this time?"

"His name is Linc. He plays shortstop for his summer ball

team. Has a chocolate lab named Maurie." He could see it. She was close.

Her hands slapped the desk. "Ring, dammit!"

Hayden continued to stare at her.

With a growl she finally booted up her computer. "I'm getting you the name." Her fingers flew over the computer keys. "I'd rather go to jail than hell."

* * *

Once upon a time Hatch had loved water. He'd loved sailing across the ocean, fishing in the bay, and swimming naked in a secluded cove with Grace. But now, as he pictured water seeping into the plastic tote that held a thirteen-year-old boy, he despised it.

He despised most of mankind, including himself. When he'd learned Alex, Linc, and Gabe had broken into the shrimp shack, he should have dragged all three of them into the sheriff's office and demanded they be locked up until they passed puberty.

Then Linc would be safe.

And Grace...

He pictured the drawing of the stick figure in pearls with the crossed out eyes. Grace was a few breaths from being the Gravedigger's next target.

"Liiiiinc!" Hatch continued to boat along the Cypress Bend River, and he got the same response as every other shout in the past three hours. Silence.

CHAPTER THIRTY-ONE

Alex worked for two full hours, clearing shrubs and weeds from both sides of the creek where he would build Mrs. Rubidoux's bridge, before the first tear fell.

Grace, who'd been at his side hauling the debris to a flatbed trailer, took off her gloves and took the boy in her arms. The thirteen-year-old, who didn't need anyone and hated most of the world, pressed his sweaty, dirty face into her shirt as loud, hiccupy sobs fell from his mouth. Her body automatically curled around his, and they swayed, a soothing, rocking motion with the creek bubbling softly around them.

Too soon Alex pulled away, leaving her arms painfully empty. He swiped a dirty arm across his nose. "I'm sorry. Man, I'm such a wuss."

"No, Alex, you're a friend, someone worried about a buddy in a bad situation."

"Hatch wouldn't be caught dead crying like a baby, nor would anyone on his team. It's me who's the loser."

"Stop."

"Stop what?"

"Beating up yourself. It's not going to help Linc."

"You think maybe we can go out and look for him?"

Grace normally had a hard time letting others do the work, but joining the searchers in Tate's Hell would be foolish. She was the Gravedigger's ultimate victim, and she refused to be an easy target. "I think we should check on Allegheny Blue. He didn't look too happy when we left him at the shack. Why don't we knock off for the day?"

Alex's fingers tightened around the shovel handle. "Can't. I promised Black Jack I'd get all the ground prepped today for Mrs. Rubidoux's bridge."

"I'm sure Black Jack will understand."

Alex drew a line in the oyster shell path with the tip of the shovel. "Yeah, Black Jack would. Okay, let me put this stuff away, and we'll go check on Blue."

Grace was glad to get out of the cemetery. Too many buried bodies.

Back at the shack, they found Blue on the front porch curled on his rag rug in a pool of sun. He greeted them with a single tail thump and rolled onto his back. Both she and Alex rubbed his belly.

Inside her shack, she set out a pitcher of sun tea to brew, cleaned and filled Blue's water and food bowls, and checked the mailbox, her phone, and both her personal and private e-mails.

"You're not good at being still, are you?" Alex asked.

"No, but I'm working on it."

He aimed his chin at the kitchen window and the creek beyond. "We could take the boat out."

"After we find Linc." She had supreme confidence in the team she'd assembled, particularly in the man at the helm.

Alex took a deep breath and nodded. "Yeah, after we find Linc."

She dug into the mail that had been accumulating over the week. Her fingers slid over the invitation from the older couple who'd bought her dad's old place, Emmaline and Oliver Lassen. The new owners had found some things that had belonged to her dad, and they'd given her an open invitation to stop by for tea any time this week. "You're right. I suck at doing nothing. Let's go."

"Are we going to look for Linc?"

"Nope. We're going to a tea party." She tucked the invitation from the Lassens in her purse.

Alex's lip curled in one of those half snarls teens had perfected over the centuries. "You're kidding, right?"

"No. But the cool factor is there will be gators. We're going to my old home, a place called Gator Slide."

The snarl disappeared. "Cool."

Blue followed them to the SUV, his tail wagging.

* * *

Grace pulled into the circular drive of the two-story Victorian with mint-green trim and a giant oak with a tire swing.

Alex craned his neck out the window. "I don't see no gators."

"They're usually out back in the grassy area between the house and the river," Grace explained. "You'll see at least a dozen glide marks where the alligators get in and out of the river. That's how it got the name Gator Slide. I remember looking out my bedroom window one time and seeing four gators lounging in the sun on the tennis court. Another time, someone left the garage door open, and when I went to get my bike to ride to school, I found an alligator cozied up next to the dryer."

"Cool." Alex nodded his head. "Nice house, too. All big and fancy. You grew up here?"

"Yep." She'd spent the first eighteen years of her life in this house. When her father died five years ago, she'd thought about selling, but every time she picked up the phone and dialed the real estate agent's number, she couldn't push the send button. Only when she'd set her sights on the Giroux place could she part with Gator Slide, and even then, it had been hard. On the day she'd removed every last item from this house, including a box of forgotten Christmas ornaments in the attic, she'd had a good cry. With everything packed up, carted off, and cleaned-up, Gator Slide now should only hold memories, which was why she was so surprised to get Emmaline Lassen's note about the personal items left behind.

Grace got out of the SUV with Alex. Blue raised his knobby head, looked out the rear window, and went back to sleep. Tired old guy. She scrubbed his head.

She rang the bell while Alex walked along the wraparound porch. "Hey, there's a boat and dock out back." When he walked back he mumbled something about everyone in the world but him having a boat. At a time like this, Grace would take brooding Alex over Alex terrified for his friend. She rang the bell again.

"Maybe they're not home," Alex said. "Can we still look for gators?"

This time she knocked and peeked through a crack in the curtains on the long, narrow windows on either side of the door. Every shutter and curtain in the house must be closed because all she saw was black. She cupped her hands to the sides of her head and squinted. Through the gloom she could make out dozens of boxes and mounds draped in sheets.

"Looks like their stuff arrived," she said. "Let's take a quick peek out back."

When the Lassens first saw the property, they'd fallen in love with the backyard and its river view, tennis court, boat dock, and gardens. Grace was surprised to see knee-high grass and weeds poking up along the walkways. On the day the sale closed, Oliver had visited the home improvement store and brought home a riding lawn mower while Emmaline carted home not one but four different bird feeders. They'd looked so cute, so excited. Grace had known her family's home would be in good hands.

"Now that's the kind of boat I want," Alex said. "Not too big, nothing fancy."

A warm wave of nostalgia washed over Grace. Since her father's death five years ago, the fourteen-foot aluminum skiff had been stored in the garage. She'd planned to keep the boat and get a new motor because the old one was shot. But when the Lassens offered to throw in a few extra thousand for the skiff, she'd jumped on the cash. She was glad to see them using it now.

She watched as Alex bounded down the sloping yard to the river. Although the Lassens weren't home, she'd give him this carefree time. She rolled her head in circles around her neck. She, too, needed a little carefree time. After they found Linc, she'd take a real vacation. She leaned against the porch railing. Maybe she and Hatch would hop aboard *No Regrets* and sail to wherever the winds would take them.

Behind her, the door creaked open, and she jumped.

"Uh, can I help you with something?" A single eye half covered with a sleep mask peeked through a crack in the door.

"Good morning," Grace said. "I'm here to see Emmaline Lassen."

The single eye squinted. "And you're..."

"Grace Courtemanche, the former owner of Gator Slide. Mrs. Lassen sent me an invitation to stop by any morning this week. She said she found some things that belonged to my father."

The door inched wider, and Grace made out short blond hair with a sea of frothy curls. The girl was tiny—probably a teenager—and wore a baggy nightshirt with a drawing of a mosquito and the words *Minnesota's State Bird*.

"If this is a bad time, I can come back later," Grace said.

The girl slapped the sides of her cheeks, as if trying to wake herself up. "No, no, don't go. I'll get the stuff for you. Let me get dressed." She took off through the darkened kitchen and up the stairs.

Grace called to Alex, who ran up from the river. "I spotted two gators, including a sixteen-footer. I can't wait to tell Gabe and Linc..." His grin fell away.

She squeezed his shoulder. "You will, Alex, because Linc's going to be okay." She pointed to his shoes, covered in the red, loamy earth found along this part of the river. "Wipe your feet."

After they entered the house, she shut the door, a shadow falling over the kitchen.

"Wow, this place is big," Alex said as he slipped through the shadows, poking his nose into the dining room, library, and living room. "I bet you didn't have to share a bedroom."

"Nope. Just me." Must be tough, a thirteen-year-old boy sharing a room with the rambunctious twins. Hatch loved his son and was clearly dedicated to his well-being. Grace wouldn't be surprised if he helped Alex's granny into a big-

ger place. Grace slid her hand along a stack of boxes in the
kitchen. And maybe he'd stick around longer.

"Hey, Grace, this way," a voice called from just beyond
the kitchen.

Grace jumped. The girl had been so quiet, Grace hadn't
heard her come down the stairs. With Alex in tow, she
picked her way through the dark kitchen and laundry room,
weaving around packing boxes.

"Oomph!" Alex cried behind her.

Grace spun, her arms searching the shadows for the boy.
"Are you okay?"

"Yeah. I bumped into a stupid wall."

"Sorry," the girl said from down the hall. "I had the electric company turn on the power a few days ago, but there's
something wonky with a few of the circuit breakers."

"Who are you?" Grace asked.

A door squeaked, and a murky wedge of light slipped
into the hall from the garage. "JoBeth Lassen. Oliver and
Emmaline are my grandparents. I came down to help them
unpack."

Grace reached the garage, which was stuffed with more
boxes, lawn furniture, and in the far bay a long vehicle.
Someone had taped blackout paper over the narrow windows
at the top of the three garage doors. The paper sagged on the
nearest window, a sliver of light cutting through the sea of
black. The girl, who now wore skinny jeans with her mosquito T-shirt, climbed over a low stack of boxes near the
door.

"Where are your grandparents?" Grace asked.

"Still in Minnesota. Grandpa took a fall. The doctors
wanted him to rest for a few days. They should be here this
weekend." The girl climbed over two lawn chairs and up to
another stack of boxes.

"I can come back then."

"No, it's okay." Fast and agile, she hopped off the boxes. "I know where the stuff is. Grandma put it in the basement."

"Basement? This house doesn't have a basement."

"Sure it does. It's below the garage."

The girl was obviously still half asleep. Grace had lived here her whole life and never went into any basement. The only storage area in the garage was the massive wall of cabinets where her father kept his fishing gear. "There is nothing below the garage. Absolutely nothing."

The girl stopped in front of the wall of cabinets and spun toward Grace, her chin lifted. "You're wrong. Absolutely wrong."

Grace edged closer to Alex. This conversation in the dark about basements that didn't exist was strange. And the girl—there was something not only strange, but familiar, about her. Alex took off and climbed over the boxes and lawn chairs. On the second stack of boxes, he slipped and fell to the ground. "Ow!"

This was ridiculous. He could get hurt. Grace ran her fingers along the wall until she found the light switch. She flicked, but the shop lights on the ceiling didn't flicker.

"I told you, the breakers blew," JoBeth said, her words snappish.

"Where are my father's things?" Grace wasn't in any mood to deal with temperamental teen theatrics.

"I told you, they're in the basement."

Grace rubbed at the center of her forehead. "I'll come back when your grandparents are here."

"Or you can get the things yourself. You're so good at that, aren't you?" The words came out with a hard, staccato edge.

"We're leaving, Alex," Grace said.

Alex picked himself off the ground but stopped as JoBeth

opened one of the cabinet doors, a tall shallow space that for decades had held her father's fishing poles. Grace had cleaned out that cabinet six months ago and had given her dad's fishing gear to the senior center over in Apalach.

"Now, Alex," Grace said.

She was halfway through the door when Alex mumbled, "Cool. A secret door."

"Alex, get back here and—" Grace turned. JoBeth had swung out the back panel of the cabinet, revealing a plain brown door. The girl took a key from her necklace, unlocked the door, and swung it inward into a wall of pitch black.

What the...

"There are two boxes, one with your dad's old trophies and the other with books, including a family album from a cruise you took to the Caribbean."

When Grace cleaned out the house, she'd searched for that album and sadly hadn't been able to find it. That album was special because it held the last photos ever taken of her mother who died three months later.

JoBeth reached into the maw of blackness. *Flick.* A soft yellow glowed far below. "Good, the basement breakers didn't trip." She motioned to Grace and Alex. "Boxes are on the counter."

"Wow, a secret room." Alex loped down the steps.

Grace hesitated at the top of the narrow stairwell. How could she have lived here all those years and not known this room existed? Rooms, she amended when she reached the bottom of the wooden steps. She stood in an oblong room with a sofa, TV, and computer desk at one end and a small kitchen on the other. Off one wall were two doors, one to a bathroom, the other to a bedroom just big enough to hold a queen-sized bed. On the counter were two boxes, one bursting with gold and bronze and wood trophies.

"I had no idea all of this was here," she said.

"I know." JoBeth's voice had lost all sleepy softness. "I'm so glad you finally get to see it, Gracie."

Grace turned and stared up the stairwell. JoBeth stood in the middle of the shadowy stairway, but Grace could clearly see the gun in her hand.

CHAPTER THIRTY-TWO

Near Genesee, Colorado

Deputy Danny Arredondo banged on the door for the fourth time. No one home. He brushed his fingers along the gooseflesh at the back of his neck. Then why did it feel like someone was watching him? He checked over his shoulder. Up here so high in the clouds, it was probably a whitetail deer or mountain lion. He turned to his cruiser and skidded to a halt. Or maybe it was the camera perched under the eve. On boots coated in mountain grit, he spun slowly. Or the camera near the garage. Or the camera tucked into a potted pine near the front door.

Some strange people lived up here on the mountain. He knocked for the fifth time. Unfortunately, the one he needed to chat with didn't seem to be home, or if she was home, she was hiding behind a camera. Hayden Reed, the special agent with the FBI's Special Criminal Investigative Unit, would be interested to know that. Agent Reed had called the Jefferson County Sheriff's Department a half hour ago wanting information on this woman ASAP. Something to do with the Gravedigger murders in Florida.

Danny maneuvered his car down one switchback and pulled into the driveway of an A-frame with a four-foot elk rack above the door. "Morning, sir," he said to the man working in a garden on the side of the house. "I'm with the sheriff's department and I'd like to talk to you about your neighbor."

"Neighbor?"

He checked the name he got from Special Agent Hayden Reed. "JoBeth Poole."

"JoBeth Poole? Don't have many neighbors up here a mile and a half in the sky, but I'm sure I don't have one by that name."

"She'd be the woman in the house just above you on the last switchback."

"Okay, sure. Dark-haired gal with the big pickup truck. I know who you're talking about. Don't see her much. She's kind of a hermit."

"But you've seen her?"

"Few times."

The deputy took out the sketch Agent Reed had sent him. "This her?"

"Yep. Dead ringer. Has those great big deer eyes."

"Have you seen her recently?"

"No, not for quite a few weeks, but that's not unusual."

"You said she drives a pickup? What color?"

"White, I think. Deputy, is my neighbor in some kind of danger or something?"

"No, but she may be a danger to others."

* * *

Grace slid across the room until she stood squarely between Alex and JoBeth Lassen. "Who are you, and what do you want?"

"Hmmm...that's two questions. Which one would you like me to answer first? Maybe we should play a game of eenie-meenie-minie-mo."

"What the—" Alex started, but Grace shushed him by holding up the palm of her hand.

The girl's bare feet shuffled down the steps, the glint of the gun brightening as it drew closer. Grace, with Alex at her back, inched toward the kitchen table.

The soft light crawled up the woman's legs, her waist, her neck, and for the first time, shadows did not bathe JoBeth's face. She was not a teenager but quite a few years older, closer to Grace's age than Alex's. She appeared young because she was short and lean. Not skinny. That would denote frailness. There was nothing frail or weak about this woman.

Grace's feet turned to ice. "Camellia," Grace said, her voice a strangled whisper. "I mean CoraBeth. I mean..."

"You're zero for two, Gracie. Not impressive. You're racking up your share of losses these days. My name's JoBeth. CoraBeth would be my..." She spun her hand in a circle, motioning for Grace to go on.

"Your mother."

JoBeth clapped, her eyes oddly bright. "Good girl. You finally got something right. I was starting to worry about you."

Alex reached for her hand, twining his shaking fingers with hers. "Whatever this is," Grace said, "it's between you and me. Let the boy go."

JoBeth laughed. Her body convulsed, the gun barrel

bouncing. "Oh, God, you sound so bossy, just like an older sister should."

"Sister?"

"You seriously have no idea who I am?"

"Let the boy go, please."

"He never mentioned me? Never showed you my picture or told you about my dreams and accomplishments?" Wistfulness, raw and real, tumbled out with her breathy words.

"Who are you talking about?"

"Henri Courtemanche, our father."

"I don't know what kind of sick game you're playing, but—"

"Oh, this is not a game. It's very, very real."

"What are you talking about?"

JoBeth let out a dreamy sigh. "You know, I used to dream about you and me talking. Long, sisterly chats where we bared souls to each other in the middle of the night. Excited talks before the first day of school. Nervous talks about boys and exams. Hopeful talks about our dreams and futures."

The kitchen chair was within arm's reach. One step and Grace would be at the counter where the box of trophies sat, including a marble football mounted on a square of wood. The chair or the trophy could serve as a weapon, knocking this crazy woman out or down long enough to grab Alex and push him up the stairs.

Tapping the tip of the gun against her chin, JoBeth nodded. "Okay, I'm game, Sister. Let's talk." Her hand rock steady, she pointed the gun at the kitchen chair. "Sit."

The issue was the shape of the room. No more than ten feet wide, it would be hard to shove past that gun. A person from the outside, someone coming down the darkened steps, could easily take out JoBeth. She'd texted Hatch that she was visiting the Lassens' house, but he and most of the town were hunting for Linc, and he had no idea she'd landed herself and his son in the killer's hands. And Blue, her trusty companion, was outside, lounging in the sun. It was her and Alex and a crazy woman who claimed to be her sister.

Grace slid her hands, damp with sweat, down the front of her pants. "I'll sit if you let the boy go."

"You're not in a position to strike a deal, counselor. Now do as I say and sit." She turned the gun on Alex. "Or Sunshine Boy gets his light put out."

Grace pulled in a quick breath, but the room had no oxygen. Slammed with a wave of dizziness, Grace shoved Alex behind her then perched herself on the edge of the chair.

JoBeth's face twisted in a warped smile.

"Who are you?" Grace asked.

"I told you, Gracie. Weren't you listening? I'm your sister." Her hair stuck out in a wild halo of blond, brassy curls, the kind that come from a box. She had big brown eyes and full lips. But she also had Henri Courtemanche's angular cheekbones and strong chin, features Grace herself had. Was that why Berkley's sketch looked so familiar? Because pieces of that face stared back at Grace every morning in the mirror?

"My mother was our father's dirty little secret, a girl from the swamp with passions but no purse, not like your blue blood mother. But you know Daddy dearest. He thought he could have it all. Two women to love, and eventually two daughters. I was born in this room and lived for fifteen years beneath your feet."

A shudder grabbed Grace's spine. "No. That's not possible. I would have known. My mother would have..."

The bad guys are on the streets, in our neighborhood, beneath our home. They're watching me, following me, touch-

ing me while I sleep. Make them go away, Gracie, please, please make them go away. Momma.

Grace grabbed both sides of the chair to keep from spinning as the room careened.

"Your mother wasn't the crazy one, was she?"

"No. Yes. I..." Grace's stomach flip-flopped and something chunky and vile churned in her gut.

"At a loss for words? Usually you're so much more articulate and poised and in control. The Golden Child." JoBeth sat on the arm of the sofa but kept the gun trained on Alex. "For the longest time, I wanted to be you. I wanted your shiny gold tennis trophies and closet full of princess dresses and sparkly shoes. When you and your mom were away at tennis tournaments he would let us out. My mom would sleep in your mom's bed. Once I even found her using your mom's toothbrush. Kind of sick, huh? As for me, I used to go into your bedroom and try on your clothes. The pretty church dresses, the snappy little tennis outfits, the silky princess nightgowns. My favorite was the blue one with the ivory lace. Sorry about the tear in the hem. You were always so much taller than me. Three cheers for sunshine and better nutrition." The half-smile twisting her lips was anything but apologetic.

"I wanted your trips to summer camp and weekly tennis lessons," JoBeth continued with words that sickened. "I wanted best friends like Gina and Nanette, who would make me beaded BFF friendship bracelets. But I could never be you, Gracie. *Daddy* only had one favorite child. So I spent almost every minute of every hour of fifteen years in a hole in the ground being me. A skinny girl who played with computers and rarely saw the sun because I was only allowed out at night."

Grace pressed her palms into the plastic chair as the

world continued to spin. Was JoBeth telling the truth? Had her father, the man who taught her about strength and power, perpetrated this heinous crime? "What kind of mother would allow that?"

"A mother who was desperately in love with a charming, powerful man who promised her the sky." She momentarily jabbed the gun at the ceiling before settling it back on Alex. "He kept telling my mom that she was the love of his life but that your mother was too sick and fragile for him to leave. Load of bullshit, huh? Your mom was actually quite strong. My mom spent years chipping away at her, taking hair barrettes and the last piece of lemon meringue pie. My mom was the queen of patience and hope, giving her power to a man who promised her heaven but kept her buried in hell."

"And you?" Grace asked around the horror clawing up her throat. "While your mom waited, what did you do?"

"Lived my version of a normal life. Played games, watched TV, drew pictures. He brought down books, and mom did her best to teach me. Did I mention mom never went to school and really didn't like her home-school lessons? After I learned to read, he bought me a computer, and that small box with all those pixels became my world. Which was good, because a year or so later, Mom had the baby and kind of lost it."

Grace pictured those tiny bones on the M.E's table. "The infant buried with your mother."

"Mom let me name her, and I called her Skye. She lived for two hours. That's when mom asked me to break her neck." JoBeth jabbed a finger into a tiny hole on the sofa, but the gun never moved from Alex. "Let me tell you something about living underground. There's this thing called absolute darkness. You lose all perception of direction and space. Underground you also have absolute silence. No birds, no cars, not even the whisper of wind. Imagine the noise when I snapped Skye's neck. It echoed through my head for years." JoBeth's wild hair jerked as she shook her head. "Our loving father wasn't due to visit for another three days, so when Skye started to stink, I put her in the refrigerator."

Alex swayed, and Grace swallowed the vile chunkiness edging up her throat. This was sick and wrong, and the man she called her father was a part of it. She must have made noise because Alex pressed his hip against her arm.

"Honestly, having me kill Skye was one of my mother's saner moves. In some part of her brain, she realized that this"—she swept her gun-less hand in an arc about the room—"was wrong. She didn't want another daughter to grow up without ever seeing the sun. But do you know the sick part?" JoBeth inched closer, like she had a secret. "Little Skye's dead eyes got to see the sun because Daddy didn't bury her deep enough in your backyard with all your mother's pretty flowers. A dog got to her, but lucky for Skye, he let me out that night, and I found her. Well, everything but her right arm. And when I reburied my baby sister, I did it right. I dug deep."

"But when your mother died, you dug up baby Skye."

"It seemed right, keeping my family together."

Grace shook her head, trying to get her mind wrapped around what was coming out of this woman's mouth. "I can't imagine what you went through."

"Oh, I could tell you more stories, tales of what it was like to live just inches from people who will never see you, never hear you, never reach into the ground and pull you from a living hell. Of course, at the time I didn't realize it was hell, because that was my normal. Do you hear me, Grace? Hell. Was. My. Normal." The words were rough and sharp and old, like the pointed end of a rusty shovel.

Grace pressed her hands to her twisting stomach.

"I never thought to run away. Only when I got away from that basement and that man did I realize the wrong that had been done to me from the moment of my birth." Spit shot from JoBeth's lips at the last word. "And you're right, Gracie, you will never know what I went through, because you were born and raised in a world of the light and living. But thanks to our little game, you got to hear and feel a tiny bit of the terror of being buried alive."

A sob caught in Grace's throat. "Lia. Janis. Linc. How? Why?"

"Took months of planning and careful execution, but yeah, I did it all. For years I dreamed of putting Daddy Dear in a box in the ground. In my dreams I'd set up a little camera and microphone so I could watch him and hear him. But you know what's really sick, Sister Gracie? I never could go through with it. Talk about father issues, huh?"

"You started this, this game to get back at our father?"

"*I* didn't start this game!" She jumped from the sofa, the still air swishing as the gun drew closer to Alex. "You did. When you bought the Giroux land, *you* started it. I was content to live on my mountain a mile and a half in the sky. I was content to come back once a year and drop a handful of camellia blossoms on my mother and Skye's grave. I was happy, Grace, or at least as happy as a person like me could be. You were the one who wasn't happy. You were the one who changed things. I tried to buy the land, to keep my family from suffering further at the hands of the Courtemanche family, but you won." A trickle of liquid ran from her nose, and she swiped it with the back of her hand.

"You killed Lia Grant and Janis Jaffee!" Grace's horror gave way to fury.

"Pawns. They were pawns!"

Grace wanted to shake the crazy out of this woman. "They were young women who lived and breathed and dreamed. You took that away. You killed them."

"They were part of The Game."

"Murder isn't a game!"

"It's a game." JoBeth sniffed, but the mucous continued to drip from her nose. "It's all a game."

"You tortured two young women. They died brutal, painful deaths. A boy could be drowning as we speak."

"A game. It's a game! No one gets hurt in games."

Grace opened her mouth to argue but pictured Hatch. This wasn't about right or wrong. Judgment would come later in a court of law. It was about diffusing a crisis situation. She needed to listen, to hear JoBeth's story, and to commiserate with her. Then it would be time to help her find a way out of that misery. "Okay, you're right. No one gets hurt in games."

CHAPTER THIRTY-THREE

Tucker parked his rental car behind the sheriff's SUV in the circular drive at Gator Slide, the winter home of the late Oliver and Emmaline Lassen. As he got out of the car, he saw no signs of gators...or a killer. Who was he kidding? This trip to Cypress Bend was a longer shot than pie.

He wondered about the sheriff's SUV, though. Was a local already checking on the home in response to his visit to the station? Had there been some kind of disturbance? Must be important to take a man off the hunt for the little boy.

A blue speckled hound lounged in a wedge of sunlight in the SUV's backseat, his tail thumping at the sight of Tucker. He slipped a hand through the open window and scratched the dog's head. "What are you doing out here all by your lonesome?" The dog yawned and went back to sleep.

Gator Slide was a three-story house in the ritzy part of Cypress Bend, situated at the end of River Run Road and perched on the banks of the Cypress Bend River. The closest neighbor was a half block away. The grass needed a good mowing, and dead leaves and yellowed palmetto fronds gathered on the steps and in the corners of the porch. Every shutter in the house was drawn. He walked up the porch steps and peeked through the curtains flanking the glass panes on either side of the front door. Storage boxes and draped furniture. On the surface this appeared to be a house waiting for its new owners.

He knocked, noting two sets of footprints along the dusty wraparound porch. No answer.

Around back sloped a lawn leading to the river. A single gator bathed on a flattened patch of grass near the dock. Nice little boat at the dock. A fourteen-foot aluminum skiff with a shiny new electric motor. Would be the perfect size for him and the kids.

The footprints ended at the back door. Again he knocked. The gator lifted its head.

A three-car garage sat on the far side of the house. Windows all covered with paper.

He took out his phone and called the sheriff's department. "This is Tucker Holt of the Kentucky State Police. Did you dispatch an officer to 707 E. River Run Road?"

After a short pause, the woman said, "No. Is this an emergency, detective?"

"No, not yet. One of your department SUVs is in the drive, but I haven't found the responding officer."

She took the license plate number. "Let me pass this on to one of the lieutenant deputies, and he'll get back with you."

Tucker checked the clock on his phone. Hannah's dance recital was still hours away. He was in no hurry to leave, but he was itching to get in that house. He jammed his phone in his pocket and headed to the front door.

* * *

The doorbell rang, a faint chime that sent a rush of hope through Grace's chest.

"Someone's here," Alex said on a croak. "Maybe it's Hatch or one of his FBI pals."

Grace's arm tightened around Alex. JoBeth still had the gun aimed at the boy's head.

"Maybe not," JoBeth said. "I heard on the news they're still in Tate's Hell on Level Three." Keeping the gun aimed at Alex, she backed up the steps.

"Dad!" Alex screamed.

JoBeth clicked shut the door.

"Down here, Dad! We're down here! She's got a gun, and we're down here!"

Grace grabbed the boy and cupped her hand over his mouth.

JoBeth polished the gun's barrel with the hem of her T-Shirt. "You're wasting your breath, Sunshine Boy."

He broke free from Grace. "Daaaaad! Daaaaaaaaaad!"

Grace lunged across the tiny kitchen and knocked the box of trophies onto the floor, metal and wood and stone crashing. She grabbed the football trophy, the marble heavy and solid.

"And you, too, Big Sis."

Grace banged the marble against the wall. Alex continued to scream.

"You don't get it, do you?" JoBeth said. "Whoever that is can't hear you. No one can hear you." JoBeth tapped the gun's grip on the door, on the wall, and on the ceiling. "This place is soundproof. No one above heard the first time a gun went off down here. Want to test it a second time?" She aimed the gun at Alex.

The trophy crashed to the floor. Grace had to get that gun out of JoBeth's hand. "Gun? A gun went off down here?"

"Oooo, you want to chat some more, Sister Gracie? You want to hear about the gun? A gun went off down here once. Took just one bullet for my mother to blow her brains out." She swept her free hand to the tiny Formica table. "It happened here in our lovely, elegant dining room. Mom stood right where you're standing, Sunshine Boy." JoBeth walked to where Alex stood and raised the gun. "She held the gun to her head like this." The gun barrel settled on Alex's temple.

A whimper slipped from his lips.

Grace's palms grew slick and hot. Sweat broke out along her upper lip.

"Then Mom—poor, sick, crazy Mom—pulled the trigger and..." JoBeth paused while Grace dropped her shoulder. "Boom," JoBeth whispered then took a step back and smiled.

Alex sunk onto one of the chairs, his shoulders heaving in a silent sob. Grace threw herself between him and her half-sister.

JoBeth waved her free hand in an arc. "Bits of her brain flew there, and there, and even way over there. Did you know brains look like clear Jell-O with worms? I know because I stared at them for nine days as I screamed my lungs out, trying to get someone down here. I banged on the door and even took a knife and tried to dig my way out. Couldn't get through all that concrete and metal. But no one came. Unfortunately, I couldn't fit mom in the refrigerator. Do you know what a dead body looks like after nine days, what it feels like, what it *smells* like? I do, and so does *Daddy*, because when he came down, he passed out. I loved seeing him prone and powerless. But just to make sure he stayed out long enough for me to grab Mom and Skye, I knocked him upside the head with one of his stupid trophies. Great minds think alike, huh, sis? Anyway, then I waltzed out with only the clothes on my back and a pocket full of money I'd stolen from Henri's wallet over the years."

JoBeth stared up the steps, tapping her leg. "You know, I need to go check on our visitor. He may have heard Sunshine Boy's first cry." She kneaded her stomach with a knotted fist. "I should have shut the door. I should have shot Sunshine Boy. See, Gracie, you're not the only one who's making dumb moves today." JoBeth bent to pick up the purse Grace had dropped on the floor when she'd lunged for the box, but she kept her eyes trained on them the entire time. "Wouldn't want to leave you with a phone."

* * *

Hatch hopped out of the boat and ran toward Hayden, who had just pulled into the parking lot at Tate's Hell State Park. Hatch desperately wanted to get his hands on thirteen-year-old Lincoln Henderson, but if he couldn't, his teammate Hayden was the next best thing. Hayden had finally tracked down Grace's real estate agent and got the name of the private bidder for the Giroux land. "What's her name? What the hell is her name?"

"JoBeth Poole," Hayden said. "I didn't find much on her, but she fits the profile. Lives on a mountain in the Colorado Rockies. No significant other. No kids. No apparent job. Five years ago she worked for a geek group in Denver. Appears to know her way around both computer software and hardware. Jefferson County sent a deputy to search for her. She and her white pickup truck are gone. Hasn't been seen for weeks."

Because the twisted woman had been too deep into the game. "Did you get anything? A cell phone we can trace or credit card statement showing a purchasing trail."

"Completely off-grid." A hint of a smile curved Hayden's mouth. "But her truck isn't."

Hatch snatched the piece of paper with the truck's license plate number. He'd done more with less, like donuts. If they found the truck, they'd most likely find JoBeth Poole, and if they found JoBeth Poole, he was going to get her to talk, and he wouldn't let her stop until she told him where she'd buried Linc.

* * *

Linc pinched the squishy, squirming body between his fingers and pulled the tick from his neck. Warm blood squirted across his hand, and he swished his fingers in the water.

The water, stinkin' and filled with ticks and slugs, had reached his neck. He'd torn apart his shirt, his pants, even rubber off the bottom of his tennis shoes, and tried to plug the holes. Wasn't working. Water came in faster now. He stretched his neck, his face scraping the top of the plastic box. He had four, maybe five inches of space left. Not sure what that meant in terms of hours. Or was he looking at minutes?

His chin shook. Tears, big sissy ones, rolled down his cheeks. "Don't be a wuss. Don't cry." He didn't need any more water in the stinkin' laundry tote.

* * *

Grace yanked open the kitchen drawer, her fingers flying across spoons, forks, a spatula, and an ice cream scoop. She slammed the drawer and threw open the next, where she found a pair of butter knives and one steak knife. She palmed the steak knife. When JoBeth returned, Grace would be armed. The issue was Alex. During their twisted version of sisterly bonding, JoBeth had the gun aimed exclusively at the boy.

"When she comes back, Alex, I want you to stay in the bedroom under the bed."

The boy poked through the drawer alongside her and pulled out one of the butter knives.

Her heart lurched as she watched a boy trying to be a man. "You'll do me more good if you hide," she added. "When she doesn't see you, she'll be surprised." And hopefully off her game.

He rummaged through the next two drawers until he found a paperclip and ball point pen. With the knife in his hand, Hatch's son ran up the stairs. He squatted in front of the door.

"Sweetie, I know you want to help, but she's going to see you. You're not going to do either of us any good up there."

"Shut up, Grace," Alex said with an exasperated puff. "I need it quiet so I can concentrate."

Hatch's wayward son, the boy who knew how to break into shrimp shacks and hair salons, stuck the paper clip between his lips and jammed the butter knife at the door handle.

Grace grabbed the lamp from the table next to the sofa and hurried to the foot of the stairs, giving the boy more light.

CHAPTER THIRTY-FOUR

JoBeth squinted down the hall, trying to see through the small windows on either side of the front door. The visitor on the front porch was still banging on the doorbell. She needed to shut him up before anyone else came to this hell house.

She didn't want to do this. She shouldn't *have* to do this. It was Grace's fault, making her talk and waste time. The stories and horrors of her childhood should stay buried. She mussed her hair and poked the gun into the back of her jeans. She cracked open the door and yawned.

"Detective Tucker Holt of the Kentucky State Police. I'm here about Oliver and Emmaline Lassen."

She pressed a fist into her stomach. How did this man find her? She'd planned carefully. No one had seen her dispose of the Lassens, and she had left nothing behind, not even footprints and tire tracks because of the dogs she'd lured to the area with a few meaty bones. The worms burrowed deeper into her gut, tiny toothy needles. "Uh, they're not here."

"And you are..."

"A friend. The Lassens invited me to stop by their new place. I'm in Florida on vacation this month."

"Where are you from?"

"Denver area."

"Where are the Lassens?"

"Haven't showed up yet. They're driving down from Minnesota. I'm expecting them any day."

He squinted at her. "What did you say your name was?"

She didn't. Damn. This wasn't part of The Game. She wasn't prepared for this. "JoBeth Poole. Is there something wrong with Oliver and Emmaline?"

"I'm afraid so, Ms. Poole, and I'd like to ask you a few more questions."

She needed to get this cop out of the way. But he was a cop who was bigger and stronger. Unfortunately for him, he couldn't turn himself invisible. "Uh...sure." Once he was inside the house, she could take him out of The Game and then disappear. She'd done it once already. But she wasn't good with people, not like Sister Grace. She fiddled with the chain at her neck. What would Grace do? "Uh, would you like some sweet tea?"

"The tea won't be necessary," the detective said. "But I'd appreciate it if you'd turn on some lights."

Most cops were stupid, but a few, like the Kentucky detective standing in the entryway and backlit by the vicious morning sun, had a few brain cells. Not as many as her. No, never as many as her. "Of course." She flicked the switch in the entryway, but the wall sconce didn't flare to life. "Breakers have been screwy for the past few days. Let me get the light in the living room near my computer. I know that one works."

"Is there anyone else in the house?"

"No." *Not* inside *the house. But you'd be shocked, Mr. Smarty-Pants Detective, to learn who is* under *the house.* If JoBeth took off now, Grace would die eventually, but... She fidgeted with the chain at her neck. But Grace wouldn't play out The Game *alone.* Sunshine Boy would be with her. Grace needed to be alone.

"There's a sheriff's department vehicle in the drive. Do you know where the driver of that vehicle is?"

"No. If he rang the bell, I didn't hear. I've been sleeping all morning." Quiet as a cat. Into the black. She slipped through the living room, her foot purposefully catching the card table leg. She went down. Her two computers went down.

Detective Holt took a single step into the entry way. "Ms. Poole?"

"Gah! I'm still half asleep. Can you get the light switch near the fireplace?"

He took another step, gun drawn. Smart cop. But not as smart as her. Hidden by the wonderful dark, she lifted her gun.

Boom.

Kentucky cop down. Too bad she didn't have a holler to roll him into.

* * *

"Was that a gunshot?" Alex asked as they tumbled through the cabinet and into the garage.

"Don't know. Don't care." Grace grabbed the boy and dragged him through the garage away from her half-sister and the gun she carried. Someone could be shot and bleeding to death. Hell, someone could be dead, but she needed to get Alex away from this place. She needed to get to Hatch. JoBeth knew where Linc was, and Hatch might be able to talk to her, to build a bridge and reach the boy before he drowned.

They reached the side door and Grace threw the deadbolt. She and Alex plunged into the brilliant light, their feet kicking up crushed shells on the circular driveway. The SUV sat twenty yards ahead. No purse. No keys. But they didn't need a vehicle. They needed a phone.

With Alex at her side, she raced down the drive. The Crismons lived a half block down the road. They rounded the SUV. Alex's foot slipped into a pothole, and he pitched forward. She lunged for him but he slammed into the ground, his ankle bending at an unnatural angle.

"Get up, Alex!" She reached for him and pulled him to his feet.

"Aaargh!" He pitched forward, and she caught him. Tucking her shoulder under his arm, she hurried him along the drive. They rounded the SUV and into the sight of JoBeth's gun.

Her wild eyes blinked rapidly, as if pained by the daylight. "You know, you're turning out to be a real pain in the ass, Sunshine Boy." She turned the gun on Alex, squinting. "Time for you to leave the Game."

Grace pushed Alex toward the road and lunged at JoBeth.

A giant mass of black and white knocked her to the ground, a rumbling bellow ripping the air. JoBeth spun toward Grace, her gun hand arcing.

"Nooooooo!" Grace screamed.

The gun fired and jerked. Allegheny Blue froze in midair, a line of drool streaked across the side of his face, his ears fanned out. His body lifted and thudded to the ground at JoBeth's feet.

JoBeth screamed and jumped back, her eyes wide with terror. "Get it away!"

Alex hauled himself upright but fell back to the ground, clutching his ankle.

"Get up!" Grace said with a hiss.

JoBeth didn't seem to notice. She scrambled back, her hands, including the one holding the gun, clawing the air. "Get the dog away!"

Grace crawled to the mound of black and white speckled fur. Blood poured from Allegheny Blue's chest, and his body heaved as he panted heavily. She dug her hands into the silken folds of his neck. His sandpapery tongue slipped across her arm as big, droopy eyes that had seen way too many doggie years settled on her. "My dog..."

His tail thumped. She dug her hands under his shoulders and was about to drag when the panting stopped. His eyelids fluttered and closed.

"Blue!" Her frantic fingers slid along his neck and to the barrel of his chest.

Still.

For a half-second, she stared at the blood on her hands. "My dog," she said in a choked whisper.

Out of the corner of her eye, she saw Alex drag himself to his hands and knees. He was heading east, straight into the rising sun. She wiped her hands on the great knobby head and jumped to her feet. With JoBeth frozen in terror and blinded by the sun, now was the time to grab Alex and run. She took two steps when a body slammed into her back. Hands landed on her pearl necklace and twisted. Pearls dug into her throat. Grace clawed at the strand, loosening the pressure and gasping for air.

Alex looked over his shoulder. "Grace?"

She opened her mouth, but couldn't scream. She punched the air. *Go! Go!*

Alex inched forward. "Aaargh!"

The pearls tightened. Grace swung an elbow, but JoBeth shifted. Dizziness grabbed her head, her chest, her feet. A gray haze slid over her vision, but not enough to block out Alex who was crawling away. The boy was a fighter. He would get away. She swayed on her feet. The gray haze thickened.

Next to her JoBeth raised an arm, something bright and shiny glinting in the sun. *Boom!* Alex jerked and fell face-first into the gravel drive.

"Goody. Bonus points for me. Now we can finish The Game, Sister Gracie. High score always wins."

* * *

The broadcast reporter brought the microphone to her mouth. "In the latest news on the search for the Gravedigger, authorities are looking for a white, late model Ford pickup with Colorado plates and the license number..."

Hatch turned away from the live broadcast airing from the Tate's Hell parking lot. So far that made three television stations and five radio stations that were running the appeal for the public's help in tracking down JoBeth Poole's truck.

Hatch wasn't a numbers guy. He didn't rely on them too much in his work, but two numbers were flying through his head: nine and six. Lia grant had lived nine hours in her box while Janis had lasted only six. Linc had just clocked in his fifth hour.

But Linc was a fighter. It came with being thirteen and thinking you ruled the world.

Hatch took out his phone. No new texts from Grace. Last he'd heard was that she and Alex were looking for gators and having tea with the folks who'd bought her dad's old place. He was grateful Grace was keeping Alex busy. That boy

idn't need to be getting deep into his head over this. Something like this—the terror and madness of burying someone
ive—could screw with a person's mind. After they found
inc, he and Alex were going to have a long talk—about his
iends, his free time, and the role Hatch would play in his
fe, because Hatch wasn't about to walk away from the boy
ow.

Nine hours. Six hours. So little time. He wanted forever.

And Grace. He wanted Grace. All these years he'd shied
way from family because he didn't want to die burdened
ith regrets. But Grace had called his team what they were,
s family. And she'd helped smooth the waters between him
nd Alex. He couldn't imagine forever without her.

His phone rang, and he cleared the thickness in his throat
efore speaking to Lieutenant Lang. "Hatcher here."

"Just got a possible hit on the white truck," she said. "A
ypress Bend resident, a man named Paul Crismon, said he
aw a muddy white truck twice in his neighborhood over the
ast week. Said he remembered it because the truck was so
irty. He couldn't verify the Colorado plates, though."

"Where's he live?"

"Off River Run Road."

"I know the area." Grace's family home had been on
iver Run, and it was possible she and Alex were there. He
ad no time to talk, but when this was over, he hoped Grace
ould listen to what he had to say. "I'll take this one. See if
can talk any more details out of the guy who saw the white
uck."

* * *

With Sunshine Boy ruining the basement lock, The Game
as once again changed," JoBeth announced as she dragged

Grace into the entryway of Gator Slide and slammed the front door, finally letting up on the pearl choker.

Grace gulped breath after breath, her raw throat convulsing. Oxygen flooded her lungs, her veins, her brain. She steadied her hand on a packing box in the entryway. The gray haze lifted.

Something cold and sharp settled between Grace's shoulder blades. JoBeth's gun. The one that had just shot Alex. A tremor rocked Grace's jaw. She shifted her head to look out the narrow windows framing both sides of the door. She couldn't see past the SUV. She pressed her palms, still wet with her dog's blood, into her thighs. Was the boy alive? JoBeth knew how to shoot, but she'd been struggling to see in the bright sunlight.

"Move to the middle of the living room." JoBeth jammed the gun into her flesh. "And don't mind the dead guy. He wanted to play, but I told him he couldn't."

Grace dropped her gaze to the floor, and a soft gasp tore up her throat. A dark-haired man in a sport coat and jeans was sprawled on the entryway floor. A gun holster peeked out from his jacket. Blood pooled beneath his upper body. His chest wasn't moving. Her heart dropped to her stomach. Dead. Like Lia and Janis and Allegheny Blue. And Alex?

"You see, the plan all along was to lock you in that tiny set of rooms under the garage and leave you to die. Alone, all alone. The water and air vent systems to the rooms are running, so I'm guessing you would have died of starvation. What do you think?"

Time was her ally. Maybe her neighbor Mr. Crismon had heard the shot. Maybe Hatch had called, and when she hadn't answered her phone, had decided to track her down. Maybe Alex was not severely injured and made it to a phone or passing car.

Her job was to keep JoBeth talking.

"Or maybe the air duct system would break down, and I'd die of carbon monoxide poisoning," Grace said.

"Ooh, that would be a good one, too."

"You're insane." Grace couldn't keep the words from stumbling out.

She grinned. "Like mother, like daughter."

Grace pictured her own mother—a strong woman at one time, a woman who'd seen what no one else had seen. Her father...Her insides twisted and knotted. She didn't even want to think about that man.

"Okay, so you're going to kill me. Are you going to shoot me?" Grace's fingers slid to her neck. "How about hanging me with my own pearls?"

"Ooh, I like that one. Your daddy told me he got you your first set of pearls on your thirteenth birthday. Do you know what he got me? Nothing. Yep, Daddy forgot about the dirty daughter buried in the cellar. At the time I didn't realize the total thoughtlessness, the cruelty of his action, but after I got out, I did." She slid her fingers along her neck. "So you know what I did after I got away and built a life for myself under the sun? I bought me my own necklace." She untucked the chain from the front of her shirt. On it hung the key she'd used on the basement door. "Great little reminder of where I came from and where I ended up. While I love the symbolism of you dying by pearls, I'm afraid I'll have to use my gun. Much more expedient. I'm thinking about shooting you in the stomach and maybe catching a little bit of bowel. I hear that's a nasty way to go."

Panic skirted down her spine. Grace raised her hands. This was it. Her last move. "Okay, JoBeth, you win."

"And?"

"I lose."

JoBeth clasped her hands to her chest and giggled. "I love the sound of those two words on your lips."

"I'd like you to promise me one thing. When you're done with me, please don't hurt Hatch and Alex."

"The Sunshine Boys? I have no bone to pick with them. Yes, Sister Gracie, after I pump a bullet into your gut so you can fester and decay, I'll leave. Won't be easy, as your mighty team has been hard at work, but I've overcome some considerable obstacles in life."

Not really. The horrors of JoBeth's childhood still held her prisoner. Her half-sister had escaped the dark, tiny rooms under the big house, but not the horrors of her mind. Could anyone go through what she went through and live a normal life? If that had been Grace hidden in the basement, deprived of sunlight and friends and an education, how would she have turned out? Would she have let the hate fester and eat away at her sanity?

JoBeth aimed the gun at Grace's stomach. "Game over."

Her gut tightened. "You've overcome so many obstacles," Grace said. "It's amazing, JoBeth, what you came from and where you're at now. How did you do it? How did you manage to beat me? No one has. Not at work, not on the courts. Only you."

JoBeth preened under the praise. "Quiet as a cat. Into the black. It's a game Mom taught me on the nights I got out of the basement. I can move without anyone seeing me. And of course I have good reflexes and hand-eye coordination, and I'm a damn good shot. Video games aren't all that bad."

"And Lia and Janis and Linc?" People, not pawns in a game. JoBeth didn't seem to get they were living, breathing human beings. "They never saw you?"

"The first two levels, easy-peasy. But Level Three was a

little tougher. That pawn was small and fast, the only one to slip away from me at first. Yaaaay for Team Small."

"Do you think he's still alive?"

JoBeth shrugged, the gun rising and falling in a jerky bounce. "Probably. The culvert where he's at has a steady flow of water, and when I did my calculations I figured he'd have about six hours. Of course that last hour would be pretty uncomfortable."

"The culvert. The one by the dwarf cypress forest. Good choice."

"Not that one. The one near Trout Creek." JoBeth blinked, then laughed. "Excellent move, Gracie. You got Linc's location from me. Too bad you won't be able to tell anyone about it."

CHAPTER THIRTY-FIVE

Hatch curled his hand in a fist and banged on Paul Crismon's door.

A jay screeched at him from a sycamore.

He continued to bang as Hayden backed the car out of the drive and took off to search the neighborhood for signs of the muddy white truck. Hatch stopped banging and stretched his fingers. A groan ripped the air to his right.

"Mr. Crismon!" Hatch called.

Another groan. Hatch ran along the front of the house to the side where the grass dipped into a reed-choked gully. "Mr. Crismon!"

The reeds rustled. A hand lifted, then a golden mop of hair.

"Alex!" With a single leap, Hatch landed in the gully and scooped up his son.

The boy screamed and grabbed his right leg.

"You're hurt. What happened? Where's Grace?"

"Put me down." Alex pushed at Hatch's chest, but Hatch held tight to the fighting boy.

"I'm getting you to a doctor."

"Later. First you need to—"

"No. That leg needs more than a few stitches."

"Shut up, Dad, and listen to me!"

The words roped around Hatch's feet, and he stumbled to a stop. This was no angry boy; this was a terrified boy. Hatch released his grip, and Alex slid to the ground and stood on one foot.

Alex grabbed the front of Hatch's shirt with two hands and brought his nose to within one inch of Hatch's. "Grace is at Gator Slide with her sister, JoBeth. JoBeth has a gun. She killed some guy and Allegheny Blue, and now she's going to kill Grace. She's a good shot and can see really good in the dark. I haven't heard a shot yet. There's a creepy bunker under the garage. She might take Grace there. Or...or..." The tension left Alex's fingers as a sob shook his entire body.

Hatch settled him against the giant sycamore tree. "Here's my phone. Call Hayden, tell him what you told me."

"And you?" Alex's chin trembled.

Hatch settled his hand on Alex's good leg. Like when he'd first met Alex, Hatch couldn't bullshit his son. "I'm leaving you here and going to help Grace."

* * *

"So who's the dead guy?" Grace asked. Alex had been gone at least fifteen minutes, plenty of time to get to the Crismon house and a phone. Grace nibbled at her bottom lip. He'd been limping, but he was a strong kid, tough enough to get a cut stitched up without a painkiller.

"Kentucky cop," JoBeth said. "Smart one, too."

The man hadn't moved. His face lay in a pool of blood.

She searched for frothy bubbles, for the faint stirring of that liquid. None.

"If he's so smart," Grace said, "how did he end up dead in the entryway?"

"Mr. Smarty-Pants Detective Holt figured out I killed dear old Oliver and Emmaline and tossed them in the holler."

Grace bit so hard into her bottom lip that blood spurted into her mouth. "You killed the Lassens?"

"Definitely not part of The Game. But they decided to come to Gator Slide a month early. They loved this place that much. Good thing they sent the phone guy out to hook up the phone at a time when I was just getting things started. Didn't take me long to track them down and put a little end to their journey."

* * *

Hatch crouched at the back door of Gator Slide. Leaves crunched and he spun.

"Lieutenant's got a tactical team and a sniper on the way," Hayden said as he slipped out his service revolver.

"No time. Grace and JoBeth are in the front living room. There are two points of entry: back door and side door into the garage. I'll take the back. You take the garage. Whoever has the best line of sight shoots."

"You going to try to talk her down?" Hayden asked.

Hatch rarely pulled a gun while on the job. By choice. Not by chance. He preferred resolution through words, not violent means. "Shoot to kill."

Hayden slipped around the house.

Hatch took off his shoes and slipped through the door into the kitchen. Shades of gray draped the house, but he'd been in here a handful of times when he and Grace were married and he remembered the floor plan. After letting his eyes adjust, he crouched and slid through the shadows toward the voices in the entryway.

"How did Detective Holt track you down?" Grace's voice. Calm. Cool. Classic Grace. God, he loved this woman.

"No idea. He must have some cop superpowers." The speaker giggled. Soft and high-pitched, almost maniacal.

He reached the living room and ducked behind a tower of boxes. He couldn't see the entryway yet, but he could smell it. Blood and fear. He dropped to the floor and slid on his stomach to a long, bulky piece of furniture draped in a sheet. Keeping his face on the floor he could make out the dead man's face and two sets of feet—one bare, the other outfitted in a pair of blue silk pumps.

Hatch lifted his gun. He couldn't get the right angle from here. Had Hayden found a better angle? Probably not. His teammate would need to come down a long, empty hall. Damn.

"You know, Gracie, these sisterly chats are about twenty years too late."

"No they're not. It's never too late." Passion, not desperation or fear, edged Grace's words. "I can help you."

JoBeth's nostrils flared. "I don't need your help! I don't need anyone's help! Do you hear me? I'm fine on my own!"

"No, JoBeth, you're not. You can have more. You deserve more." Grace's words were the same ones she'd thrown at him. True then and now. "Let me be your sister. Let me love you."

"Love me? You don't even know me."

"Give me time."

"Time? Can't do that. The game clock's run out." She lifted her arm.

"They know who you are, JoBeth." Grace's words rushed out in a burst of clear panic. "They know where you live. You can't go back to your old life."

"And you think that's a problem for someone like me?" JoBeth spat the words. "God, you're stupid, and I'm done with this conversation." Her gun hand swung forward.

"Wait!" Grace cried on a sob. She pushed her hair back from her face and frantically searched the room. For a weapon? A distraction? Divine intervention? Hatch could see she wasn't going down without a fight.

He reached into his pocket, his fingers wrapping around the linking rings. He palmed them, metal clinking.

Grace froze.

JoBeth hadn't heard the soft clinks, or if she had, she paid them no heed. "Gracie, The Game is over, and I want to get out of this place."

Grace slid her hands along her thighs. "I know. You won. You're done. After...after you get where you need to go, can you get word to a friend of mine? His name's Theodore Hatcher."

"Come on, Gracie. I'm not stupid, and I'm not going to contact an FBI agent."

"No. In this case he's not an FBI agent, but the man I love. Leave a note on his windshield or call him on a non-traceable prepaid phone. Just please let Hatch know I don't want to be buried in the cemetery next to my father." Her voice broke. "Can...can you ask him to take my ashes and take me out on *No Regrets* and...and spread them on the ocean?"

No. As long as he had breath in his body, there was no way that was going to happen.

Still on his stomach, Hatch crawled to another tower of boxes. He peeked around the corner. Damn! Grace stood with her back to him, directly in his target line. JoBeth, with her wild hair and wild eyes, stood still.

As he got to his knees, two wide eyes landed on him. The man on the floor blinked three times.

Holy hell, the man was alive.

Hatch mouthed, *One, two, three...*

"Hey, Asswipe." The bloody man raised his hand and waggled his fingers.

JoBeth spun toward the downed man. Grace dove at a stack of boxes. Hatch shot.

JoBeth's mouth twisted in a silent scream, her upper body jerked, and her curls flew out from her head, like a gruesome clown. She crumpled to the floor.

Hayden rushed around the corner, kicked the gun from her hand, and dropped to his knees next to the man. Hatch ran to Grace, who was scrambling up from a jumble of boxes. The front of her shirt was soaked in blood, the pearls missing from her neck. "Are you okay? Did she shoot you? Where—"

Grace pushed his hands away. "Your phone. Where's your phone?"

"You're bleeding, Grace. Have you been shot?"

She jammed her hand into his pocket. "Where the hell is your phone?"

"I gave it to Alex to call Hayden."

"Well, find another phone and call Jon MacGregor. I know where he can find Linc."

CHAPTER THIRTY-SIX

Daisies, Grace." Detective Tucker Holt clenched Grace's hand as a pair of surgical attendants wheeled him down the hall. "Hannah's favorite flowers are daisies."

"You bet, a dozen daisies. I'll order them as soon as you let go of my hand."

"Yellow ones to..."

"...match her yellow bumblebee tutu," Grace added. "Got it, Tuck. Hannah's flowers will be at the Center for the Arts by seven tonight and will include a note that reads, *Love Dad.*"

"Yeah...love dad. That's what it needs to read." His hands climbed higher up her arm. Grace was surprised he had such a tight grip. He'd lost so much blood. He should be weak. "And the kids' mom, Mara, you got in touch with her, explained things so she can tell Hannah I really want to be at the dance recital, but I can't, right?"

"Mara understands but is going to wait to tell the kids

until after the surgery. That way she'll be able to tell them things went great and Daddy will be home soon."

"Home. Soon. Yeah, that sounds good."

They reached a set of double doors. "I'm sorry, Detective Holt, but you'll need to say good-bye," one of the attendants said. "The doctors are ready for you."

Grace patted his hand. "Everything's going to go fine."

"Yeah, good thing I got a tough gut." He patted his stomach then winced. "Doc said me and Jackson will be out on the lake fishing in less than two weeks."

She'd said it before, but she needed to say it again. "Thanks, Tucker. You're a good cop, and you saved more than my life today."

He winked as the cart wheeled through the doors of the operating room. "Hey Grace," he called as he lifted himself on one elbow and looked over his shoulder.

"Yeah, Tuck?"

"Good guys: One. Asswipes: Zero."

* * *

Grace stopped at a doorway to the sunny room on the second floor of the hospital and leaned her shoulder against the doorframe.

"...and then *snap*, my leg busts," Alex was saying to the twin boys sitting on the end of his hospital bed and eating banana popsicles. "I mean it's useless, and I'm pretty sure at this point the doctors will have to amputate."

"Amputate," Ricky and Raymond said in unison.

"But I keep going. I know Grace needs me. The detective needs me. But most of all, Linc needs me." Alex pointed a Popsicle at a freckle-faced boy in a hospital gown, an IV in his arm and his feet propped on a rung on the IV stand. "He's trapped in a plastic box with the water rising to his neck. It's only minutes before he drowns. You got that? Minutes."

The twins' eyes grew wide. "Minutes."

"At that point, I know I have to find a way to get to my dad. Even if it kills me. So I drop to the ground and I crawl on my hands and knees. The Gravedigger spots me, aims, and fires." He patted the bandage on his right arm. "But I can't stay down because she's got Grace and is choking her with her own pearls."

"Pearls." The twins edged closer together.

"I dig deep, finding that last burst of strength and drag myself on my elbows through reeds and mud and deadly plants." Alex held up his right arm, swollen with angry welts.

"Deadly plants," the twins echoed.

Grace smiled. Alex had been lucky. He'd walked away from JoBeth Poole with only a sprained ankle, a flesh wound on his upper arm, and an armful of welts from a close encounter with poison sumac. But the horrific experience was going to make for a great story the rest of his life. The boy had been brave and resourceful and just bad enough to be good.

Alex finally spotted her and waved. "Come on in, Grace. The nurse brought us a load of Popsicles. They're all worried about Linc getting his electrolytes back up. We got one more left."

"Ain't got none for me?" A tall boy with black hair and a big grin bounded into the room and grabbed the Popsicle.

"Gabe!" Alex and Linc called out.

"Where the hell have you been, pal?" Alex asked. "You missed all the action."

Alex took the Popsicle from Gabe and offered it to Grace, who waved it off. "I'll take a rain check," she said. "I just got a text from Hatch. He wrapped up his report at the sheriff's station and is on his way."

"Okay," Gabe said as he ripped off the Popsicle wrapper and sat on the windowsill. "Now start from the beginning, Alex. I want to hear the whole story."

The power of a good story, Grace couldn't help but think as she left Alex's room. Hatch was a masterful storyteller, and it looked like his son had the talent, too. She knew things weren't going to be smooth sailing with Hatch and Alex. They were too much alike, but Grace had no problem being a buffer or a soft place to land when they took swipes at each other.

On a puff of antiseptic air, Grace left the medical center and scanned the steps where Hatch was supposed to be waiting. No blond head, but she knew he hadn't left town. That was the old Hatch.

She found him at the bottom of the steps sitting next to a gray-haired woman in a wheelchair. A plastic hospital bag rested on her lap. He reached behind the woman's ear and pulled out a hibiscus bloom. He bowed and held it out to her. She giggled, took the flower in her veiny hand, and kissed his cheek.

A red minivan pulled up to the curb, and a man got out and helped the woman inside. Hatch stood waving until the van disappeared. The fading sun dipped in and out of his hair, creating rolling waves of gold. She couldn't imagine a life without that golden hair and those eyes like a summer sky.

As she'd faced the end of JoBeth's gun, she knew she'd take Hatch for ten minutes, an hour, a year, or two. He might not be willing to offer her forever, but she'd take whatever he'd give her because although she wanted a family and a job fighting bad, she *needed* Hatch.

Her feet barely touched concrete as she raced down the steps and slipped her hands around his neck. "Despite the day we've been through," Grace said, "you're still charming the lipstick off the ladies."

Hatch spun and took her in his arms. "*Because* of the day we've been though, I'd appreciate a bit of lipstick from you."

Without a second thought she lifted her hands to Hatch's neck and pulled his head toward hers. Their tongues and breath tangled long enough to take off most of Grace's lipstick, and it felt wonderful.

"Everything go okay?" Grace asked when they finally came up for air.

"Lieutenant Lang is filing the last of the paperwork, and Lou Poole is making arrangements with Black Jack to have JoBeth's body, along with CoraBeth's and Skye's remains, buried near a set of tupelo trees on her property."

"The bees okay with that?" Grace asked with a hint of jest.

"Lou said it was the bees' idea."

Who was Grace to question Lou Poole's version of normal? Normal was what one lived and breathed day after day. Slipping her hand into Hatch's, they walked through the approaching dusk to the SUV, and within fifteen minutes they were seated on the bow of *No Regrets* watching the sunset.

"You okay?" Hatch asked.

"Tired. A little sore around the neck." She slipped her finger across the bruises circling her throat. "But relieved. I'm so glad it's over."

"Your eyes look a little red."

Grace bit into her bottom lip, focusing on the pain and forcing back another flood of tears. "I cried for two hours, Hatch. Two. Stupid. Hours."

Hatch raised his longneck in the air. "He was a good dog."

"He drooled and he dug and he followed me everywhere." Grace raised her longneck. "But Allegheny Blue was a *great* dog." Their beer bottles clinked.

"His legendary status is reaching all new proportions," Hatch said. "One of the broadcast reporters at the press conference told me one of the national networks is doing a feature on him for one of their news magazines. I'm sure they'll be contacting you for an interview."

"About my *dog*?"

"About *your* dog?"

She laughed, shaking her head. She brought the beer to her mouth but didn't drink.

Hatch slid his arm along the back of her neck and pulled her into the curve of his shoulder. He rested his lips on her head, and she just sat there, focusing on the soft heat of his breath rushing through her hair.

Her hand curled around the longneck. Beads of water slid down the icy cold beer and ran in rivulets onto her hand, splashing onto her thigh.

"Talk," he said softly.

"I haven't cried yet for the others, not for JoBeth and or... for him." Grace reached for her necklace before remembering she'd thrown it in the river. She pushed out of the safe circle of his arms. "Hatch, how could I not have known what my father was doing? JoBeth and her mother lived below my feet for fifteen years. Fifteen years! That makes me some kind of monster, doesn't it?"

"No, it makes you just as much a victim as JoBeth."

"But—"

"Grace, Henri Courtemanche was a strong, confident, smart man. He bamboozled you and hundreds of other people, including congressmen and judges and business associates. He was a powerful man who believed in the power of self, which can be good."

"Until you take it to an extreme."

"Exactly. He passed on that strength to both of his daughters. Despite his twisted way of thinking, he raised two incredibly strong, smart, and confident daughters. JoBeth couldn't have done what she did, and I'm talking about pulling herself up out of that basement, without an innate belief in herself. I honestly think if she had decided to talk to someone, to cut open what was festering and release the poison, she wouldn't have done what she did."

"I noticed a few things about...her." Grace couldn't say it yet, but someday she may be able to call JoBeth Poole *sister*. "She fiddled with her necklace and jutted out her chin when making a point."

"Sounds like someone I know." He took her hand. "And love."

She twined her fingers with his. "And a few times she looked at me with these big wide eyes, like she wanted something from me. Answers. Direction. Maybe even love." Grace settled her head on Hatch's shoulder. "I could have loved her, Hatch, if she'd given me a chance."

"I know. Family's important to you." He tossed his empty longneck into the bait bucket. "Me, too. There's no way I can walk away from you and Alex—not now, not ever. So when are we moving into the house on the hill?"

Grace thought she'd exhausted a decade's supply of tears over that dog—her dog—but liquid swelled in her eyes. If the defense attorneys she battled every day in the courtroom could see her now, she'd never win another case. "That means you're staying for a while?"

"Yep. Already talked to Parker about opening up the

Florida branch of Apostles Inc. I don't have any details yet, but I can guarantee you're going to have a hard time getting rid of me." He cradled her chin in his palm, the calluses familiar and wonderful, and turned her face to his. "I'm going to be like Blue, dogging you the rest of your life."

"As long as you don't drool, I think we can make it work."

Her lips crushed his, and despite the windless night, *No Regrets* lurched.

EPILOGUE

He was a great dog," Alex said as he settled a single white lily on the smooth square of freshly turned earth.

"The best," Ricky and Raymond answered in unison as they tossed in four handfuls of wilted sneezeweed.

Grace cast an exasperated look over her shoulder. Where was Hatch? The funeral for Allegheny Blue had been Alex's idea, and Hatch's son had spent an inordinate amount of time and energy planning and executing the ceremony on a sunny strip of land between Lamar Giroux's shack and the creek. In attendance were the twins, the boys' grandmother, Black Jack, Gabe, and a spry Linc. Alex had even sent a memorial service announcement to old Lamar Giroux, who'd sent a blue pine sapling to be planted over the grave. Grace was proud of the young boy, who was clearly showing respect and responsibility.

"Gabe, you get the pine," Alex said. "Linc, get the shovel. Ricky and Raymond, you can get the hoe and rake. We're going to plant the tree here." Hatch's son pointed to a spot near the head of the grave and shot a glance to Black Jack who gave a solemn nod. With Alex at the helm, Linc dug.

When Alex asked where they should bury the dog's ashes, Grace knew there was only one place: her land. Twice the old dog had walked a hundred miles to this square of earth on bloody paws. Like the bees, he had a message. This was where he wanted to die.

Grace had called off construction of her new home, at least for now. A week had passed since JoBeth had died, but the dust still needed to settle. Grace wasn't sure if she'd ever build anything on this land, especially a dream home sketched on the back of a cocktail napkin by a man she didn't know.

She still had a hard time coming to grips with her father's twisted side. Hatch, of all people, had come to her father's defense. "He wasn't all bad, Grace. He did a lot of right things by you, and maybe someday you'll be able to see that."

Again she looked over her shoulder. "Where's Hatch?"

"He said something about a surprise for you," Trina Milanos said.

"Maybe it'll be a car that actually runs," Alex said. "That one you have's a real pain."

"I doubt it," Grace said as she took a bottle of sunscreen from her purse. The back of Raymond's neck was already turning pink, and after they finished planting the blue pine, they were heading out for a sail and picnic lunch. A leery Hatch had spent all morning preparing *No Regrets* for the Twin Terrors and picking up a *surprise* for Grace. "Your dad knows I just took the compact in to get the starter, battery, and entire ignition system replaced."

"I'm placing my money on a fancy new diamond ring," Trina Milanos said as she sat on the trunk of a downed cypress log.

"Gaaaaaag," Ricky said as he shoved his finger down his throat.

"Does that mean you'll be kissing even more?" Raymond asked with a groan.

"Probably." Grace slathered sunscreen on Raymond's ears. She and Hatch had agreed on forever, but they hadn't talked about marriage yet. She'd be shocked if Hatch showed up with an engagement ring. But he'd been full of surprises the past few days. He'd taken personal time from work and had spent hours with Trina and all three boys.

As for Alex, not too many surprises there. He and Hatch were figuring out the father-son dance, but they were spending a good deal of time scuffling on the floor. Just yesterday, after his shift at the cemetery ended, Alex had gone kayaking with Gabe and hadn't bothered to check in. When Alex finally came home after a four-hour romp through the swamp, Hatch took away Alex's new kayak for a week. Alex had sulked, but the boy had also stolen looks at Hatch through dinner that night, like he was amazed he had a dad, and one who loved him enough to make a fuss.

Today Alex was smiling. Like his dad, he loved getting out on the ocean with the wind in his hair. Grace corralled Ricky, doused him with sunscreen and gave the bottle to Alex. He shook his head, but she shook hers longer. Just as Alex finished with the sunscreen, Hatch came down the path with a picnic basket.

"Looks like he brought something for the picnic," Grace said. "I bet it's a dessert. I hope it's peach pie."

"I hope it's chocolate cream," Alex said.

"Apple!" Ricky.

"No, pumpkin with extra whipped cream!" Raymond.

"I got a real hankering for strawberry-rhubarb," Trina said with a wink.

Hatch set the basket on top of the log. With a dramatic swoosh of his hand, he opened the lid.

"Uh, what is that?" Trina asked as she wrinkled her nose.

Hatch rubbed a hand along his neck. "It's probably the biggest mistake of my life."

The twins dropped the hoe and rake and dropped to their knees before the basket. "A puppy!" they cried in unison.

A lump of blue and white speckled fur crawled over the lip, the basket spilling. A puppy with ears to the ground and feet as big as Grace's palm tumbled out.

"He has plenty of Allegheny Blue in him," Hatch said. "Got the papers to prove it."

Grace reached for the pup, which was about to leap off the log. "Seriously?"

"Seriously. I'm telling you, the old dog's spawn is every-where. Do you know how many times old man Giroux sent that dog out to procreate? No wonder Blue was so doggone tired in his old age."

Grace laughed, the chunky glass bead necklace at the V of her T-shirt swinging. The puppy batted at the necklace. She grabbed the paw and brushed the silky, warm fur against her cheek. The pup settled into her arms, yawned, and closed its eyes.

"See. Just like his great, great grandpa." Hatch looped an arm around her shoulder. "You ready?"

She breathed in all that was Hatch: sun and summer and sweetness. But he was also steadfast, and he wanted for-ever. She kissed Hatch's smiling lips, shifted the dog to one arm, and motioned to the pack of boys who'd just finished smoothing dirt around the blue pine. "Okay everyone, let's sail."

Please see the next page for a preview
of the next chilling book in the
Apostles series

THE BLIND

CHAPTER ONE

Wake up, sleeping beauty." Carter Voles cradled the woman's face in his hand. "The clock is ticking."

Tick tock, like a clock, ready, set, go!

The woman—didn't she say her name was Maria?—moaned but didn't open her eyes. Even if her name wasn't Maria, he would call her Maria. Mary. The Madonna. Beautiful. His fingers caressed the split on her lower lip. So, so beautiful.

His lips trailed along her throat. Soft. The tip of his tongue slid along her jaw. Sweet. His cheek brushed hers. Warm. Like heated cream. He nibbled her ear, then bit. Hard.

Her eyes flew open, and she tried to scream. The duct tape held, a scream-catcher of sorts.

"Excellent. You're awake." He settled onto the edge of the futon that reeked of body fluid stew. "How's your head? Sorry about that nasty bump. I didn't mean to hit you so hard." His fingers sifted through the thick fall of honey-colored hair, and his nails dug into the swollen flesh at her temple. Her eyes bulged. "Okay, that was a lie. Now get up." He fisted a handful of hair and pulled her upright.

"So here's the deal, Maria." He dangled an eighteen-gauge wire in front of her face. "Tiny little thing, isn't it? But with it you have the power to live or die." He attached the wire to the mercury switch secured to the fanny pack he'd belted around her exquisite hips. Not beautiful. But necessary. Just the right size for five pounds of RDX. He taped the wire up her ribcage and along her neck.

His fingers lingered over the corner of the duct tape. Two schools of thought here. He could slowly ease back the tape, pulling out fine hair and the top layer of skin as he went, prolonging the pain. Or he could give it one long yank. That would hurt like hell.

Riiiiiiip!

"You son of a bitch. You sadistic, fu—"

Smack!

"Such ugly words from such a beautiful mouth," he said with a soft cluck as he taped the wire to the corner of her mouth. "Now let's talk about that beautiful mouth. From this moment on, if you open your mouth, the wire will trip the anti-movement switch." He ran his finger along the wire. "After a thirty-second delay, enough time for me to get away, an electric loop will close, setting off the initiator and starting the firing train. The train—*choo-choo*—chugs over to the primary explosive, which will detonate the main charge. And boom!" His fisted fingers fanned out in front of her face. Visuals were so useful to get across one's point. "Bottom line, Maria. You open your mouth, you die. Understand?"

She sat before him, a still life.

"Blink once for yes. Twice for no."

One blink. One terrified, beautiful blink.

"Excellent. Now it's time to go." He pulled her to her feet and hid all that was beautiful with a white satin robe.

Tick tock, like a clock, ready, set, blow!

* * *

Three weeks later

Evie Jimenez planted one red leather cowboy boot on the edge of the pool. She could do this. Her other boot followed. She *had* to do this.

Curls of steam rose from the lap pool perched on a cliff overlooking the Atlantic, and Parker Lord, head of the FBI's Special Criminal Investigative Unit, touched up for the last of his daily laps. One hundred. Evie had counted every one.

His head broke the water, his chest heaving as he sucked in a series of deep breaths. She snagged one of her own. Contrary to legend, Parker Lord wasn't a god. He was just a man. Her boss.

Despite the frosty morning air, sweat trickled down the back of her neck. She unbuttoned her denim jacket. "Got a call from a buddy at Bar Harbor PD. One of the local high schools received a bomb threat."

"Bar Harbor?" Parker pushed himself out of the water and took a seat on the lip of the pool. "Not too far from here."

"Explosive detection canine spotted up on a backpack inside the gymnasium. Surrounding area has been evacuated and perimeter set."

"Good. Preservation of life is key." He swiped a towel along the ripped muscle of his chest.

"Bar Harbor PD doesn't have a bomb squad, and the

aine State Police Hazardous Devices Unit is tied up with
at threat at the airport."

"That's rather unfortunate." He cupped his fingers around
curved railing at the edge of the pool.

She ground the heel of her boot into the deck. A spider-
eb of cracks splintered the ice. "It's a simple grab and
ow. I do this type of stuff in my sleep."

"I'm sure you do." Hand over hand, he swung along the
il, his arms and chest tightening into rock-hard curves.
arker Lord was one of the strongest men she knew, in body
d in spirit, which is why she was in her version of hell.

"Dammit, Parker, I want in on this one. I'm ready."

Reaching behind him, he grabbed two handles, swung
to his wheelchair, and rolled across the patio, shooting her
glance over his shoulder.

Her gut twisted. She'd seen that look before, on the faces
her dad and brothers the day she walked away from the
lbuquerque Police Academy. But she'd come a long way
nce Albuquerque.

She raced after Parker, her boots sliding on the ice. "I've
en sitting on my ass for two months. Internal Affairs
rapped up their investigation last week. Officer Gilley took
ll responsibility for his actions in Houston, and IA cleared
e of any wrongdoing or negligence."

Parker pushed a button, and a wall of glass slid open. She
rdled herself in front of him, backpedaling into the giant
om of polished concrete, glass, and leather. "Do you want
e to say it again? Fine." She drilled her fingertips into her
est. "I screwed up. I was the command of the Houston
mb disrupt, and under my command a two-year-old al-
ost died."

"And?"

What more did he want? She lifted her hands in the

air, her fingers flicking wide. "And boom! An IED went off destroying property and *whittling away at the American public's confidence in law enforcement to protect against bomb threats, both foreign and domestic.*"

The media had loved that last bit. And in Houston, the media had been out in full force because the job had sexy written all over it: a fanatic anti-abortionist, a bomb made with directions downloaded from the Internet, and her, a female bomb and weapons specialist who clearly didn't have the respect and command of her men. The bubbleheads on the network news had lambasted her and questioned the ability and effectiveness of Parker's team, which years ago the media had nicknamed the Apostles. That had been the biggest blow, putting a black mark on a team known for it damn-near miraculous execution.

Parker rested his chin on his steepled fingers. "And would you do the same thing again?"

Save the baby! Two months ago the words ricocheted through her head and heart. Still did. "In a heartbeat."

Parker spun toward the window where the early morning sun shot lances into the churning water, setting the Atlantic on fire.

"Do you want me to lie?" Evie paced, determined to stay one step ahead of the tremor in her voice. "I knew the force of that IED, the distance, and my rate of speed. I could have grabbed that child without incident. I had it all under control."

"But you didn't have your men under control."

"I gave the order. I told everyone to stay put." Even now frustration bubbled in her veins.

"But one man didn't. One officer didn't obey your command."

"Gilley was a chauvinistic pig."

"But he was *your* pig, Evie. You should have stuck him a pen or locked him in a barn. You should have prevented n from going after that child." A vein thickened at rker's temple where a splash of silver feathered into jet ck waves. "Therefore you did not have the situation under ntrol. You were not doing your job."

"My job was to preserve life. That little boy was heading aight for the IED, and I was in the best position to avert d rescue." Her shoulders sunk with a sigh, and she pped to her knees before her boss. "Park, I can't change o I am. Do you want me to beg? To lie and promise I'll ver, ever run after a human being whose life is at risk?" cold, hard knot gathered in her throat. "To hand in my eld?"

Parker shifted his gaze from the fiery ocean to her. Three ars ago this man had put his neck and reputation on the line her. Did he regret it? The knot dropped to her stomach.

Parker cupped the side of her head, his thumb running ng the scar dissecting her eyebrow. "I hand-chose you, ie, because you are *you*, and I want you to keep doing at you do so well, and do it so *everyone* is safe."

"Then let me go to Bar Harbor. It's not like I'm asking to n the First Friday Bomber investigation in Los Angeles." t yet. She desperately wanted to be in on the hunt for the ial bomber who strapped bombs to live victims and had eady killed seven people, but first she needed to prove to rker that she was ready to get back in the field.

Parker let loose a long sigh, so long she was surprised it ln't fog the glass. At last he waved the back of his hand at r. "Get out of here, Evie. Go. Go to Bar Harbor."

She jammed the heavy waves of hair on either side of r head behind her ears. During her Army days she'd been ordnance disposal specialist, and she'd suffered a hearing loss in her left ear. "You're allowing me back in the field" Now?"

A wry smile curved his lips. "With a bomb ticking, now would be a good time."

She threw both arms around his neck, landing a noisy kiss on his cheek before running to her office.

"And Evie," Parker called out.

Her cowboy boots skidded to a halt. "Yeah?"

"Your job is to preserve life, all life, including yours."

* * *

Evie hauled her emergency response duffel from the back of her truck and rushed past the hazardous devices unit parked in front of the gym.

"Hold up there, young lady." A uniformed officer grabbed her arm. "You can't go back there. We have a bomb on the premises."

Evie reached for her creds, but the officer snagged her other arm. Having long ago resolved to life at five-foot-two, she craned her neck so he could see every inch of her face. "I'm not young, and I'm not feeling very ladylike, so get your fucking hands off me so I can disrupt that bomb."

The officer dropped her arms as if she were on fire. At the inner perimeter she found the lieutenant in charge of the scene, a silver-haired man who scrubbed a thumb across his chin after she introduced herself.

"You're Parker Lord's guy?" the lieutenant asked.

"Yes, sir. Has the bomb robot been unloaded?"

"Five minutes ago."

"Excellent." Evie pulled her hair into a knot on top of her head, securing it with a rubber band, and dug into the duffel for her bomb suit.

Fall in Love with Forever Romance

UNLEASHED
by Rachel Lacey

Cara has one rule: Don't get attached. It's served her well with the dogs she's fostered and the children she's nannied. But one smile from her sexy neighbor has her thinking some rules are made to be broken. Fans of Jill Shalvis will fall in love with this sassy, sexy debut!

MADE FOR YOU
by Lauren Layne

's met her match...she just sn't know it yet. Fans of Jennifer Probst and Rachel Van ken will fall head over heels the second book in the Best take series.

Fall in Love with Forever Romance

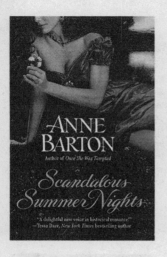

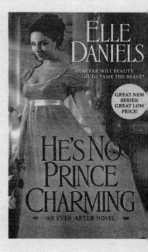

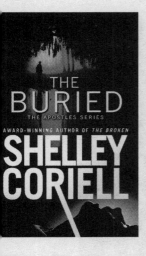

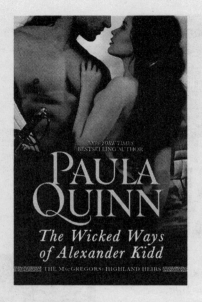